THE ADVENTUROUS SIMPLICISSIMUS

Frontispiece of the First Edition
from the Ducal Library Wolf Buettel.

The Adventurous
SIMPLICISSIMUS

*Being the description of the life
of a strange vagabond named
Melchoir Sternfels von Fuchshaim*

H. J. C. VON GRIMMELSHAUSEN

Translated by

A. T. S. Goodrick

A BISON BOOK

UNIVERSITY OF NEBRASKA PRESS ● Lincoln

First Bison Book printing June, 1962
Second Bison Book printing August, 1965

Bison Book edition reprinted by arrangement with
William Heinemann Ltd.

PREFACE

SIMPLICISSIMUS, which has more than once been called the greatest of all German novels, has a terrible relevance in the America of the nineteen sixties.

The United States, which has never yet been devastated by any modern weapons of war, is now contemplating the possibility of being devastated by a war which will make those of 1914-1918 and 1939-1945 seem trivial. Already one is told that, if one has plenty of money and a plot of land, one can dig a shelter and prepare to live underground. One can even buy a machine gun to keep crowds of poorer people from sharing that shelter. . . .

At this point, the SIMPLICISSIMUS becomes a modern book again. For the Thirty Years' War, which is its subject, was not just any war. It was a war which inflicted death not on individuals only but on cities, on populations, and it was a war in which life went on, between battles, in the seventeenth-century equivalent of deep shelters protected from the neighbors by machine guns: a war which, even more than other wars, brought out the worst in human nature. And around it, as today, in supreme irony: the highest of high ideals. Historians, in their oblivious way, call it the last of the wars of religion.

The people who are today urging readiness for war in the name of freedom and courage overlook what war will do to people. I am not one of those who think the next war will kill everyone. I only hope to be among the killed. For the survivors will suffer something much worse than death. They will suffer something worse than suffering: namely, the deepest degradation. It was a surprise for many to learn in 1945 that the inmates of the concentration camps, those much-pitied, innocent victims, had often behaved like beasts. In the devastated cities of the next war what awaits us—all suffering and death aside—is bestiality. The *talk* is all of freedom and courage but the *meaning* may well prove to be: bestiality.

Preface

I do not, by the way, write these lines in the faith of a pacifist arguing that we should disarm unilaterally. I write, not as a statesman with a policy, but as a man of letters committed to the belief that the truth is always important: if we are going to contemplate war, let us at least know what it is we are contemplating. There is a great literature of war, and very much of it speaks poignantly today. The SIMPLICISSIMUS may well be the most poignant book in all this literature because its war, alas, is our war, our *kind* of war.

The book suggested to Bertolt Brecht, not indeed the plot and characters, but the tone and milieu of his *Mother Courage,* the greatest of modern war plays. And re-reading SIMPLICISSIMUS recently I was reminded of some words which Simone Weil wrote about another war book, *The Iliad:* "The wantonness of the conqueror that knows no respect for any creature or thing that is at its mercy or is imagined to be so, the despair of the soldier that drives him on to destruction, the obliteration of the slave or the conquered man, the wholesale slaughter—all these elements combine to make a picture of uniform horror of which force is the sole hero."

It might be retorted that while such a picture is instructive it is also intolerable. At moments, the SIMPLICISSIMUS may be too painful to read, and its relevance too much to bear thinking of, but it is a classic function of literature to make the unbearable bearable, the painful—and not perversely—pleasurable. There is a transcendence here, and, in the case of the SIMPLICISSIMUS, not just an aesthetic one. We shall not end the horrors of war by refusing to let the mind dwell on them. On the contrary, it is people who refuse to let the mind dwell on them who can enter upon a war imagining they are making the world easier for ideals to live in. Simone Weil, who was no absolute pacifist, but who returned to Europe in 1942 to help De Gaulle, wrote: ". . . the sense of human misery is a pre-condition of justice and love. He who does not realize to what extent shifting fortune and necessity hold in subjection every human spirit, cannot regard as fellow creatures nor love as he loves himself those whom chance separated from him by an abyss. The variety of constraints pressing upon man give rise to the illusion of several distinct species that cannot communicate. Only he who has measured the dominion of force, and knows how not to respect it, is capable of love and justice."

ERIC BENTLEY

New York City
September 14, 1961

INTRODUCTION

THE translation here presented to the public is intended rather as a contribution to the history, or perhaps it should be said the sociology, of the momentous period to which the romance of "Simplicissimus" belongs, than as a specimen of literature. Effective though its situations are, consistent and artistic though its composition is (up to a certain point), its interest lies chiefly in the pictures, or rather photographs, of contemporary manners and characters which it presents. It has been said with some truth that if succeeding romancers had striven as perseveringly as our author to embody the spirit and reflect the ways of the people, German fiction might long ago have reached as high a development as the English novel. As it is, there is little of such spirit to be discovered in the prose romances which appeared between the time of Grimmelshausen and that of Jean Paul Richter. But the influence of the latter was completely swept away in the torrent of idealism by which the fictions of the idolised Goethe and his followers were characterised, and his domestic realism has only of late made its reappearance in disquieting and sordid forms.

It should be remembered as an apology for the stress now laid upon the sociological side of the history of the Thirty Years War, that that side has by historians been resolutely thrust into the background. The most detailed and painstaking narratives of the war are either bare records of military operations or, worse still, represent merely meticulous and valueless unravellings of the web of intrigue with which the pedants of the time deceived themselves into the belief that they were very Machiavels of subtlety and resource. While the Empire was bleeding to death, the chancelleries of half Europe were intent on the detaching from one side or the other of a venal general, or the patching up of some partial armistice that might afford breathing-time to organise further mischief. It does not

Introduction

matter much to any one whether Wallenstein was knave
or fool, but it did matter and does matter that the war
crippled for two hundred years the finances, the agriculture,
and the enterprise of the German people, and dealt
a blow to their patriotism from the like of which few
nations could have recovered. Even the character of the
civil administration was completely altered when the
struggle ended. An army of capable bourgeois secretaries
and councillors had for centuries served their princes and
their fellow subjects well. It is wonderful that throughout
the devastating wars waged by Wallenstein and Weimar,
and even later on during the organised raids of Wrangel
and Königsmark, the records were kept, the village business
administered (where there was a village left), and even
revenue collected with wellnigh as much regularity as in
time of peace. These functionaries, who had worked so well,
were at the end of the war gradually dispossessed of their
influence, and their posts were taken by a swarm of
young place-hunters of noble birth whom the peace had
deprived of their proper employment, and whose pride
was only equalled by their incapacity. But neither particulars nor generalisations bearing on such subjects
are to be found in the pages of professional historians;
they must be sought in the contemporary records of the
people, of which the present work affords one of the few
existing specimens, or else in the work of picturesque
writers who, laying no claim to the title of scientific
investigators, yet possess the power of selecting salient
facts and deducing broad conclusions from them. Freitag's
"Bilder aus der Deutschen Vergangenheit" indicates a
wealth of material for sociological study which has as
yet been but charily used; and recent German works
dealing directly with the subject are more remarkable for
elegance of production than for depth of research.

Such being the purpose for which this translation
has been undertaken, an Introduction to it must neces-
sarily be concerned not so much with the bibliography
of the book or even the sources, if any, to which the
author was beholden for his material, as with his own

personality and the amount of actual fact that underlies the narrative of the fictitious hero's adventures. In respect of the first point, we are presented with a biography almost as shadowy and elusive as that of Shakespeare. In many ways, indeed, the particulars of the lives of these two which we possess are curiously alike. Both were voluminous writers; both enjoyed considerable contemporary reputation; and in both cases our knowledge of their actual history is confined to a few statements by persons who lived somewhat later than themselves, and a few formal documents and entries. In Grimmelshausen's case this obscurity is increased by his practice of publishing – under assumed names. In the score of romances and tracts which are undoubtedly his work, we find only two to – which his real name is attached. He has nine other pseudonyms, nearly all anagrams of the words "Christoffel von Grimmelshausen." Of these, "German Schleifheim von Sulsfort" and "Samuel Greifnsohn vom Hirschfelt" are the best known; the latter being the name to which he most persistently clung, and under which "Simplicissimus" was published, though the former appears on the title-page as that of the "editor." Only as the signature to a kind of advertisement at the end do we find the initials of "Hans Jacob Christoffel von Grimmelshausen," his full name. Until the publication of a collection of his works by Felsecker at Nuremberg in 1685, the true authorship of most of them remained unknown. But that editor, by his allusions in the preface, practically identified the writer as the "Schultheiss of Renchen, near Strassburg," whom he seems to have known personally. The reasons for anonymity were, no doubt, firstly, the fact that "Simplicissimus" at least dealt with the actions of men yet alive; and sec – ondly, with regard to the other books, the continual references to details of the author's own life and opinions. His dread of offending a contemporary is shown by his disguising of the name of St. André, the commandant of Lippstadt, as N. de S. A. of L. (bk. iii., chap. 15).

It is unnecessary here to enter into a discussion of the authorities from whom the meagre particulars of Grimmelshausen's life are drawn. It may suffice for our present purpose to indicate the main events of that life. He was ✦ born at Gelnhausen, near Hanau, about 1625—probably of a humble family. At the age of ten he was captured by Hessian (that is, be it remembered, anti-Imperialist) troops, and became a member of that "unseliger Tross"—the unholy crew of horseboys, harlots, sutlers, and hangers-on who followed the armies on both sides, and sometimes outnumbered them three to one. In 1648, the last year of the war, the whole Imperial army only numbered 40,000 fighting men, and the recognised camp-followers, who were commanded and kept in order by officers significantly named the "Provosts of the Harlots," no less than 140,000. In the preface to one of his works called the "Satyrical Pilgrim," Grimmelshausen speaks of himself as having been "a musqueteer" at the age of ten—a statement which is obviously to be taken in the same sense in which Simplicissimus tells us (bk. ii., chap. 4) how he "served the crown of Sweden" at a similar age as a soldier, and drew pay for it. As a matter of fact, Grimmelshausen probably served a musqueteer or several musqueteers, just as the "Boy" in Henry V. serves Ancient Pistol and his comrades. From another book, the "Everlasting Almanack," we learn that he was a soldier under the Imperialist general Götz, lay in garrison at Offenburg, the free city alluded to in book v., chapter 20, and also for a long time in the famous fortress of Philippsburg, of his residence in which he tells various anecdotes. There are traces both in "Simplicissimus" and his other books of a wide and unusual acquaintance with many lands, German and non-German. He knows both Westphalia and Saxony well: Bohemia also: and certainly Switzerland. The journey to Russia may have some foundation in fact, though the statement put into the mouth of Simplicissimus that he has himself seen the fabulous "sheep plant" (bk. v., chap. 22) growing in Siberia considerably detracts from his trustworthiness here. But when he left the army, and whether he ever attained to any reputable rank therein, is quite uncertain. If 1625 be the correct date of his birth he would be but twenty-three years old at the conclusion of peace.

Besides his military expeditions, it is pretty clear from his works that he had visited Amsterdam and Paris and knew them fairly well; but for nineteen years we have no further trace of his career, till he suddenly appears as Schultheiss, under the Bishop of Strassburg, of Renchen, now in the Grand Duchy of Baden, a town of which he deliberately conceals the name exactly as he does his own, by anagrams, calling it now Rheinec, now Cernheim. In October 1667 he appears as holding this office and issuing an order concerning the mills of the town, which is still in existence. His wife was Katharina Henninger, and entries have been found of the birth of two children, a daughter and a son, in 1669 and 1675. A curious episode in the first part of the "Enchanted Bird's-nest," quoted hereafter, seems to indicate a grave family disappointment. In 1676 he died, aged fifty-one only, but having reached what may almost be called a ripe age for the battered and spent soldier of the Thirty Years War. The entry of his death is peculiarly full and even discursive, and tells how though he had again entered on military service—no doubt on the occasion of the French invasion in 1674—and though his sons and daughters were living in places widely distant from each other, they were all present at his death, in which he was fortified by the rites of Holy Church. A final touch of uncertainty is added by the fact that we do not even know whether Grimmelshausen was his true name: it is more likely to be that of some small estate which he had acquired, and of which he assumed the name when, as we learn, he was raised to noble rank.

It is plain even from this brief outline of his life that Grimmelshausen was emphatically a self-taught man; and it is partly to this fact that we owe the originality of his work; for he had never fallen under the baleful influence of the pedantry of his time. He had, it is true, picked up a deal of out-of-the-way knowledge, which he is willing enough to set before us to the verge of tediousness. But his learning is very superficial; he was a poor Latinist;

and it is likely that for most of his erudition he was indebted to the translations which were particularly plentiful during that golden period of material prosperity in Germany which preceded the terrible war. It is clear enough that everywhere he thought more of the content than of the literary form of his own or any other work; and for the times his scientific and mathematical knowledge was considerable. In the field of romance he knows, and does not hesitate to borrow from, Boccaccio, Bandello ("Simplicissimus," bk. iv., chaps. 4, 5), and the "Cent Nouvelles Nouvelles," while in his minor works he shows ample acquaintance with old German legend and also with stories like that of King Arthur of England. Lastly, we find him commending the "incomparable Arcadia" of Sir Philip Sidney (which he would have read in the translation of Martin Opitz) as a model of eloquence, but corrupting and enervating in its effect upon the manly virtues ("Simplicissimus," bk. iii., chap. 18).

Yet his own earlier works are themselves in the tedious, unreal, and stilted style of the romances of chivalry. "The Chaste Joseph," "Dietrich and Amelind," and "Proximus and Limpida," though widely different in subject, are alike in this, and show no sign of the genius which created Simplicissimus. Yet for the first-named work—the "Joseph" —its author cherished an unreasoning affection, and even alludes to it in our romance as the work of the hero himself (bk. iii., chap. 19). But it is no discredit to Grimmelshausen's originality if we conjecture that the translations of Spanish picaresque novels (chiefly by the untiring Aegidius Albertini), which appeared during the first two decades of the seventeenth century, gave him the idea—they gave him little or nothing more—of a vagabond hero. Mateo Aleman's famous "Guzman de Alfarache" had been succeeded by two miserably poor "Second Parts" by different authors, and in one of these there appears a tedious episode containing the submarine adventures of the hero under the form of a tunny-fish, to which we may conceivably owe the equally tedious story of Simplicissimus and the sylphs of the Mummelsee. At the end of the original book (bk. v., chap. 24) is an unblushing copy of a passage from a work of Antonio Quevara or Guevara, also translated by Albertini.

That Grimmelshausen died a Romanist is pretty clear from the entry of his death quoted above; nor is it likely that a Protestant could have held the office of Schultheiss under the Bishop of Strassburg. There is also extant a curious dialogue ascribed to Grimmelshausen in which Simplicissimus's arguments against changing his religion are combated and finally overthrown by a certain Bonamicus, who effects his complete conversion. It is far from improbable that the account of his rescue from sinful indifference at Einsiedel which Simplicissimus gives (bk. v., chap. 2)—of course apart from the miraculous incident of the attack on him by the unclean spirit—roughly represents the experience of his author. That the latter had been brought up a Protestant we simply assume from the fact that Simplicissimus is understood to have been so; the first indication which we have of a change in his opinions being his exclamation of "Jesus Maria!" (bk. iii., chap. 20), which draws upon him the suspicions of the pastor at Lippstadt. But Papist or not, our author's superstition is unmistakable.

It was indeed a time, like all periods of intense human misery, in which men, it might almost be said, turned in despair to the powers of hell because they had lost all faith in those of heaven. That numbers of the unhappy wretches who suffered in their thousands for witchcraft during the first period of the war actually believed themselves in direct communication with the devil is certain. The Bishop of Würzburg's fortnightly "autos-da-fé" were only stopped when some of the victims denounced the prelate himself as their accomplice, apparently believing it. Grimmelshausen is ready to believe anything. His description of the Witches' Sabbath is that of a scene which he is firmly convinced is a possible one; and he stoutly defends by a multitude of preposterous stories the reasonableness of such conviction ("Simplicissimus," bk. ii., chaps. 17, 18). But among soldiers the most widely spread superstition was that concerned with invulnerability. Not only separate in-dividuals, but whole bodies of troops were supposed to be "frozen," or proof, at all events, against leaden bullets. Christian of Brunswick actually employed his ducal bro-ther's workers in glass to make balls of that material to be used against Tilly's troops, who were credited with this supernatural property; and when the small fortress of Rogäz, near Dessau, was captured by Mansfeld in 1626, the assailants were forbidden to use their fire-arms as use-less; the members of the garrison, being wizards all, were clubbed to death with hedge-stakes or the butt-ends of musquets. In all probability this superstition arose mainly from observation of the very small penetrating power of the ammunition of the time. Oliver (bk. iv., chap. 14) is merely bruised on the forehead by a bullet fired a few paces off: and bullets then weighed ten to the pound. It is true that he has, as it seems, been rendered ball-proof by the wicked old Provost Marshal, whose skull Herzbruder (bk. ii., chap. 27) caused his own servant to split with an axe at Wittstock, when no pistol could slay him: but the peasant in book i., chapter 14, cannot be killed by a bullet fired close to his head, perhaps by reason of the thickness of his skull. To celebrated persons particularly the repu-tation of being "gefroren" attached. Count Adam Terzky, Wallenstein's confidant, was supposed to be so protected: the superstition regarding Claverhouse, who could only be killed with a silver bullet, is well known: and even as late as 1792 there was a belief among his soldiers that Frederick William II, of Prussia was invulnerable. Grim-melshausen's adventuress "Courage" (of whom more here-after) is supposed to be "sword- and bullet-proof": and towards the end of the war "Passau Tickets," or amulets protecting against wounds, were manufactured and sold, while a host of minor magic arts, more or less connected with invulnerability, were believed to exist. For such tricks the passage from the generally uninteresting "Continua-tio," which is given as Appendix B of this book, is a kind of "locus classicus."

Another whole cycle of superstitions centres round the

belief in possible invisibility of persons. Of this we have no example in "Simplicissimus," though the whole plot of the delightful double romance of the "Enchanted Bird's-nest" (also fully discussed hereafter) depends on it. On the other hand, the story of the production of the puppies from the pockets of the colonel's guests by the wizard Provost in book ii., chap. 22, is narrated by a man who plainly believed such things possible; and absolute credence is given to the powers of prophecy possessed both by old Herzbruder (bk. ii., chaps. 23, 24) and by the fortune-teller of Soest (bk. iii., chap. 17), who is apparently a well-known character of the times. It is noteworthy that Herzbruder thinks meanly of the art of palmistry.

Coming to the actual career of Simplicissimus as chronicled in the romance which bears his name, we are at the outset confronted by some strange chronology. The boy is born just after the battle of Höchst in 1622, and is captured by the troopers when ten years old; he is with the hermit two years (bk. i., chap. 12) till the latter's death, and makes his first "spring into the world" after the battle of Nördlingen in the autumn of 1634. He is in Hanau during Ramsay's rule, and spends there the winter of 1634-5. In the spring of 1635 (there was still ice on the town-moat) he was captured by Croats. The following eighteen months are occupied by his adventures as a forest-thief and as a servant-girl, and the next certain note of time we have is that of the battle of Wittstock, September 24, 1636. There follow the happenings at Soest and the six months internment at Lippstadt. But at the time of the siege of Breisach, in the winter of 1638, he has long been back from Paris; his marriage, therefore, must have taken place before the completion of his sixteenth year. Strange as this may appear, the story appears to be deliberately so arranged. For it will be observed that just before the lad's capture by the Swedes it is plainly implied (bk. iii., chap. 11) that he has not yet arrived at the age of puberty. Grimmelshausen intends him to be a "Wunderkind"—a youthful prodigy; and such an explanation is far more likely than that the author is simply careless and counting on the carelessness of his readers to conceal the incongruity. For the continual references to the time of year at which various events happen seem to prove that he had sketched for himself something like a chronology of his fictitious hero's life. And it is exceedingly difficult ever to detect him in the smallest false note of time. The date of the banquet and dance at Hanau is exactly fixed by the capture of Braunfels in January 1635 (bk. i., chap. 29): and Orb and Staden *had* both been captured before Simplicissimus could well have delivered his oration on the miseries of a governor (bk. ii., chap. 12). These may seem small matters, but it must be remembered that Grimmelshausen had no Dictionary of Dates before him. The battle of Jankow in 1645 gives us the last exact date to be found in the book, and Tittmann is probably right in assuming that with that engagement the author's personal connection with the war ceased. By the time Simplicissimus returns from his Eastern wanderings the "German Peace" had been concluded.

At the very beginning of Simplicissimus's story he is brought in contact with at least one historical personage— James Ramsay, the Swedish commandant of Hanau, whose heroic defence of that town is well known. Simplicissimus is said to be the son of his brother-in-law, one Captain Sternfels von Fuchsheim. This man's Christian name is nowhere given; the boy is expressly said by his foster-father (bk. v., chap. 8) to have been christened Melchior after himself, and the fictitious character of the supposed parentage seems amply proved by the fact that the whole name, "Melchior Sternfels von Fugshaim" (as it is often spelt), is an exact anagram of "Christoffel von Grimmelshausen." We may therefore pass over as unmeaning the attribution to this supposed father of "estates in Scotland" by the pastor in book i., chapter 22, and must probably consign to the realms of imagination the lady-mother, Susanna Ramsay, also. That Grimmelshausen was really brought in contact, possibly as a page, with the commandant of Hanau, seems likely. He knows a good deal of him. But of his later career he is quite ignorant; he even repeats as true the malignant calumny circulated by the Jesuits of Vienna to the effect that Ramsay had gone mad with rage at the loss of Hanau (bk. v., chap. 8). As a matter of fact, the poor man died partly of his wounds and partly of a broken heart. The only other historic personage in the story who can be identified with certainty is Daniel St. André, a Hessian soldier of fortune (bk. iii., chap. 15) of Dutch descent, and commanding at Lippstadt for the "Crown of Sweden."

For what reason Grimmelshausen wrote the "Continuatio," a dull medley of allegories, visions, and stories of knavery, brightened only by the "Robinsonade" at the end, it is hard to say; probably at the urgent request of his publisher, when the striking success of the original work became assured. It appeared at Mömpelgard (Montbéliard) in the very same year, viz. 1669, as the first known edition, or more probably editions, of the first five books, and is sometimes quoted as a sixth book. Two years later there were issued three more "Continuations," even more unworthy of their author, and laying stress chiefly on the least estimable side of the hero's character—the roguery by which he paid his way on his journey back from France. The worthlessness of these sequels is the more remarkable when we consider the excellence of the other books which make up what may be called the Simplicissimus-cycle. These are "Trutzsimplex," "Springinsfeld," the two parts of the "Enchanted Bird's-nest," and the "Everlasting Almanack." They are all deserving of attention.

The first, which is also known as the "Life of the Adventuress 'Courage,'" appeared immediately after "Simplicissimus," with which it is connected by the fact that the heroine is none other than the light-minded lady of the Spa at Griesbach, the alleged mother of Simplicissimus's bastard son; she is also at one time the wife or companion of "Springinsfeld" or "Jump i' th' Field," Simplicissimus's old servant. Her history, which is narrated with extraordinary vivacity, covers nearly the whole period of the war, and is interwoven with the remaining books of the cycle in a sufficiently ingenious manner. A secretary out of employ is driven by the cold into the warm guest-room of an inn in a provincial town. Here he finds a huge old man armed with a cudgel "that with one blow could have administered extreme unction to any man." This is Simplicissimus, with the famous club that had so terrified the resin-gatherers of the Black Forest ("Simplicissimus," bk. v., chap. 17). Either the episode of the Desert Island is left out of account altogether—possibly not yet invented—or he has not yet started on his final journey. The latter is unlikely, for the date is indicated as 1669 or 1670. To these two enters an old wooden-legged fiddler who turns out to be Simplicissimus's faithful knave, "Jump i' th' Field." Of the former hero the secretary had read; of the latter he himself had written; for meeting, as a poor wandering scholar, with a gang of gipsies in the Schwarzwald, he had been engaged by their queen, an aged but still handsome woman, to write her history, on the promise of a pretty wife and good pay. He is cheated of both, and the gipsies disappear with their queen, who is in fact the famous "Courage" or "Kurrasche."

The daughter of unknown parents, this heroine was living in a small Bohemian town with an old nurse when the Imperialists, under Bucquoy, conquered the country in 1620. She was then thirteen years old, and thus fifteen years senior to Simplicissimus. The nurse, to protect her chastity, disguises her as a boy, and in this garb she becomes page to a young Rittmeister, to whom, her secret having been all but discovered in a scuffle, she reveals her sex and becomes his mistress. The name Courage is, for amusing but quite unmentionable reasons, given to her in consequence of this episode. To her first lover she is actually married on his death-bed, and now begins her career nominally as an honourable widow, but in reality as an accomplished courtesan. She still follows the army, for which she has an invincible love, and being, of course, "frozen" or invulnerable, takes part in various fights, in one of which she captures a major, who, when she in turn is taken prisoner, revenges himself on her in the vilest fashion. He is preparing to hand her over, according to custom ("Simplicissimus," bk. ii., chap. 26), "to the horse-boys," when she is rescued by a young Danish nobleman, who proposes to make her his wife. The terrible story is told with an exactness of detail, which plainly can only be the work of the witness of similar scenes, and it is to be feared represents only too faithfully the truth as to the treatment of women in the war. It is remarkable, however, that few officers of high rank on either side are accused of wanton offences against public morals. Holk and Königsmark are the only two who are charged with publicly keeping their mistresses; and they were the two most brutal commanders of their time. As a rule superior officers took their wives with them ("Simplicissimus," bk. ii., chap. 25) even to the field of battle, and if such ladies fell into the enemy's hands, as did many after Nördlingen, they were treated with all possible respect.

But to return to "Courage." Her Danish lover is about to marry her when he too dies, and after this disappointment she sinks lower and lower in the social scale, forming temporary connections successively with a captain, a lieutenant, a corporal and finally with a musqueteer, who is no other than our old friend "Jump i' th' Field," for whose name she gives us a very complete and quite untranslatable reason. With him she journeys, as a Marketenderin or female sutler, to Italy, following the army of Colalto and Gallas, and there, with his assistance, she plays a variety of tricks, always knavish and often highly diverting. Grown rich, the vivandière dismisses poor "Jump i' th' Field" with a handsome present, and again resumes her trade of a superior courtesan in the town from which she journeys to the Spa, where she found and beguiled Simplicissimus. Her luck now turns; owing to a scandalous adventure under a pear-tree—the story is a mere copy of a well-known one in the "Hundred New Novels"—she is expelled from the town with the loss of all her money and almost of her life—so severe in the matter of public morals were the laws, in the midst of the general welter of wickedness then prevailing. Her beauty lost, she becomes a petty trader in wine and tobacco, and finally marries a gipsy chief; in which position we find her and leave her.

Introduction

This story ended, the secretary and his friends in the inn are joined by Simplicissimus's old foster-father and mother—the "Dad" and "Mammy" of our romance—and also by young Simplicissimus, Courage's alleged son. She has avenged herself on her faithless lover, as she tells us in her own history, by laying at his door the child of her maid. It is for this reason that she entitles her narrative "Trutzsimplex," or "Spite Simplex." Her revenge, however, for reasons plainly hinted at, miscarries; the child is her lover's after all. The merry company of six then divert themselves during the short winter afternoon with a profitable exhibition of Simplicissimus's tricks in the market-place, and the night is pleasantly spent in listening to Springinsfeld's account of his own life and adventures.

The son of a Greek woman and an Albanian juggler, he follows in early boyhood his father's trade. Carried away from the port of Ragusa by an accident, he is landed in the Spanish Netherlands, and there serves under Spinola, then with that general's army in the Rhine Palatinate, and then in Pappenheim's cavalry. He is present at Breitenfeld and Lützen, and while temporarily out of the service falls in with "Courage" as above narrated. On leaving her, he sets up as an inn-keeper, and prospers, but is ruined through his own incorrigible knavery. Serving against the Turks, he is wounded, and takes to fiddling to support himself, marrying also a hurdy-gurdy girl of loose character. In the course of their vagabond life there occurs the incident which leads to the most ingenious and attractive of all the romances of the cycle.

Sitting by a stream, they see in the water the shadow of a tree with a lump on one of the branches: on the tree itself there is no such lump. It is a bird's-nest, invisible itself, which makes its possessor invisible also. The wife seizes it and at once disappears, with all their money in her pocket. She does not, however, abandon her husband altogether, but when he goes into the neighbouring town of Munich she slips a handful of money into his pocket. He finds that this is a part of the proceeds of an impudent robbery just committed in the house of a merchant, and will have none of it, but is compelled to be witness of numerous amusing and mischievous pranks played by his wife of which he alone knows the secret. He goes to the wars again and loses a leg, after which he begs his way back to Munich and finds his wife dead. She has befooled a young baker's man into believing her to be the fairy Melusina, and after a sanguinary chance-medley in the baker's chamber, whither she is pursued for thefts committed for his sake, is slain by a young halberdier of the watch sent to arrest her. Her body is burned as that of a witch, and her slayer disappears bodily. His story thus ended, Springinsfeld is taken home by Simplicissimus to his farm, where he dies in the odour of sanctity.

Here begins the first part of the history of the "Enchanted Bird's-nest." The young halberdier is an honest lad, who uses his powers for good only, and his experiences are of exceeding interest as giving a picture of the manners of the time viewed in their most intimate particularities by an invisible witness We have matrimonial infelicities circumstantially described, as likewise the efforts of an impoverished family of nobles to keep up appearances in their tumble-down old castle. The halberdier prevents hideous and unspeakable crime, captures burglars who are effecting their purpose by a device similar to that of the "hand of glory," wreaks vengeance upon loose-living pastors and rescues the intended victims of footpads. The adventures follow one upon another in quick succession, but are ended by a somewhat unnecessary fit of remorse, during which the halberdier tears up the nest. It is, however, found, and the portion which contains its magic properties kept, by a passer-by. This First Part ends with a fresh appearance of Simplicissimus, who is in deep grief over the rejection by a neighbouring nobleman of his application for a post for his son, whom the invisible halberdier has seen and helped out of trouble in the convent where he was studying. This scene is so utterly unconnected with the course of the narrative that it is conjectured to refer to some real family misfortune of Grimmelshausen, of which he is anxious to give an explanation to the public.

Introduction

The new owner of the enchanted nest is the merchant whom Springinsfeld's wife had robbed at Munich, and the "Second Part" is occupied with the story of his wicked misuse of his powers. His actions are the very opposite of the halberdier's, though the contrast is not so pointed as to become inartistic. He makes use of his supernatural facilities to seduce his own servant, to perpetrate a peculiarly filthy act of revenge upon his faithless wife, and finally to accomplish the crowning deception of his whole career. He makes his way into the family of a respectable Portuguese Jew, in the first instance with a view to robbery, but becoming enamoured of the beautiful daughter of the house, he employs his invisibility to practise a most blasphemous piece of knavery. He succeeds in making the unfortunate parents believe that the maiden is destined to be the mother of the future Messiah by the prophet Elias. The latter part he of course plays himself, and enjoys the society of his victim till at length a child is born, which turns out, to the general horror, to be a girl. The motive is not new and the story is a sordid one; but it is most artistically recounted, and an intimate knowledge of Jewish manners and ideas is displayed. The narrative is also diversified by an element found in none of the other romances of the cycle—acute and far-sighted political discourses and reasonings on European affairs as likely to be affected by the war then impending with France, which ended with the treaty of Nimwegen in 1678.

Rendered desperate by his sins, though now deeply enamoured of the unfortunate Jewess Esther, the merchant is on the verge of surrendering himself to the power of "black magicians" of the worst and most diabolical kind when he escapes by betaking himself to the wars. Possessing besides his invisibility the power of rendering himself invulnerable, he is nevertheless wounded by a "consecrated" bullet, and finally makes his way home in poverty and misery accompanied by a pious monk. The nest is thrown into the Rhine and disappears for ever, and the merchant prepares to spend the remainder of his life in prayer and penitence.

The connection of the fifth work, the "Everlasting Almanack," with Simplicissimus is nominal only. It appeared in 1670, and is a perfect specimen of what may be called the best class of chapbooks of that day. It is the Whitaker's Almanack of the period. Each day has its special saints given: there are rules of good husbandry and weather prognostics; recipes for the house, the kitchen, and the farmyard; together with matters adapted for the higher class of readers, such as brief scientific notices, fragments of historical interest, narratives of marvellous occurrences, and, of course, in the spirit of the time, a mass of particulars as to astrology and the casting of horoscopes. Ingenious as it all is, and not without interest from the sociological point of view the book reminds us of Simplicissimus only by its connection with that side of his character which we would willingly forget, but for which Grimmelshausen seems to have cherished an unreasoning admiration, and on which he insisted more and more in his successive works —namely his qualities as a quack and mountebank.

As already pointed out, the interest of the central romance of "Simplicissimus" is less literary than historic, whereas German critics in their estimate of its value have considered the first aspect only, and their opinions are consequently little worth recording. Gervinus, for example, looking at the book from a purely artistic point of view, finds it wanting. Other critics have followed him blindly and with a considerable amount of underlying ignorance to boot. The accurate Dahlmann, for example, though he reckons the romance among his "historical sources," speaks of it as published at Mömpelgard in 1669 in six "volumes." Plainly he had never seen a copy, but had heard of the six books (five and the "Continuation") and mistook them for volumes. Tittmann, one of the latest editors of the work, sums up its chief merits when he says: "Simplicissimus and the Simplician writings are almost our only substitute, and that a poor one, for the contemporary memoirs in which our western neighbours are so rich."

The bibliography of the book is for our purpose not important. For a year or two editions seem to have succeeded each other with such rapidity that it is difficult to distinguish between them; but the only additional value which those printed later than 1670 possess is the questionable one of including the three worthless little sequels above referred to. Of modern editions the best, perhaps, is that of Tittmann (Leipzig, 1877), which has been principally used for this translation. The annotations, however, leave much to be desired: many difficulties are left unexplained, and there are some positive mistakes, of which a single instance may suffice. In book v., chapter 4, we find the expression "in prima plana," which is a sufficiently well-known military phrase of the time and means "on the first page" (of the muster-roll), which contained the names of the officers of a company written separately from those of the rank and file. It is explained by Tittmann to mean "at the first estimate," and succeeding editors have copied this, adding as a possible alternative "in the first engagement," or "at the first start". The editions for school and family reading which are current in Germany are, as a rule, so expurgated as to deprive the book of much of its interest. In this translation it has been found necessary to omit a single episode only, which is as childishly filthy as it is utterly uninteresting.

A. T. S. GOODRICK

CONTENTS

Contents

BOOK II

Contents

Contents

Chap. i : TREATS OF SIMPLICISSIMUS'S RUSTIC DESCENT AND OF HIS UPBRINGING AN-SWERING THERETO

THERE appeareth in these days of ours (of which many do believe that they be the last days) among the common folk, a certain disease which causeth those who do suffer from it (so soon as they have either scraped and higgled together so much that they can, besides a few pence in their pocket, wear a fool's coat of the new fashion with a thousand bits of silk ribbon upon it, or by some trick of fortune have become known as men of parts) forthwith to give themselves out gentlemen and nobles of ancient descent. Whereas it doth often happen that their ancestors were day-labourers, carters, and porters, their cousins donkey-drivers, their brothers turnkeys and catch-polls, their sisters harlots, their mothers bawds—yea, witches even : and in a word, their whole pedigree of thirty-two quarterings as full of dirt and stain as ever was the sugar-bakers' guild of Prague. Yea, these new sprigs of nobility be often themselves as black as if they had been born and bred in Guinea.

With such foolish folk I desire not to even myself, though 'tis not untrue that I have often fancied I must have drawn my birth from some great lord or knight at least, as being by nature disposed to follow the nobleman's trade had I but the means and the tools for it. 'Tis true, moreover, without jesting, that my birth and upbringing can be well compared to that of a prince if we overlook the one great difference in degree. How ! did not my dad (for so they call fathers in the Spessart) have his own palace like any other, so fine as no king could build with his own hands, but must let that alone for ever. 'Twas painted with lime, and in place of unfruitful tiles, cold lead and red copper, was roofed with that straw whereupon the noble corn doth grow, and that he, my dad, might make a proper show of nobility and riches, he had his wall round his castle built, not of stone, which men do find upon the road or dig out of the earth in barren places, much less of miserable baked bricks that in a brief space can be made and burned (as other great lords be wont to do), but he did use oak, which noble and profitable tree, being such that smoked sausage and fat ham doth grow upon it, taketh for its full growth no less than a hundred years ; and where is the monarch that can imitate him therein ? His halls, his rooms, and his chambers did he have thoroughly blackened with smoke, and for this reason only, that 'tis the most lasting colour in the world, and doth take longer to reach to real perfection than an artist will spend on his most excellent paintings. The tapestries were of the most delicate web in the world, wove for us by her that of old did challenge Minerva to a spinning match. His windows were dedicated to St. Papyrius for no other reason than that that same paper doth take longer to come to perfection, reckoning from the sowing of the hemp or flax whereof 'tis made, than doth the finest and clearest glass of Murano : for his trade made him apt to believe that whatever was produced with much paint was also more valuable and more costly ; and what was most costly was best suited to nobility. Instead of pages, lackeys, and grooms, he had sheep, goats, and swine, which often waited upon me in the pastures till I drove them home. His armoury was well furnished with ploughs, mattocks, axes, hoes, shovels, pitchforks, and hayforks, with which weapons he daily exercised himself ; for hoeing and digging he made his military discipline, as did the old Romans in time of peace. The yoking of oxen was his generalship, the piling of dung his fortification, tilling of the land his campaigning, and the cleaning out of stables his princely pastime and exercise. By this means did he conquer the whole round world so far as he could reach, and at every harvest did draw from it rich spoils. But all this I account nothing of, and am not puffed up thereby, lest any should have cause to jibe at me as at other new-fangled nobility, for I esteem myself no higher than was my dad, which had his abode in a right merry land, to wit, in the Spessart, where the wolves do howl good-night to each other. But that I have as yet told you nought of my dad's family, race and name is for the sake of precious brevity, especially since there is here no question of a foundation for gentlefolks for me to swear myself into ; 'tis enough if it be known that I was born in the Spessart.

Now as my dad's manner of living will be perceived to be truly noble, so any man of sense will easily understand that my upbringing was like and suitable thereto : and whoso thinks that is not deceived, for in my tenth year had I already learned the rudiments of my dad's princely exercises : yet as touching studies I might compare with the famous Amphistides, of whom Suidas reports that he could not count higher than five : for my dad had perchance too high a spirit, and therefore followed the use of these days, wherein many persons of quality trouble themselves not, as they say with bookworms' follies, but have their hirelings to do their inkslinging for them. Yet was I a fine performer on the bagpipe, whereon I could produce most dolorous strains. But as to knowledge of things divine, none shall ever persuade me that any lad of my age in all Christendom could there beat me, for I knew nought of God or man, of Heaven or hell, of angel or devil, nor could discern between good and evil. So may it be easily understood that I, with such knowledge of theology, lived like our first parents in Paradise, which in their innocence knew nought of sickness or death or dying, and still less of the Resurrection. O noble life ! (or, as one might better say, O noodle's life !) in which none troubles himself about medicine. And by this measure ye can estimate my proficiency in the study of jurisprudence and all other arts and sciences. Yea, I was so perfected in ignorance that I knew not that I knew nothing. So say I again, O noble life that once I led ! But my dad would not suffer me long to enjoy such bliss, but deemed it right that as being nobly born, I should nobly act and nobly live : and therefore began to train me up for higher things and gave me harder lessons.

Chap. ii : *OF THE FIRST STEP TOWARDS THAT DIGNITY TO WHICH SIMPLICISSIMUS ATTAINED, TO WHICH IS ADDED THE PRAISE OF SHEPHERDS AND OTHER EXCELLENT PRECEPTS*

FOR he invested me with the highest dignity that could be found, not only in his household, but in the whole world : namely, with the office of a shepherd : for first he did entrust me with his swine, then his goats, and then his whole flock of sheep, that I should keep and feed the same, and by means of my bagpipe (of which Strabo writeth that in Arabia its music alone doth fatten the sheep and lambs) protect them from the wolf. Then was I like to David (save that he in place of the bagpipe had but a harp), which was no bad beginning for me, but a good omen that in time, if I had any manner of luck, I should become a famous man : for from the beginning of the world high personages have been shepherds, as we read in Holy Writ of Abel, Abraham, Isaac, Jacob, and his sons : yea, of Moses also, which must first keep his father-in-law his sheep before he was made law-giver and ruler over six hundred thousand men in Israel.

And now may some man say these were holy and godly men, and no Spessart peasant-lads knowing nought of God ? Which I must confess : yet why should my then innocence be laid to my charge ? Yet, among the heathen of old time you will find examples as many as among God's chosen folk. So among the Romans were noble families that without doubt were called Bubulci, Vituli, Vitellii, Caprae, and so forth, because they had to do with the cattle so named, and 'tis like had even herded them. 'Tis certain Romulus and Remus were shepherds, and Spartacus that made the whole Roman world to tremble. What ! was not Paris, King Priam's son, a shepherd, and Anchises the Trojan prince, Aeneas's father ? The beautiful Endymion, of whom the chaste Luna was enamoured, was a shepherd, and so too the grisly Polypheme. Yea, the gods themselves were not ashamed of this trade : Apollo kept the kine of Admetus,

4

King of Thessaly ; Mercurius and his son Daphnis, Pan and Proteus, were all mighty shepherds : and therefore be they still called by our fantastic poets the patrons of herdsmen. Mesha, King of Moab, as we do read in II Kings, was a sheep-master ; Cyrus, the great King of Persia, was not only reared by Mithridates, a shepherd, but himself did keep sheep ; Gyges was first a herdsman, and then by the power of a ring became a king ; and Ismael Sophi, a Persian king, did in his youth likewise herd cattle. So that Philo, the Jew, doth excellently deal with the matter in his life of Moses when he saith the shepherds' trade is a preparation and a beginning for the ruling of men, for as men are trained and exercised for the wars in hunting, so should they that are intended for government first be reared in the gentle and kindly duty of a shepherd : all which my dad doubtless did understand : yea, to know it doth to this hour give me no little hope of my future greatness.

But to come back to my flock. Ye must know that I knew as little of wolves as of mine own ignorance, and therefore was my dad the more diligent with his lessons : and "lad," says he, "have a care ; let not the sheep run far from each other, and play thy bagpipe manfully lest the wolf come and do harm, for 'tis a four-legged knave and a thief that eateth man and beast, and if thou beest anyways negligent he will dust thy jacket for thee." To which I answered with like courtesy, "Daddy, tell me how a wolf looks : for such I never saw yet." "O thou silly blockhead," quoth he, "all thy life long wilt thou be a fool : thou art already a great looby and yet knowest not what a four-legged rogue a wolf is." And more lessons did he give me, and at last grew angry and went away, as bethinking him that my thick wit could not comprehend his nice instruction.

Chap. iii : TREATS OF THE SUFFERINGS OF A FAITHFUL BAGPIPE

SO I began to make such ado with my bagpipe and such noise that 'twas enough to poison all the toads in the garden, and so methought I was safe enough from the wolf that was ever in my mind : and remembering me of my mammy (for so they do use to call their mothers in the Spessart and the Vogelsberg) how she had often said the fowls would some time or other die of my singing, I fell upon the thought to sing the more, and so make my defence against the wolf stronger ; and so I sang this which I had learned from my mammy :

1. O peasant race so much despised,
How greatly art thou to be priz'd ?
Yea, none thy praises can excel,
If men would only mark thee well.

2. How would it with the world now stand
Had Adam never till'd the land ?
With spade and hoe he dug the earth
From whom our princes have their birth.

3. Whatever earth doth bear this day
Is under thine high rule and sway,
And all that fruitful makes the land
Is guided by thy master hand.

4. The emperor whom God doth give
Us to protect, thereby doth live :
So doth the soldier : though his trade
To thy great loss and harm be made.

5. Meat for our feasts thou dost provide :
Our wine by thee too is supplied :
Thy plough can force the earth to give
That bread whereby all men must live.

6. All waste the earth and desert were
Didst thou not ply thy calling there :
Sad day shall that for all be found
When peasants cease to till the ground.

7. So hast thou right to laud and praise,
For thou dost feed us all our days.
Nature herself thee well doth love,
And God thy handiwork approve.

8. Whoever yet on earth did hear
Of peasant that the gout did fear ;
That fell disease which rich men dread,
Whereby is many a noble dead.

9. From all vainglory art thou free
   (As in these days thou well mayst be),
   And lest thou shouldst through pride have loss,
   God bids thee daily bear thy cross.

10. Yea, even the soldier's wicked will
    May work thee great advantage still :
    For lest thou shouldst to pride incline,
    " Thy goods and house," saith he, " are mine."

So far and no further could I get with my song : for in a moment was I surrounded, sheep and all, by a troop of cuirassiers that had lost their way in the thick wood and were brought back to their right path by my music and my calls to my flock. " Aha," quoth I to myself, " these be the right rogues ! these be the four-legged knaves and thieves whereof thy dad did tell thee ! " For at first I took horse and man (as did the Americans the Spanish cavalry) to be but one beast, and could not but conceive these were the wolves ; and so would sound the retreat for these horrible centaurs and cond them a-flying : but scarce had I blown up my bellows to that end when one of them catches me by the shoulder and swings me up so roughly upon a spare farm horse they had stolen with other booty that I musts need fall on the other side, and that too upon my dear bagpipe, which began so miserably to scream as it would move all the world to pity : which availed nought, though it spared not its last breath in the bewailing of my sad fate. To horse again I must go, it mattered not what my bagpipe did sing or say : yet what vexed me most was that the troopers said I had hurt my dear bagpipe, and therefore it had made so heathenish an outcry. So away my horse went with me at a good trot, like the " primum mobile," for my dad's farm.

Now did strange and fantastic imaginations fill my brain ; for I did conceive, because I sat upon such a beast as I had never before seen, that I too should be changed into an iron man. And because such a change came not, there arose in me other foolish fantasies : for I thought these strange creatures were but there to help me drive my sheep home ; for none strayed from the path, but all, with one accord, made for my dad's farm. So I looked anxiously when my dad and

my mammy should come out to bid us welcome : which yet
came not : for they and our Ursula, which was my dad's only
daughter, had found the back-door open and would not wait
for their guests.

*Chap. iv : HOW SIMPLICISSIMUS'S PALACE WAS
STORMED, PLUNDERED, AND RUINATED,
AND IN WHAT SORRY FASHION THE
SOLDIERS KEPT HOUSE THERE*

ALTHOUGH it was not my intention to take the
peaceloving reader with these troopers to my dad's
house and farm, seeing that matters will go ill
therein, yet the course of my history demands
that I should leave to kind posterity an account of what
manner of cruelties were now and again practised in
this our German war : yea, and moreover testify by
my own example that such evils must often have been
sent to us by the goodness of Almighty God for our profit.
For, gentle reader, who would ever have taught me that
there was a God in Heaven if these soldiers had not
destroyed my dad's house, and by such a deed driven me
out among folk who gave me all fitting instruction thereupon ? Only a little while before, I neither knew nor could
fancy to myself that there were any people on earth save
only my dad, my mother and me, and the rest of our household, nor did I know of any human habitation but that
where I daily went out and in. But soon thereafter I understood the way of men's coming into this world, and how they
must leave it again. I was only in shape a man and in name
a Christian : for the rest I was but a beast. Yet the Almighty
looked upon my innocence with a pitiful eye, and would bring
me to a knowledge both of Himself and of myself. And
although He had a thousand ways to lead me thereto, yet
would He doubtless use that one only by which my dad and
my mother should be punished : and that for an example to
all others by reason of their heathenish upbringing of me.

The first thing these troopers did was, that they stabled
their horses : thereafter each fell to his appointed task :

which task was neither more nor less than ruin and destruction. For though some began to slaughter and to boil and to roast so that it looked as if there should be a merry banquet forward, yet others there were who did but storm through the house above and below stairs. Others stowed together great parcels of cloth and apparel and all manner of household stuff, as if they would set up a frippery market. All that they had no mind to take with them they cut in pieces. Some thrust their swords through the hay and straw as if they had not enough sheep and swine to slaughter : and some shook the feathers out of the beds and in their stead stuffed in bacon and other dried meat and provisions as if such were better and softer to sleep upon. Others broke the stove and the windows as if they had a never-ending summer to promise. Houseware of copper and tin they beat flat, and packed such vessels, all bent and spoiled, in with the rest. Bedsteads, tables, chairs, and benches they burned, though there lay many cords of dry wood in the yard. Pots and pipkins must all go to pieces, either because they would eat none but roast flesh, or because their purpose was to make there but a single meal.

Our maid was so handled in the stable that she could not come out ; which is a shame to tell of. Our man they laid bound upon the ground, thrust a gag into his mouth, and poured a pailful of filthy water into his body : and by this, which they called a Swedish draught, they forced him to lead a party of them to a another place where they captured men and beasts, and brought them back to our farm, in which company were my dad, my mother, and our Ursula.

And now they began : first to take the flints out of their pistols and in place of them to jam the peasants' thumbs in and so to torture the poor rogues as if they had been about the burning of witches : for one of them they had taken they thrust into the baking oven and there lit a fire under him, although he had as yet confessed no crime : as for another, they put a cord round his head and so twisted it tight with a piece of wood that the blood gushed from his mouth and nose and ears. In a word each had his own device to torture the peasants, and each peasant his several torture. But as it seemed to me then, my dad was the luckiest, for he with a laughing face confessed what others must out with in the midst of pains and miserable lamentations : and such honour without doubt fell to him because he was the householder. For they set him before a fire and bound him fast so that he could neither stir hand nor foot, and smeared the soles of his feet with wet salt, and this they made our old goat lick off, and so tickle him that he well nigh burst his sides with laughing. And this seemed to me so merry a thing that I must needs laugh with him for the sake of fellowship, or because I knew no better. In the midst of such laughter he must needs confess all that they would have of him, and indeed revealed to them a secret treasure, which proved far richer in pearls, gold, and trinkets than any would have looked for among peasants. Of the women, girls, and maidservants whom they took, I have not much to say in particular, for the soldiers would not have me see how they dealt with them. Yet this I know, that one heard some of them scream most piteously in divers corners of the house ; and well I can judge it fared no better with my mother and our Ursel than with the rest. Yet in the midst of all this miserable ruin I helped to turn the spit, and in the afternoon to give the horses drink, in which employ I encountered our maid in the stable, who seemed to me wondrously tumbled, so that I knew her not, but with a weak voice she called to me, " O lad, run away, or the troopers will have thee away with them. Look to it well that thou get hence : thou seest in what plight . . . " And more she could not say.

Chap. v : HOW SIMPLICISSIMUS TOOK FRENCH LEAVE, AND HOW HE WAS TERRIFIED BY DEAD TREES

NOW did I begin to consider and to ponder upon my unhappy condition and prospects, and to think how I might best help myself out of my plight. For whither should I go ? Here indeed my poor wits were far too slender to devise a plan. Yet they served me so far that towards evening I ran into the woods. But then whither was I to go further ? for the ways of the wood were as little known to me as the passage beyond Nova Zembla through the Arctic Ocean to China. 'Tis true the pitch-dark night was my protection : yet to my dark wits it seemed not dark enough ; so I did hide myself in a close thicket wherein I could hear both the shrieks of the tortured peasants and the song of the nightingales ; which birds regarded not the peasants either to show compassion for them or to stop their sweet song for their sakes : and so I laid myself, as free from care, upon one ear, and fell asleep. But when the morning star began to glimmer in the East I could see my poor dad's house all aflame, yet none that sought to stop the fire : so I betook myself thither in hopes to have some news of my dad ; whereupon I was espied by five troopers, of whom one holloaed to me, " Come hither, boy, or I will shoot thee dead."

But I stood stock-still and open-mouthed, as knowing not what he meant or would have ; and I standing there and gaping upon them like a cat at a new barn-door, and they, by reason of a morass between, not being able to come at me, which vexed them mightily, one discharged his carbine at me : at which sudden flame of fire and unexpected noise, which the echo, repeating it many times, made more dreadful, I was so terrified that forthwith I fell to the ground, and for terror durst not move a finger, though the troopers went their way and doubtless left me for dead ; nor for that whole day had I spirit to rise up. But night again overtaking me, I stood up and wandered away into the woods until I saw afar off a dead tree that shone : and this again wrought in me a new fear : wherefore I turned me about poste-haste and ran till I saw another such tree, from which I hurried away again, and in this manner spent the night running from one dead tree to another. At last came blessed daylight to my help, and bade those trees leave me untroubled in its presence : yet was I not much the better thereby ; for my heart was full of fear and dread, my brain of foolish fancies, and my legs of weariness, my belly of hunger, and mine eyes of sleep. So I went on and on and knew not whither ; yet the further I went the thicker grew the wood and the greater the distance from all human kind. So now I came to my senses, and perceived (yet without knowing it) the effect of ignorance and want of knowledge : for if an unreasoning beast had been in my place he would have known what to do for his sustenance better than I.

Yet I had wit enough when darkness again overtook me to creep into a hollow tree and there take up my quarters for the night.

Chap. vi : IS SO SHORT AND SO PRAYERFUL THAT SIMPLICISSIMUS THEREUPON SWOONS AWAY

BUT hardly had I composed myself to sleep when I heard a voice that cried aloud, " O wondrous love towards us thankless mortals ! O mine only comfort, my hope, my riches, my God ! " and more of the same sort, all of which I could not hear or understand. Yet these were surely words which should rightly have cheered, comforted, and delighted every Christian soul that should find itself in such plight as did I. But O simplicity ! O ignorance ! 'Twas all gibberish* to me, and all in an unknown tongue out of which I could make nothing : yea, was rather terrified by its strangeness. Yet when I heard how the hunger and thirst of him that spake should be satisfied, my unbearable hunger did counsel me to join myself to him as a guest. So I plucked up heart to come out of my hollow tree and to draw nigh to the voice I had heard, where I was ware of a tall man with long greyish hair which fell in confusion over his shoulders : a tangled beard he had shapen like to a Swiss cheese ; his face yellow and thin yet kindly enough, and his long gown made up of more than a thousand pieces of cloth of all sorts sewn together one upon another. Round his neck and body he had wound a heavy iron chain like St. William,† and in other ways seemed in mine eyes so grisly and terrible that I began to shake like a wet dog. But what made my fear greater was that he did hug to his breast a crucifix some six spans long. So I could fancy nought else but that this old grey man must be the wolf of whom my dad had of late told me : and in my fear I whipped out my bagpipe, which, as mine only treasure, I had saved from the troopers,

* *Lit.*, " Bohemian Villages," *i.e.*, with unpronounceable names.
† William, Duke of Aquitaine, and afterwards a Saint noted for the acerbity of his penances.

and blowing up the sack, tuned up and made a mighty noise to drive away that same grisly wolf : at which sudden and unaccustomed music in that lonely place the hermit was at first no little dismayed, deeming, without doubt, 'twas a devil come to terrify him and so disturb his prayers, as happened to the great St. Anthony. But presently recovering himself, he mocked at me as his tempter in the hollow tree, whither I had retired myself : nay, plucked up such heart that he advanced upon me to defy the enemy of mankind.

" Aha ! " says he, " thou art a proper fellow enough, to tempt saints without God's leave " : and more than that I heard not : for his approach caused in me such fear and trembling that I lost my senses and fell forthwith into a swoon.

Chap. vii : HOW SIMPLICISSIMUS WAS IN A POOR LODGING KINDLY ENTREATED

AFTER what manner I was helped to myself again I know not ; only this, that the old man had my head on his breast and my jacket open in front, when I came to my senses. But when I saw the hermit so close to me I raised such a hideous outcry as if he would have torn the heart out of my body. Then said he, " My son, hold thy peace : be content : I do thee no harm." Yet the more he comforted me and soothed me the more I cried, " Oh, thou eatest me ! Oh ! thou eatest me : thou art the wolf and wilt eat me." " Nay, nay," said he, " my son, be at peace : I eat thee not."

This contention lasted long, till at length I let myself so far be persuaded as to go into his hut with him, wherein was poverty the housekeeper, hunger the cook, and want clerk of the kitchen : there was my belly cheered with herbs and a draught of water, and my mind, which was altogether distraught, again brought to right reason by the old man's comfortable kindness. Thereafter then I easily allowed myself to be enticed by the charm of sweet slumber to pay my debt to nature. Now when the hermit perceived my need of sleep he left me to occupy my place in his hut alone : for one only could lie therein. So about midnight I awoke again and heard him sing the song which followeth here, which I afterwards did learn by heart.

> " Come, joy of night, O nightingale :
>   Take up, take up thy cheerful tale :
>   Sing sweet and loud and long.
>   Come praise thine own Creator blest,
>   When other birds are gone to rest,
>   And now have hushed their song.

> (Chorus)   With thy voice loud rejoice ;
>   For so thou best canst shew thy love
>   To God who reigns in heaven above.

> For though the light of day be flown,
> And we in darkness dwell alone,
> Yet can we chant and sing
> Of God his power and God his might :
> Nor darkness hinders us nor night
> Our praises so to bring.
> Echo the wanderer makes reply
> And when thou singst will still be by
> And still repeat thy strain.
> All weariness she drives afar
> And sloth to which we prisoners are,
> And mocks at slumber's chain.
> The stars that stand in heaven above,
> Do shew to God their praise and love
> And honour to Him bring ;
> And owls by nature reft of song
> Yet shew with cries the whole night long
> Their love to God the king.
> Come hither then, sweet bird of night,
> For we will share no sluggard's plight
> Nor sleep away the hours ;
> But, till the rosy break of day
> Chase from these woods the night away,
> God's praise shall still be ours."

Now while this song did last it seemed to me as if nightingale, owl, and echo had of a truth joined therein, and had I ever heard the morning star or had been able to play its melody on my bagpipe, I had surely run out of the hut to take my trick also, so sweet did this harmony seem to me : yet I fell asleep again and woke not till day was far advanced, when the hermit stood before me and said, " Up, child, I will give thee to eat and thereafter shew thee the way through the wood, so that thou comest to where people dwell, and also before night to the nearest village."

So I asked him, what be these things, " people " and " village " ?

" What," says he, " hast never been in any village and knowest not what people or folks be ? "

" Nay," said I, " nowhere save here have I been : yet tell me what be these things, folk and people and village."

" God save us," answered the hermit, " art thou demented or very cunning ? "

" Nay," said I, " I am my mammy's and dad's boy, and neither Master Demented or Master Cunning,"

Then the hermit shewed his amazement with sighs and crossing of himself, and says he, " 'Tis well, dear child, I am determined if God will better to instruct thee."

So then our questions and answers fell out as the ensuing chapter sheweth.

Chap. viii : HOW SIMPLICISSIMUS BY HIS NOBLE
DISCOURSE PROCLAIMED HIS EXCELLENT
QUALITIES

ERMIT. What is thy name ?
Simplicissimus. My name is " Lad."
H. I can see well enough that thou art no girl :
but how did thy father and mother call thee ?
S. I never had either father or mother.

H. Who gave thee then thy shirt ?

S. Oho ! Why, my mammy.

H. What did thy mother call thee ?

S. She called me " Lad," ay, and " rogue, silly gaby, and gallowsbird."

H. Who, then, was thy mammy's husband ?

S. No one.

H. With whom, then, did thy mammy sleep at night ?

S. With my dad.

H. What did thy dad call thee ?

S. He called me " Lad."

H. What was his name ?

S. His name was Dad.

H. What did thy mammy call him ?

S. Dad, and sometimes also " Master."

H. Did she never call him aught besides ?

S. Yea, that did she.

H. And what then ?

S. " Beast," " coarse brute," " drunken pig," and other the like, when she would scold him.

H. Thou beest but an ignorant creature, that knowest not thy parents' name nor thine own.

S. Oho ! neither dost thou know it.

H. Canst thou say thy prayers ?

S. Nay, my mammy and our Ursel did uprear the beds.

H. I ask thee not that, but whether thou knowest thy Paternoster ?

S. That do I.

H. Say it then.

S. Our father which art heaven, hallowed be name, to thy kingdom come, thy will come down on earth as it says heaven, give us debts as we give our debtors : lead us not into no temptation, but deliver us from the kingdom, the power, and the glory, for ever and ever.   Amen.

H. God help us !   Knowest thou naught of our Blessed Lord God ?

S. Yea, yea : 'tis he that stood by our chamber-door ; my mammy brought him home from the church feast and stuck him up there.

H. O Gracious God, now for the first time do I perceive what a great favour and benefit it is when Thou impartest knowledge of Thyself, and how naught a man is to whom Thou givest it not !   O Lord, vouchsafe to me so to honour Thy holy name that I be worthy to be as zealous in my thanks for this great grace as Thou hast been liberal in the granting of it. Hark now, Simplicissimus (for I can call thee by no other name), when thou sayest thy Paternoster, thou must say this : " Our Father which art in heaven, hallowed be Thy name : Thy kingdom come : Thy will be done in earth as it is in heaven : give us this day our daily bread . . ."

S. Oho there ! ask for cheese too !

H. Ah, dear child, keep silence and learn that thou needest more than cheese : thou art indeed loutish, as thy mammy told thee : 'tis not the part of lads like thee to interrupt an old man, but to be silent, to listen, and to learn. Did I but know where thy parents dwelt, I would fain bring thee to them, and then teach them how to bring up children.

S. I know not whither to go. Our house is burnt, and my mammy ran off and was fetched back with our Ursula, and my dad too, and our maid was sick and lying in the stable.

H. And who did burn the house ?

S. Aha ! there came iron men that sat on things as big as oxen, yet having no horns : which same men did slaughter sheep and cows and swine, and so I ran too, and then was the house burnt.

H. Where was thy dad then ?

S. Aha ! the iron men tied him up and our old goat was set to lick his feet. So he must needs laugh, and give the iron men many silver pennies, big and little, and fair yellow things and some that glittered, and fine strings full of little white balls.

H. And when did this come to pass ?

S. Why, even when I should have been keeping of sheep : yea, and they would even take from me my bagpipe.

H. But when was it that thou shouldst have been keeping sheep ?

S. What, canst thou not hear ? Even then when the iron men came : and then our Anna bade me run away, or the soldiers would carry me off : and by that she meant the iron men : so I ran off and so I came hither.

H. And whither wilt thou now ?

S. Truly I know not : I will stay here with thee.

H. Nay, to keep thee here is not to the purpose, either for me or thee. Eat now ; and presently I will bring thee where people are.

S. Oho ! tell me now what manner of things be " people."

H. People be mankind like me and thee : thy dad, thy mammy, and your Ann be mankind, and when there be many together then are they called people : and now go thou and eat.

So was our discourse, in which the hermit often gazed on me with deepest sighs : I know not whether 'twas so because he had great compassion on my simplicity and ignorance, or from that cause, which I learned not until some years later.

Chap. ix : *HOW SIMPLICISSIMUS WAS CHANGED FROM A WILD BEAST INTO A CHRISTIAN*

SO I began to eat and ceased to prattle ; all which lasted no longer than till I had appeased mine hunger : for then the good hermit bade me begone. Then must I seek out the most flattering words which my rough country upbringing afforded me, and all to this end, to move the hermit that he should keep me with him. Now though of a certainty it must have vexed him greatly to endure my troublesome presence, yet did he resolve to suffer me to be with him ; and that more to instruct me in the Christian religion, than because he would have my service in his approaching old age : yet was this his greatest anxiety, lest my tender youth should not endure for long such a hard way of living as was his.

A space of some three weeks was my year of probation : in which three weeks St. Gertrude* was at war with the gardeners : so was it my lot to be inducted into the profession of these last : and therein I carried myself so well that the good hermit took an especial pleasure in me, and that not so much for my work's sake (whereunto I was before well trained) but because he saw that I myself was as ready greedily to hearken to his instructions as the waxen, soft, and yet smooth tablet of my mind shewed itself ready to receive such. For such reasons he was the more zealous to bring me to the knowledge of all good things. So he began his instructions from the fall of Lucifer : thence came he to the Garden of Eden, and when we were

* A proverb : On Saint Gertrude's day spinning ceases and garden-work begins.

thrust out thence with our first parents, he passed through the law of Moses and taught me, by the means of the ten commandents and their explications—of which commandments he would say that they were a true measure to know the will of God, and thereby to lead a life holy and well pleasing to God —to discern virtue from vice, to do the good and to avoid the evil. At the end of all he came to the Gospel and told me of Christ's Birth, Sufferings, Death, and Resurrection : and then concluded all with the Judgment Day, and so set Heaven and hell before my eyes : and this all with befitting circumstance, yet not with superfluity of words, but as it seemed to him I could best comprehend and understand. So when he had ended one matter he began another, and therewithal contrived with all patience so to shape himself to answer my questions, and so to deal with me, that better he could not have shed the light of truth into my heart. Yet were his life and his speech for me an everlasting preaching : and this my mind, all wooden and dull as it was, yet by God's grace left not fruitless. So that in three weeks did I not only understand all that a Christian should know, but was possessed with such love for this teaching that I could not sleep at night for thinking thereon.

I have since pondered much upon this matter and have found that Aristotle, in his second book " Of the Soul," did put it well, whereas he compared the soul of a man to a blank unwritten tablet, whereon one could write what he would, and concluded that all such was decreed by the Creator of the world, in order that such blank tablets might by industrious impression and exercise be marked, and so be brought to completeness and perfection. And so saith also his commentator Averroes (upon that passage where the Philosopher saith that the Intellect is but a possibility which can be brought into activity by naught else than by Scientia or Knowledge: which is to say that man's understanding is capable of all things, yet can be brought to such knowledge only by constant exercise), and giveth this plain decision : namely, that this knowledge or exercise is the perfecting of souls which have no power at all in themselves. And this doth Cicero confirm in his second book of the " Tusculan Disputations," when he compares the soul of a man without instruction, knowledge, and exercise, to a field which, albeit fruitful by nature, yet if no man till it or sow it will bring forth no fruit.

And all this did I prove by my own single example : for that I so soon understood all that the pious hermit shewed to me arose from this cause : that he found the smooth tablet of my soul quite empty and without any imaginings before entered thereupon, which might well have hindered the impress of others thereafter. Yet in spite of all, that pure simplicity (in comparison with other men's ways) hath ever clung to me : and therefore did the hermit (for neither he nor I knew my right name) ever call me Simplicissimus. Withal I learned to pray, and when the good hermit had resolved himself to satisfy my earnest desire to abide with him, we built for me a hut like to his own, of wood, twigs and earth, shaped well nigh as the musqueteer shapes his tent in camp or, to speak more exactly, as the peasant in some places shapes his turnip-hod, so low, in truth, that I could hardly sit upright therein ; my bed was of dried leaves and grass, and just so long as the hut itself, so that I know not whether to call such a dwelling-place or hole, a covered bedstead or a hut.

Chap. x : IN WHAT MANNER HE LEARNED TO READ AND WRITE IN THE WILD WOODS

NOW when first I saw the hermit read the Bible, I could not conceive with whom he should speak so secretly and, as I thought, so earnestly ; for well I saw the moving of his lips, yet no man that spake with him : and though I knew naught of reading or writing, nevertheless I marked by his eyes that he had to do with somewhat in the said book. So I marked where he kept it, and when he had laid it aside I crept thither and opened it, and at the first assay lit upon the first chapter of Job and the picture that stood at the head thereof, which was a fine woodcut and fairly painted : so I began to ask strange questions of the figures, and when they gave me no answer waxed impatient, and even as the hermit came up behind me, " Ye little clowns," said I, " have ye no mouths any longer ? Could ye not even now prate away long enough with my father (for so must I call my hermit) ? I see well enough that ye are driving away the gaffer's sheep and burning of his house : wait awhile and I will quench your fire for ye," and with that rose up to fetch water, for there seemed to me present need of it. Then said the hermit, who I knew not was behind me : " Whither away, Simplicissimus ? " " O father," says I, " here be more soldiers that will drive off sheep : they do take them from that poor man with whom thou didst talk : and here is his house a-burning, and if I quench it not 'twill be consumed " : and with that I pointed with my finger to what I saw. " But stay," quoth the hermit, " for these figures be not alive " ; to which I, with rustic courtesy, answered him : " What, beest thou blind ? Do thou keep watch lest that they drive the sheep away while I do seek for water." " Nay," quoth he again, " but they be not alive ; they be made only to call up before our eyes things that happened long ago." " How " ; said I, " thou didst even now talk with them : how then can they be not alive ? " At that the hermit must, against his will and contrary to his habit, laugh · and " Dear child," says he, " these figures cannot talk : but what they do and what they are, that can I see from these black lines, and that do men call reading. And when I thus do read, thou conceivest that I speak with the figures : but 'tis not so."

Yet I answered him : " If I be a man as thou art, so must I likewise be able to see in these black lines what thou canst see : how then may I understand thy words ? Dear father, teach me in truth how to understand this matter."

So said he : " 'Tis well, my son, and I will teach thee so that thou mayest speak with these figures as well as I : only 'twill need time, in which I must have patience and thou industry."

With that he wrote me down an alphabet on birch-bark, formed like print, and when I knew the letters, I learned to spell, and thereafter to read, and at last to write better than could the hermit himself : for I imitated print in everything.

Chap. xi : DISCOURSETH OF FOODS, HOUSEHOLD STUFF, AND OTHER NECESSARY CONCERNS, WHICH FOLK MUST HAVE IN THIS EARTHLY LIFE

IN that wood did I abide for about two years, until the hermit died, and after his death somewhat longer than a half-year. And therefore it seemeth me good to tell to the curious reader, who often desireth to know even the smallest matters, of our doings, our ways and works, and how we spent our life.

Now our food was vegetables of all kinds, turnips, cabbage, beans, pease, and the like : nor did we despise beech-nuts, wild apples, pears, and cherries : yea, and our hunger often made even acorns savoury to us ; our bread or, to say more truly, our cakes, we baked on hot ashes, and they were made of Italian rye beaten fine. In winter we would catch birds with springes and snares ; but in spring and summer God bestowed upon us young fledglings from their nest. Often must we make out with snails and frogs : and so was fishing, both with net and line, convenient to us : for close to our dwelling there flowed a brook, full of fish and crayfish, all which did help to make our rough vegetable diet palatable. Once on a time did we catch a young wild pig, and this we penned in a stall, and did feed him with acorns and beech-nuts, so fatted him and at last did eat him ; for my hermit knew it could be no sin to eat that which God hath created to such end for the whole human race.

Of salt we needed but little and spices not at all : for we might not arouse our desire to drink, seeing that we had no cellar : what little salt we wanted a good pastor furnished us who dwelt some fifteen miles away from us, and of whom I shall yet have much to tell.

Now as concerns our household stuff, we had enough : for we had a shovel, a pick, an axe, a hatchet, and an iron pot for cooking, which was indeed not our own, but lent to us by the said pastor : each of us had an old blunt knife, which same were our own possessions, and no more : more than that needed we naught, neither dishes, plates, spoons, nor forks :

neither kettles, frying-pans, gridirons, spits, salt-cellars, no, nor any other table and kitchen ware: for our iron pot was our dish, our hands our forks and spoons : and if we would drink, we could do so through a pipe from the spring or else we dipped our mouths like Gideon's soldiers. Then for garments : of wool, of silk, of cotton, and of linen, as for beds, table-covers, and tapestries, we had none save what we wore upon our bodies : for we deemed it enough if we could shield ourselves from rain and frost. At other times we kept no rule or order in our household, save on Sundays and holy-days, at which time we would start on our way at midnight, so that we might come early enough to escape men's notice, to the said pastor's church, which was a little away from the village, and there might attend service. When we came thither we betook ourselves to the broken organ, from which place we could see both altar and pulpit : and when I first saw the pastor go up to the pulpit I asked my hermit what he would do in that great tub ! So, service finished, we went home as secretly as we had come, and when we found ourselves once more at home, with weary body and weary feet, then did we eat foul food with fair appetite : then would the hermit spend the rest of the day in praying and in the instructing of me in holy things.

On working days we would do that which seemed most necessary to do, according as it happened, and as such was required by the time of year and by our needs : now would we work in the garden : another time we gathered together the rich mould in shady places and out of hollow trees to improve our garden therewith in place of dung ; again we would weave baskets or fishing-nets or chop firewood, or go a-fishing, or do aught to banish idleness. Yet among all these occupations did the good hermit never cease to instruct me faithfully in all good things : and meanwhile did I learn, in such a hard life, to endure hunger, thirst, heat, cold, and great labour, and before all things to know God and how one should serve Him best, which was the chiefest thing of all. And indeed my faithful hermit would have me know no more, for he held it was enough for any Christian to attain his end and aim, if he did but constantly pray and work : so it came about that, though I was pretty well instructed in ghostly matters, and knew my Christian belief well enough, and could speak the German language as well as a talking spelling-book, yet I remained the most simple lad in the world : so that when I left the wood I was such a poor, sorry creature that no dog would have left his bone to run after me.

Chap. xii : TELLS OF A NOTABLE FINE WAY, TO DIE HAPPY AND TO HAVE ONESELF BURIED AT SMALL COST

SO had I spent two years or thereabouts, and had scarce grown accustomed to the hard life of a hermit, when one day my best friend on earth took his pick, gave me the shovel, and led me by the hand, according to his daily custom, to our garden, where we were wont to say our prayers.

" Now Simplicissimus, dear child," said he, " inasmuch as, God be praised, the time is at hand when I must part from this earth and must pay the debt of nature, and leave thee behind me in this world, and whereas I do partly foresee the future course of thy life and do know well that thou wilt not long abide in this wilderness, therefore did I desire to strengthen thee in the way of virtues which thou hast entered on, and to give thee some lessons for thy instruction by means of which thou shouldest so rule thy life that, as though by an unfailing clue, thou mightest find thy way to eternal happiness, and so with all elect saints mightest be found worthy for ever to behold the face of God in that other life."

These words did drown mine eyes in tears, even as once the enemy's device did drown the town of Villingen ; in a word, they were so terrible that I could not endure them, but said : " Beloved father, wilt thou then leave me alone in this wild wood ? Must I then. . . . ? " And more I could not say, for my heart's sorrow was, by reason of the overflowing love which I bore to my true father, so grievous that I sank at his feet as if I were dead. Yet did he raise me up and comfort me so far as time and opportunity did allow, and would shew me mine own error, in that he asked, would I rebel against the decree of the Almighty ? " and knowest thou not," says he, " that neither heaven nor hell can do that ?

Nay, nay, my son ! Why dost thou propose further to burden
my weak body, which of itself is but desirous of rest ? Thinkest thou to force me to sojourn longer in this vale of tears ?
Ah no, my son, let me go, for in any case neither with lament-
ation and tears, nor still less with my good will, canst thou
compel me to dwell longer in this misery when I am by God's
express will called away therefrom : instead of all this useless
clamour, follow thou my last words, which are these : the
longer thou livest seek to know thyself the better, and if thou
live as long as Methuselah, yet let not such practice depart
from thy heart : for that most men do come to perdition
this is the cause—namely, that they know not what they have
been and what they can or must be." And further he ex-
horted me, I should at all times beware of bad company :
for the harm of that was unspeakable. Of that he gave me
an example, saying : " If thou puttest a drop of malmsey
into a vessel full of vinegar, forthwith it turns to vinegar :
but if thou pour a drop of vinegar into malmsey, that drop
will disappear into the wine. Beloved son, before all things
be steadfast : for whoso endureth to the end he shall be
saved : but if it happen, contrary to my hopes, that thou
from human weakness dost fall, then by a fitting penitence
raise thyself up again."

Now this careful and pious man gave me but this brief
counsel, not because he knew no more, but because in sober
truth I seemed to him, by reason of my youth, not able to
comprehend more in such a case, and again, because few
words be better to hold in remembrance than long discourse,
and if they have pith and point do work greater good when
they be pondered on than any long sermon, which a man may
well understand as spoken and yet is wont presently to
forget. And these three points : to know oneself : to avoid
bad company : and to stand steadfast ; this holy man,
without doubt, deemed good and necessary because he had
made trial of them in his own case and had not found them
to fail : for, coming to know himself, he eschewed not only
bad company but that of the whole world, and in that plan
did persevere to the end, on which doubtless all salvation
doth depend.

So when he had thus spoken, he began with his mattock

to dig his own grave : and I helped as best I could in whatever way he bade me ; yet did I not conceive to what end all this was. Then said he : " My dear and only true son (for besides thee I never begat creature for the honour of our Creator), when my soul is gone to its own place, then do thy duty to my body, and pay me the last honours : cover me up with these same clods which we have even now dug from this pit." And thereupon he took me in his arms and, kissing me, pressed me harder to his breast than would seem possible for a man so weak as he appeared to be. And, " Dear child," says he, " I commend thee to God his protection, and die the more cheerfully because I hope He will receive thee therein." Yet could I do naught but lament and cry, yea, did hang upon the chains which he wore on his neck, and thought thereby to prevent him from leaving me. But " My son," says he, " let me go, that I may see if the grave be long enough for me." And therewith he laid aside the chains together with his outer garment, and so entered the pit even as one that will lie down to sleep, saying, " Almighty God, receive again the soul that Thou hast given : Lord, into Thy hands I commend my spirit." Thereupon did he calmly close his lips and his eyes : while I stood there like a stockfish, and dreamt not that his dear soul could so have left the body : for often I had seen him in such trances : and so now, as was my wont in such a case, I waited there for hours praying by the grave. But when my beloved hermit arose not again, I went down into the grave to him and began to shake, to kiss, and to caress him : but there was no life in him, for grim and pitiless death had robbed the poor Simplicissimus of his holy companionship. Then did I bedew or, to say better, did embalm with my tears his lifeless body, and when I had for a long time run up and down with miserable cries, began to heap earth upon him, with more sighs than shovelfuls : and hardly had I covered his face when I must go down again and uncover it afresh that I might see it and kiss it once more. And so I went on all day till I had finished, and in this way ended all the funeral ; an " exequiae " and " ludi gladiatorii " wherein neither bier, coffin, pall, lights, bearers, nor mourners were at hand, nor any clergy to sing over the dead.

*Chap. xiii : HOW SIMPLICISSIMUS WAS DRIVEN
ABOUT LIKE A STRAW IN A WHIRLPOOL*

NOW a few days after the hermit's decease I betook myself to the pastor above-mentioned and declared to him my master's death, and therewith besought counsel from him how I should act in such a case. And though he much dissuaded me from living longer in the forest, yet did I boldly tread on in my predecessor's footsteps, inasmuch as for the whole summer I did all that a holy monk should do. But as time changeth all things, so by degrees the grief which I felt for my hermit grew less and less, and the sharp cold of winter without quenched the heat of my steadfast purpose within. And the more I began to falter the lazier did I become in my prayers, for in place of dwelling ever upon godly and heavenly thoughts, I let myself be overcome by the desire to see the world : and inasmuch as for this purpose I could do no good in my forest, I determined to go again to the said pastor and ask if he again would counsel me to leave the wood. To that end I betook myself to his village, which when I came thither I found in flames : for a party of troopers had but now plundered and burned it, and of the peasants killed some, driven some away, and some had made prisoners, among whom was the pastor himself. Ah God, how full is man's life of care and disappointment ! Scarce hath one misfortune ended and lo ! we are in another. I wonder not that the heathen philosopher Timon set up many gallows at Athens, whereon men might string themselves up, and so with brief pain make an end to their wretched life.

These troopers were even now ready to march, and had the pastor fastened by a rope to lead him away. Some cried, " Shoot him down, the rogue ! " Others would have money from him. But he, lifting up his hands to heaven, begged, for the sake of the Last Judgment, for forbearance and Christian compassion, but in vain ; for one of them rode him down and dealt him such a blow on the head that he fell flat, and commended his soul to God. Nor did the remainder of the captured peasants fare any better. But even when it seemed these troopers, in their cruel tyranny, had clean lost their wits, came such a swarm of armed peasants out of the wood that it seemed a wasps'-nest had been stirred. And these began to yell so frightfully and so furiously to attack with sword and musket that all my hair stood on end ; and never had I been at such a merrymaking before : for the peasants of the Spessart and the Vogelsberg are as little wont as are the Hessians and men of the Sauerland and the Black Forest to let themselves be crowed over on their own dunghill. So away went the troopers, and not only left behind the cattle they had captured, but threw away bag and baggage also, and so cast all their booty to the winds lest themselves should become booty for the peasants : yet some of them fell into their hands. This sport took from me well-nigh all desire to see the world, for I thought, if 'tis all like this, then is the wilderness far more pleasant. Yet would I fain hear what the pastor had to say of it, who was, by reason of wounds and blows received, faint, weak, and feeble. Yet he made shift to tell me he knew not how to help or advise me, since he himself was now in a plight in which he might well have to seek his bread by begging, and if I should remain longer in the woods, I could hope no more for help from him ; since, as I saw with my own eyes, both his church and his parsonage were in flames. Thereupon I betook myself sorrowfully to my dwelling in the wood, and because on this journey I had been but little comforted, yet on the other hand had become more full of pious thoughts, therefore I resolved never more to leave the wilderness : and already I pondered whether it were not possible for me to live without salt (which the pastor had until now furnished me with) and so do without mankind altogether.

Chap. xiv: A QUAINT COMEDIA OF FIVE PEASANTS

SO now that I might follow up my design and become a true anchorite, I put on my hermit's hair-shirt which he had left me and girded me with his chain over it : not indeed as if I needed it to mortify my unruly flesh, but that I might be like to my fore-runner both in life and in habit, and moreover might by such clothes be the better able to protect myself against the rough cold of winter. But the second day after the above-mentioned village had been plundered and burnt, as I was sitting in my hut and praying, at the same time roasting carrots for my food over the fire, there surrounded me forty or fifty musqueteers : and these, though amazed at the strangeness of my person, yet ransacked my hut, seeking what was not there to find : for nothing had I but books, and these they threw this way and that as useless to them. But at last, when they regarded me more closely and saw by my feathers what a poor bird they had caught, they could easily reckon there was poor booty to be found where I was. And much they wondered at my hard way of life, and shewed great pity for my tender youth, specially their officer that commanded them : for he shewed me respect, and earnestly besought me that I would shew him and his men the way out of the wood wherein they had long been wandering. Nor did I refuse, but led them the nearest way to the village, even where the before-mentioned pastor had been so ill handled ; for I knew no other road.

Now before we were out of the wood, we espied some ten peasants, of whom part were armed with musquets, while the rest were busied with burying something. So our musqueteers ran upon them, crying, " Stay ! stay ! " But they answered with a discharge of shot, and when they saw they were outnumbered by the soldiers, away they went so quick that none of the musqueteers, being weary, could overtake them. So then they would dig up again what the peasants had been burying : and that was the easier because they had left the mattocks and spades which they used lying there. But they had made few strokes with the pick when they heard a voice from below crying out, " O ye wanton rogues, O ye worst of villains, think ye that Heaven will leave your heathenish cruelty and tricks unpunished ? Nay, for there live yet honest fellows by whom your barbarity shall be paid in such wise that none of your fellow men shall think you worth even a kick of his foot." So the soldiers looked on one another in amazement, and knew not what to do. For some thought they had to deal with a ghost : to me it seemed I was dreaming : but the officer bade them dig on stoutly. And presently they came to a cask, which they burst open, and therein found a fellow that had neither nose nor ears, and yet still lived. He, when he was somewhat revived, and had recognised some of the troop, told them how on the day before, as some of his regiment were a-foraging, the peasants had caught six of them. And of these they first of all, about an hour before, had shot five dead at once, making them stand one behind another ; and because the bullet, having already passed through five bodies, did not reach him, who stood sixth and last, they had cut off his nose and ears, yet before that had forced him to render to five of them the filthiest service in the world.* But when he saw himself thus degraded by these rogues without shame or knowledge of God, he had heaped upon them the vilest reproaches, though they were willing now to let him go. Yet in the hope one of them would from annoyance send a ball through his head, he called them all by their right names : yet in vain. Only this, that when he had thus chafed them they had clapped him in the cask here present and buried him alive, saying, since he so desired death they would not cheat him of his amusement.

Now while the fellow thus lamented the torments he had endured, came another party of foot-soldiers by a cross road through the wood, who had met the above-mentioned boors, caught five and shot the rest dead : and among the prisoners were four to whom that maltreated trooper had been forced to do that filthy service a little before. So now, when both parties had found by their manner of hailing one another that they were of the same army, they joined forces, and again must hear from the trooper himself how it had fared with him and his comrades. And there might any man tremble and quake to see how these same peasants were handled : for some in their first fury would say, " Shoot them down," but others said, " Nay : these wanton villains must we first properly torment : yea, and make them to understand in their own bodies what they have deserved as regards the person of this same trooper." And all the time while this discussion proceeded these peasants received such mighty blows in the ribs from the butts of their musquets that I wondered they did not spit blood. But presently stood forth a soldier, and said he : " You gentlemen, seeing that it is

* Viz. " ihnen den Hintern zu lecken."

a shame to the whole profession of arms that this rogue (and therewith he pointed to that same unhappy trooper) have so shamefully submitted himself to the will of five boors, it is surely our duty to wash out this spot of shame, and compel these rogues to do the same shameful service for this trooper which they forced him to do for them." But another said : " This fellow is not worth having such honour done to him ; for were he not a poltroon surely he would not have done such shameful service, to the shame of all honest soldiers, but would a thousand times sooner have died." In a word, 'twas decided with one voice that each of the captured peasants should do the same filthy service for ten soldiers which their comrade had been forced to do, and each time should say, " So do I cleanse and wash away the shame which these soldiers think they have endured."

Thereafter they would decide how they should deal with the peasants when they had fulfilled this cleanly task. So presently they went to work : but the peasants were so obstinate that neither by promise of their lives nor by any torture could they be compelled thereto. Then one took the fifth peasant, who had not maltreated the trooper, a little aside, and says he : " If thou wilt deny God and all His saints, I will let thee go whither thou wilt." Thereupon the peasant made reply, " he had in all his life taken little count of saints, and had had but little traffic with God," and added thereto with a solemn oath, " he knew not God and had no art nor part in His kingdom." So then the soldier sent a ball at his head : which worked as little harm as if it had been shot at a mountain of steel. Then he drew out his hanger and " Beest thou still here ? " says he. " I promised to let thee go whither thou wouldst : see now, I send thee to the kingdom of hell, since thou wilt not to heaven " : and so he split his head down to the teeth. And as he fell, " So," said the soldier, " must a man avenge himself and punish these loose rogues both in this world and the next."

Meanwhile the other soldiers had the remaining four peasants to deal with. These they bound, hands and feet together, over a fallen tree in such wise that their back-sides (saving your presence) were uppermost. Then they stript off their breeches, and took some yards of their match-string

and made knots in it, and fiddled them therewith so merci-
lessly that the blood ran. So they cried out lamentably,
but 'twas sport for the soldiers, who ceased not to saw away
till skin and flesh were clean sawn off the bones. Me they let
go to my hut, for the last-arrived party knew the way well.
And so I know not how they finished with the peasants.

*Chap. xv : HOW SIMPLICISSIMUS WAS PLUN-
DERED, AND HOW DE DREAMED OF THE
PEASANTS AND HOW THEY FARED IN
TIMES OF WAR*

NOW when I came home I found that my fire-
place and all my poor furniture, together with
my store of provisions, which I had grown
during the summer in my garden and had kept
for the coming winter, were all gone. " And whither now ? "
thought I. And then first did need teach me heartily to
pray : and I must summon all my small wits together, to
devise what I should do. But as my knowledge of the world
was both small and evil, I could come to no proper conclusion,
only that 'twas best to commend myself to God and to put
my whole confidence in Him : for otherwise I must perish.
And besides all this those things which I had heard and seen
that day lay heavy on my mind : and I pondered not so
much upon my food and my sustenance as upon the enmity
which there is ever between soldiers and peasants. Yet
could my foolish mind come to no other conclusion than this
—that there must of a surety be two races of men in the
world, and not one only, descended from Adam, but two,
wild and tame, like other unreasoning beasts, and therefore
pursuing one another so cruelly.

With such thoughts I fell asleep, for mere misery and cold,
with a hungry stomach. Then it seemed to me, as if in a dream,
that all the trees which stood round my dwelling suddenly
changed and took on another appearance : for on every tree-
top sat a trooper, and the trunks were garnished, in place of
leaves, with all manner of folk. Of these, some had long
lances, others musquets, hangers, halberts, flags, and some

drums and fifes. Now this was merry to see, for all was neatly
distributed and each according to his rank. The roots, moreover, were made up of folk of little worth, as mechanics and
labourers, mostly, however, peasants and the like ; and these
nevertheless gave its strength to the tree and renewed the
same when it was lost : yea more, they repaired the loss of
any fallen leaves from among themselves to their own great
damage : and all the time they lamented over them that sat
on the tree, and that with good reason, for the whole weight
of the tree lay upon them and pressed them so that all the
money was squeezed out of their pockets, yea, though it was
behind seven locks and keys : but if the money would not
out, then did the commissaries so handle them with rods
(which thing they call military execution) that sighs came
from their heart, tears from their eyes, blood from their
nails, and the marrow from their bones. Yet among these
were some whom men call light o' heart ; and these made
but little ado, took all with a shrug, and in the midst of their
torment had, in place of comfort, mockery for every turn.

Chap. xvi : OF THE WAYS AND WORKS OF SOLDIERS NOWADAYS, AND HOW HARDLY A COMMON SOLDIER CAN GET PROMOTION

S O must the roots of these trees suffer and endure
toil and misery in the midst of trouble and com-
plaint, and those upon the lower boughs in yet
greater hardship : yet were these last mostly merrier
than the first named, yea and moreover, insolent and swaggering, and for the most part godless folk, and for the roots
a heavy unbearable burden at all times. And this was the
rhyme upon them :

" Hunger and thirst, and cold and heat, and work and
    woe, and all we meet ;
  And deeds of blood and deeds of shame, all may ye
    put to the landsknecht's name."

Which rhymes were the less like to be lyingly invented in
that they answered to the facts. For gluttony and drunken-

ness, hunger and thirst, wenching and dicing and playing, riot and roaring, murdering and being murdered, slaying and being slain, torturing and being tortured, hunting and being hunted, harrying and being harried, robbing and being robbed, frighting and being frighted, causing trouble and suffering trouble, beating and being beaten : in a word, hurting and harming, and in turn being hurt and harmed—this was their whole life. And in this career they let nothing hinder them : neither winter nor summer, snow nor ice, heat nor cold, rain nor wind, hill nor dale, wet nor dry ; ditches, mountain-passes, ramparts and walls, fire and water, were all the same to them. Father nor mother, sister nor brother, no, nor the danger to their own bodies, souls, and consciences, nor even loss of life and of heaven itself, or aught else that can be named, will ever stand in their way, for ever they toil and moil at their own strange work, till at last, little by little, in battles, sieges, attacks, campaigns, yea, and in their winter quarters too (which are the soldiers' earthly paradise, if they can but happen upon fat peasants) they perish, they die, they rot and consume away, save but a few, who in their old age, unless they have been right thrifty rievers and robbers, do furnish us with the best of all beggars and vagabonds.

Next above these hard-worked folk sat old henroost-robbers, who, after some years and much peril of their lives, had climbed up the lowest branches and clung to them, and so far had had the luck to escape death. Now these looked more serious, and somewhat more dignified than the lowest, in that they were a degree higher ascended : yet above them were some yet higher, who had yet loftier imaginings because they had to command the very lowest. And these people did call coat-beaters, because they were wont to dust the jackets of the poor pikemen, and to give the musqueteers oil enough to grease their barrels with.

Just above these the trunk of the tree had an interval or stop, which was a smooth place without branches, greased with all manner of ointments and curious soap of disfavour, so that no man save of noble birth could scale it, in spite of courage and skill and knowledge, God knows how clever he might be. For 'twas polished as smooth as a marble pillar or a steel mirror. Just over that smooth spot sat they

with the flags : and of these some were young, some pretty
well in years : the young folk their kinsmen had raised so
far : the older people had either mounted on a silver ladder
which is called the Bribery Backstairs or else on a step which
Fortune, for want of a better client, had left for them. A
little further up sat higher folk, and these had also their toil
and care and annoyance : yet had they this advantage, that
they could fill their pokes with the fattest slices which they
could cut out of the roots, and that with a knife which they
called " War-contribution." And these were at their best
and happiest when there came a commissary-bird flying over-
head, and shook out a whole panfull of gold over the tree
to cheer them : for of that they caught as much as they could,
and let but little or nothing at all fall to the lowest branches :
and so of these last more died of hunger than of the enemy's
attacks, from which danger those placed above seemed to be
free. Therefore was there a perpetual climbing and swarming
going on on those trees ; for each would needs sit in those
highest and happiest places : yet were there some idle, worthless rascals, not worth their commissariat-bread, who troubled
themselves little about higher places, and only did their duty.
So the lowest, being ambitious, hoped for the fall of the highest,
that they might sit in their place, and if it happened to one
among ten thousand of them that he got so far, yet would
such good luck come to him only in his miserable old age
when he was more fit to sit in the chimney-corner and roast
apples than to meet the foe in the field. And if any man
dealt honestly and carried himself well, yet was he ever
envied by others, and perchance by reason of some unlucky
chance of war deprived both of office and of life. And nowhere was this more grievous than at the before-mentioned
smooth place on the tree : for there an officer who had had
a good sergeant or corporal under him must lose him, however
unwillingly, because he was now made an ensign. And for
that reason they would take, in place of old soldiers, ink-
slingers, footmen, overgrown pages, poor noblemen, and at
times poor relations, tramps and vagabonds. And these
took the very bread out of the mouths of those that had
deserved it, and forthwith were made Ensigns.

Chap. xvii : HOW IT HAPPENS THAT, WHEREAS IN WAR THE NOBLES ARE EVER PUT BEFORE THE COMMON MEN, YET MANY DO ATTAIN FROM DESPISED RANK TO HIGH HONOURS

ALL this vexed a sergeant so much that he began loudly to complain : whereupon one Nobilis answered him : " Knowst thou not that at all times our rulers have appointed to the highest offices in time of war those of noble birth as being fittest therefore. For greybeards defeat no foe : were it so, one could send a flock of goats for that employ : We say :

' Choose out a bull that's young and strong to lead and keep the herd,
  For though the veteran be good, the young must be preferred.
  So let the herdsman trust to him, full young though he appears :
  'Tis but a saw, and 'tis no law, that wisdom comes with years.'

Tell me," says he, " thou old cripple, is't not true that nobly born officers be better respected by the soldiery than they that beforetime have been but servants ? And what discipline in war can ye find where no respect is ? Must not a general trust a gentleman more than a peasant lad that had run away from his father at the plough-tail and so done his own parents no good service ? For a proper gentleman, rather than bring reproach upon his family by treason or desertion or the like, will sooner die with honour. And so 'tis right the gentles should have the first place. So doth Joannes de Platea plainly lay it down that in furnishing of offices the preference should ever be given to the nobility, and these properly set before the commons. Such usage is to be found in all codes of laws, and is, moreover, confirmed in Holy Writ : for ' happy is the land whose king is of noble family,' saith Sirach in his tenth chapter : which is a noble testimony to the preference belonging to gentle birth. And even if one of your kidney be a good soldier enough that can smell powder and play his part well in every venture, yet is he not therefore capable of command of others : which quality is natural to gentlemen, or at least customary to them from their youth up. And so saith Seneca, ' A hero's soul hath this property, that 'tis ever alert in search of honour : and no lofty spirit hath pleasure in small and unworthy things.' Moreover, the nobles have more means to furnish their inferior officers with money and to procure recruits for their weak companies than a peasant. And so to follow the common proverb, it were not well to put the boor above the gentleman ; yea, and the boors would soon become too high-minded if they be made lords straightway ; for men say :

> ' Where will ye find a sharper sword, than peasant churl
> that's made a lord ? '

Now had the peasants, by reason of long and respectable custom, possessed all offices in war and elsewhere, of a surety they would have let no gentleman into such. Yea, and besides, though ye soldiers of Fortune, as ye call yourselves, be often willingly helped to raise yourselves to higher ranks, yet ye are commonly so worn out that when they try you and would find you a better place, they must hesitate to promote you ; for the heat of your youth is cooled down and your only thought is how ye can tend and care for your sick bodies which, by reason of much hardships, be crippled and of little use for war : yea, and a young dog is better for hunting than an old lion."

Then answered the old sergeant, " And what fool would be a soldier, if he might not hope by his good conduct to be promoted, and so rewarded for faithful service ? Devil take such a war as that ! For so 'tis all the same whether a man behave himself well or ill ! Often did I hear our old colonel say he wanted no soldier in his regiment that had not the firm intention to become a general by his good conduct. And all the world must acknowledge that 'tis those nations which promote common soldiers, that are good soldiers too, that win victories, as may be seen in the case of the Turks and Persians ; so says the verse

' Thy lamp is bright : yet feed it well with oil : an thou
dost not the flame sinks down and dies.
So by rewards repay the soldiers toil, for service brave
demands its pay likewise.' "

Then answered Nobilis : " If we see brave qualities and in
an honest man, we shall not overlook them : for at this very
time see how many there be who from the plough, from the
needle, from shoemaking, and from shepherding have done
well by themselves, and by such bravery have raised themselves up far above the poorer nobility to the ranks of counts
and barons. Who was the Imperialist John de Werth ? Who
was the Swede Stalhans ? Who were the Hessians, Little
Jakob and St. André ? Of their kind there were many yet well
known whom I, for brevity's sake, forbear to mention. So is
it nothing new in the present time, nor will it be otherwise in
the future, that honest men attain by war to great honours, as
happened also among the ancients. Tamburlaine became a
mighty king and the terror of the whole world, which was before
but a swineherd : Agathocles, King of Sicily, was son of a potter ; Emperor Valentinian's father was a ropemaker ; Maurice
the Cappadocian, a slave, was emperor after Tiberius II. ;
Justin, that reigned before Justinian, was before he was emperor a swineherd ; Hugh Capet, a butcher's son, was after-
ward King of France ; Pizarro likewise a swineherd, which
afterwards was marquess in the West Indies, where he had to
weigh out his gold in hundredweights."

The sergeant answered : " All this sounds fair enough for
my purpose : yet well I see that the doors by which we might
win to many dignities be shut against us by the nobility. For
as soon as he is crept out of his shell, forthwith your nobleman
is clapped into such a position as we cannot venture to set our
thoughts upon, howbeit we have done more than many a noble
who is now appointed a colonel. And just as among the peasants many noble talents perish for want of means to keep a lad
at his studies, so many a brave soldier grows old under the
weight of a musquet, that more properly deserved a regiment
and could have tendered great services to his general."

Chap. xviii : HOW SIMPLICISSIMUS TOOK HIS FIRST
STEP INTO THE WORLD AND THAT WITH
EVIL LUCK

I CARED no longer to listen to this old ass, but grudged
him not his complaints, for often he himself had beaten
poor soldiers like dogs. I turned again to the trees whereof the whole land was full and saw how they swayed and
smote against each other : and the fellows tumbled off them
in batches. Now a crack ; now a fall. One moment quick,
the next dead. In a moment one lost an arm, another a leg,
the third his head. And as I looked methought all trees I saw
were but one tree, at whose top sat the war-god Mars, and
which covered with its branches all Europe. It seemed to me
this tree could have overshadowed the whole world : but because it was blown about by envy and hate, by suspicion and
unfairness, by pride and haughtiness and avarice, and other
such fair virtues, as by bitter north winds, therefore it seemed
thin and transparent . for which reason one had writ on its
trunk these rhymes :

" The holmoak by the wind beset and brought to ruin,
    Breaks its own branches down and proves its own undoing.
    By civil war within and brothers' deadly feud
    All's topsy-turvy turned and misery hath ensued."

By the mighty roaring of these cruel winds and the noise of
the breaking of the tree itself I was awoke from my sleep, and
found myself alone in my hut. Then did I again begin to
ponder what I should do. For to remain in the wood was impossible, since I had been so utterly despoiled that I could
not keep myself : nothing remained to me but a few books
which lay strewn about in confusion. And when with weeping
eyes I took these up to read, calling earnestly upon God that
He would lead and guide me whither I should go, I found by
chance a letter which my hermit had writ in his lifetime, and
this was the content of it. " Beloved Simplicissimus, when
thou findest this letter, go forthwith out of the forest and save
thyself and the pastor from present troubles : for he hath done

me much good. God, whom thou must at all times have before thine eyes and earnestly pray to, will bring thee to the place which is best for thee. Only keep Him ever in thy sight and be diligent ever to serve Him as if thou wert still in my presence in the wood. Consider and follow without ceasing my last words, and so mayest thou stand firm. Farewell."

I kissed this letter and the hermit's grave many thousand times, and started on my way to seek for mankind. Yet before I could find them I journeyed straight on for two whole days, and when night overtook me, sought out a hollow tree for my shelter, and my food was naught but beech-nuts which I picked up on the way : but on the third day I came to a pretty open field near Gelnhausen, and there I enjoyed a veritable banquet, for the whole place was full of wheatsheaves which the peasants had, being frightened away after the great battle of Nördlingen, for my good fortune not been able to carry off. Inside a sheaf I set up my tent, for 'twas cruel cold, and filled my belly with the ears of corn which I rubbed in my hands : and such a meal I had not enjoyed for a long time.

Chap. xix : HOW SIMPLICISSIMUS WAS CAPTURED BY HANAU AND HANAU BY SIMPLICISSIMUS

WHEN 'twas day I fed myself again with wheat, and thereafter betook myself to Gelnhausen, and there I found the gates open and partly burnt, yet half barricaded with dung. So I went in, but was ware of no living creature there. Indeed the streets were strewn here and there with dead, some of whom were stripped to their shirts, some stark naked. This was a terrifying spectacle, as any man can imagine. I, in my simplicity, could not guess what mishap had brought the place to such a plight. But not long after I learned that the Imperialists had surprised a few of Weimar's folk there. And hardly had I gone two-stones'-throw into the town when I had seen enough : so I turned me about and went across the meadows, and presently I came to a good road which brought me to the fine fortress of Hanau. When I came to the first sentries I tried to pass ; but two musqueteers made at me, who seized me and took me off to their guard-room.

Now must I first describe to the reader my wonderful dress at that time, before I tell him how I fared further. For my clothing and behaviour were altogether so strange, astonishing, and uncouth, that the governor had my picture painted. Firstly, my hair had for two years and a half never been cut either Greek, German, or French fashion, nor combed nor curled nor puffed, but stood in its natural wildness with more than a year's dust strewn on it instead of hair plunder or powder, or whatever they call the fools' work—and that so prettily that I looked with my pale face underneath it, like a great white owl that is about to bite or else watching for a mouse. And because I was accustomed at all times to go bare-headed and my hair was curly, I had the look of wearing a Turkish turban. The rest of my garb answered to my head-gear ; for I had on my hermit's coat, if I may now call it a coat at all, for the stuff out of which 'twas fashioned at first was now clean gone and nothing more remaining of it but the shape, which more than a thousand little patches of all colours, some put side by side, some sewn upon one another with manifold stitches, still represented. Over this decayed and yet often improved coat I wore the hair-shirt mantle-fashion, for I needed the sleeves for breeches and had cut them off for that purpose. But my whole body was girt about with iron chains, most deftly disposed crosswise behind and before like the pictures of St. William ; so that all together made up a figure like them that have once been captured by the Turks and now wander through the land begging for their friends still in captivity. My shoes were cut out of wood and the laces woven out of strips of lime-bark : and my feet looked like boiled lobsters, as I had had on stockings of the Spanish national colour or had dyed my skin with logwood. In truth I believe if any conjurer, mountebank, or stroller had had me and had given me out for a Samoyede or a Greenlander, he would have found many a fool that would have wasted a kreutzer on me. Yet though any man in his wits could easily conclude, from my thin and starved looks and my decayed clothes, I came neither from a cook-shop nor a lady's bower, and still less had played truant from any great lord's court, nevertheless I was strictly examined in the guard-room, and even as the soldiers gaped at me so was I filled with wonder at the mad apparel of their officer to whom I must answer and give account. I knew not if it were he or she : for he wore his hair and beard French fashion, with long tails hanging down on each side like horse-tails, and his beard was so miserably handled and mutilated that between mouth and nose there were but a few hairs, and those had come off so ill that one could scarce see them. And not less did his wide breeches leave me in no small doubt of his sex, being such that they were as like a woman's petticoats as a man's breeches. So I thought, if this be a man he should have a proper beard, since the rogue is not so young as he pre-tends : but if a woman, why hath the old witch so much stubble round her mouth ? Sure 'tis a woman, thought I, for no honest man would ever let his beard be so lamentably bedevilled, seeing that even goats for pure shamefacedness venture not a step among a strange flock when their beards are clipped. So as I stood in doubt, knowing not of modern fashions, at last I held he was man and woman at once. And this mannish woman or this womanish man had me thoroughly searched, but could find nothing on me but a little book of birch-bark wherein I had written down my daily prayers, and had also left the letter which my pious hermit, as I have said in the last chapter, had bequeathed me for his farewell : that he took from me : but I, being loath to part from it, fell down before him and clasped both his knees and, " O my good Hermaphrodite," says I, " leave me my little prayer-book." " Thou fool," he answered, " who the devil told thee my name was Hermann ? " And therewith commanded two soldiers to lead me to the Governor, giving them the book to take with them : for indeed this fop, as I at once did note, could neither read nor write himself.

So I was led into the town, and all ran together as if a sea-monster were on show ; and according as each one regarded me so each made something different out of me. Some deemed me a spy, others a wild man, and some even a spirit, a spectre, or a monster, that should portend some strange happening. Some, too, there were that counted me a mere fool, and they had indeed come nearest to the mark had I not had the know-ledge of God our Father.

*Chap. xx : IN WHAT WISE HE WAS SAVED FROM
PRISON AND TORTURE*

NOW when I was brought before the Governor he asked me whence I came. I said I knew not. Then said he again " Whither wilt thou ? " and again I answered, " I know not." " What the devil dost thou know, then ? " says he, " What is thy business ? " I answered as before, I knew not. He asked, " Where dost thou dwell ? " and as I again answered I knew not, his countenance was changed, I know not whether from anger or astonishment. But inasmuch as every man is wont to suspect evil, and specially the enemy being in the neighbourhood, having just, as above narrated, captured Gelnhausen and therein put to shame a whole regiment of dragoons, he agreed with them that held me for a traitor or a spy, and ordered that I should be searched. But when he learned from the soldiers of the watch that this was already done, and nothing more found on me than the book there present which they delivered to him, he read a line or two therein and asked who had given me the book. I answered it was mine from the beginning : for I had made it and written it. Then he asked, " Why upon birch-bark ? " I answered, because the bark of other trees was not fitted therefore. " Thou rascal," says he, " I ask why thou didst not write on paper." " Oh ! " I answered him, " we had none in the wood." The Governor asked, " Where, in what wood ? " And again I paid him in my old coin and said I did not know. Then the Governor turned to some of his officers that waited on him and said, " Either this is an archrogue, or else a fool : and a fool he cannot be, that can write so well." And as he spake, he turned over the leaves to shew them my fine hand-writing, and that so sharply that the hermit's letter fell out : and this he had picked up, while I turned pale, for that I held for my chiefest treasure and holy relic. That the Governor noted and conceived yet greater suspicion of treason, specially when he had opened and read the letter, " for," says he, " I surely know this hand and know that it is written by an officer well known to me : yet can I not remember by whom." Also the contents seemed to him strange and not to be understood :

for he said, " This is without doubt a concerted language, which none other can understand save him to whom it is imparted." Then asking me my name, when I said Simplicissimus, " Yes, yes," says he, " thou art one of the right kidney. Away, away : put him at once in irons, hand and foot."

So the two before-mentioned soldiers marched off with me to my bespoken lodging, namely, the lock-up, and handed me over to the gaoler, which, in accordance with his orders, adorned me with iron bands and chains on hands and feet, as if I had not had enough to carry with those that I had already bound round my body. Nor was this way of welcoming me enough for the world, but there must come hangmen and their satellites, with horrible instruments of torture, which made my wretched plight truly grievous, though I could comfort myself with my innocence. " O ! God ! " says I to myself, " how am I rightly served ! To this end did Simplicissimus run from the service of God into the world, that such a misbirth of Christianity should receive the just reward which he hath deserved for his wantonness ! O, thou unhappy Simplicissimus, whither hath thine ingratitude led thee ! Lo, God hath hardly brought thee to the knowledge of Him and into His service when thou, contrariwise, must run off from His employ and turn thy back on Him. Couldst thou not go on eating of acorns and beans as before, and so serving thy Creator ? Didst thou not know that thy faithful hermit and teacher had fled from the world and chosen the wilderness ? O stupid stock, thou didst leave it in the hope to satisfy thy loose desire to see the world. And behold, while thou thinkest to feed thine eyes, thou must in this maze of dangers perish and be destroyed. Couldst thou not, unwise creature, understand before this, that thy everblessed teacher would never have left the world for that hard life which he led in the desert, if he had hoped to find in the world true peace, and real rest, and eternal salvation ? O poor Simplicissimus, go thy way and receive the reward of the idle thoughts thou hast cherished and thy presumptuous folly. Thou hast no wrong to complain of, neither any innocence to comfort thee with, for thou hast hastened to meet thine own torment and the death to follow thereafter." So I bewailed myself, and besought God for forgiveness and commended my soul to Him. In the meanwhile we drew near to the prison, and when my need was greatest then was God's help nearest : for as I was surrounded by the hangman's mates, and stood there before the gaol with a great multitude of folk to wait till it was opened and I could be thrust in, lo, my good pastor, whose village had so lately been plundered and burned, must also see what was toward (himself being also under arrest). So as he looked out of window and saw me, he cried loudly, " O Simplicissimus, is it thou ? "

When this I heard and saw, I could not help myself, but must lift up both hands to him and cry, " O father, father, father." So he asked what had I done. I answered, I knew not : they had brought me there of a certainty because I had deserted from the forest. But when he learned from the bystanders that they took me for a spy, he begged they would make a stay with me till he had explained my case to the Lord Governor, for that would be of use for my deliverance and for his, and so would hinder the Governor from dealing wrongfully with both of us, since he knew me better than could any man.

Chap. xxi : HOW TREACHEROUS DAME FORTUNE CAST ON SIMPLICISSIMUS A FRIENDLY GLANCE

SO 'twas allowed him to go to the Governor, and a half-hour thereafter I was fetched out likewise and put in the servitors' room, where were already two tailors, a shoemaker with shoes, a haberdasher with stockings and hats, and another with all manner of apparel, so that I might forthwith be clothed. Then took they off my coat, chains and all, and the hair-shirt, by which the tailors could take their measure aright : next appeared a barber with his lather and his sweet-smelling soaps, but even as he would exercise his art upon me came another order which did grievously terrify me : for it ran, I should put on my old clothes again. Yet 'twas not so ill meant as I feared : for there came presently a painter with all his colours, namely vermilion and cinnabar for my eyelids, indigo and ultramarine for my coral lips, gamboge and ochre and yellow lead for my white teeth, which I was licking for sheer hunger, and lamp-black and burnt umber for my golden hair, white lead for my terrible eyes and every kind of paint for my weather-coloured coat : also had he a whole handful of brushes. This fellow began to gaze upon me, to take a sketch, to lay in a background and to hang his head on one side, the better to compare his work exactly with my figure : now he changed the eyes, now the hair, presently the nostrils ; and, in a word, all he had not at first done aright, till at length he had executed a model true to nature ; for a model Simplicissimus was. And not till then might the barber whisk his razor over me : who twitched my head this way and that and spent full an hour and a half over my hair : and thereafter trimmed it in the fashion of that day : for I had hair enough and to spare. After that he brought me to a bathroom and cleansed my thin, starved body from more than three or four years' dirt. And scarce was he ended when they brought me a white shirt, shoes and stockings, together with a ruff or collar, and hat and feather. Likewise the breeches were finely made and trimmed with gold lace ; so all that was wanted was the cloak, and upon that the tailors were at work with all haste. Then came the cook with a strong broth and the maid with a cup of drink : and there sat my lord Simplicis-simus like a young count, in the best of tempers. And I ate heartily though I knew not what they would do with me : for as yet I had never heard of the " condemned man's supper," and therefore the partaking of this glorious first meal was to me so pleasant and sweet that I cannot sufficiently express, declare, and boast of it to mankind ; yea, hardly do I believe I ever tasted greater pleasure in my life than then. So when the cloak was ready I put it on, and in this new apparel shewed such an awkward figure that it might seem one had dressed up a hedge-stake : for the tailors had been ordered of intent to make the clothes too big for me, in the hope I should presently put more flesh on, which, considering the excellence of my feeding, seemed like to happen. But my forest dress, together with the chains and all appurtenances, were con-veyed away to the museum, there to be added to other rare objects and antiquities, and my portrait, of life size, was set hard by.

So after his supper, his lordship myself was put to bed in

such a bed as I had never seen or heard of in my dad's house or while I dwelt with my hermit : yet did my belly so growl and grumble the whole night through that I could not sleep, perchance for no other reason than that it knew not yet what was good or because it wondered at the delightful new foods which had been given to it : but for me, I lay there quiet until the sweet sun shone bright again (for 'twas cold) and reflected what strange adventures I had passed through in a few days, and how God my Father had so truly helped me and brought me into so goodly an heritage.

Chap. xxii : WHO THE HERMIT WAS BY WHOM SIMPLICISSIMUS WAS CHERISHED

THE same morning the Governor's chamberlain commanded me, I should go to the before-mentioned pastor, and there learn what his lordship had said to him in my affair. Likewise he sent an orderly to bring me to him. Then the pastor took me into his library, and there he sat down and bade me also sit down, and says he, " My good Simplicissimus, that same hermit with whom thou didst dwell in the wood was not only the Lord Governor's brother-in-law, but also his staunch supporter in war and his chiefest friend. As it pleased the Governor to tell me, the same from his youth up had never failed either in the bravery of an heroical soldier nor in that godliness and piety which became the holiest of men : which two virtues it is not usual to find united. Yet his spiritual mind, coupled with adverse circumstances, so checked the course of his earthly happiness that he rejected his nobility and resigned certain fine estates in Scotland where he was born, and despised such because all worldly affairs now seemed to him vain, foolish, and contemptible. In a word, he hoped to exchange his earthly eminence for a better glory to come, for his noble spirit had a disgust at all temporal display, and all his thoughts and desires were set on that poor miserable life wherein thou didst find him in the forest and wherein thou didst bear him company till his death. " And in my opinion," said the pastor, " he had been seduced thereto by his reading of many popish books concerning the lives of the ancient eremites. Yet will I not conceal from thee how he came into the Spessart, and, in accord with his wish, into such a miserable hermit's life, that thou mayest hereafter be able to tell others thereof : for the second night after that bloody battle of Höchst was lost, he came alone and un-attended to my parsonage-house, even as I, my wife, and children were fallen asleep, and that towards morning, for because of the noise all over the country which both pursuers and pursued are wont to make in such cases, we had been awake all the night before and half of this present one. At first he knocked gently, and then sharply enough, till he wakened me and my sleep-drunken folk : and when I at his request, and after short exchange of words, which was on both sides full cautious, had opened the door, I saw the cavalier dismount from his mettlesome steed. His costly clothing was as thickly sprinkled with the blood of his enemies as it was decked with gold and silver ; and inasmuch as he still held his drawn sword in his hand, fear and terror came upon me. Yet when he sheathed his sword and shewed nothing but courtesy I must wonder that so noble a gentleman should so humbly beg a poor village pastor for shelter. And by reason of his handsome person and his noble carriage I addressed myself to him as to the Count of Mansfield himself : but said he, he could for this once be not only compared to the Count of Mansfield in respect of ill fortune but even preferred before him. Three things did he lament : first, the loss of his lady, and her near her delivery, and then the loss of his battle ; and last of all, that he had not had the luck to die therein, as did other honest soldiers, for the Evangelical cause. Then would I comfort him, but saw that his noble heart needed no comfort : so I set before him what the house afforded and bade them make for him a soldier's bed of clean straw, for in no other would he lie though much he needed rest. The next morning, the first thing he did was to give me his horse and his money (of which he had with him no mean sum in gold), and did share divers costly rings among my wife, children, and servants. This could I not understand in him, seeing that soldiers be wont far rather to take than to give : and therefore I had doubts whether to receive so great presents, and gave as a pretext that I had not deserved so much from him nor could again repay him : besides, said I, if folks saw such riches, and specially the splendid horse, which could not be hid, in my possession, many would conclude I had robbed or murdered him. But he said I should live without care on that score, for he would protect me from such danger with his own handwriting, yea, and he would desire to carry away out of my parsonage not even his shirt, let alone his clothes : and therewith he opened his design to become a hermit. I fought against that with might and main, for methought such a plan smacked of Popery, reminding him that he could serve the Gospel more with his sword, but in vain . for he argued so long and stoutly with me that at last I gave in and provided him with those books, pictures, and furniture which thou didst find in his hut. Yet would he take nothing in return for all that he had presented to me save only the coverlet of wool, under which he had slept on the straw that night : and out of that he had a coat made. And my wagon chains (those which he always wore) must I exchange with him for a golden one whereon he wore his lady's portrait, so that he kept for himself neither money nor money's worth. Then my servant led him to the wildest part of the wood, and there helped him to build his hut. And in what manner he there spent his life, and with what help at times I did assist him, thou knowest as well as I, yea, in part better.

" Now when lately the Battle of Nördlingen was lost and I, as thou knowest, was clean stripped of all and also evilly handled, I fled hither for safety ; besides, I had here my chief possessions. And when my ready money was about to fail me, I took three rings and the before-mentioned chain, together with the portrait that I had from the hermit, among which was his signet-ring, and took them to a Jew, to turn them into money. But he, on account of their value and fine workmanship, took them to the Governor to sell, who forthwith knew the arms and portrait, and sent for me and asked where I had gotten such treasures. So I told him the truth and shewed him the hermit's handwriting or deed of gift, and narrated to him all his story ; also how he had lived and died in the wood. Such a tale he could not believe, but put me under arrest, till he could better learn the truth ; and while he was at work sending out a party to take a survey of the dwelling and to fetch thee hither, here I beheld thee brought to the tower. Now seeing that the Governor hath no longer cause to doubt of my story, and seeing that I can call to witness the place where the hermit dwelt, and likewise thee and other living deponents, and most of all my sexton, which so often admitted thee and him to the church before day, and specially since the letter which he found in thy book of prayer doth afford an excellent testimony not only of the truth, but of the late hermit's holiness : therefore he will shew favour to me and thee for the sake of his dear departed brother-in-law. And now hast thou only to decide what thou wouldest he should do for thee. An thou wilt study, he pays the cost : desirest thou to learn a trade, he will have thee taught one : but if thou wilt stay with him he will hold thee as his own child : for he said if even a dog came to him from his departed brother-in-law he would cherish it." So I answered, 'twas all one to me what the Lord Governor would do with me.

Chap. xxiii : HOW SIMPLICISSIMUS BECAME A PAGE : AND LIKEWISE, HOW THE HERMIT'S WIFE WAS LOST

NOW did the pastor keep me at his lodging till ten of the clock before he would go with me to the Governor, to tell him of my resolve : for so could he be his guest at dinner : for the Governor kept open house : 'tis true Hanau was then blockaded, and with the common folk times were so hard (especially with them that had fled for refuge to the fortress) that some who seemed to themselves to be somewhat, were not ashamed to pick up the frozen turnip-peelings in the streets, which the rich had cast away. And my pastor was so lucky that he got to sit by the Governor at the head of the table, while I waited on them with a plate in my hand as the chamberlain taught me, to which business I was as well fitted as an ass to play chess. Yet my pastor made good with his tongue what the awkwardness of my person failed in. For he said I had been reared in the wilderness, and had never dwelt among men,

and therefore must be excused, because I could not yet know
how to carry myself : yet the faithfulness I had shewn to
the hermit and the hard life I had endured with him were
wonderful, and that alone deserved that folk should not
only have patience with my awkwardness but should even
put me before the finest young nobleman. Furthermore, he
related how the hermit had found all his joy in me because,
as he often said, I was so like in face to his dear lady, and that
he had often marvelled at my steadfastness and unchangeable
will to remain with him as also at many other virtues which
he praised in me. Lastly, he could not enough declare with
what earnest fervency the hermit had, just before his death,
commended me to him (the pastor) and had confessed he
loved me as his own child. This tickled my ears so much
that methought I had already received satisfaction enough
for all I had endured with the hermit.

Then the Governor asked, did not his late brother-in-law
know he was commandant of Hanau. " Yea, truly," answered
the pastor, " for I told him myself : but he listened as coldly
(yet with a joyful face and a gentle smile) as he had never
known any Ramsay, so that even now when I think thereupon,
I must wonder at this man's resolution and firm purpose, that
he could bring his heart to this : not only to renounce the
world but even to put out of his mind his best friend, when
he had him close at hand."

Then were the Governor's eyes full of tears, who yet had
no soft woman's heart but was a brave and heroical soldier ;
and says he, " Had I known he was yet alive and where he
was to be found, I would have had him fetched even against
his will, that I might repay his kindnesses : but since Fortune
hath denied me that, I will in his place cherish his Simplicissimus." And " Ah !" says he again, " the good cavalier
had cause enough to lament his wife, great with child as she
was ; for in the pursuit she was captured by a party of
Imperialist troopers, and that too in the Spessart. Which
when I heard, and knew not but that my brother-in-law was
slain at Höchst, at once I sent a trumpeter to the enemy to
ask for my sister and ransom her : yet got no more thereby
than to learn the said party of troopers had been scattered
in the Spessart by a few peasants, and that in that fight my

sister had again been lost to them, so that to this hour I know not what became of her." This and the like made up the table-talk of the Governor and the pastor regarding my hermit and his lady-wife : which pair were the more pitied because they had enjoyed each other's love but a year. But as to me, I became the Governor's page, and so fine a fellow that the people, specially the peasants when I must announce them to my master, called me the young lord already : though indeed one seldom sees a youngster that hath been a lord, but oftentime lords that have been youngsters.

Chap. xxiv : HOW SIMPLICISSIMUS BLAMED THE WORLD AND SAW MANY IDOLS THEREIN

NOW at that time I had no precious possession save only a clear conscience and a right pious mind, and that clad and surrounded with the purest innocence and simplicity. Of vice I knew no more than that I had at times heard it spoken of or read of it, and if I saw any man commit such sin then was it to me a fearful and a terrible thing, I being so brought up and reared as to have the presence of God ever before my eyes and most earnestly to live according to His holy will : and inasmuch as I knew all this, I could not but compare men's ways and works with that same will : and methought I saw naught but vileness. Lord God ! How did I wonder at the first when I considered the law and the Gospel and the faithful warnings of Christ, and saw, on the contrary part, the deeds of them that gave themselves out to be His disciples and followers ! In place of the straightforward dealing which every true Christian should have, I found mere hypocrisy ; and besides, such numberless follies among all dwellers in the world that I must needs doubt whether I saw before me Christians or not. For though I could see well that many had a serious knowledge of God's will : yet could I mark but little serious purpose to fulfil the same. So had I a thousand puzzles and strange thoughts in my mind, and fell into grievous difficulty upon that saying of Christ, which saith, " Judge not, that ye be not judged." Nevertheless there came into my mind the words of St. Paul in the fifth chapter of Galatians, where he saith : " The works of the flesh are manifest, which are these : adultery, fornication, uncleanness, lasciviousness," and so on : " of the which I tell you before as I have also told you in time past, that they which do such things shall not inherit the kingdom of God." Then I thought : every man doeth all these things openly : wherefore then should I not in this matter conclude from the apostle's word that there shall be few that are saved ?

Moreover, pride and greed with their worthy accompaniments, gorging and swilling and loose living, were a daily occupation for them of substance : yet what did seem to me most terrible of all was this shameful thing, that some, and specially soldiers, in whose case vice is not wont to be severely punished, should make of both these things, their own godlessness and God's holy will, a mere jest. For example, I heard once an adulterer which after his deed of shame accomplished would treat thereof, and spake these godless words : " It serves the cowardly cuckold aright," says he, " to get a pair of horns from me : and if I confess the truth, I did the thing more to vex the husband than to please the wife, and so to be revenged on them."

" O pitiful revenge ! " says one honest heart that stood by, " by which a man staineth his own conscience and gaineth the shameful name of adulterer and fornicator ! "

" What ! fornicator ! " answered he, with a scornful laughter, " I am no fornicator because I have given this marriage a twist : a fornicator is he that the sixth commandment* speaks of, where it forbids that any man get into another's garden and nick the fruit before the owner." How to prove that this was so to be understood, he forthwith explained according to his devil's catechism the seventh commandment, wherein it is said, " Thou shalt not steal." And of such words he used many, so that I sighed within myself and thought, " O God-blaspheming sinner, thou callest thyself a marriage-twister : and so then God must be a marriage-breaker, seeing that He doth separate man and wife by death." And out of mine overflowing zeal and

* The commandments are here numbered according to the Roman arrangement, but the meaning is obscure.

anger I said to him, officer though he was, "Thinkest thou not, thou sinnest more with these godless words than by thine act of adultery." So he answered me, "Thou rascal, must I give thee a buffet or two?" Yea, and I believe I had received a handsome couple of such if the fellow had not stood in fear of my lord. So I held my peace, and thereafter I marked it was no rare case for single folk to cast eyes upon wedded folk and wedded folk upon such as were unwedded.

Now while I was yet studying, under my good hermit's care, the way to eternal life, I much wondered why God had so straitly forbidden idolatry to his people: for I imagined, if any one had ever known the true and eternal God, he would never again honour and pray to any other, and so in my stupid mind I resolved that this commandment was unnecessary and vain. But ah! Fool as I was, I knew not what I thought I knew: for no sooner was I come into the great world, than I marked how (in spite of this commandment) wellnigh every man had his special idol: yet some had more than the old and new heathen themselves. Some had their god in their money-bags, upon which they put all their trust and confidence: many a one had his idol at court, and trusted wholly and entirely on him: which idol was but a minion and often even such a pitiable lickspittle as his worshipper himself; for his airy godhead depended only on the April weather of a prince's smile: others found their idol in popularity, and fancied, if they could but attain to that they would themselves be demi-gods. Yet others had their gods in their head, namely, those to whom the true God had granted a sound brain, so that they were able to learn certain arts and sciences: for these forgot the great Giver and looked only to the gift, in the hope that gift would procure them all prosperity. Yea, and there were many whose god was but their own belly, to which they daily offered sacrifice, as once the heathen did to Bacchus and Ceres, and when that god shewed himself unkind or when human failings shewed themselves in him, these miserable folk then made a god of their physician, and sought for their life's prolongation in the apothecary's shop, wherefrom they were more often sped on their way to death. And many fools made goddesses for themselves out of flattering harlots: these they called by all manner of outlandish names, worshipped them day and night with many thousand sighs, and made songs upon them which contained naught but praise of them, together with a humble prayer they would have mercy upon their folly and become as great fools as were their suitors.

Contrariwise were there women which had made their own beauty their idol. For this, they thought, will give me my livelihood, let God in heaven say what He will. And this idol was every day, in place of other offerings, adorned and sustained with paint, ointments, waters, powders, and the like daubs.

There too I saw some which held houses luckily situated as their gods. for they said, so long as they had lived therein had they ever had health and wealth : and many said these had tumbled in through their windows. At this folly I did more especially wonder because I would well perceive the reason why the inhabitants so prospered. I knew one man who for some years could never sleep by reason of his trade in tobacco ; for to this he had given up his heart, mind and soul, which should be dedicate to God alone : and to this idol he sent up night and day a thousand sighs, for 'twas by that he made his way in life. Yet what did happen ? The fool died and vanished like his own tobacco-smoke. Then thought I, O thou miserable man ! Had but thy soul's happiness and the honour of the true God been so dear to thee as thine idol, which stands upon thy shop-sign in the shape of a Brazilian, with a roll of tobacco under his arm and a pipe in his mouth, then am I sure and certain that thou hadst won a noble crown of honour to wear in the next world.

Another ass had yet more pitiful idols : for when in a great company it was being told by each how he had been fed and sustained during the great famine and scarcity of food, this fellow said in plain German : the snails and frogs had been his gods : for want of them he must have died of hunger. So I asked him what then had God Himself been to him, who had provided such insects for his sustenance. The poor creature could answer nothing, and I wondered the more because I had never read that either the old idolatrous Egyptians or the new American savages ever called such vermin their gods, as did this prater.

I once went with a person of quality into his museum, wherein were fine curiosities : but among all none pleased me better than an " Ecce Homo " by reason of its moving portraiture, by which it stirred the spectator at once to sympathy. By it there hung a paper picture painted in China, whereon were Chinese idols sitting in their majesty, and some in shape like devils. So the master of the house asked me which piece in this gallery pleased me most. And when I pointed to the said " Ecce Homo " he said I was wrong : for the Chinese picture was rarer and therefore of more value : he would not lose it for a dozen such " Ecce Homos." So said I, " Sir, is your heart like to your speech ? " " Surely," said he. " Why then," said I, " your heart's god is that one whose picture you do confess with your mouth to be of most value." " Fool," says he, " 'tis the rarity I esteem." Whereto I replied, " Yet what can be rarer and more worthy of wonder than that God's Son Himself suffered in the way which this picture doth declare ? "

Chap. xxv : HOW SIMPLICISSIMUS FOUND THE WORLD ALL STRANGE AND THE WORLD FOUND HIM STRANGE LIKEWISE

EVEN as much as these and yet a greater number of idols were worshipped, so much on the contrary was the majesty of the true God despised : for as I never saw any desirous to keep His word and command, so I saw contrariwise many that resisted him in all things and excelled even the publicans in wickedness : which publicans were in the days when Christ walked upon earth open sinners. And so saith Christ : " Love your enemies ; bless them that curse you. If ye do good only to your brethren, what do ye that the publicans do not ? " But I found not only no one that would follow this command of Christ, but every man did the clean opposite. " The more a man hath kindred the more a man is hindered " was the word : and nowhere did I find more envy, hatred, malice, quarrel, and dispute than between brothers, sisters, and other born friends, specially if an inheritance fell to them. Moreover, the handicraftsmen of every place hated one another, so that I could plainly see, and must conclude, that in comparison the open sinners, publicans and tax-gatherers, which by reason of their evil deeds were hated by many, were far better than we Christians nowadays in exercise of brotherly love : seeing that Christ bears testimony to them that at least they did love one another. Then thought I, if we have no reward because we love our enemies, how great must our punishment be if we hate our friends ! And where there should be the greatest love and good faith, there I found the worst treachery and the strongest hatred. For many a lord would fleece his true servants and subjects, and some retainers would play the rogue against the best of lords. So too between married folk I marked continual strife : many a tyrant treated his wedded wife worse than his dog, and many a loose baggage held her good husband but for a fool and an ass. So too, many currish lords and masters cheated their industrious servants of their due pay and pinched them both in food and drink : and contrariwise I saw many faithless servitors which by theft or neglect brought their kind masters to ruin. Tradesfolk and craftsmen did vie with each other in Jewish roguery : exacted usury : sucked the sweat of the poor peasant's brow by all manner of chicanery and overreaching. On the other hand, there were peasants so godless that if they were not thoroughly well and cruelly fleeced, they would sneer at other folks or even their lords themselves for their simplicity.

Once did I see a soldier give another a sore buffet ; and I conceived he that was smitten would turn the other cheek (for as yet I had been in no quarrel), but there was I wrong, for the insulted one drew on him, and dealt the offender a crack of the crown. So I cried at the top of my voice, " Ah ! friend, what dost thou ? " " A coward must he be," says he, " that would not avenge himself : devil take me but I will, or I care not to live. What ! he must be a knave that would let himself be so fobbed off." And between these two antagonists the quarrel waxed greater, for their backers on both sides, together with the bystanders, and any man moreover that came by chance to the spot, were presently by the ears : and there I heard men swear by God and their own souls, so lightly, that I could not believe they held those souls for their dearest treasure. But all this was but child's play : for they stayed not at such children's curses but presently 'twas so : " Thunder, lightning, hail : strike me, tear me, devil take me," and the like, and not one thunder or lightning but a hundred thousand, " and snatch me away into the air." Yea, and the blessed sacraments for them must have been not seven but a hundred thousand, and there with so many " bloodies," " damnes," and " cursemes " that my poor hair stood on end thereat. Then thought I of Christ's command wherein He saith, " Swear not, let your speech be yea yea ; and nay nay ; for whatsoever is more is evil."

Now all this that I saw and heard I pondered in my heart : and at the last I firmly concluded, these bullies were no Christians at all, and therefore I sought for other company. And worst of all it did terrify me when I heard some such swaggerers boast of their wickedness, sin, shame, and vice. For again and again I heard them so do, yea, day by day ; and thus they would say : " 'S blood, man, but we were foxed yesterday : three times in the day was I blind drunk and three times did vomit all." " My stars," says another, " how did we torment the rascal peasants ! " And " Hundred thousand devils ! " says a third, " what sport did we have with the women and maids ! " And so on. " I cut him down as if lightning had struck him." " I shot him—shot him so that he shewed the whites of his eyes ! " Or again : " I rode him down so cleverly, the devil only could fetch him off," " I put such a stone in his way that he must needs break his neck thereover."

Such and such-like heathen talk filled my ears every day : and more than that, I did hear and see sins done in God's name, which are much to be grieved for. Such wickedness was specially practised by the soldiers, when they would say, " Now in God's name let us forth on a foray," viz., to plunder, kidnap, shoot down, cut down, assault, capture and burn, and all the rest of their horrible works and practices. Just as the usurers ever invoke God with their hypocritical " In God's name " : and therewithal let their devilish avarice loose to flay and to strip honest folk. Once did I see two rogues hanged, that would break into a house by night to steal, and even as they had placed their ladder one would mount it saying, " In God's name, there comes the householder " : " and in the devil's name " says he also, and therewithal threw him down : where he broke a leg and so was captured, and a few days after strung up together with his comrade. But I, if I saw the like, must speak out, and out would I come with some passage of Holy Writ, or in other ways would warn the sinner : and all men therefore held me for a fool. Yea, I was so often laughed out of countenance in return for my good intent that at length I took a disgust at it, and preferred altogether to keep silence, which yet for Christian love I could not keep. I would that all men had been reared with my hermit, believing that then many would look on the world's ways with Simplicissimus' eyes as I then beheld them. I had not the wit to see that if there were only Simplicissimuses in the world then there were not so many vices to behold : meanwhile 'tis certain that a man of the world, as being accustomed to all vices and himself partaker thereof, cannot in the least understand on what a thorny path he and his likes do walk.

Chap. xxvi : *A NEW AND STRANGE WAY FOR MEN TO WISH ONE ANOTHER LUCK AND TO WELCOME ONE ANOTHER*

HAVING now, as I deemed, reason to doubt whether I were among Christians or not, I went to the pastor and told him all that I had heard and seen, and what my thoughts were : namely, that I held these people for mockers of Christ and His word, and no Christians at all, with the request he would in any case help me out of my dream, that I might know what I should count my fellow men to be. The pastor answered : " Of a surety they be Christians, nor would I counsel thee to call them otherwise." " O God," said I, "how can that be ? for if I point out to one or the other his sin that he committeth against God, then am I but mocked and laughed at." " Marvel not at that," answered the pastor ; " I believe if our first pious Christians, which lived in the time of Christ—yea, if the Apostles themselves should now rise from the grave and come into the world, that they would put the like question, and in the end, like thee, would be accounted of many to be fools : yet that thou hast thus far seen and heard is but an ordinary thing and mere child's play compared with that which elsewhere, secretly and openly, with violence against God and man, doth happen and is perpetrated in the world. Let not that vex thee ! Thou wilt find few Christians such as was the late Master Samuel." *

Now even as we spake together, some of the opposite party which had been taken prisoner were led across the market-place, and this broke up our discourse, for we too must go to look on the captives. Here then I was ware of a folly whereof I could never have dreamed, and that was a new fashion of greeting and welcoming one another : for one of our garrison, who also had beforetime served the emperor, knew one of the prisoners : so he goes up to him, gives him his hand, and pressed his for sheer joy and heartiness, and says he : " Devil take thee ! art still alive, brother ? 'S blood, 'tis surely the devil that brings us together here ! Strike me blind, but I believed thou wert long since hanged." Then answered the other : " Curse me, but is it thee or not ? Devil take thee, how camest thou here ? I never thought in all my born days I should meet thee again, but thought the devil had fetched thee long ago." And when they parted, one says to the other (in place of " God be wi' you "). " Gallows' luck ! Gallows' luck ! to-morrow will we meet again, and be nobly drunk together."

" Is not this a fine pious welcome ? " said I to the pastor ; " be not these noble Christian wishes ? Have not these men a godly intent for the coming day? Who could know them for Christians or hearken to them without amazement ? If they so talk with one another for Christian love, how will it fare if they do quarrel ? Sir Pastor, if these be Christ's flock, and thou their appointed shepherd, I counsel thee to lead them in better pastures." " Yea," answered the pastor, " dear child, 'tis ever so with these godless soldiers. God help us ! If I said a word, I might as well preach to the deaf ; and should gain nought from it but the perilous hatred of these godless fellows."

* The hermit.

At that I wondered, but talked yet awhile with the pastor, and went then to wait upon the Governor ; for at times had I leave to view the town and to visit the pastor, for my lord had wind of my simplicity, and thought such would cease if I went about seeing this and hearing that and being taught by others or, as folks say, being broken to harness.

Chap. xxvii : *HOW SIMPLICISSMUS DISCOURSED WITH THE SECRETARY, AND HOW HE FOUND A FALSE FRIEND*

NOW my lord's favour towards me increased daily, and the longer the greater, because I looked more and more like, not only to his sister whom the hermit had had to wife, but also to that good man himself, as good food and idleness made me sleeker. And this favour I enjoyed in many quarters : for whosoever had business with the governor shewed me favour also, and especially my lord's secretary was well affected to me ; and as he must teach me my figures, he often found pastime in my simpleness and ignorance : he was but now fresh from the University, and therefore was cram-full of the jokes of the schools, which at times gave him the appearance of being a button short or a button too many : often would he convince me black was white or white black : so it came about that at first I believed him in everything and at last in nothing. Once on a time I blamed him for his dirty inkhorn : so he answered 'twas the best piece of furniture in his office, for out of it he could conjure whatever he desired ; his fine ducats of gold, his fine raiment, and, in a word, whatsoever he possessed, all that had he fished out of his inkhorn. Then would I not believe that out of so small and inconsiderable a thing such noble possessions were to be had : so he answered all this came from the Spiritus Papyri (for so did he name his inks), and the inkhorn was for this reason named an ink-holder, because it held matters of importance. Then I asked, how could a man bring them out since one could scarce put a couple of fingers in. To that he answered, he had an arm in his head fit to do such business, yea, and hoped presently to fish out a rich and handsome wife, and if he had luck he trusted also to bring out land of his own and servants of his own, as in earlier times would surely have happened. At these tricks of craft I wondered, and asked if other folk knew such arts.

" Surely," says he, " all chancellors, doctors, secretaries, proctors or advocates, commissaries, notaries, traders and merchants, and numberless others besides, which commonly, if they do but fish diligently in it, become rich lords thereby." Then said I, " In this wise the peasants and other hard-working folk have no wit, in that they eat their bread in the sweat of their brow, and do not also learn this art." So he answered, " Some know not the worth of an art, and therefore have no desire to learn it : some would fain learn it, but lack that arm in their head, or some other necessary thing ; some learn the wit and have the arm, but know not the knack which the art requireth if a man will be rich thereby : and others know all and can do all that appertains thereto, yet they dwell on the unlucky side and have no opportunity, like me, to exercise this art properly."

Now as we reasoned in this fashion of the ink-holder (which of a truth reminded me of Fortunatus his purse) it happened that the book of dignities came into my hand and therein, as it seemed to me then, I found more follies than had ever yet come before mine eyes. " And these," said I to the secretary, " be all Adam's children and of one stuff, and that dust and ashes ? Whence cometh, then, so great a difference ; —his Holiness, his Excellency, his Serenity ! Be these not properties of God alone ? Here is one called ' Gracious ' and another ' Worshipful.' And why must this word ' born ' noble or ' well born ' be ever added ? We know well that no men fall from heaven and none rise out of the water and none grow out of the earth like cabbages." The secretary must needs laugh at me, and took the trouble to explain to me this and that title and all the words separately. Yet did I insist that the titles did not do men right : for sure 'twas more credit to a man to be called merciful than worshipful : so, too, if the word " noble " signify in itself all incalculable virtues, why should it when placed in the midst of the word " high-born," which applieth only to princes, impair the dignity of the title. And as to the word " well-born," why 'twas a flat untruth : and that could any baron's mother testify ; for if one should ask her if he was well born she could say whether 'twas " well " with her when she brought him into the world.

And so we talked long : yet could he not convince me. But this favour of the secretary towards me lasted not long, for by reason of my boorish and filthy habits I presently, after his foregoing discourse, behaved myself so foully (yet without evil intent) in his presence that he must bid me betake myself to the pigs as to my best comrades. Yet his disgust would have been the easier to bear had I not fallen into yet greater disgrace ; for it fared so with me as with every honest man that cometh to court where the wicked and envious do make common cause against him.

For my lord had besides me a double-dyed rascal for a page, which had already served him for two years : to him I gave my heart, for he was of like age with myself. " And this is Jonathan," I thought, " and thou art David."

But he was jealous of me by reason of the great favour that my lord shewed me, and that greater day by day : so he was concerned lest I should step into his shoes ; and therefore in secret looked upon me with malicious and envious eyes, and sought occasion how he might put a stumbling-block for me and by my fall prevent his own. Yet mine were eyes as doves' eyes* and my intent far different from his : nay, I confided to him all my secrets, which yet consisted in naught else than in childish simplicity and piety. But he, innocent as I was, persuaded me to all manner of folly, which yet I accepted for truth and honesty, followed his counsels, and through the same (as shall not fail to be duly treated of in its proper place) fell into grievous misfortunes.

* *i.e.* full of innocence.

Chap. xxviii : *HOW SIMPLICISSIMUS GOT TWO EYES OUT OF ONE CALF'S HEAD*

THE next day after my discourse with the secretary my master had appointed a princely entertainment for his officers and other good friends ; for he had received the good news that his men had taken the strong castle of Braunfels without loss of a single man : and there must I, as at that time 'twas my duty, like any other table-server, help to bring up dishes, pour out wine, and wait at table with a plate in my hand. The first day there was a big fat calf's-head (of which folk are wont to say no poor man may eat) handed to me to carry up. And because this calf's-head was soft-boiled, therefore he must needs have his whole eye with the appurtenance thereof hanging out ; which was to me a charming and a tempting sight, and the fresh perfume of the bacon-broth and ginger sprinkled thereon alluring me, I felt such appetite that my mouth did water at it. In a word, the eye smiled at once on mine eyes, my nostrils, and my mouth, and besought me that I would incorporate it into my hungry belly. Nor did I need long forcing, but followed my desires ; for as I went, with a spoon that I had first received on that same day I did scoop the eye so masterly out, and sent it so swiftly and without let or hindrance to its proper place, that none perceived it till the dish came to table and there betrayed itself and me. For when they would carve it up, and one of its daintiest members was wanting, my lord at once perceived what made the carver start : and he was not a man to endure such mockery as that any should dare to say to him he had served up a calf's-head with one eye. So the cook must appear at table, and they that should have brought the dishes up were with him examined : and last of all it came out that 'twas to poor Simplicissimus the calf's-head had last been entrusted, and that with two eyes : how it had fared thereafter no man could say. Then my lord, as it seemed to me with a terrible countenance, asked what I had done with the calf's eye. So I whipt my spoon out of my pouch again and gave the calf's-head the second turn, and shewed briefly and well what they asked of me, for I swallowed the second eye like the first, in a wink.

" Pardieu," quoth my lord, " this trick savoureth better than ten calves." And thereupon all the gentlemen present praised that saying and spoke of my deed, which I had done for pure simplicity, as a wondrous device and a presage of future boldness and fearless and swift resolution : so that for this time, by the repeating of the very trick for which I had deserved punishment I not only escaped that punishment, but from a few merry jesters, flatterers, and boon companions gained the praise of acting wisely, inasmuch as I had lodged both eyes together, that so they might in the next world, as in this, afford help and company to each other, to which end they were at first appointed by nature. Yet my lord warned me to play him no more such tricks.

*Chap. xxix : HOW A MAN STEP BY STEP MAY AT-
    TAIN UNTO INTOXICATION AND FINALLY
    UNAWARES BECOME BLIND DRUNK*

A T this banquet (and I take it it happens likewise at others) all came to table like Christians. Grace was said very quietly, and to all appearance very piously. And this pious silence lasted as long as they had to deal with the soup and the first courses, as one had been at a Quakers' meeting. But hardly had each one said " God's blessing ! " three or four times when all was already livelier. Nor can I describe how each one's voice grew louder and louder : I could but compare the whole company to an orator, that beginneth softly at the first and endeth with thunder. Then dishes were served called savour-ies, which, being strongly seasoned, are appointed to be eaten before the drinking begin, that it may go the livelier, and likewise dessert, to give a flavour to the wine, to say nothing of all manner of French pottages and Spanish olla podridas, which by a thousand artful preparations and unnumbered ingredients were in such wise spiced, devilled, disguised, and seasoned (and all to further the drinking) that they, by such added ingredients and spices, were altogether changed in their substance and different from what Nature had made them, so that Gnaeus Manlius* himself, though he had come direct from Africa and had with him the best of cooks, yet had not recognised them. Then thought I : " Is't not like enough that these things should disturb the senses of any man who can take delight in them and the drink too (whereto they be specially appointed) and change him, or even transform him, to a beast ? Who knows if even Circe used any other means but these when she did change Ulysses his companions into swine ? For I saw how these guests at one time devoured the food like hogs and then swilled like sows, then carried themselves like asses, and last of all were as sick as farmers' dogs. The noble wines of Hochheim, of Bacharach, and of Klingenberg they tipped into their bellies in glasses as big as buckets, which presently shewed their effects higher up, in the head. And thereupon I saw with wonder how all changed ; for here were reputable folk, which just before were in possession of their five senses and sitting in peace by one another, now beginning of a sudden to act the fool and to play the silliest tricks in the world. And the great follies which they did commit and the huge draughts which they drank to each other became bigger as time went on, so that it seemed as if fooleries and draughts strove with each other which of them should be accounted the greater : but at last this contest ended in a filthy piggishness. 'Twas not wonderful that I understood not whence their giddiness came : inasmuch as the effect of wine, and drunkenness itself, were until now quite unknown to me : and this left in my roguish remembrance thereafter all manner of merry pranks and fantastic imaginings : their strange looks I could see ; but the cause of their condition I knew not. Indeed up till then each one had emptied the pot with a good appetite : but when now their bellies were full 'twas as hard with them as with a waggoner, that can fare well enough with his team over level ground, yet up the hill can scarcely toil. But though their heads were bemused, their want of strength was made good : in one man's case by his courage, well soaked in wine : in another the loyal desire to drink yet one health to his friend : in a third that German chivalry which must do his neighbour

* Given as an example of a Roman of luxurious tastes.

right. But even such efforts must fail in the long run. Then would one challenge another to pour the wine in in buckets to the health of the princes or of dear friends or of a mistress. And at this many a one's eyes turned in his head, and the cold sweat broke out : yet still the drinking must go on ; yea, at the last they must make a noise with drums, fifes, and stringed instruments, and shot off the ordnance, doubtless for this cause, because the wine must take their bellies by assault. Then did I wonder where they could be rid of it all, for I knew not that they would turn out the same before 'twas well warm within them (and that with great pains) out of the very place into which they had just before poured it to the great danger of their health.

At this feast was also my pastor : and because he was a man like other men, he must retire for a while. So I followed him and " Pastor," said I, " why do these folk behave so strangely ? How comes it that they do reel this way and that ? Sure it seems to me they be no longer in their senses ; for they have all eaten and drunken themselves full, and cwoar devil take them if they can drink more, and yet they cease not to swill. Be they compelled thereto, or is it in God's despite that they of their free will waste all things so wantonly ? "

" Dear child," answered the pastor, " when the wine is in the wit is out. This is nought compared with what is to come. To-morrow at daybreak 'twill be hardly time for them to break up ; for though they have already crammed their bellies, yet they are not yet right merry."

So I answered, " Then do not their bellies burst if they stuff them so continually ? Can, then, their souls, which are God's image, abide in such fat hog's bodies, in which they lie, as it were, in dark cells and verminous dungeons, imprisoned without knowledge of God ? Their precious souls, I say, how can they so let themselves be tortured ? Be not their senses, of which their souls should be served, buried as in the bowels of unreasoning beasts ?"

" Hold thou thy tongue," answered the pastor, " or thou mayest get thee a sound thrashing : here 'tis no time to preach, or I could do it better than thou." So when I heard this I looked on in silence further, and saw how they wantonly spoiled food and drink, notwithstanding that the poor Lazarus, that might have been nourished therewith, languished, before our gates in the shape of many hundred expelled peasants of the Wetterau, whose hunger looked out through their eyes : for in the town there was famine.

Chap. xxx : STILL TREATS OF NAUGHT BUT OF DRINKING BOUTS, AND HOW TO BE RID OF PARSONS THEREAT

SO this gormandising went on as before, and I must wait on them as from the beginning of the feast. My pastor was still there, and was forced to drink as well as the rest : yet would he not do like them, but said he cared not to drink in so beastly a fashion : so a valiant pot companion takes him up and shews him that he, a pastor, drinks like a beast, and he, the drunkard and others present, drink like men. " For," says he, " a beast drinks only so much as tastes well to him and quenches his thirst, for he knows not what is good, nor doth he care to drink wine at all. But 'tis the pleasure of us men to make the drink profit us, and to suck in the noble grape-juice as our fore-fathers did." " Yes, yes," says the pastor, " but for me 'tis proper to keep due measure." " Right," says the other, " a man of honour must keep his word " : and thereupon he has a beaker filled which held a full measure, and with that in his hand he reels back to the pastor. But he was gone and left the tippler in the lurch with his wine-bucket.

So when they were rid of the pastor all was confusion, and 'twas for all the world in appearance as if this feast was an agreed time and opportunity for each to disgrace his neigh-bour with drunkenness, to bring him to shame, or to play him some scurvy trick : for when one of them was so well settled that he could neither sit, walk, nor stand, the cry was, " Now we are quits ! Thou didst brew a like draught for me : now must thou drink the like " ; and so on. But he that could last longest and drink deepest was full of pride thereat, and seemed to himself a fellow of no mean parts ; and at the last they tumbled about, as they had drunk henbane. 'Twas indeed a wonderful pantomime to see how they did fool, and yet none wondered but I. One sang : one wept : one laughed : another moaned : one cursed : another prayed : one shouted " Courage ! " another could not even speak. One was quiet and peaceable : another would drive the devil out by swaggering : one slept and was silent, another talked so fast that none could stand up against him. One told stories of tender love adventures, another of his dreadful deeds in war. Some talked of church and clergy, some of the constitution, of politics, of the affairs of the empire and of the world. Some ran hither and thither and could not keep still : some lay where they were and could not stir a finger, much less stand up or walk. Some were still eating like ploughmen, and as if they had been a week without food, while others were vomiting up what they had eaten that very day. In a word, their whole carriage was comical, strange and mad : and moreover sinful and godless. At the last there arose at the lower end of the table real quarrels, so that they flung glasses, cups, dishes, and plates at each other's heads and fought, not with fists only, but with chairs and legs of chairs, yea, with swords and whatever came to hand, till some had the red blood running down their ears : but to that my lord presently put an end.

Chap. xxxi : HOW THE LORD GOVERNOR SHOT A VERY FOUL FOX

SO when order was restored, the master-drinkers took with them the minstrels and the women-folk, and away to another house wherein was a great room chosen and dedicated for another sort of folly. But my lord throws himself on his pallet-bed, for either from anger or from over-eating he was in pain : so I let him lie where he was, to rest and sleep, but hardly had I come to the door of the room when he musts needs whistle to me : and that he could not. Then he would call ; but naught could he say but " Simple ! " So I ran back to him and found his eyes turn in his head as with a beast that is slaughtered : and there stood I before him like a stock-fish, neither did I know what to do. But he pointed to the washstand and stammered out. " Bra-bra-bring me that, thou rogue : ha-ha-ha-hand me the basin. I mu-mu-must shoot a fo-fo-fo-fox ! "

So with all haste I brought him the silver wash-basin, but ere I could come to him he had a pair of cheeks like a trumpeter. Then he took me quickly by the arm and made me so to stand that I must hold the basin right before his mouth. Then all must out, with grievous retchings, and such foul stuff was discharged into the said basin that I near fainted away by reason of the unbearable stench, and specially because some fragments spurted up into my face. And nearly did I do the same : but when I marked how deadly pale he was, I gave that over for sheer fright and feared only his soul would leave him with his vomit. For the cold sweat broke out upon his forehead, and his face was like a dying man's. But when he recovered himself he bade me fetch fresh water, that with that he might rinse out the wine-skin into which he had made his belly.

Thereafter he bade me take away the fox : and because I knew not where I should bestow such a precious treasure, which, besides that it was in a silver dish, was composed of all manner of dainties that I had seen my lord eat, I took it to the steward : to him I shewed this fine stuff and asked what I should do with the fox. " Thou fool," says he, " go and take it to the tanner to tan his hides therewith." So I asked where could I find the tanner : but he perceiving my simplicity. " Nay," says he, " take it to the doctor, that he may see from it what our lord's state of health is." And such an April fool's journey had I surely gone, but that the steward was affrighted at what might follow : he bade me therefore take the filth to the kitchen, with orders that the maids should serve it up with seasoning. And this I did in all good faith, and was by those baggages soundly laughed at for my pains.

*Chap. xxxii : HOW SIMPLICISSIMUS SPOILED THE
DANCE*

JUST as I was free of my basin my lord was going forth :
so I followed him to a great house, where in a room
I saw gentlemen and ladies, bachelors and maidens,
twisting about so quickly that everything spun round :
with such stamping and noise that I deemed they were all
gone mad, for I could not imagine what they could intend
with this rage and fury : yea, the very sight of them was
so terrible, so fearful, and so dreadful that all my hair stood
on end, and I could believe nothing but that they were all
bereft of reason. And as we came nearer I was aware that
these were our guests, which had up till noon been in their
right senses. " Good God," thought I, " what do these poor
folk intend to do ? Surely madness is come upon them."
Yet presently I thought these might perchance be hellish
spirits, which under this disguise did make a mock of the
whole human race by such wanton capers and monkey-tricks :
for I thought, had they human souls and God's image in
them, sure they would not act so unlike to men.

When my lord came in and would enter the room, the
tumult ceased, save that there was such bowing and ducking
with the heads and such curtseying and scraping with the
feet on the floor that methought they would scrape out the
foot-tracks they had trodden in their furious madness. And
by the sweat that ran down their faces, and by their puffing
and blowing, I could perceive they had struggled hard : yet
did their cheerful countenances declare that such labours had
not vexed them. Now was I fain to know what this mad
behaviour might mean, and therefore asked of my comrade
and trusted confidant what such lunatic doings might signify,
or for what purpose this furious ramping and stamping was
intended. And he, as the real truth, told me that all there
present had agreed to stamp down the floor of the room.
" For how," says he, " canst thou otherwise suppose that
they would so stamp about ? Hast thou not seen how they
broke all the windows for pastime ? Even so will they break
in this floor." " Good heavens ! " quoth I, " then must we

also fall, and in falling break our legs and our necks in their company ? " " Yea," quoth my comrade, " 'tis their purpose, and therefore do they work so devilishly hard. And thou wilt see that when they do find themselves in danger of death each one seizes upon a fair lady or maiden, for 'tis said that to couples that fall holding one another in this way no grievous harm is wont to happen."

Now as I believed all this tale, there fell upon me such anguish and fear of death that I knew not where I should stand, and when the minstrels, which I had not before seen, made themselves likewise heard, and every man ran to his lady as soldiers run to their guns or to their ranks when they hear the drums beat the alarm, and each man took his partner by the hand, 'twas to me even as if I saw the floor already a-sinking, and my neck and those of many others a-breaking. But when they began to jump so that the whole building shook (for they played just then a lively galop), then thought I, " Now is thy life at stake." For I thought nought else but that the whole building would suddenly tumble in : so in my deadly fear I seized upon a lady of high nobility and eminent virtues with whom my lord was even then conversing. Her I caught all unawares by the arm, like a bear, and clung to her like a burr, but when she struggled, as not knowing what foolish fancies were in my head, I acted as one desperate, and for sheer despair began to scream as if they would murder me. Now did the music cease of a sudden : the dancers and their partners stopped dancing, and the honourable lady to whose arm I still clung deemed herself grievously insulted ; for she fancied my lord had had all this done for her annoyance, who thereupon commanded that I should be soundly whipped and then locked up somewhere, " for," said he, " 'twas not the first trick I had played on him that day." Yet the grooms which were to carry out his orders had sympathy with me, and spared me the whipping and locked me up in a goose-pen under the staircase.

BOOK II

Chap. i : *HOW A GOOSE AND A GANDER WERE MATED*

S O in my goose-pen I pondered on all that I have set down in black and white in my first part ; of which, therefore, there is no need in this place to say more. Yet can I not choose but say that even then I doubted whether the dancers in truth were so mad to stamp the floor down or whether I was only so led to believe. Now will I further relate how I came again out of my goose prison. For three whole hours, namely, till that " Praeludium Veneris " (I should have said that seemly dance) was ended, I must perforce sit till one came softly and fumbled with the bolt : so I listened as quiet as any mouse, and presently the fellow that was at the door not only opened it but whipped in himself as quick as I would fain have whipped out, and with him by the hand he led in a lady, even as I had soon done at the dancing. I knew not what was to happen : but because I was now accustomed to all such strange adventures as had happened to me, poor fool, on that one day, and had made up my mind to bear with patience and silence whatever my fate might bring me, I crept close to the door and with fear and trembling waited for the end. So presently there was between these two a whispering, whereof I could understand naught save that the one party complained of the evil air of the place, and on the other hand the second party would console the first.

Thereupon I heard kisses and observed strange postures, yet knew not what this should mean, and therefore still kept still as a mouse. Yet when a comical noise arose and the goose-pen, which was but of boards nailed together below the staircase, began to shake and crack, and moreover the lady seemed in trouble, I thought, surely these be two of those mad folk which helped to stamp on the floor, and have now betaken themselves hither to behave in like manner, and bring thee to thy death.

As soon as these thoughts came into my head, I seized upon the door, so to escape death, and out I whipt with a cry of " Murder " as loud as that which had brought me to that place. Yet had I the sense to bolt the door behind me and make for the open house-door.

This was now the first wedding I was ever present at in my life, and even to that I had not been invited : on the other hand, I needed to give no wedding-gift, though the bridegroom did mark up a heavy score against me, which I honourably discharged.

Gentle reader, I tell this story not that thou mayest laugh thereat, but that my History may be complete, and my readers may take to heart what honourable fruits are to be expected from this dancing. For this I hold for certain, that in these dances many a bargain is struck up, whereof the whole company hath cause thereafter to be shamed.

Chap. ii : CONCERNING THE MERITS AND VIRTUES OF A GOOD BATH AT THE PROPER SEASON

AND now, when I had luckily escaped from my goose-pen, I was then first aware of my sad plight. In my master's quarters all was sound asleep : so dared I not address myself to the sentry that stood before the house : and at the Mainguard assuredly they would not entertain me : while to abide in the streets was too cold : so I knew not whither to betake myself. Long past midnight it was when it came into my head to seek refuge with the pastor so often spoken of before ; and this thought I followed so far as to knock at his door : and therein was so importunate that at last the maid, with much ill will, admitted me. But forthwith she began to chide with me ; and this her master, who had by this time wellnigh slept off his wine, heard. So he called us both to him as he lay in his chamber : and ordered his maid, to put me to bed : for he could well perceive that I was numbed with the cold. Yet was I hardly warm in my bed when day began to break and the good pastor stood by my bedside to hear how it had gone with me and how my business had fared, for I could not rise to go to him. So I told him all, and began with the tricks which my comrade the page had taught me, and how ill they had turned out. Thereafter I must tell him how the guests, after he, the pastor, had left the table, had lost their wits and (as my comrade had told me) determined to stamp down the floor of the house : item into what fearful terror I thereupon fell, and in what fashion I tried to save my life : how thereafter I was shut up in a goose-pen and what I had noted in words and works of those two which had delivered me, and in what manner I had locked them both up in my stead.

" Simplicissimus," said the pastor, " thy case stands but lousily : thou hadst a good opportunity ; but I fear, I fear thou hast fooled it away. Get thee quick out of bed and pack out of my house, lest I come with thee under my lord's displeasure if thou be found here with me." So I must away, with my wet clothes, and now for the first time must understand how well he stands with all and sundry who doth but possess his master's favour : yet how askance he is looked upon when that favour halteth.

Away I went to my master's lodging, wherein all were yet sound asleep save the cook and a maid or two : these last were ordering the room wherein the day before had been the carouse, and the first was preparing from the remains of the feast a breakfast, or rather a luncheon. So first I betook myself to the maids : they had to deal with all manner of drinking-glasses and window-glass strewn up and down. In some places all was foul with what the guests had voided both upwards and downwards : in other places were great pools of spilt wine and beer, so that the floor looked like a map wherein a man could trace separate seas, islands, and continents. And in that room was the smell far worse than in my goose-pen : and therefore I delayed not long there but betook myself to the kitchen, and there had my clothes dried on my body before the fire, expecting with fear and trembling what tricks fortune would further play with me when my lord should awake. Then did I reflect upon all the folly and senselessness of the world, and ran over in my mind all that happened to me in the past day and night and what I had seen and heard in that time. So when I thought thereon

I did even deem the poor and miserable life which my old hermit led a happy one, and heartily I wished him and myself back in our old place.

*Chap. iii : HOW THE OTHER PAGE RECEIVED PAY-
MENT FOR HIS TEACHING, AND HOW
SIMPLICISSIMUS WAS CHOSEN TO BE A
FOOL*

WHEN my lord rose he sent his orderly to fetch me from the goose-pen : who brought news he had found the door open and a hole cut with a knife behind the bolt, by which means the prisoner had escaped. But before such report came my lord understood from others that I had for a long time been in the kitchen. Meanwhile the servants must run hither and thither to fetch yesterday's guests to breakfast : among whom was also the pastor, who must appear earlier than the rest because my master would talk with him concerning me before they went to table. He asked him first, did he account me sane or mad, and whether I was in truth so simple or not the rather mischievous ; and told him all : how unseemly I had carried myself all the day and evening before, which was in part taken amiss by his guests, and so regarded as if this had been done of malice and in their despite ; item, that he had caused me to be shut up in a goose-pen to protect himself against such tricks as I might yet further have played him ; which prison I had broken and now held my state in the kitchen like a gentleman who need no longer wait on him : in his lifetime no such trick had ever happened to him as I had played him in the presence of so many honourable persons : he knew not what to do with me save to have me soundly beaten, and, since I behaved myself so clownishly, to send me to the devil.

Meantime, while my master so complained of me, the guests assembled by degrees ; so when he had said his say the pastor answered, if the Lord Governor would please to hearken to him with patience for a little while, he would tell him this and that regarding Simplicissimus, from which not only his innocence could be known, but also all unfavourable thoughts removed from the minds of them that had taken a disgust at his conduct.

Now while they thus discoursed of me in the chamber above, that same mad ensign whom I in mine own person had imprisoned in my place makes a treaty with me below-stairs in the kitchen, and by threats and by a thaler which he put in my pouch, brought me to this, that I promised him to keep a still tongue concerning his doings.

So the tables were set, and, as on the day before, furnished with food and with guests. There wormwood, sage wine, elecampane, quince and lemon drinks, with hippocras, were to clear the heads and stomachs of the drinkers ; for for one and all there was the devil to pay. Their first talk was of themselves, and that chiefly of how brave a bout of drinking they had had yesterday : nor was there any among them that would truly confess he had been drunk, albeit the evening before some had called the devil to witness they could drink no more. Some indeed confessed that they had headaches : yet others would have it 'twas only since men had ceased to drink themselves full in the good old mode that such aches had come in fashion. But when they were tired both of hearing and talking of their own follies, poor Simplicissimus must bear the brunt. And the Governor himself reminded the pastor to tell of those merry happenings which he had promised.

So the pastor begged first that none should take offence inasmuch as he must use words which might be accounted unbefitting his holy office. Then he went on to tell how sorely I was plagued by nature, how I had caused great disgust thereby to the secretary in his office, and how I had learned, together with the art of prophecy, also certain enchantments* against such mishaps, and how ill such arts had turned out when they were tried ; item, how the dancing had seemed so strange to me, because I had never seen the like before, what an explication thereof I had heard from my comrade, and for what reason I had seized upon the noble lady, and thereupon had found my way into the goose-pen. All this he enounced with such a civil and discreet way of speaking

* Refers to an episode omitted in this translation.

that they were fit to split with laughing, and so completely forgave my simplicity and ignorance that I was restored to my master's favour and was allowed to wait at table again. But of what had happened to me in the goose-pen and how I was delivered therefrom would he say nought, for it seemed to him some old antediluvian images might have taken offence at him, which believe that pastors should always look sour. Then again my master, to make sport for his guests, asked me what had I given to my comrade that had taught me those pretty tricks : so I said, " Nothing at all." Then says he, " I will pay him the school fees for thee." So he had him clapt in a winnowing basket and there soundly trounced : even as I had been dealt with the day before, when I tried those magical arts and found them false.

So now my master had proof enough of my simplicity, and would fain give me the more occasion to make sport for him and his guests : he saw well that all the minstrels availed nothing so long as the company had me to make sport for them, for to every one it seemed that I, with my foolish fancies, was better than a dozen lutes. So he asked me why I had cut a hole in the door of the goose-pen. I answered, " Another may have done it." " Who then ? " says he. " Why," says I, " he that came to me." " And who came to thee ? " quoth he. " Nay," says I, " that may I tell no man." Now my master was a man of a quick wit, and he saw well how one must go about with me : so he turns him about and of a sudden he asks me who it was that had forbidden me, and I of a sudden answered, " The mad ensign."

Then, when I perceived by the laughter of all that I had mightily committed myself, and the mad ensign who sat at table also grew red as a hot coal, I would say no more till by him it should be allowed. Yet this was but a matter of a nod, which served my master instead of a command, to the ensign, and forthwith I might tell all I knew. And thereupon my master questioned me what the mad ensign had had to do with me in the goose-pen. " Oh," says I, " he brought a young lady to me there."

And thereupon there arose among all that were present such laughter that my master could hear me no longer, let alone ask me more questions ; and 'twas not needful, for if he had, that honourable young maiden (forsooth) might have been put to shame.

Thereafter the Controller of the Household told all at table how a little before I had come home from the ramparts and had said I knew now where the thunder and lightning came from : for I had seen great beams on half-waggons, which were all hollow inside : into these, men rammed in onion-seed with an iron turnip with the tail off, and then tickled the beams behind with a spit, whereupon there was driven out in front smoke and thunder and hell-fire. Then they told many more such stories of me, so that for the whole of that breakfast-time there was no other employ but to talk of me and laugh at me. And this was the cause of a general conclusion, to my destruction ; which was that I should be soundly befooled. For with such treatment I should in time prove a rare jester, by whose means one could do honour to the greatest princes in the world and cause laughter to a dying man.

Chap. iv : CONCERNING THE MAN THAT PAYS THE MONEY, AND OF THE MILITARY SERVICE THAT SIMPLICISSIMUS DID FOR THE CROWN OF SWEDEN : THROUGH WHICH SERVICE HE GOT THE NAME OF SIMPLICISSIMUS

BUT now, as they began to carouse and to make merry as they had done the day before, the watch brings news, together with the delivery of letters to the Governor, of a commissary that was at the gate, which same was appointed by the war council of the Crown of Sweden to review the garrison and survey the fortress. Such news spoiled all jesting, and all jollity died away like the bellows of a bagpipe when the wind is gone out. The minstrels and the guests dispersed themselves even as tobacco-smoke, which leaves but a smell behind it : while my lord, with the adjutant who kept the keys, betook himself, together with a detachment from the Mainguard and many torches, to the very gates, himself to give admittance to the Blackguts, as he called him : he wished, he said, the devil had broke his neck in a thousand pieces ere ever he came to the city. Yet so soon as he had let him in and welcomed him upon the inner drawbridge it wanted but a little, or nothing at all, but he would hold his stirrup for him to shew his devotion ; yea, the courtesy to all outward shew was between the two so great that the Commissary must dismount and walk on foot with my lord even to his lodging ; and as they walked each would have the left-hand place.

Then thought I, " Oh, what a wondrous spirit of falsehood doth govern all mankind, and so doth make one a fool through another's help."

So we drew near to the Mainguard, and the sentinel must call " Who goes there ? " though well he knew it was my lord : who would not answer but would leave the honour to that other : yet when the sentinel grew more impatient and repeated his challenge, the Commissary answered to the last " Who goes there ? " " The man who pays the money."

Now as we passed the sentry-box, and I came last of all, I heard the before-mentioned sentry, which was a new recruit, and before that by profession a well-to-do young farmer on the Vogelsberg, thus murmur to himself : " Yea, and a lying customer thou art : a man, forsooth, that pays the money ? a skin-the-flint that takes the money, that art thou. So much money hast thou wrung from me that I would to God thou wert struck dead before thou shouldst leave this town."

So from that hour I conceived this belief that this foreign lord with the silk doublet must be a holy man : for not only did no curse harm him, but also even they that hated him shewed him all honour and love and kindness : and that night was he princely entreated and made blind drunk, and thereafter put to bed in a noble bedplace.

Next day, then, at the review of the troops everything was at sixes and sevens. And even I, poor simple creature, was clever enough to cheat that clever commissary (for to such offices and administrations ye may well know they do choose no simple babes). Which same deceit I learned in less than a hour ; for the whole art consisted therein, to beat five with the right hand and four with the left on a drum. For yet I was too little to represent a musqueteer. So they furnished me forth to that end with borrowed clothes (for my short page's breeches were in no wise military to look upon) and with a borrowed drum : without doubt for this reason, that I myself was but borrowed : and with all this I came happily through the inspection. Thereafter, nevertheless, would no one trust my simple mind to keep in my memory any unaccustomed name, hearing which I should answer to it and step out of the ranks : and so must I keep the name of Simplicius ; and for a surname the Governor himself added that of Simplicissimus, and so had me written down in the muster-roll. And so he made me like a bastard, the first of my family ; and that although, after his own shewing, I looked so like his own sister. So ever thereafter I bore this name and surname, until I knew my right name : and under that name I played my part pretty well to the profit of the Governor and small danger to the Crown of Sweden. And this is all the service that ever I rendered to the Crown of Sweden in all my life : and the enemies of that Crown can at least not lay more than this to my charge.

Chap. v : HOW SIMPLICISSIMUS WAS BY FOUR DEVILS BROUGHT INTO HELL AND THERE TREATED WITH SPANISH WINE

NOW when the Commissary had gone the abovementioned pastor bade me come secretly to him to his lodging ; and then said he, " O Simplicissimus : for thy youth I am sorry, and thy future misery moveth me to sympathy. Hear, my child, and know of a surety, that thy master hath determined to deprive thee of all reason and so to make of thee a fool : yea, and to that end hath he already commanded raiment to be made ready for thee. So to-morrow must thou go to school : and in that school thou art to unlearn thy reason : and in that school without doubt they will so grievously torment thee, that, unless God help thee and other means be used against it, without doubt thou wilt become a madman. Now, because such is a wrong and dangerous manner of dealing ; and likewise because I, for thy hermit's piety's sake and for thine own innocence' sake, desire to serve thee, and with true Christian love to assist thee with counsel and all necessary help, and to give thee relief in trouble, therefore follow thou now my teaching and take this powder, which will in such wise strengthen thy brain and wits that thou, without danger to thine understanding, mayst endure all things most easily. Here likewise hast thou an ointment, with which thou must smear thy temples, thy spine and the nape of thy neck, and also thy nostrils; and both these things must thou use at evening-time when thou goest to bed, seeing at no time thou wilt be safe against being fetched forth from thy bed: but look thou that no one be ware of this my warning and the remedy that I impart to thee; else might it go ill with me and thee. And when they shall have thee under their accursed treatment, do thou heed not nor believe not all of which they will strive to persuade thee, and yet so carry thyself as if thou believest all. Say but little, lest thine attendants mark in thy conduct that they do but thresh straw; for then will they change the fashion of thy torments; though in truth I know not in what manner they will go about to deal with thee. But when thou shalt be clad in thy plumes and thy fool's coat, then come again to me that I may further serve thee with counsel. And meanwhile will I pray God for thee, that He may protect thine understanding and thy health of body."

With that he gives me the said powder and ointment, and so I betook myself home.

Now even as the pastor had said, so it happened. In my first sleep came four rogues disguised with frightful devils' masks into my room and to my bed, and there they capered around like mountebanks and twelfth-night fools. There had one a red-hot hook and another a torch in his hands; but the other two fell upon me and dragged me out of bed and danced around with me for a time, and then forced me to put on my clothes: while I so pretended as if I had taken them for true and natural devils, shrieked murder at the top of my voice, and shewed all the effects of the greatest terror. So they told me I must go with them: and with that they bound a napkin round my head so that I could neither see, hear nor cry out. Then they led me by many winding ways up and down many stairs, and at last into a cellar wherein was a great fire burning, and when they had unbound the napkin then they began to drink to me in Spanish wine and malmsey. And fain would they persuade me I was dead, and what is more, in the depths of hell : for I was careful to keep such a carriage as if I believed all that they pretended.

Then said they, " Drink lustily ; for thou must for ever abide with us : but if thou wilt not be a good fellow and take thy part, thou must forthwith into this fire that thou seest."

These poor devils would have disguised their speech and voice : yet I marked at once they were my lord's grooms : yet I let them not perceive this, but laughed in my sleeve that they that would make me a fool must themselves be my fools. So I drank my share of the Spanish wine ; but they drank more than I, for such heavenly nectar cometh rarely to such customers ; insomuch that I could swear they would be drunk sooner than I. But when it seemed to me to be the right time I so behaved myself with reeling this way and that, as I had seen my master's guests lately do, and at last would drink no more, but sleep ; but no : they began to chase me all round the cellar and prick me with their prong, which all the time they had left to lie in the fire, till it seemed as if they themselves had gone mad, and that to make me drink more or at least not go to sleep. And whenever, being thus baited, I fell down (and this I often did purposely), then they seized upon me and made as if they would cast me into the fire. So was it with me as with a hawk that is kept from sleep* : and this was my great torment. 'Tis true I could have lasted them out both in respect of drunkenness and sleep ; but they stayed not all the time altogether, but relieved one another's watch ; and so at last must I have failed. Three days and two nights did I spend in that smoky cellar, which had no other light but that which the fire gave out : and so my head began to hum and to feel as if 'twould burst, so that at last I must contrive some device to rid me at once of my torment and of my tormentors. And this did I even as does the fox when he cannot escape the hounds, and that so well that my devils could no longer endure to be near me. So to punish me they laid me in a sheet and trounced

* Allusion to a cruel practice in use in falconry.

me so unmercifully that all my inward parts might well have come out, soul and all. And what they did further with me I know not, so gone was I from my senses.

Chap. vi : HOW SIMPLICISSIMUS WENT UP TO HEAVEN AND WAS TURNED INTO A CALF

NOW when I came to myself I found myself no longer in the gloomy cellar with the devils, but in a fine room under the charge of three of the foulest old wives that ever the earth bore : I held them at first, when I opened my eyes a little, for real spirits of hell : but had I then read the old heathen poets I should have deemed them to be the Furies, or at least have taken one for Tisiphone come from hell to rob me, like Athamas, of my wits (for well I knew I was there to be turned into a fool). For she had a pair of eyes like two will-o'-the-wisps, and between the same a long, thin hawk's nose whose end or point reached at least to her lower lip : and two teeth only could I see in her mouth, and those so perfect, long, round, and thick that each might for its form be likened to a ring-finger, and for its colour to the gold ring itself. In a word, there was enough to make up a mouthful of teeth, yet ill distributed. Her face was like Spanish leather, and her grey hair hung in a strange confusion about her head, for they had but just fetched her from her bed. In truth it was a fearsome sight, which could serve for nought else but as an excellent remedy against the unreasonable lust of a salacious goat. The other two were no whit handsomer, save that they had blunt apes' noses and had put on their clothes somewhat more orderly. So when I had a little recovered myself, I perceived that the one was our dish-washer and the other two wives of two grooms. I pretended as though I could not move (and in truth I was in no condition for dancing) : whereupon these honest old beldames stripped me stark naked and cleansed me from all filth like a young child ; yea, while the work was a-doing they shewed me great patience and much compassion, insomuch that I nearly revealed to them how it truly stood with me : yet I thought, " Nay, Simplicissimus, trust thou in no old women ; but consider thou hast victory enough if thou in thy youth canst deceive three such crafty old hags, with whose help one could catch the devil in the open field : from such beginnings thou mayest hope in thine old age to do yet greater things."

So when they had ended with me they laid me in a splendid bed wherein I fell asleep without rocking : but they departed and took their tubs and other things wherewith they had washed me away with them, and my clothes likewise. Then according to my reckoning did I sleep at one stretch twenty-four hours : and when I awoke there stood two pretty lads with wings before my bed, which were finely decked out with white shirts, taffety ribbons, pearls and jewels, as also golden chains and the like dazzling trinkets. One had a gilded trencher full of cakes, shortbread, marchpane, and other confectionery ; but the other a gilded flagon in his hand. These two angels (for such they gave themselves out to be) sought to persuade me I was now in heaven, for that I had happily endured purgatory and had escaped from the devil and his dam : so need I only ask what my heart desired, for all that I could wish was at hand or, if not, they could presently fetch it. Now I was tormented by thirst, and as I saw the beaker before me I desired only drink, which was willingly handed to me. Yet was it no wine but a gentle sleeping-draught which I drank at one pull, and with that again fell asleep so soon as it grew warm within me.

The next day I woke once more (for else had I still been sleeping), yet found myself no longer in bed nor in the aforesaid room, but in my old goose-pen. There too was hideous darkness even as in the cellar, and besides that I had on a garment of calf-skins whereof the rough side was turned outwards : the breeches were cut in Polish or Swabian fashion and the doublet too shaped in a yet more foolish wise : and on my neck was a head-piece like a monk's cowl ; this was drawn down over my head and ornamented with a fine pair of great asses' ears. Then must I perforce laugh at mine own plight ; for well I saw by the nest and the feathers what manner of bird I was to be. And at that time I first began to reason with myself and to reflect what I had best do. So this I determined : to play the fool to the uttermost, as I might have the chance now and again, and meanwhile to wait with patience how my fate would shape itself.

Chap. vii : HOW SIMPLICISSIMUS ACCOMMODATED HIMSELF TO THE STATE OF A BRUTE BEAST

NOW it had been easy for me, by means of the hole which the mad ensign had cut in the door before, to free myself. But because I must now be a fool, I let that alone : and not only did I behave like a fool who hath not the wit of his own motion to release himself, but did even present myself as a hungry calf that pineth for its mother : nor was it long before my bleating was heard of them that were appointed to watch me ; for presently there came two soldiers to the goose-pen and asked who was in there. So I answered : " Ye fools, hear ye not that a calf is in here." And with that they opened the pen and brought me out, and wondered how a calf could so speak : which forced performance became them even as well as doth the awkward attempt of a new-recruited comedian who cannot play his part ; and that so much so that I thought often I must help them to play their jest out. So they took counsel what they should do with me, and agreed to make me a present to the Governor as one who would give them a larger reward if I could speak than the butcher would pay for me. Then they questioned me how I did, and I answered, " Sorrily enough." So they asked why, and I said, " For this reason, that here it is the fashion to shut up honest calves in goose-pens. Ye rogues must know that a proper ox will in due time come of me ; and so must I be brought up as becometh an honourable steer."

So after this brief discourse they had me with them across the street to the Governor's quarters : a great crowd of boys following us, and inasmuch as they, like myself, all bleated loud like a calf, the very blind could have guessed by the hearing that a whole herd of calves was being driven past : whereas by our looks we might be likened to a pack of young fools and old.

Then was I by my two soldiers presented to the Governor, for all the world as if they had taken me as plunder : them he rewarded with a gratification, but to me he promised the best post that I could have about him. So I thought of the Goldsmith's* apprentice and answered thus : " Good, my lord, but none must clap me into goose-pens : for we calves can endure no such treatment if we are to grow and to turn into fine heads of cattle." The Governor promised me better things, and thought himself a clever fellow to have made so presentable a fool out of me. " But no," thought I, " wait thou, my dear master ; I have endured the trial by fire and therein have I been hardened : now will we try which of us two can best trick the other."

Now just then a peasant that had fled into the city was driving his cattle to drink. Which when I saw forthwith I left the Governor and ran to the cows, bleating like a calf, even as though I would suck : but they, when I came to them, were more terrified at me than a wolf, albeit I wore hair of their kind ; yea, they were so affrighted and scattered so quickly from one another as if a hornet's nest had been let loose among them in August, so that their master could not again bring them together at the same place ; which occasioned pretty sport. And in a wink a crowd of folk ran together to see this fool's jape, and as my lord laughed till he was fit to burst, at last he said, " Truly one fool maketh a hundred more."

But I thought to myself, " Yea, and thou speakest this truth of thine own self."

And as from that time forward each must call me the calf, so I for my part had a scoffing nickname for every one : which same, according to the opinion of all and especially of my lord, turned out most wittily ; for I christened each as his qualities demanded. In a word ; many did count me for a witless madman, while I held all for fools in their wits. And to my thinking this is still the way of the world : for each one is content with his own wits and esteemeth that he is of all men the cleverest.

The said jest which I played with the peasant's cattle made a short forenoon still shorter : for 'twas then about the winter

* Proverbial : an allusion to a popular story.

solstice. At dinner-time I waited as before, but besides that I played many quaint tricks : as that when I must eat no man could force me to take man's food or drink : for I said roundly I would have only grass, which at that time 'twas impossible to come by. So my lord had a fresh pair of calf-skins fetched from the butcher, and the same pulled over the heads of two little boys : and these he set by me at table, and for a first course set before us a dish of winter salad and bade us fall to lustily : yea, he commanded to bring a live calf and entice him with salt to eat the salad. So I looked on staring as if I wondered at this, but the thing gave me occasion to play my part the better.

" Of a certainty," said they, when they saw me so unmoved, " 'tis no new thing if calves do eat flesh, fish, cheese, and butter ; yea, and at times drink themselves soundly drunk : nowadays the beasts do know what is good. Ay, and 'tis nowadays come to that, that but little difference is to be found between them and mankind. Wilt thou not play thy part therein ? " And to that I was the more easily persuaded in that I was hungry, and not because I had before seen with mine own eyes how men could be more swinish than pigs, more savage than lions, more lustful than goats, more envious than dogs, more unruly than horses, more stupid than asses, more mad for drink than the brutes, craftier than foxes, greedier than wolves, sillier than apes, and more poisonous than asps and toads ; yet all alike partook of men's food, and only by their shape were discerned from the beasts, and specially in respect of innocence were they to be counted far below the poor calf. So I ate my fill with my fellow calves as much as my appetite demanded : and if a stranger had unexpectedly thus beheld me sitting at table, without doubt he had imagined that Circe of old had risen up again to turn men into beasts ; which art my master then knew and practised. And as I took my dinner, so was I treated at my supper, and even as my fellow guests or parasites fed with me, so must they with me to bed, though my lord would not permit that I should pass the night in the cow-byre. Now all this I did to befool them that would have held me for a fool, and this sure conclusion did I make, that the most gracious God doth lend and impart to every man in his station to which He hath called him, so much wit as he hath need of there to maintain himself : yea, and moreover, that many do vainly imagine, doctors though they be or not, that they alone be men of wit and they only fit for every trade, whereas there be as many good fish* in the sea yet.

Chap. viii : DISCOURSETH OF THE WONDROUS MEMORY OF SOME AND THE FORGET-FULNESS OF OTHERS

NOW when I awaked next morning were both my becalfed bedfellows up and away : so I rose up likewise, and when the adjutant came to fetch away the keys to open the town gates, out I slipped to my pastor ; and to him I told all that had happened to me, as well in heaven as in hell. So when he saw that it vexed my conscience that I should deceive so many folk, and specially my master, whereas I pretended to be a fool, " why, upon that point," says he, " thou needest not to trouble thyself : this foolish world will be befooled, and if they have left thee thy wits, so use thou those same wits to thine own advantage, and imagine to thyself as if thou, like to the Phœnix, hast been newly born from folly to understanding through fire, and so to a new human life. Yet know thou withal thou art not yet out of the wood, but with risk of thy reason hast slipped into this fool's cap. Yea, and these times be so out of joint that none can know whether thou yet escape without loss of thy life. For a man can run quickly into hell, but to get out again doth need a deal of puffing and blowing : and thou art not yet—no, not by a long way— man enough to escape the danger that lies before thee, as well thou mightest suppose. So wilt thou have need of more foresight and wit than in those days when thou knewest not what reason or unreason was : bide thou thy time and wait on the turn of the tide."

Now was his manner of speaking different from what it had been, and that because, I believe, he had read it in my countenance that I fancied myself to be somewhat, since I had

* Lit. there are folk dwelling beyond the mountains too.

with such masterly deceit and art slipped through the net. Nay, I gathered this from his face, that he was sick and tired of me, for his looks shewed it ; and indeed what part had he in me ? With that I changed my discourse also, and busied myself to give him great thanks for the excellent remedies which he had imparted to me for the preserving of my wits : yea, and I made him impossible promises to repay him all that my debt to him demanded. Now this tickled him and brought him again to a different humour, wherein he bepraised his medicine and told me Simonides of Melos had invented an art which Metrodorus of Skepsis had perfected, and that not without great pains, whereby he could teach men at the repeating of a single word to recount all that they had ever heard or read, and such a thing, said he, " were not possible without medicines to strengthen the head such as he had ministered to me."

" Yea," thought I, " my good master parson : yet have I read in thine own books, when I dwelt with my hermit, a different tale of that wherein the Skepsian's mnemonic did consist."

Yet was I crafty enough to hold my peace : for if I must speak truth, 'twas now first, when I must be counted a fool, that I became keen-witted and more guarded in my talk. So the pastor continued, and told me how Cyrus could call every one of his 30,000 soldiers by his right name ; how Lucius Scipio could do the like with every citizen of Rome ; and how Cineas, Pyrrhus's ambassador, on the very day after he came to Rome could repeat in their order the names of all the senators, and nobles. Mithridates, the King of Pontus, said he, had in his realm men speaking twenty-two languages, to all of which he could minister judgment in their own tongue : yea, and talk with each separately. So, too, the learned Greek Charmides could tell a man what each would know out of all the books in a whole library if he had but read them once through. Lucius Seneca could say 2000 names in order if they were once recited before him and, as Ravisius tells, could repeat 200 verses spoken by 200 scholars from the last back to the first. So Esdras knew the five books of Moses by heart, and could dictate the same word by word to the scribes. Themistocles in one year did learn the Persian Speech, and Crassus, in Asia, could talk the five separate dialects of the Greek language, and in each administer the law to his subjects. Julius Cæsar could at the same time read, dictate, and give audiences. The holy Jerome knew both Hebrew, Chaldee, Greek, Persian, Median, Arabic and Latin, and the eremite Antonius knew the whole Bible by heart only from hearing it read. And so we know of a certain Corsican that he could hear 6000 men's names recited and thereafter repeat them in proper order.

" And all this I tell thee," said he further, " that thou mayest not hold it for an impossible thing that a man's memory should be excellently strengthened and maintained, even as it may, on the other hand, be in many ways weakened and even altogether destroyed. For in man there is no faculty so fleeting as that of memory : for by reason of sickness, terror, fear, or trouble and grief, it either vanisheth away or loseth a great part of its virtue. So do we read of a learned man at Athens that after a stone had fallen on his head he forgot all he had ever learned, even to his alphabet. So too another, by reason of sickness, came to this, that he forgot his own servant's name : and Messala Corvinus knew not his own name, though aforetime he had a good memory. And a priest who had sucked blood from his own veins thereupon forgot how to read and write, yet otherwise kept his memory, and when after a year's time he had again drunken of the same blood at the same place and the same time, could again write and read. So if a man eat bear's brains, 'tis said he will fall into such a craze and strong delusion as if he himself were turned into a bear ; as is shewn by the example of a Spanish nobleman who, having eaten of it, ran wild in the woods and could believe nought else but that he was a bear. My good Simplicissimus, had thy master but known this art, thou mightest well have been changed into a bear like Callisto, rather than into a bull like Jupiter."

The pastor told me much more of the same sort, gave me more of his medicament, and instructed me as to my carriage for the time to come. So with that I betook myself home again, and with me more than one hundred boys, which all ran after me and again cried after me like calves : insomuch that my master, who was now risen, ran to the window, and when he saw so many fools all at once, was so gracious as to laugh heartily thereat.

Chap. ix : CROOKED PRAISE OF A PROPER LADY

NOW no sooner was I come into the house but I must forthwith to the parlour, for there were noble ladies with my lord which desired much to see and to hear his new fool. There I appeared and stood a-gaping like a dummy : whereupon she whom I had before caught at the dance took occasion to say she had been told this calf could speak, but now she did plainly perceive 'twas not true. Whereto I made answer I had also heard apes could not speak, but now could plainly hear 'twas not so.

"What ; " says my lord, " opinest thou, then, that these ladies be apes ? "

So I answered, " Be they not so already, yet they soon will be : for who knowest how things will go ; Yea, I myself had never expected to become a calf ; and yet am I that same."

Then my lord would ask me whereby I could tell that these ladies should become apes : so I answered him, " Our ape here carrieth his hinder parts naked, but these ladies do so carry their bosom : which other maidens be wont to cover."

" Ah, rogue," saith my lord, " thou beest but a foolish calf, and as thou art so thou talkest : for these ladies do of purpose shew what 'tis worth men's while to gaze upon ; whereas the poor ape goeth naked for sheer want of clothing. And now be thou quick to make good that wherein thou hast offended : else will we so bastinado thee and so hunt thee to thy goose-pen with dogs as men use to do with calves that know not how to behave themselves. Yet let us hear if thou canst praise a lady as is becoming."

So I looked upon the lady from head to foot and again from foot to head, and gazed upon her so fixedly and so lovingly as I would take her to wife : and at last, " Sir," said I, " I see clearly where the fault lieth ; for the rascal tailor is the cause of all. The villain hath left those parts, which should cover the neck and the breast, below in the skirts : and therefore do these so trail behind. The botcher should have his hand hewn off that can tailor no better than this." And "Lady," quoth I to her, "be rid of him, or he will shame you ; and have a care that you do deal with my dad's tailor, which same was hight Master Powle : for he could fashion fine plaited gowns for my mammy, our Ann, and our Ursula, and all cut even round about below. So did they never drag in the mud like yours : nay, and ye cannot believe what fine clothes he would make for the hussies."

So says my lord, "Were now thy father's Ann and thy father's Ursula handsomer than these ladies ? "

"Nay," said I, "my lord, that may not be : this young maiden hath hair as yellow as sulphur, and the parting of her hair so white and smooth as though one had cut bristle-brushes therefrom ; yea, and her hair so sweetly done up in rolls that it is like unto pipe-stems ; yea, and as if one had hanged upon each side of her head a pound of candles or a dozen of sausages. Look you now, what a smooth, fair brow she hath ! is it not rounder than a plum-pudding and whiter than a dead man's skull that has hung long on the gallows in wind and rain. 'Tis pity indeed that her tender skin is so stained by puff-powder ; for when people see this who understand not such things, surely they will think this lady had the king's evil, which is wont to produce such a scaly humour ; and this were surely pity : for look upon those sparkling eyes : they shine as black as did the soot on my dad's chimney ; for that did use to shine so terribly when our Ann stood there before it with a wisp of straw to warm the room as if fire were therein enough to set the world in a blaze. Her cheeks be rosy enough, yet not so red as the red garters with which the Swabian waggoners at Ulm did truss up their breeches. Yet the bright red which she hath on her lips doth far surpass the colour of those garters, and if she speak or laugh (I pray my masters give heed thereto), then can one see in her mouth two rows of teeth, so orderly and so sugary as if they were with one snip cut out of a white turnip. Oh, lovely creature ! I cannot believe that any one should feel pain if thou shouldst bite him therewith ! So, too, her neck is as white as curdled milk and her bosom, which lieth beneath, of like colour. And oh, my masters, look upon her hands and fingers : they be so slender, so long, so slim, so supple, and so cunning as for all the world like a gipsy's fingers, ready to thrust into any man's pockets and there go a-fishing."

With that there arose such a laughter that none could hear me, nor I talk : so I took French leave and off I went : for I would be mocked by others so long as I would, and no longer.

Chap. x : DISCOURSETH OF NAUGHT BUT HEROES AND FAMOUS ARTISTS

THEREAFTER followed the midday meal, whereat I again did good service : for now had I made it my purpose to rebuke all follies and to chastise all vanities, to which end my present condition was excellent well fitted : for no guest was too exalted for me to reprove and upbraid his vices, and if there were any that shewed displeasure, then was he laughed out of countenance by the rest, or else my master would demonstrate to him that no wise man is wont to be vexed at a fool. As to the mad ensign, which was my worst enemy, him I put on the rack at once. Yet the first who (at my lord's nod) did answer me reasonably was the secretary ; for when I called him a " title-forger " and asked what title, then, had our first father Adam, " Thou talketh," answered he, " like an unreasoning calf : for thou knowest not how after our first parents different folk lived in the world, which by rare virtues such as wisdom, manly deeds of arms, and invention of useful arts, did in such wise ennoble themselves and their family that they by others were exalted above all earthly things, yea even above the stars to be gods : and wert thou a man, or hadst thou at least, like a man, read the histories, thou wouldst understand the difference that lies between men, and so wouldst thou gladly grant to each his title of honour ; but since thou art but a calf, and so neither worthy nor capable of human honour, thou talketh of this matter like a stupid calf, and grudgest to the noble human race that wherein it can rejoice."

So I answered : " I was once a man as much as thou, and

I have read pretty much also, and so can I judge that thou either understandeth not this business aright, or art for thine own advantage compelled to speak otherwise than as thou knowest. For tell me, what deeds so noble and what arts so fine have ever been devised as to be enough to give nobility to a whole family for hundreds of years after the death of these great heroes and craftsmen ? Did not the strength of the heroes and the wisdom and high understanding of the craftsmen die with them ? And if thou seest not this, and if the qualities of the parents do descend to their children, then must I believe thy father was a stockfish and thy mother a plaice."

" Oho ! " answered the secretary, " if the matter is to be settled by our reviling of each other, then can I cast in thy teeth thy father was but a clownish peasant of the Spessart, and though in thy home and in thy family there be many famous blockheads, yet thou hast made thyself yet lower, seeing that thou art become an unreasoning calf."

So I answered : " Thou art right ; 'tis even that that I would maintain ; namely, that the virtues of the parents descend not always to the children, and that therefore the children be not alway worthy of their parent's titles of honour. For me it is no shame to have become a calf, seeing that in such case I have the honour to follow the great king Nebuchadnezzar. Who knoweth whether it may not please God that I, like him, may again become a man, yea, and a far greater one than my dad ? Yet do I praise those only that by their own virtues do make themselves nobles."

" Let it be so for the sake of argument," said the secretary, " that the children should not alway inherit the titles of their parents, yet thou must acknowledge that they are worthy of all praise which do earn their nobility by a good conduct : and if that be so, it followeth that we do rightly honour the children for the parents' sake, since the apple falleth not far from the tree. And who would not honour in the descendants of Alexander the Great, if such there were to hand, their ancient forefather's high courage in the wars. For this man shewed in his youth his desire for fighting, in that he wept (though not yet able to bear arms) grieving lest his father might conquer all and leave him nothing to

subdue. Did not he before the thirtieth year of his age overcome all the world and wish for another to conquer ? Did
not he in a battle against the Indians, when he was deserted
by his men, for sheer rage sweat blood ? And was he not so
terrible to look upon (as though he were all begirt with flames
of fire) that even the savages must flee before him in battle ?
Who would not esteem him higher and nobler than other
men, of whom Quintus Curtius tells that his breath was like
perfume and his sweat like musk and that his dead body
smelt of precious spiceries ? Here could I cite the case of
Julius Cæsar and Pompeius, of whom the one, besides the
victories which he won in the civil wars, did fifty times engage
in pitched battles, and defeated and slew 1,520,000 men :
while the other, besides the taking of 940 ships from the
pirates, did from the Alps to the uttermost parts of Spain
capture and subdue 376 cities and towns. Lucius Siccius,
the Roman people's tribune, was engaged in 120 pitched
battles, and did eight times conquer them that challenged
him : he could shew forty-five scars on his body, and those
all in front and none behind : with nine generals-in-chief did
he enter Rome in their triumphs, which they did clearly earn
by their courage. Yea, and Manlius Capitolinus's honour in
war were no less had he not at the end of his life himself abased
his fame : for he too could shew thirty-three scars, without
counting that he once did alone save the capitol with all its
treasures from the French. What of Hercules the Strong and
Theseus and the rest, whose undying praise it is wellnigh
impossible both to describe and to tell of ? Should not these
be honoured in their descendants ? But I will pass over war
and weapons and turn to the arts, which, though they seem
to make less noise in the world, yet do achieve great fame
for the masters of them. What skill do we find in Zeuxis,
which by his ingenious brain and skilful hand did deceive the
very birds of the air ; and likewise in Apelles, who did paint
a Venus so natural, so fine, so exquisite, and in all features
so nice and so delicate that all bachelors did fall in love with
her ! Doth not Plutarch tell us how Archimedes did draw
with one hand and by a single rope through the midst of the
market-place at Syracuse a great ship laden with merchants'
ware as if he had but led a packhorse by the bridle ? which

thing not twenty oxen, to say nothing of two hundred calves like thee, could have effected. And should not this honest craftsman be endowed with a title of honour fitted to his art ? This Archimedes made a mirror wherewith he could set on fire an enemy's warship in mid-sea. And who would not praise him which first did invent letters ? Yea, who would not exalt him far above all artists who devised the noble and, for all the world, useful art of printing ? If Ceres was accounted a goddess because she is said to have invented agriculture and the grinding of corn, why were it not fair that others should have their praise with titles of honour allowed them ? Yet in truth it mattereth little whether thou, thou stupid calf, canst take such things into thy unreasoning bullock's brain or not. For 'tis with thee as with the dog which lay in the manger and would not let the ox eat of the hay, yet could not enjoy the same himself : thou art capable of no honour, and for that very cause thou grudgest such to those that do deserve it."

With all this I found myself sorely bestead, yet made answer : " These mighty deeds were indeed highly to be praised were they not accomplished with the destruction and damage of other men. But what manner of praise is this which is stained with the bloodshed of so many innocents ; and what manner of nobility that which is achieved and won by the ruin of so many thousand other folk ! And as concerns the arts, what be they save merely vanities and follies ! Yea, they be as vain, idle, and unprofitable as the title of honour which might come to any man from these craftsmen ; for they do but serve the greed, or the lust, or the luxury, or the corruption of others, like to those vile guns which lately I beheld on their half-waggons. Yea, and well could we spare both printing and writing, according to the sentence and opinion of that holy man who held that the whole wide world was book enough for him, wherein to study the wonders of his Creator and thereupon to recognise the almighty power of God."

Chap. xi : OF THE TOILSOME AND DANGEROUS OFFICE OF A GOVERNOR

THEN my lord would also have his jest with me, and said : " I do well perceive that because thou trusteth not thyself to be of gentle birth, therefore thou despisest the honourable titles of gentility." " Sir," answered I, " if I could at this very hour enter upon your place of honour, yet would I not take it."

My lord laughed and said ; " That I believe, for for the ox his oaten straw is well enough : but an thou hadst a high spirit such as hearts of gentles should have, then wouldst thou with zeal aspire to high honours and dignities. I for my part count it no small thing that fortune raises me above my fellows."

Then did I sigh, and " O toilsome felicity ! " said I. " Sir, I assure you, ye are the most miserable man in Hanau."

" How so ; how so, calf ? " said my lord. " Give me thy reasons, for such I find not in myself."

So I answered, " If you know not and feel not that you are Governor in Hanau, and with how many cares and uneasiness in that account burdened, then either the devouring thirst of honour blinds you or else are you of iron and quite insensible ; ye have, 'tis true, the right to command, and whosoever comes within your ken the same must obey you. But do they serve ye for naught ? Are ye not all men's servant ? Must ye not specially take care for each and all ? See, ye are girded round with foes, and the safeguarding of this stronghold depends on you alone. Ever must ye be devising how to do some damage to your opposites : and therein must ever be on your guard that your plans be not spied upon. Must ye not often stand on guard like a common sentinel ? Besides, ye must ever be concerned that there be no failure in money, ammunition, food and folk, and for that reason be ever holding the whole land to contribution by continual exactions and extortions. Send ye your men out to such an end, then is robbery, plunder, stealing, burning, and murder their highest task. Even now of late they have plundered Orb, captured Braunfels, and laid Staden in ashes.

Thence 'tis true they brought back booty, but ye have laid on them a grievous responsibility before God. I grant this, that those enjoyments which accompany thine honour do please thee well; but knowest thou who will enjoy such treasures as doubtless thou gatherest? And granted that such riches remain thine (whereof a man may doubt), yet must thou leave them in this world and takest nothing with thee but the sin whereby thou hast gained them. And even if thou hast the good luck to enjoy thy booty, yet thou dost but spend the sweat and blood of the poor, who do now in misery suffer want or even perish and die of hunger. How often do I see that thy thoughts, by reason of the cares of thine office, are distracted hither and thither, while I and other calves do sleep in peace without any care, and if thou dost not so, it shall cost thee thy head if aught be overlooked that should have been provided for the preservation of thy subject people and this fortress. Look you, I am raised above such cares! and so, knowing that I do owe the debt of death to nature, I fear not lest an enemy should storm my stall or lest I should have with pains to fight for life. If I die young, so am I delivered from the toilsome life of a yoke-ox. But for thee men lay snares in a thousand fashions: and therefore is thy life naught but a continual care and sleeplessness; for thou must fear both friend and foe, which be ever devising to cheat thee of thy life or thy money, or thy reputation or thy command, or somewhat else whatever it be; even as thou thinkest to do by others. The enemy doth attack thee openly: and thy supposed friends do secretly envy thee thy good luck, and even as regards thy subjects art thou in no manner of safety.

" I say naught of this, that daily thy burning desires do torment thee and drive thee hither and thither, whilst thou plannest to gain for thyself still greater name and fame, to rise higher in rank, to gather greater riches, to play the enemy a trick, to surprise this or that place; in a word, to do wellnigh everything that may vex others and prove harmful to thine own soul and grievous to God's majesty. Yea, and the worst is this, that thou art so spoiled by thy flatterers that thou knowest not thyself, but art by them so captivated and drugged that thou canst not see the dangerous way thou

goest ; for all that thou doest they say is right and all thy
vices are by them turned into virtues and so proclaimed ;
thy cruelty is to them stern justice : and when thou plunderest
land and folk, thou art a brave soldier, say they, and do urge
thee on to others' harm, that they may keep in thy favour
and fill their purses too."

" Thou malingerer," said my lord, " who taught thee so
to preach ? "

" Good my lord," answered I, " say I not truly that thou
art so spoiled by thine ear-wiggers and sycophants that already
thou art past help ? Whereas contrariwise other folk do soon
detect thy faults and condemn thee not only in high and
mighty matters, but find enough to blame in thee in small
things which are of little account. And of this hast thou not
examples enough in the case of great men of old time ? So
the Lacedaemonians railed at their own Lycurgus for walking
with his head bowed : the Romans deemed it a foul fault
in Scipio that he snored so loud in his sleep : it seemed to
them an ugly fault in Pompey that he did scratch himself
but with one finger : at Cæsar they mocked for wearing his
girdle awry ; and the good Cato was slandered for eating
too greedily with both jaws at once ; yea, the Carthaginians
spoke evil of Hannibal for going with his breast bare and
uncovered. How think ye now, my dear master ? Think
ye I would change places with one that, besides twelve or
thirteen boon companions, flatterers and parasites, hath more
than one hundred, yea, 'tis like enough more than ten thousand, both open and secret foes, slanderers, and malicious
enviers ? Besides, what happiness, what pleasure, and what
joy can such a head have under whose care, protection, and
guard so many men do live ? Is't not a duty laid upon thee
to watch for all thy folk, to care for them, and listen to each
one's complaints and grievances ? Were that not of itself
troublesome enough even though thou hadst neither foes nor
secret enemies ? I can see well enough how hard 'tis for thee
and yet how many grievances thou must endure. And, good
my lord, what in the end will be thy reward ? Tell me what
hast thou for it all ? If thou canst not say, then suffer the
Grecian Demosthenes to tell thee, who after he had bravely
and loyally furthered and defended the common weal and

rights of the Athenians, was, contrary to all law and justice, banished the land and driven into miserable exile as an evil-doer. So Socrates was requited with poison, and Hannibal so ill rewarded by his countrymen that he must wander in the world as a poor wretched outlaw ; yea, the Greeks repaid Lycurgus in such fashion that he was stoned and had an eye beaten out. Do thou, therefore, keep thy high office to thyself, with the reward thou wilt have from it : seek not to share it with me ; for even if all go well with thee, yet hast thou naught to carry home with thee but an ill conscience. And if thou art minded to obey that conscience, then wilt thou be quickly deposed from thy commands as incapable, for all the world as if thou too wert become a stupid calf."

While I thus spake, the rest of the company looked hard upon me and wondered much that I should be able to hold such discourse, which, as they openly confessed, would have taxed the wits of a man of sense if he had been forced so to speak without preparation.

Chap. xii : OF THE SENSE AND KNOWLEDGE OF CERTAIN UNREASONING ANIMALS

SO I ended my discourse thus : " Therefore," said I, " my excellent master, will I not change with thee : for indeed I have no call to do so since the brook affords me a healthy drink instead of thy costly wines ; and He who allowed me to be turned into a calf will also in such wise know how to bless the fruits of the earth to my use, that they be to me as to Nebuchadnezzar, no unfitting provision for food and sustenance : even so hath nature provided me with a good coat of fur ; while as for thee, often thou loathest thy meat, thy wine splitteth thy head, and soon will bring thee into one sickness or another."

Then my lord answered : " I know not what I have in thee ; meseemeth thou art for a calf far too wise : nay, I do surmise thou hast under that calf-skin clad thyself with a rogue-skin."

With that I made as if I were angry, and said : " Do ye men think then, that we beasts be all fools ? That may

101

ye not imagine. I do maintain that if older beasts could speak as well as I, that they would tell you a very different story. If ye deem we are so stupid, then tell me who hath taught the wild wood-pigeons, the jays, the blackbirds, and the partridges to purge themselves with laurel-leaves, and doves, turtle-doves, and fowls with dandelions. Who teacheth cat and dog to eat the dewy grass when they desire to purge a full belly ? Who hath taught the tortoise to heal a bite with hemlock or the stag when he is shot to have recourse to the dictamnus or calamint ? Who taught the weasel to use the rue when she will fight with bat or snake ? Who maketh the wild boar to know the ivy and the bear the mandrake, and saith to them it is their medicine ? Who giveth the swallow to understand that she should heal her fledglings' dim eyes with chelidonium ? Who did instruct the snake to eat of fennel when she will cast her slough and heal her darkened eyes ? Who teacheth the stork to purge himself, the pelican to let himself blood and the bear to get himself scarified by bees ? Nay, I might almost say, ye men have learned your arts and sciences from us beasts. Ye eat and drink yourselves to death, and that we beasts do never do. Lion or wolf, when he is by way of growing too fat, then he fasteth till again he is thin, active, and healthy. And which party dealeth most wisely herein ? Yea, above and beyond all this, consider the fowls of the air ; regard the various architecture of their cunning nests, and inasmuch as all your labours can never imitate them, therefore ye must acknowledge they be both wiser and more ingenious than ye men yourselves. Who telleth to our summer birds when they should come to us for the spring and hatch their young, or for the autumn, when they should again betake themselves from us to warmer climes ? Who teacheth them they must choose a gathering-place to that end ? Who leadeth them or sheweth them the way ? Do ye men lend them, perchance, a compass that they fall not out by the way ? Nay, my good friends, they do know the way without your help, and how long they must spend therein, and when they must depart from this place and the other, and therefore have no need of your compass nor your almanack. Further, behold the industrious spider, whose web is wellnigh a miracle : look if you find a single knot in all her weaving. What hunter or fisher hath taught her how to spread her net, and when she hath laid that net to catch her prey, to set herself either in the furthest corner or else full in the centre ? Ye men do admire the raven of whom Plutarchus writeth that he threw into a vessel that was half full of water so many stones that the water rose until he could conveniently drink thereof. What would ye do if ye were to dwell among the beasts and there behold all the rest of their dealings, their doings, and their not-doings ? Then at all events would ye acknowledge 'twas plain that all beasts had somewhat of especial natural vigour and virtue in all their desires and instincts, as being now prudent, now strenuous, now gentle, now timid, now fierce, for your learning and instruction. Each knoweth the other ; they discern each from other ; they seek after that which is useful to them, flee from what is harmful, avoid danger, gather together what is necessary for their sustenance—yea, and at times do befool you men yourselves. Therefore have many ancient philosophers seriously pondered of such matters and have not been ashamed to question and to dispute whether unreasoning brutes might not have understanding. But I care not to speak further of these matters : get ye to the bees and see how they make wax and honey, and then come again and tell me how ye think of it."

Chap. xiii : *OF VARIOUS MATTERS WHICH WHO-EVER WILL KNOW MUST EITHER READ THEM OR HAVE THEM READ TO HIM*

THEREUPON various judgments were pronounced upon me by my lord's guests. The Secretaries were of opinion I should be counted a fool because I esteemed myself a reasoning beast, and because they that had a tile or two slipped, and yet seemed to themselves wise, were the most complete and comical fools of all. Others said, if 'twere possible to drive out of me the idea that I was a calf, or one could persuade me I was again turned into a man, I should surely be held reasonable, or at least sane enough. But my lord himself said, " I hold him for a fool because he telleth every man the truth so shamelessly ; yet are his speeches so ordered that they belong to no fool." (Now all this they spake in Latin, that I might not understand.) Then he asked me, had I studied while I was yet a man ? I answered, I knew not what study was, " but, dear sir," said I further, " tell me what manner of things are these studs with which men study ? Speakest thou, perchance, of the balls with which men bowl." Then answered he they called the " mad ensign," " What will ye with the fellow ? 'a hath a devil, 'a is possessed ? 'tis sure the devil talking through his mouth." And on that my lord took occasion to ask me, since I had been turned into a calf, whether I still was accustomed to pray like other men and trusted to go to heaven. " Surely," answered I, " Yet have I my immortal human soul, which, as thou canst easily believe, will not lightly desire to come to hell again, specially since I fared therein so evilly once before. I am but changed as once was Nebuchadnezzar, and in God's good time I might well become a man again." " And I hope thou mayst," said my lord, with a pretty deep sigh, whereupon I might easily judge that he repented him of having allowed me to be driven mad. " But let us hear," he went on, " how art thou wont to pray ? " So I kneeled down and raised my eyes and hands to heaven in good hermit fashion, and because my lord's repentance which I had perceived touched my heart with exceeding comfort, I could not refrain my tears, and so to outward appearance prayed with deepest reverence, after the Paternoster, for all Christendom, for my friends and my enemies, and that God would vouchsafe to me so to live in this world that I might be worthy to praise Him in eternal bliss. My hermit had taught me such a prayer in devout and well-ordered words. At that some soft-hearted onlookers were also nigh to weeping, for they had great pity for me, yea, my lord's own eyes were full of water.

After dinner my lord sends for the pastor, and to him he told all that I had uttered, and gave him to understand that he was concerned lest all was not well* with me, and perchance the devil had a finger in the pie, seeing that at first I had shewn myself altogether simple and ignorant yet now

* I.e. he was bewitched.

could utter things to make men wonder. The pastor, who knew my qualities better than any other, answered, that should have been thought on before 'twas allowed to make me a fool, for, " men," said he, " were made in the image of God, and with such, and especially with such tender youth, one must not make sport as with beasts " : yet would he never believe 'twas permitted to the evil spirit to interfere, seeing that I had ever commended myself to God with fervent prayer. Yet if against all likelihood such a thing were decreed and permitted, then had men a sore account to answer for before God, inasmuch as there would scarcely be greater sin than for one man to rob another of his reason and thus withdraw him from the praise and service of God, whereto he was chiefly created. " I gave ye beforehand my assurance," said he, " that he had wit enough, but that he could not fit himself to the world was caused by this, that he was brought up first with his father, a rough peasant, and then with your brother-in-law in the wilderness, in all simplicity. Had folk had but a little patience with him at first, he would with time have learned a better carriage ; he was but a simple, God-fearing child, such as the evil-disposed world knew not. Yet do I not doubt he can again be brought to his right mind, if we can but take from him this fantasy and bring him to believe no longer that he was turned into a calf. We read of one which did firmly believe he was changed into an earthen pot, and would beseech his friends to put him high on a shelf lest he should be trodden on and broken. Another did imagine he was a cock, and in his infirmity crowed both day and night. And yet another fancied he was already dead and a wandering spirit, and therefore would partake of no medicine nor food nor drink, till a wise physician hired two fellows which gave themselves out likewise to be spirits, yet hearty drinkers, who joined themselves to him and persuaded him that nowadays spirits were wont to eat'and drink, whereby he was brought to his senses. Yea, I myself had a sick peasant in my parish, who, when I visited him, complained to me he had three or four barrels of water in his body ; and could he be rid of that he trusted to be well again, and begged me either to have him ripped up, that the water might run away, or have him hung up in the smoke to dry it up. So

I spoke him fair, and persuaded him I could draw off the water from him in another fashion ; and with that I took a tap such as we use for wine and beer casks, bound a strip of pig's guts to it, and the other end I fastened to the bung hole of a great puncheon, which to that end I had had filled with water ; then I pretended as if I had stuck the tap into his belly, which he had had swathed in rags lest it should burst. Then I let the water run out of the puncheon through tubes ; whereat the poor creature rejoiced heartily and, throwing away his rags, was in a few days whole again. Again, one that imagined he had all manner of horse-furniture, bits and the like, in his body, was in this wise cured : for his physician, having given him a strong purge, conveyed such things into the night-stool so that the fellow must needs believe he was rid of them by the purging. So, too, they tell of one madman that believed his nose was so long that it reached to the ground : for him they hung a sausage to his nose, and cut it away by little and little till they came to the real nose : who, as soon as he felt the knife touch his flesh, cried out the nose was in its right shape again. And our good Simplicissimus can therefore be cured even as were these of whom I have spoken."

"All this can I believe," answered my master, " only this gives me concern, that he was before so ignorant, and now can talk of all matters, and that in such perfect fashion as one cannot easily find even among persons older, more practised, and better read than he is : for he hath told me of many properties of beasts, and described mine own person so exactly as he had been all his life in the busy world, so that I must needs wonder and hold his speeches wellnigh for an oracle or a warning of God."

"Sir," answered the pastor, " this may well be true and yet natural : I know that he is well read, seeing that he, as well as his hermit, went through all my books which I had, and which were not few ; and because the lad hath a good memory, and is now at leisure in his mind and forgetful of his own person, therefore he can utter what aforetime he stored in his brain : and therefore I do cherish the firm hope that with time he may again be brought to right reason."

In this wise the pastor left the Governor between hope and

fear : and me and my cause he defended in the best way, and gained for me days of happiness and for himself (by the way) access to the Governor. Their crowning resolve was this, to deal with me for a time quietly ; and that the pastor did more for his own sake than mine, for by going to and fro and acting as if he bestirred himself for my sake and felt great care for me, he gained the Governor's favour, who gave him office and made him chaplain to the garrison, which in those hard times was no small matter : neither did I grudge it him.

Chap. xiv : *HOW SIMPLICISSIMUS LED THE LIFE OF A NOBLEMAN, AND HOW THE CROATS ROBBED HIM OF THIS WHEN THEY STOLE HIMSELF*

SO from this time forward I possessed in full the favour, grace, and love of my lord, of which I can boast with truth : nought I wanted to complete my good fortune but that my calf-skin was too much and my years too little, though I knew it not myself. Besides, the pastor would not yet have me brought to my senses, but it seemed to him not yet time, neither as yet profitable for his interest. But my lord, seeing my taste for music, had me to learn it, and hired for me an excellent lute-player, whose art I presently well understood and in this excelled him, that I could sing to the lute better than he. So could I serve my lord for his pleasure, for his pastime, delight, and admiration. Likewise all the officers shewed me their respect and goodwill, the richest burghers sent me gratifications, and the household, like the soldiers, wished me well because they saw how well inclined my master was to me. One treated me here, another there ; for they knew that often jesters have more power with their masters than honest men : and to this end were all their gifts ; for some gave to me lest I should slander them, others for that very reason—namely, that I should slander others for their sake. In which manner I put together a pretty sum of money, which for the most part I handed to the pastor ; for I knew not yet to what end it could be used. And as none dared look at me askance, so from this time forward I had no jealousy, care, or trouble to encounter with. All my thoughts I gave to my music, and to devising how I might courteously point out to one and the other his failings. So I grew like a pig in clover, and my strength of body increased palpably : soon could one see that I was no longer starving my body in the wood with water and acorns and beech-nuts and roots and herbs, but that over a good meal I found the Rhenish wine and the Hanau double-beer to my taste, which was indeed in those miserable times to be accounted a great favour of God : for at that time all Germany was aflame with war and harried by hunger and pestilence, and Hanau itself besieged by the enemy, all which disturbed me not in the least. But after the raising of the siege my master designed to make a present of me either to Cardinal Richelieu or Duke Bernhard of Weimar, for besides that he hoped to earn great thanks for the gift, he said plainly 'twas not possible for him to bear the sight of me longer, because I presented to him in that fool's raiment the face of his lost sister, to whom I grew more like every day. In that the pastor opposed him, for he held that the time was not yet come when he was to do a miracle and make me a reasonable creature again, and therefore counselled the Governor he should have a couple of calf-skins prepared and put on two other boys, and thereafter appoint some third person who, in the shape of a physician, prophet or conjurer, should strip me and the said two boys and pretend he could make beasts into men and men into beasts : in this manner I might be restored, and without great pains might be brought to believe I had, like others, again become a man. Which proposal when the Governor approved, the pastor told me what he had agreed with my master, and easily persuaded me to consent thereto. But envious Fortune would not so easily free me of my fool's clothes nor leave me longer to enjoy my noble life of pleasure. For while tanners and tailors were already at work on the apparel that appertained to this comedy, I was even then sporting with some other boys on the ice in front of the ramparts. And there some one, I know not who, brought upon us a party of Croats, which seized upon us all, set us upon certain riderless farm-horses which they had just stolen, and carried us all off together. 'Tis true they were at first in doubt whether to take me with them or not, till at last one said in Bohemian, " Mih werne daho blasna sebao, bowe deme ho gbabo Oberstowi " (" Take we the fool : bring we him to our colonel "). And another answered him, " Prschis am bambo ano, mi ho nagonie possadeime wan rosumi niemezki, won bude mit Kratock wille sebao " (" Yes, by God, set we him on the horse. The colonel speaks German : he will have sport with him "). So I must to horse, and must learn how a single unlucky hour can rob one of all welfare and so separate him from all luck and happiness that all his life he must bear the consequences.

Chap. xv : OF SIMPLICISSIMUS' LIFE WITH THE TROOPERS, AND WHAT HE SAW AND LEARNED AMONG THE CROATS

THOUGH 'tis true the Hanauers raised an alarm at once, sallied forth on horseback, and for a while detained the Croats and harassed them with skirmishing, yet could they get from them none of their booty ; for being light troops, they escaped very cleverly, and took their way to Büdingen, where they baited, and delivered to the burghers there the rich Hanauers' sons to put to ransom, and there sold their stolen horses and other wares. From thence they decamped again before it was even fully night, let alone day again, and rode hard through the Büdingen forest into the abbey-lands of Fulda, and seized on the way all they could carry with them. For robbery and plunder hindered them not in the least in their swift march : like the devil, that can do mischief as he flies. And the same evening they arrived in the abbey-lands of Hirschfeld, where they had their quarters, with great store of plunder. And this was divided ; but me their colonel Corpes took as his share.

In the service of this master all appeared to me as unpleasing and wellnigh barbarous : the dainties of Hanau had changed into coarse black bread and stringy beef, or by good luck a bit of stolen pork : wine and beer were now turned to water, and instead of a bed I must be content to lie by the horses in the straw. Instead of that lute-playing which had delighted all men, now must I at times creep under the table like the other lads, howl like a dog, and suffer myself to be pricken with their spurs, which was for me but a poor jest. Instead of my promenades at Hanau, I must now ride on foraging parties, groom horses and clean out their stalls. Now this same foraging is neither more nor less than attacking of villages (with great pains and labour : yea, often with danger to life and limb), and there threshing, grinding, baking, stealing, and taking all that can be found ; harrying and spoiling the farmers, and shaming of their maids, their wives, and their daughters. And if the poor peasants did murmur, or were bold enough to rap a forager or two over the fingers, finding them at such work (and at that time were many such guests in Hesse,) they were knocked on the head if they could be caught, or if not, their houses went up in smoke to heaven. Now my master had no wife (for campaigners of his kidney be not wont to take ladies with them), no page, no chamberlain, no cook, but on the other hand a whole troop of grooms and boys which waited both on him and his horse ; nor was he himself ashamed to saddle his own horse or give him a feed : he slept ever on straw or on the bare ground, and covered himself with a fur coat. So it came about that one could often see great fleas or lice walk upon his clothes, of which he was not ashamed at all, but would laugh if any one picked one out. Short hair he had, but a broad Switzer's beard, which served his turn well, for he was wont to disguise himself as a peasant and so to go a-spying. Yet though, as I have said, he kept no great household, yet was he by his own folk and others that knew him honoured, loved, and feared. Never were we at rest, but now here, now there : now we attacked and now we were attacked : never for a moment were we idle in damaging the Hessians' resources : nor on his part did Melander* leave us in peace : but cut off many a trooper and sent him prisoner to Cassel.

This restless life was not to my liking, and often I did wish myself back in Hanau, yet in vain : my greatest torment was that I could not talk with the men, and must suffer myself to be kicked, plagued, beaten, and driven by each

* Hessian General.

and all : and the chiefest pastime that my colonel had was that I should sing to him in German, and puff my cheeks like the other stable-lads, which 'tis true happened but seldom, yet then I got me such a shower of buffets that the red blood flowed, and I soon had enough. At last I began to do somewhat of cooking, and to keep my master's weapons clean, whereon he laid great stress : for I was as yet useless for foraging. And this answered so well that in the end I gained my master's favour, insomuch that he had a new fool's coat of calf-skins made for me, with much greater asses' ears than I wore before. Now as my master's palate was not delicate, I needed the less skill for my cookery : yet because I was too often without salt, grease or seasoning, I wearied of this employ also, and therefore devised day and night how I might most cleverly escape—and that the more because 'twas now springtime. So to accomplish this I undertook the work of clearing away the guts of sheep and oxen, with heaps of which our quarters were surrounded, so that they should no longer cause so foul a smell : and this the colonel approved. And being busied with this, I stayed outside altogether, and when it was dark slipped away to the nearest wood.

Chap. xvi : HOW SIMPLICISSIMUS FOUND GOODLY SPOILS, AND HOW HE BECAME A THIEV-ISH BROTHER OF THE WOODS

YET to all appearance my condition grew worse and worse the further I went ; yea, so grievous that I conceived I was born but for misfortune : for I was but a few miles distant from the Croats when I was caught by highwaymen, which, without doubt, thought they had captured in me somewhat of value, for by reason of the dark night they could not see my fool's coat, and forthwith bade two of their number take me to their trysting-place in the forest. So when they had brought me thither, and 'twas still pitch-dark, one fellow would at once have money from me : to which end he laid aside his gauntlets and his fire-arms and began to search me, asking, " Who art thou ? Hast thou money ? "

Yet so soon as he was ware of my hairy clothing and the long asses' ears on my cap, which he took for horns, and at the same time perceived the shining sparks which the hides of beasts do commonly shew when they are stroked in the dark, he was so terrified that he shrank into himself. That did I presently mark : so before he could recover himself or devise aught, I stroked down my hide with both hands to such good purpose that it glittered as if I had been stuffed full of burning sulphur, and then I answered him in a terrible voice, "I am the devil, and I will break thy neck and thy fellow's too."

Which so terrified both that they fled through the thicket as swiftly as if the fires of hell were pursuing them ; yea, though they dashed themselves against sticks and stones and trunks of trees, and yet more often tumbled, they were up again with all speed. So they went on till I could hear them no longer ; while I laughed so loud that it echoed through the whole forest, which, without doubt, in that dark wilderness was horrible to hear.

Now when I would be gone I tripped over the musket ; and that I took for myself, for already I had learned from the Croats how to manage fire-arms : then as I walked on I came upon a knapsack which, like my coat, was made of calf-skin : that too I took up, and found that a cartridge-pouch, well stored with powder and shot and all appurtenance, hung below it. All this I hung on me, took the musket on my shoulder like a soldier, and hid myself not far off in a thicket, intending to sleep there awhile ; but at daybreak came the whole crew to the spot, searching for the musket that was lost and the knapsack : so I pricked up mine ears like a fox and kept still as a mouse ; and when they found nothing they mocked at those two that had fled before me. " Shame," said they, " ye craven fools : shame on your very heart that ye could so suffer yourselves to be frighted and chased, and have your arms taken by a single man." Yet one fellow swore the devil should take him if 'twere not the devil himself : his horns and his hairy hide he had well perceived ; and the other waxed angry and said, " It may have been the devil or his dam, if I had but my knapsack back again." Then one of them whom I took to be their captain answered him ; and says he, " What thinkest thou the devil should do with thy knapsack and thy musket ? I would wager my neck the rascal that ye so shamefully let go hath taken both with him." Yet another took the contrary part, and said it might well happen that some countrymen had since passed that way who had found the things and taken them : and in the end all approved this, and 'twas believed by all the band they had had the devil himself in their hands, especially because the fellow that would search me in the darkness not only swore the same with horrid oaths, but also was able powerfully to describe and to magnify the rough and glittering skin and the two horns as certain signs of the devil's quality. Nay, I do conceive that had I shewn myself again unawares the whole band would have run. So at last, when they had sought long enough and had found nothing, they went on their way again : but I opened the knapsack to make my breakfast thereof, and at the first trial I brought out a pouch in which were some 360 ducats. And that I rejoiced thereat none need question, yet may the reader be assured that the knapsack pleased me yet more than this fine sum of money, since I found it well stored with provisions. And as such yellow-boys are far too sparsely strewn among common soldiers for them to take such with them on a raid, I judge that the fellow must have just snapped up these on that very excursion, and quickly whipped them into his knapsack that he might not be compelled to share them with the rest.

Thereupon I made a cheerful breakfast, and found too a merry little spring, at which I refreshed myself and counted my fine ducats. And if my life depended thereon, to say, in what land or place I then found myself, I could not tell. And first I stayed in the wood as long as my food lasted, with which I dealt right sparingly : then when my knapsack was empty, hunger drove me to the farmers' houses. And there I crept by night into cellar and kitchen and took what food I found and could carry off ; and this I conveyed away to the wildest part of the wood. And so I led a hermit's life as before, save that I stole much and therefore prayed less, and had, moreover, no fixed abode, but wandered now here, now there. 'Twas well for me indeed that it was now the beginning of summer, though I could kindle a fire with my musket whenever I would.

Chap. xvii : *HOW SIMPLICISSIMUS WAS PRESENT AT A DANCE OF WITCHES*

DURING these my wanderings there met me once and again in the woods different country-folk, who at all times fled from me. I know not if the cause was that they were by reason of the war turned so timid and were so hunted, and never left in peace in one place, or whether the highwaymen had spread abroad in the land the adventure they had had with me, so that all which saw me thereafter believed the evil one was of a truth prowling about in that part. But for this reason I must needs fear lest my provisions should fail and so I be brought to the uttermost misery ; for then must I begin again to eat roots and herbs, to which I was no longer accustomed. As I pondered on this I heard two men cutting of wood, which rejoiced me mightily. So I followed the sound of the blows, and when I came in sight of the men I took a handful of ducats out of my pouch and, creeping nearer to them, shewed them the alluring gold and cried, " My masters, if ye will but wait for me I will give you this handful of gold." But as soon as they saw me and my gold, at once they took to their heels, and left their mallets and wedges together with their bag of bread and cheese ; with this I filled my knapsack, and so betook myself back to the wood, doubting if in my life I should ever come to the company of men again. So after long pondering thereupon, I thought, " Who knoweth what may chance to thee ? Thou hast money, and if thou comest in safety with it to honest folk, thou canst live on it a long while." So it came into my head to sew it up ; and to that end I made, out of my asses' ears which made the folk so fly from me, two armlets, and companying my Hanau ducats with those of the banditti, I packed all together into these armlets and bound them on mine arms above the elbow. And now, as I had thus secured my treasure, I attacked the farms again, and got from them what I needed and what I could snap up. And though I was but simple, yet I was sly enough never to come a second time to a place where I had stolen anything ; and therefore was I very lucky in my thefts and was never caught pilfering.

It fell out at the end of May, as I sought to replenish my store by my customary yet forbidden tricks, and to that end had crept into a farmyard, that I found my way into the kitchen, but soon perceived that there were people still awake (and here note that where dogs were I wisely stayed away) ; so I set the kitchen door, which opened into the yard, ajar, that if any danger threatened I could at once escape, and stayed still as a mouse till I might expect the people would go to bed. But meanwhile I took note of a crack that was in the kitchen-hatch that led to the living-room ; thither I crept to see if the folk would not soon go to rest ; but my hopes were deceived, for they had but now put on their clothes, and in place of a light there stood a sulphurous blue flame on a bench, by the light of which they anointed sticks, brooms, pitchforks, chairs, and benches, and on these flew out of the window one after another. At this I was horribly amazed, and felt great terror ; yet, as being accustomed to greater horrors, and, moreover, in my whole life having never heard nor read of witches, I thought not much of this, and that chiefly because 'twas all so done in such stillness ; but when all were gone I betook myself also to the living-room, and devising what I could take with me and where to find it, in such meditation sat me down straddle-wise upon a bench ; whereon I had hardly sat down when I and the bench together flew straight out of the window, and left my gun and knapsack, which I had laid aside, as pay for that magical ointment. Now my sitting down, my departure, and my descent were all in one moment, for I came, methought, in a trice to a great crowd of people ; but it may be that from fear I took no count how long I took for this long journey. These folk were dancing of a wondrous dance, the like of which I saw never in my life, for they had taken hands and formed many rings within one another, with their backs turned to each other like the pictures of the Three Graces, so that all faced outwards. The inmost ring was of some seven or eight persons ; the second of as many again : the third contained more than the first two put together, and so on, so that in the outermost ring there were over two hundred persons ; and because one ring danced towards the right and the next towards the left, I could not see how many rings they formed, nor what was

in the midst around which they danced. Yet all looked
monstrous strange, because all the heads wound in and out
so comically. My bench that brought me alighted beside
the minstrels which stood outside the rings all round the
dancers, of which minstrels some had, instead of flutes, clari-
nets and shawms, nothing but adders, vipers and blind-worms,
on which they blew right merrily : some had cats into whose
breech they blew and fingered on the tail, which sounded like
to bagpipes : others fiddled on horses' skulls as on the finest
violins, and others played the harp upon a cow's skeleton
such as lie in the slaughter-house yards : one was there, too,
that had a bitch under his arm, on whose tail he fiddled and
fingered on the teats ; and throughout all the devils trumpeted
with their noses till the whole wood resounded therewith :
and when the dance was at an end, that whole hellish crew
began to rave, to scream, to rage, to howl, to rant, to ramp,
and to roar as they were all mad and lunatic. And now can
any man think into what terror and fear I fell.

In this tumult there came to me a fellow that had under
his arm a monstrous toad, full as big as a kettledrum, whose
guts were dragged out through its breech and stuffed into its
mouth, which looked so filthy that I was fit to vomit at it.
"Lookye, Simplicissimus," says he, " I know thou beest a
good lute-player : let us hear a tune from thee." But I
was so terrified (because the rogue called me by name) that
I fell flat : and with that terror I grew dumb, and fancied
I lay in an evil dream, and earnestly I prayed in my heart I
might awake from it. Now the fellow with the toad, whom
I stared at all the time, went on thrusting his nose out and
in like a turkey-cock, till at last it hit me on the breast, so
that I was near choked. Then in a wink 'twas all pitch-dark,
and I so dismayed at the heart that I fell on the ground and
crossed myself a good hundred times or more.

Chap. xviii : DOTH PROVE THAT NO MAN CAN LAY
TO SIMPLICISSIMUS' CHARGE THAT HE
DOTH DRAW THE LONG BOW

NOW since there be some, and indeed some learned folk among them, that believe not that there be witches and sorcerers, still less that they can fly from place to place in the air, therefore am I sure there will be some to say that here the good Simplicissimus draws the long bow. With such folk I cannot argue ; for since brag is become no longer an art, but nowadays well-nigh the commonest trade, I may not deny that I could practise this if I would ; for an I could not, I were the veriest fool. But they that deny the witches' gallop to be true, let them but think of Simon the Magician, which was by the evil spirit raised aloft into the air, and at the prayer of St. Peter fell again to earth. Nicolas Remigius, which was an honest, learned, and understanding man, who in the Duchy of Lorraine caused to be burned a good many more than a half-dozen of witches, tells us of John of Hembach, that his mother (which same was a witch) in the sixteenth year of his age took him with her to their assembly, that he might play to them as they danced—for he had learned to play the fife. That to that end he mounted on a tree, piped to them and earnestly gazed upon the dancers (and that maybe because he marvelled so at it all). But at last, " God help us ; " says he, " whence cometh all this mad and foolish folk ? " And hardly had he said that word when down he fell from the tree, twisted his shoulder, and called for help. But there was nobody there but himself.

When this was noised abroad, most held it for a fable, till a little after Catherine Prévost was arrested for witchcraft, who had been at the said dance : so she confessed all even as it had happened, save that she knew naught of the cry that Hembach had uttered. Majolus tells us of a servant that had been too common with his mistress, and of an adulterer that took his paramour's ointment-boxes and smeared himself with the same, and so both came to the witches' Sabbath. So likewise they tell of a farm-servant that arose early to grease his waggon ; but because he had taken the wrong pot of ointment in the dark, that waggon rose into the air and must be dragged down again. Olaus Magnus tells us of Hading, King of Denmark ; how he, being driven from his kingdom by rebels, journeyed far over the sea through the air on the Spirit of Odin, which had turned himself to the shape of a horse. So do we know well enough, and too well, how wives and wenches in Bohemia will fetch their paramours to them, on the backs of goats, by night and from a great distance. And what Torquemada in his Hexameron relateth of his schoolfellow may in his own words be read. So, too, Ghirlandus speaketh of a nobleman which, when he marked that his wife anointed herself and thereafter flew out of the house, did once on a time compel her to take him with her to the sorcerers' assembly. And when they feasted there, and there was no salt, he demanded such, and having with great pains gotten it, did cry, " God be praised, here cometh the salt ! " Whereupon the lights went out and all vanished. So when now 'twas day he understood from the shepherds in that place that he was near to the town of Benevento in the kingdom of Naples, and therefore full five hundred miles from his home. And therefore, though he was rich, must he beg his way home, whither when he came he delated his wife for a witch before the magistrate, and she was burned. How Doctor Faust, too, and others, which were no enchanters, could journey through the air from one place to another is from his history sufficiently known. So I myself knew a wife and a maid (both dead at this time of writing, but the maid's father yet alive), which maid was once greasing of her mistress's shoes by the fire, and when she had finished one and set it by to grease the other, lo ; the greased one flew up the chimney : which story, nevertheless, was hushed up.

All this I have set down for this reason only, that men may believe that witches and wizards do in truth at certain seasons in their proper bodies journey to these their assemblies, and not to make any man to believe that I, as I have told you, went myself to such : for to me 'tis all one whether a man believe me or not ; and he that will not believe may devise for himself another way for me to have come from the lands of Fulda or Hirschfeld (for I know not myself whither I had wandered in the woods) into the Archbishopric of Magdeburg, and that in so brief a space of time.

Chap. xix : HOW SIMPLICISSIMUS BECAME A FOOL AGAIN AS HE HAD BEEN A FOOL BEFORE

SO now I begin my history again with this : that I assure the reader that I lay on my belly till 'twas at least broad daylight ; as not having the heart to stand up : therewithal I doubted whether the things I have told of were a dream or not ; and though I was yet in great terror, yet was I bold enough at my waking, for I deemed I could be in no worse place than in the wild woods ; and therein I had spent the most of my time since I was separated from my dad, and therefore was pretty well accustomed thereto. Now it was about nine o'clock when there came foragers, which woke me up. And now for the first time I perceived I was in the open field. So they had me with them to certain windmills, and when they had ground their corn there, to the camp before Magdeburg, where I fell to the share of a colonel of a foot-regiment, who asked me what was my story and what manner of master I had served. So I told him all to a nicety, and because I had no name for the Croats, I did but describe their clothing and gave examples of their speech, and told how I escaped from them : yet of my ducats said I nought, and what I told of my journey through the air and of the witches' dance, that they all held to be imagination and folly, and that especially because in the rest of my discourse I seemed to talk wildly. Meanwhile a crowd of folk gathered round me (for one fool makes a thousand), and among them was one that the year before had been made prisoner at Hanau and there had taken service, yet afterwards had come back to the Emperor's army : who, knowing me again, said at once, " Hoho ! 'tis the commandant's calf of Hanau."

Thereupon the colonel questioned him further ; but the fellow knew no more save that I could play the lute well, and that I had been captured outside the walls at Hanau by the Croats of Colonel Corpes' regiment, and, moreover, that the said commandant had been vexed at losing me ; for I was a right clever fool. So then the colonel's wife sent to another colonel's wife that could play well upon the lute, and therefore always had one by her, and begged her for the loan of it : which, when it came, she handed to me with the command that I should play. But my view was they should first give me to eat ; for an empty stomach accorded not well with a fat one, such as the lute had. So this was done, and when I had eaten my fill and drunk a good draught of Zerbst beer, I let them hear what I could do both with my voice and with the lute : and therewithal I talked gibberish, all that first came into my head, so that I easily persuaded the folk to believe I was of the quality that my apparel represented. Then the colonel asked me whither I would go ; and I answering 'twas all one to me, we agreed thereupon that I should stay with him and be his page. Yet would he know where my asses' ears had gone. " Yea," said I to myself, " and thou knewest where they were : they would fit thee well enough." Yet was I clever enough to say naught of their properties, for all my worldly goods lay in them.

Now in a brief space I was well known to all both in the Emperor's and the Elector's camp, but specially among the ladies, who would deck my hood, my sleeves, and my short-cut ears with ribbons of all colours, so that I verily believe that certain fops copied therefrom the fashion of to-day. But all the money that was given me by the officers, that I liberally gave away and spent all to the last farthing, drinking it away with jolly companions in beer of Hamburg and Zerbst, which liquors pleased me well : and besides this, in all places wheresoever I came there was plenty of chance of spunging. But when my colonel procured for me a lute of my own (for he trusted to have me ever with him), then I could no longer rove hither and thither in the two camps, but he appointed for me a governor who should look after me, and I to obey him. And this was a man after mine own heart, for he was quiet, discreet, learned, of sufficient conversation yet not too much, and (which was the chief matter), exceeding God-fearing, well read, and full of all arts and sciences. At night I must sleep in his tent, and by day I might not go out of his sight : he had once been a counsellor and minister of a prince, and indeed a rich man ; but being by the Swedes utterly ruined, his wife dead, and his only son unable to continue his studies for want of money, and therefore serving as a muster-roll clerk in the Saxon army, he took service with this my colonel, and was content to serve as a lackey, to wait until the dangerous chances of war on the banks of the Elbe should change and so the sun of his former happiness again shine upon him.

Chap. xx : IS PRETTY LONG, AND TREATS OF
PLAYING WITH DICE AND WHAT HANGS
THEREBY

NOW because my governor was rather old than young, therefore could he not sleep all the night through : and that was the cause that he even in the first few weeks discovered my secret ; namely, that I was no such fool as I gave out, of which he had before observed somewhat, and had conceived such a judgment from my face, for he was skilled in physiognomia. Once I awoke at midnight, and having divers thoughts upon my life and its strange adventures, rose up, and by way of gratitude recounted all the benefits that God had done unto me, and all the dangers from which He had rescued me : then I lay down again with deep sighing and slept soundly till day.

All this my governor heard, yet made as if he were sound asleep ; and this happened several nights running, until he had fully convinced himself I had more understanding than many an older man who fancied himself to be somewhat. Yet he spake thereof nought to me in our hut, because it had walls too thin, and because he for certain reasons would not have it that as yet (and before he was assured of my innocence) any one else should know this secret. Once on a time I went to take the air outside the camp, and this he gladly allowed, because he had then the opportunity to come to look for me, and so the occasion to speak with me alone. So, as he wished, he found me in a lonely place, where indeed I was giving audience to my thoughts, and says he : " Good and dear friend, 'tis because I seek for thy welfare that I rejoice to be able to speak with thee alone. I know thou art no fool as thou pretendest, and that thou hast no desire to continue in this miserable and despised state. If now thou holdest thy welfare dear and wilt trust to me as to a man of honour, and so canst tell me plainly the condition of thy fortunes, so will I for my part, whenever I can, be ready with word and deed to help thee out of this fool's coat."

So thereupon I fell upon his neck, and so carried myself as he had been a prophet to release me from my fool's cap : and sitting both down upon the ground, I told him my whole story. Then he examined my hands, and wondered both at the strange events which had befallen me and those which were to come : yet would in no wise counsel me to lay aside my fool's coat in haste, for he said that by means of palmistry he could see that my fate threatened me with imprisonment which should bring me danger of life and limb. So I thanked him for his good will and his counsel, and asked of God that He would reward him for his good faith, and of himself that he would be and ever remain my true friend and father.

So we rose up and came to the gaming-place, where men tilt with the dice, and loudly they cursed with all the blood and thunder, wounds and damnation that they could lay their tongues to. The place was wellnigh as big as the Old Market at Cologne, spread with cloaks and furnished with tables, and those full of gamesters : and every company had its four-cornered thieves' bones, on which they hazarded their luck ; for share their money they must, and give it to one and take it from another. So likewise every cloak or table had its coupier (croupier I should have said, and might well have said * " cooperer "), whose office 'twas to be judges and to see that none was cheated ; they too lent the cloaks and tables and dice, and contrived so well to get their hire out of the winnings that they generally got the chief share : yet it bred them no advantage, for commonly they gamed it away again, or when it was best laid out, 'twas the sutler or the barber-surgeon that had it—for there were many broken heads to mend.

At these fools one might well wonder, how they all thought

* It is difficult to translate the German expression. Probably this word, meaning a maritime trader in illicit wares, represents it best.

to win, which was impossible, even if they had played at another's* risk : and though all hoped for this, yet the cry was, the more players the more skill ; for each thought on his own luck ; and so it happened that some hit and some missed, some won and some lost. Thereupon some cursed, some roared ; some cheated and others were jockeyed—whereat the winners laughed and the losers gnashed their teeth : some sold their clothes and all they valued most, and others again won even that money from them ; some wanted honest dice, and others, on the contrary part, would have false ones, and brought in such secretly, which again others threw away, broke in two, bit with their teeth, and tore the croupiers' cloaks. Among the false dice were Dutch ones, that one must cast with a good spin ; for these had the sides, whereon the fives and sixes were, as sharp as the back of the wooden horse on which soldiers be punished : others were High German, to which a man must in casting give the Bavarian swing. Some were of stag's-horn, light above and heavy below. Others were loaded with quicksilver or lead, and others, again, with split hairs, sponge, chaff, and charcoal : some had sharp corners, others had them pared quite away : some were long like logs and some broad like tortoises. All which kinds were made but for cheating : and what they were made for, that they did, whether they were thrown with a swing or trickled on to the board, and no coupling of them was of any avail ; to say nothing of those that had two fives or two sixes or, on the other hand, two aces or two deuces. With these thieves' bones they stole, filched, and plundered each other's goods, which they themselves perchance had stolen, or at least with danger to life and limb, or other grievous trouble and labour, had won.

So I as stood there and looked upon the gaming-place and the gamesters in their folly, my governor asked me how the thing pleased me. Then answered I : " That men can so grievously curse God pleases me not : but for the rest, I leave it for what 'tis worth as a matter unknown to me, and of which I as yet understand nought." " Know then," said my governor, " that this is the worst and vilest place in the whole

* Obscure lines : many of the expressions in this chapter are now inexplicable.

camp, for here men seek one another's money and lose their own in doing so. And whoso doth but set a foot here, with intent to play, hath already broken the tenth commandment, which saith, ' Thou shalt not covet thy neighbour's goods.' " And says he, " An thou play and win, specially by deceit and false dice, then thou transgressest the seventh and eighth commandments. Yea, it may well happen that thou committest murder on him from whom thou hast won his money, as, for example, if his loss is so great that by reason of it he come into poverty and into utter need and recklessness, or else fall into other foul vices : nor will this plea help thee, that thou sayest, ' I did risk mine own and won honestly.' Thou rogue, thou camest to the gaming-place with this intent, to grow rich through another's loss. And if thou lose, thou art not excused with the punishment of losing thine own, but, like the rich man in the parable, thou must answer it sorely to God that thou so uselessly hast squandered that which He lent thee for the support of thee and thine. Whosoever goeth to the gaming-place to play, the same committeth himself to the danger of losing therein, not only his money, but his body and his life also ; yea, what is most terrible of all, there can he lose his own soul. I tell thee this as news, my friend Simplicissimus (because thou sayest gaming is unknown to thee), that thou mayest be on thy guard against it all thy life long." So I answered him : " Dear sir," said I, " if gaming be so terrible and dangerous a thing, wherefore do our superiors allow it ? " My governor answered : " I will not say 'twas because our officers themselves take part therein, but for this reason, that the soldiers will not—yea, cannot— do without it ; for whosoever hath once given himself over to gaming, or whomsoever the habit or, rather, the devil of play hath seized upon, the same is by little and little (whether he win or lose) so set upon it that he can easier do without his natural sleep than that : as we see that some will rattle the dice the whole night through and will neglect the best of food and drink if they can but play—yea, even if they must go home shirtless. Yet this gaming hath already been forbidden at divers times on pain of loss of life and limb, and at the command of headquarters hath been punished with an iron hand, through the means of provost-marshals, hangmen, and their satellites—openly and violently. Yet 'twas all in vain ; for the gamesters betook themselves to secret corners and behind hedges, won each other's money, quarrelled, and brake each other's necks thereupon : so that to prevent such murders and homicides, and specially because many would game away their arms and horse, yea, even their poor rations of food, therefore now 'tis not only publicly allowed, but this particular place is appointed therefore, that the mainguard may be at hand to prevent any harm that might happen : yet they cannot always hinder that one or the other fall not dead on the spot. And inasmuch as this gaming is the tormenting devil's own device, and bringeth him no small gain, therefore hath he ordained especial gaming-devils, that prowl around in the world and have naught else to do but to tempt men to play. To these divers wanton companions bind themselves by certain pacts and agreements, that the devil may suffer them to win : yet can a man among ten thousand gamesters scarce find a rich one : nay, on the contrary part, they are poor and needy because their winnings are lightly esteemed, and therefore either gambled away again or wasted in vile pleasures. Hence is derived that true yet sad saying, ' The devil never leaveth the gamester, yet leaveth him ever poor,' for he taketh from them goods, courage, and honour, and then quitteth them no more (except God's infinite mercy save them) till he have made an end of their souls. Yea, and should there be a gamester of so merry a heart by nature and so sprightly that by no ill-luck or loss he can be brought to despair, to recklessness, and all the accursed sins that spring therefrom, then doth the sly and cunning fiend suffer him to win mightily, that in the end he may, by waste and pride and gluttony and drunkenness and loose life, bring him into his net." Thereat I crossed myself and blessed myself to think that in a Christian army such things should be allowed which the devil himself invented, and specially because visibly and palpably such damage and harm for this world and the next followed therefrom. Yet my governor said all that he had told me was as yet nought ; for he who would undertake to describe all the harm that came from gaming would begin an impossible task. For as men say, so soon as the hazard is thrown 'tis now in the devil's hands, so should I fancy that with every die, as it rolled from the player's hand upon cloak or table, there ran a little devil, to guide it and make it shew as many points as his master's interest demanded. And further, I should reflect that 'twas not for nought that the devil entered into the game so heartily, but doubtless because he contrived to make fine gains out of it himself. " And with that note thou further," says he, " that just as there are wont to stand by the gaming-place certain chafferers and Jews, which buy from the players at cheap rate what they have won, as rings, apparel or jewels, or are ready to change such for money for them to game away, so also there be devils walking to and fro, that they may arouse and foster thoughts that may destroy the souls in the gamesters that have ceased to play, be they winners or losers. For the winners the devil will build terrible castles in the air ; but into them that have lost, whose spirit is already quite distraught and therefore the more apt to receive his harmful counsels, he instilleth, doubtless, such thoughts and designs as can but tend to their eternal ruin. Yea, I assure thee, Simplicissimus, I am of the mind to write a book hereupon so soon as I can come in peace to my own again. And in that I will describe first the loss of precious time, which is squandered to no purpose in gaming, and no less the fearful curses with which men blaspheme God over their gaming-tables. Then will I likewise recount the taunts with which men provoke one another, and will adduce many fearful examples and stories which have happened in, during, and after play : and there will I not forget the duels and homicides that have happened by reason of gaming. Yea, I will portray in their true colours set before men's eyes the greed, the rage, the envy, the jealousy, the falsehood, the deceit, the covetousness, the thievery, and, in a word, all the senseless follies both of dicers and of card-players ; that they who read this book but once, may conceive such a horror of gaming as if they had drunk sows' milk (which folk are wont to give to gamesters without their knowledge, to cure their madness). So will I shew to all Christendom that the dear God is more blasphemed by a single regiment of gamesters than by a whole army with their curses." And this project I praised, and wished him the opportunity to carry it out.

Chap. xxi : IS SOMEWHAT SHORTER AND MORE
ENTERTAINING THAN THE LAST

NOW my governor grew more and more kindly
disposed to me, and I to him, yet kept we our
friendship very secret : 'tis true I acted still as
a fool, yet I played no bawdy tricks or buffoon-
eries, so that my carriage and conduct were indeed simple
enough yet rather witty than witless. My colonel, who had
a mighty liking for the chase, took me with him once when
he went out to catch partridges with the draw-net, which
invention pleased me hugely. But because the dog we had
was so hot that he would spring for the birds before we could
pull the strings, and so we could catch but little, therefore
I counselled the colonel to couple the bitch with a falcon or
an osprey (as men do with horses and asses when they would
have mules), that the young puppies might have wings, and
so could with them catch the birds in the air. I proposed
also, since it went right sleepily with the conquest of Magdeburg, which we then besieged, to make ready a long rope as
thick as a wine-cask, and encompassing the whole town therewith, to harness thereto all the men and all the cattle in the
two camps, and so in one day pull the whole city head over
heels. Of such foolish quips and fantasies I devised every
day an abundance, for 'twas my trade, and none ever found
my workshop empty. And for this my master's secretary,
which was an evil customer and a hardened rogue, gave me
matter enough, whereby I was kept on the road which fools
be wont to walk : for whatsoever this mocker told me, that
I not only believed myself but told it to others, whenas I
conversed with them, and the discourse turned on that subject.

So when I asked him once what our regimental chaplain
was, since he was distinguished from other folk by his apparel,
" that," says he, " is master *Dicis et non facis*, which is, being
interpreted into German, a fellow that gives wives to others
and takes none himself. He is the bitter enemy of thieves
because they say not what they do, but he doth not what he
says : likewise the thieves love him not because they be commonly hanged even then when their acquaintance with him

is at its best." So when I afterwards addressed the good priest by that name, he was laughed at and I was held to be a rogue as well as a fool, and at his request well basted. Further, the secretary persuaded me they had pulled down and set on fire all the houses behind the walls of Prague, that the sparks and ashes might sow all over the world the seeds of evil weeds : so, too, he said that among soldiers no brave heroes and hearty fighters ever went to heaven, but only simple creatures, malingerers, and the like, that were content with their pay : likewise no elegant a la mode cavaliers, and sprightly ladies, but only patient Jobs, henpecked husbands, tedious monks, melancholy parsons, devout women, and all manner of outcasts which in this world are good neither to bake nor to boil, and young children. He told me too a lying story of how hosts were called innkeepers only because in their business they endeavoured to keep in with both God and the devil. And of war he told me that at times golden bullets were used, and the more precious such were, the more damage they did. " Yea," said he, " and a whole army with artillery, ammunition, and baggage-train can be so led by a golden chain." Further, he persuaded me that of women more than half wore breeches, though one could not see them, and that many, though they were no enchantresses and no goddesses as was Diana, yet could conjure bigger horns on to their husbands' heads than ever Actaeon wore. In all which I believed him : so great a fool was I.

On the other hand, my governor, when he was alone with me, entertained me with far different discourse. Moreover, he brought me to know his son, who, as before mentioned, was a muster-clerk in the Saxon army, and was a man of far different quality to my colonel's secretary : for which reason my colonel not only liked him well, but thought to get him from his captain and make him his regimental secretary, on which post his own secretary before mentioned had set his mind also. With this muster-clerk, whose name, like his father's, was Ulrich Herzbruder, I struck up such a friendship that we swore eternal brotherhood, in virtue of which we would never desert each other in weal or woe, in joy or sorrow ; and because this was without his father's knowledge, therefore we held more stoutly and stiffly to our vow. By this was it made our chiefest care how I might be honourably freed from my fool's coat, and how we might honestly serve one another ; all which however the old Herzbruder, whom I honoured and looked to as my father, approved not, but said in so many words that if I was in haste to change my estate, such change would bring me grievous imprisonment and great danger to life and limb. And because he foretold for himself also and his son a great disgrace close at hand, he deemed, therefore, that he had reason to act moɪe prudently and warily than to interfere in the affairs of a person whose great approaching danger he could foresee : for he was fearful he might be a sharer in my future ill luck if I declared myself, because he had long ago found out my secret and knew me inside and out, yet he never revealed my true condition to the colonel. And soon after I perceived yet better that my colonel's secretary envied my new brother desperately, as thinking he might be raised over his head to the post of regimental secretary ; for I saw how at times he fretted, how ill will preyed upon him, and how he was always sighing and in deep thought whenever he looked uɪon the old or the young Herzbruder. Therefrom I judged he was making of calculations how he might trip and throw him. So I told to my brother, both fɪom my faithful love to him and also as my certain duty, what I suspected, that he might a little be on his guard against this Judas. But he did but take it with a shrug, as being more than enough superior to the secretary both with sword and pen, and besides enjoying the colonel's great favour and grace.

Chap. xxii: A RASCALLY TRICK TO STEP INTO ANOTHER MAN'S SHOES

'TIS commonly the custom in war to make provosts of old tried soldiers, and so it came about that we had in our regiment such a one, and to boot such a perfected rogue and villain that it might well be said of him he had seen enough and more than enough. For he was a fully qualified sorcerer, necromancer and wizard, and in his own person not only as wound-proof as steel, but could make others wound-proof also, yea, and conjure whole squadrons of cavalry into the field : his countenance was exactly like what our painters and poets would have Saturn to be, save that he had neither stilts nor scythe. And though the poor soldier prisoners that came into his merciless hands, held themselves the more unlucky because of this his character, and his ever-abiding presence, yet were there folk that gladly consorted with this spoil-sport, specially Oliver, our secretary. And the more his envy of young Herzbruder increased—who was ever of a lively humour—the thicker grew the intimacy between him and the provost : whence I could easily calculate that the conjunction of Saturn and Mercury boded no good to the honest Herzbruder. Just then my colonel's lady was rejoiced at the coming of a young son, and the christening feast spread in wellnigh princely fashion : at which young Herzbruder was brought to wait at table. Which, when he of his courtesy willingly did, he gave the longed-for opportunity to Oliver to bring into the world the piece of roguery of which he had long been in labour. For when all was over my colonel's great silver-gilt cup was missing ; and this loss he made the more ado about because 'twas still there after all stranger guests had departed : 'tis true a page said he had last seen it in Oliver's hands, but would not swear it. Upon that the Provost was fetched to give his counsel in the matter, and 'twas said aside to him that if he by his arts could discover the thief, they would so carry the matter that that thief should be known to none save the colonel : for officers of his own regiment had been present whom, even if one of them had forgotten himself in such a matter, he would not willingly bring to shame.

So as we all knew ourselves to be innocent, we came merrily enough into the colonel's great tent, and there the sorcerer took charge of the matter. At that each looked on his neighbour, and desired to know how 'twould end and whence the lost cup would reappear. And no sooner had the rogue mumbled some words than there sprang out of each man's breeches, sleeves, boots and pockets, and all other openings in their clothes, one, two, three, or more young puppies. And these sniffed round and round in the tent, and pretty beasts they were, of all manner of colours, and each with some special ornament, so that 'twas a right merry sight. As to me, my tight Croat breeches were so full of puppies that I must pull them off, and because my shirt had long before rotted away in the forest, there I must stand naked. Last of all one sprang out of young Herzbruder's pocket, the nimblest of all, and had on a golden collar. This one swallowed all the other puppies, though there were so many a-sprawling in the tent that one could not put his foot down by reason of them. And when it had destroyed all, it became smaller and smaller and the golden collar larger, till at last it turned into my colonel's cup.

Thereupon not only the colonel but all that were present must perforce believe that none other but young Herzbruder could have stolen the cup : so said the colonel to him : " Lookye, unthankful guest, have I deserved this, with my kindnesses to thee, this theft, which I had never believed of thee ? For see : I had intended to-morrow to make thee my secretary ; but thou hast this very day deserved rather that I should have thee hanged ; and that I would forthwith have done had I not had a care of thy honourable and ancient father. Now quick ; " said he, " out of my camp, and so long as thou livest let me not see thee more."

So poor Ulrich would defend himself : yet would none listen to him, for his offence was plain : and when he departed, good old Herzbruder must needs fall in a swoon ; and there must all come to succour him, and the colonel himself to comfort him, which said, " a pious father was not to answer for this sinful son." Thus, by the help of the devil did Oliver attain to that whereto he had long hoped to come, but could not in any honourable fashion do so.

Chap. xxiii : HOW ULRICH HERZBRUDER SOLD HIMSELF FOR A HUNDRED DUCATS

NOW as soon as young Herzbruder's captain heard this story he took from him his office and made a pikeman of him ; from which time forward he was so despised that any dog might bark at him, and he himself wished for death ; and his father was so vexed at the thing that he fell into a sore sickness and looked to die. And whereas he had himself prophesied that on the twenty-sixth day of July he should run risk of life and limb (which day was now close at hand), therefore he begged of the colonel that his son might come to him once more, that he might talk with him of inheritance and declare his last will. At this meeting I was not shut out, but made the third party in their grief. Then I saw that the son needed no defence as far as his father was concerned, who knew his ways and his good upbringing, and therefore was assured of his innocence. He, as a wise, understanding, and deep-witted man, judged easily from the circumstances that Oliver had laid this trap for his son through the provost : but what could he do against a sorcerer, from whom he had worse to expect if he attempted any revenge ? Besides, he looked but for death, yet could not die content because he must leave his son in such disgrace : in which plight the son desired not to live, but rather wished he might die before his father. And truly the grief of these two was so piteous to behold that I from my heart must weep. At last 'twas their common resolve to commit their cause to God in patience, and the son was to devise ways and means to be quit of his regiment, and seek his fortune elsewhere : but when they examined the matter, they had no money with which he might buy himself out of the service ; and while they considered and lamented the miserable state in which their poverty kept them fast, and cut off all hope of improving of their present condition, I then first remembered my ducats that I had sewn up in my ass's ears, and so asked how much money they wanted in their need. So young Herzbruder answered, " If there came one and brought us a hundred thalers, I could trust to be free from all my troubles." I answered him, " Brother, if that will help thee, have a good heart ; for I can give thee a hundred ducats." " Alas, brother," says he, " what is this thou sayest ? Beest thou in truth a fool, or so wanton that thou makest jests upon us in our sore affliction ? " " Nay, nay," said I, " I will provide the money." So I stripped off my coat and took one of the asses' ears from my arm, and opened it and bade him to count out a hundred ducats and take them : the rest I kept and said, " Herewith will I lend thy sick father if he need it."

Thereupon they both fell on my neck and kissed me, and knew not for very joy what they did ; then they would give me an acknowledgment and therein assure me I should be the old Herzbruder's co-heir together with his son, or that, if God should help them to their own again, they would return me the same with interest and with great thanks : of all which I would have nothing, but only commended myself to their perpetual friendship. After that, young Herzbruder would have sworn to be revenged on Oliver or to die. But his father forbade it, and prophesied that he that should slay Oliver would meet his end at the hands of me, Simplicissimus. " Yet," said he, " I am well assured that ye two will never slay each other ; for neither of you shall perish in fight." Thereafter he pressed upon us that we should swear on oath to love one another till death and stand by each other in all straits.

But young Herzbruder bought his freedom for thirty-six thalers (for which his captain gave him an honourable discharge), and betook himself with the rest of the money, a good opportunity offering, to Hamburg, and there equipped himself with two horses and enlisted in the Swedish army as a volunteer trooper, commending his father to me in the meanwhile.

Chap. xxiv : HOW TWO PROPHECIES WERE FUL-
FILLED AT ONCE

NOW none of my colonel's people shewed himself better fitted to wait on old Herzbruder in his sickness than I : and inasmuch as the sick man was also more than content with me, this office was entrusted to me by the colonel's wife, who shewed him much kindness ; and by reason of good nursing, and being relieved in respect of his son, he grew better from day to day, so that before July the twenty-sixth he was almost restored to full health. Yet would he stay in bed and give himself out to be sick till the said day, which he plainly dreaded, should be past. Meanwhile all manner of officers from both armies came to visit him, to know their future fortune, bad

or good ; for because he was a good calculator and caster of
horoscopes, and besides that an excellent physiognomist and
palmist, his prophecies seldom failed : yea, he named the
very day on which the Battle of Wittstock afterwards befel,
since many came to him to whom he foretold a violent death
on that day.

My colonel's wife he assured she would end her lying-in
in the camp, for before her six weeks were ended Magdeburg
would not be surrendered ; and to the traitorous Oliver, who
was ever troublesome with his visits, he foretold that he
must die a violent death, and that I should avenge that death,
happen it when it would, and slay his murderer : for which
cause Oliver thereafter held me in high esteem. But to me
myself he described the whole course of my life to come as
particularly as if it were already ended and he had been by
my side throughout ; which at the time I esteemed but
lightly, yet afterwards remembered many things which he
had beforetime told me of, when they had already happened
or had turned out true : but most of all did he warn me to
beware of water, for he feared I might find my destruction
therein.

When now the twenty-sixth of July came, he charged me,
and also the orderly whom the colonel at his desire had
appointed him for that day, most straitly, we should suffer
no one to enter the tent : there he lay and prayed without
ceasing : but as 'twas near to afternoon there came a lieutenant riding from the cavalry quarters and asking for the
colonel's master of the horse. So he was directed to us and
forthwith by us denied entrance : yet would he not be
denied, but begged the orderly (with promises intermixed) to
admit him to see the master of the horse, as one with whom
he must that very evening talk. When that availed not, he
began to curse, to talk of blood and thunder, and to say he
had many times ridden over to see the old man and had never
found him : now that he had found him at home, should he
not have the honour of speaking a single word with him ?
So he dismounted, and nothing could prevent him from un-
fastening the tent himself ; and as he did that I bit his hand,
and got for my pains a hearty buffet. So as soon as he saw
mine old friend, " I ask his honour's pardon," says he, " for

the freedom I have taken, to speak a word with him." " 'Tis well," says Herzbruder, " wherein can I pleasure his honour ? " " Only in this," says the lieutenant, " that I could beg of his honour that he would condescend upon the casting of my nativity." Then the old man answered : " I hope the honourable gentleman will forgive me that I cannot, by reason of my sickness, do his pleasure herein : for whereas this task needs much reckoning, my poor head cannot accomplish it ; but if he will be content to wait till to-morrow, I hope to give him full satisfaction." " Very well," says the lieutenant, " but in the meantime let your honour tell my fortune by my hand." " Sir," said old Herzbruder, " that art is uncertain and deceiving ; and so I beg your worship to spare me in that matter : to-morrow I will do all that your worship asks of me." Yet the lieutenant could not be so put off, but he goes to the bed, holds his hand before the old man's eyes, and says he, " Good sir, I beg but for a couple of words concerning my life's end, with the assurance that if they be evil I will accept the saying as a warning from God to order my life better ; and so for God's sake I beg you not to conceal the truth." Then the honest old man answered him in a word, and says he, " 'Tis well : then let the gentleman be on his guard, lest he be hanged before an hour be past." " What, thou old rogue," quoth the lieutenant, which was as drunk as a fly, " durst thou hold such language to a gentleman ? " and drew his sword and stabbed my good old friend to death as he lay in his bed. The orderly and I cried " Murder," so that all ran to arms : but the lieutenant was so speedy in his departure that without doubt he would have escaped, but that the Elector of Saxony with his staff at that very moment rode up, and had him arrested. So when he understood the business he turned to Count Hatzfeld, our general, and all he said was this : " 'Twould be bad discipline in an imperial camp that even a sick man in his bed were not safe from murderers."

That was a sharp sentence, and enough to cost the lieutenant his life : for forthwith our general caused him to be hanged by his precious neck till he was dead.

Chap. xxv : HOW SIMPLICISSIMUS WAS TRANS-
FORMED FROM A BOY INTO A GIRL
AND FELL INTO DIVERS ADVENTURES
OF LOVE

FROM this veracious history it may be seen that all prophecies are not to be despised, as some foolish folk despise them, that will believe nothing. And so can any one conclude from this that it is hard for any man to avoid his predestined end, whether his mishap be predicted to him long before or shortly before by such prophecies as I have spoken of. And to the question, whether 'tis necessary, helpful, and good for a man to have his fortune foretold and his nativity cast, I answer only this, that old Herzbruder told me much that I often wished and still wish he had told me nothing of at all : for the misfortunes which he foretold I have never been able to shun, and those that still await me do turn my hair grey, and that to no purpose, because it matters not whether I torment myself or not : they will happen to me as did the rest. But as to strokes of good luck that are prophesied to any man, of them I hold that they be ever deceitful, or at least be not so fully accomplished as the unlucky prophecies. For how did it help me that old Herzbruder swore by all that was holy I was born and bred of noble parents, since I knew of none but my dad and my mammy, which were but common peasants in the Spessart ? In like manner, how did it help Wallenstein, the Duke of Friedland, that 'twas prophesied to him he should once be crowned king with stringed music thereto ? Doth not all the world know how he was lulled to his ruin at Eger ? Others may worry their brains over such questions : but I must to my story.

So when I had lost my two Herzbruders in the manner before described, I took a disgust at the whole camp before Magdeburg, which otherwise I had been wont to call a town of flax and straw with earthen walls. For now I was as tired of mine office of a fool as I had had to eat it up with iron spoons : this only I was resolved on : to suffer no man to fool me more, but to be rid of my jester's garb should it cost me life and limb. And that design I carried out but scurvily, for otherwise I had no opportunity.

For Oliver the secretary, which after the old Herzbruder's death was appointed to be my governor, often gave me permission to ride with the servants a-foraging : so as we came once on a time to a great village, wherein was plunder very fit for the troopers' purpose, and as each went to and fro into the houses to find what could be carried off, I stole away, and searched to find some old peasant's clothing for which I could exchange my fool's cap : yet I found not what I desired but must be content with a woman's clothing : that I put on, seeing myself alone, and threw mine own away into a corner, imagining now nothing else but that I was delivered from all mine afflictions. In this dress I walked across the street, where were certain officers' wives, and made such mincing steps as perhaps Achilles did when his mother brought him disguised as a maiden to consort with Lycomedes his daughter : yet was I hardly outside the house when some foragers caught sight of me, and taught me to run faster : for when they cried "Halt, halt ; " I ran the quicker, and before they could overtake me I came to the said officers' ladies, and falling on my knees before them, besought them, in the name of all womanly honour and virtue, they should protect me from those rascals. And this my prayer not only found a good reception, but I was hired by the wife of a captain of horse, whom I served until Magdeburg and the fort at Werben and Havelberg and Perleberg were all taken by our people.

The captain's wife was no baby, but yet young, and came so to dote on my smooth face and straight limbs that at length, after long trouble and vain circumlocutions, she gave me to understand in all too plain German where the shoe pinched. But at that time I was far too conscientious, and pretended I understood not, nor would I show any outward indication by which any man might judge me to be aught but a virtuous maiden. Now the captain and his servant lay sick in that same hospital, so he bade his wife to have me better clothed that she might not be put to shame by my miserable peasant's kirtle. So that she did and more than she was bidden ; for she dressed me up like a French doll, and that did but fan the fire wherewith all three were a-burning : yea, and it waxed so that master and man begged of me that which I could not grant to them, and that which I refused to the lady, though with all manner of courtesy. At last the captain determined to take an opportunity to get by force from me that which 'twas impossible he should have : but that his wife marked, and being in hopes to overcome my resistance in the end, blocked all the ways and laid all manner of obstacles in the path, so that he thought he must in the end go mad or lunatick. Once on a time when my master and mistress were asleep, the servant came to the carriage in which I had to sleep every night, bemoaned his love for me with hot tears, and begged most solemnly for grace and mercy. But I shewed myself harder than any stone, and gave him to understand I would keep my chastity till I was married. Then he offered me marriage a thousand times over, yet all he could get from me was an assurance 'twas impossible for me to marry him. Whereupon he became desperate or pretended it, and drawing his sword, set the point at his breast and the hilt against the carriage, and acted just as if he would stab himself. So I thought, the devil is a rogue, and therefore spoke him fair and comforted him, saying I would next morning give him a certain answer : with that he was content and went to bed, but I stayed awake the longer because I reflected on my strange condition : for I could see that in the end my trick must be discovered, for the captain's wife became more and more importunate with her enticements, the captain more impudent in his designs, and the servant more desperate in his constant love : and out of such a labyrinth I could see no escape. Yet if the lady left me in peace, the captain tormented me, and when I had peace from both of them at night, then the servant beset me, so that my women's clothes were worse to wear than my fool's cap. Then indeed (but far too late) I thought of the departed Herzbruder's prophecy and warning, and could imagine nothing else but that I was already fast in the prison he spoke of and in danger of life and limb. For the woman's apparel kept me imprisoned, since I could not get out of it, and the captain would have handled me roughly if he had once found out who I was, and had caught me at the toilet with his fair wife. What should I do ? I resolved at length the same night to reveal myself to the servant as soon as 'twas day, for I thought, " his desires will then cease, and if thou art free with thy ducats to him he will help thee to man's clothes again and so out of all thy straits." Which was all well devised enough if luck would have had it so : but that was against me. For my friend Hans took day to begin just after midnight, and came to get his " Yes " from me, and began to hammer on the carriage-cover even then when I was soundest asleep, calling out a little too loud, " Sabina, Sabina, oh my beloved, rise up and keep your promise to me," and so waked the captain before me, who had his tent close by the carriage. And now he saw green and yellow before his eyes, for jealousy had already got a hold of him : yet he came not out to disturb us, but only got up, to see how the thing would end. At last the servant woke me with his importunities, and would force me either to come out of the carriage to him or to let him in to me, but I rebuked him and asked did he take me for a whore ? My promise of yesterday was on condition of marriage, without which he should have nought to do with me. He answered I must in any case rise, for it began to grow light, to prepare the food for the family in good time : then he would fetch wood and water and light the fire for me. " Well," said I, " if thou wilt do that I can sleep the longer : only go away and I will soon follow." Yet as the fool would not give over, I got up, more to do my work than to pleasure him, for methought his desperate madness of yesterday had left him. I should say that I would pass pretty well for a maid-servant in the field, for with the Croats I had learned how to boil, bake, and wash : as for spinning, soldiers' wives do it not on a campaign. All other women's work which I could not do, such as brushing and braiding hair, my mistress gladly forgave me, for she knew well I had never learned it.

But as I came out of the coach with my sleeves turned up, my Hans was so inflamed by the sight of my white arms that he could not refrain himself, but must kiss me ; and I not greatly resisting that, the captain, before whose eyes this took place, could bear it no longer, but sprang with drawn sword out of the tent to give my poor lover a thrust : but he ran off and forgot to come back ; so says the captain to me,

" Thou whore in grain," says he, " I will teach thee . . ."
and more he could not say for very rage, but struck at me
as if he were mad. But I beginning to cry out, he must needs
stop lest he should alarm the camp : for both armies, Saxon
and Imperialist, lay close together expecting the approach
of the Swedes under Banér.

Chap. xxvi : HOW HE WAS IMPRISONED FOR A TRAITOR AND ENCHANTER

AS soon as it was day my master handed me over
to the horse-boys, even as both armies were
striking their tents : these were a pack of rascals,
and therefore was the baiting which I must endure
the greater and more dreadful : for they hastened with me
to a thicket the better to satisfy their bestial desires, as is the
custom of these devils' children when a woman is given over
to them : and there followed them many fellows looking on
at their scurvy tricks, and among them my Hans, who let
me not out of his sight, and when he saw 'twould go ill with
me would rescue me by force, even should it cost him his
head : who found backers enough when he said I was his
betrothed wife ; and they, shewing pity for him and me,
were ready to help. But that the boys, who thought they
had the better right to me, and would not let such a good
prize go, would not have, and went about to repel force with
force. So blows beginning to be dealt on both sides, the
crowd and the noise became greater and greater till it seemed
almost like a tournament in which each did his best for a
fair lady's sake. All this terrible hubbub drew the Provost-
general to the spot, who came even then when my clothing
had been torn from my body and 'twas plain that I was no
woman : his coming made all quiet as mice, for he was feared
far more than the devil himself ; and those that had been at
fisticuffs scattered. But he briefly inquired of the matter,
and whereas I hoped he would save me, on the contrary he
arrested me, because it was a strange and suspicious thing
for a man to be found in an army in women's clothes. Accordingly, he and his men walked off with me to the regiments

(which were all afoot and ready to march), with intent to deliver me to the Judge-Advocate-General, or Quartermaster-General : but when we were about to pass my colonel's regiment, I was known and accosted and furnished by my colonel with some poor clothes, and so given in custody to our old provost, who put me in irons hand and foot.

It was mighty hard work for me so to march in fetters, and the old curmudgeon would have properly plagued me had not the secretary Oliver paid for me ; for I would not let my ducats, which I had thus far kept, see the light, for I should at the same time have lost them and also have fallen into greater danger. The said Oliver informed me the same evening why I was kept in such close custody, and the regimental sheriff received orders at once to examine me, that my deposition might the sooner be laid before the Judge-Advocate-General, for they counted me not only for a spy, but also for one that could use witchcraft ; for shortly after I left my colonel certain witches were burnt who confessed before their death that they had seen me at their General Assembly, when they met together to dry up the Elbe, that Magdeburg might be taken the sooner. So the points on which I was to give an answer were these. (1) Whether I had not been a student, or at least could read and write ? (2) Why I had come to the camp at Magdeburg disguised as a fool, whereas in the captain's service I had been as sane as I was now ? (3) Why I had disguised myself in women's apparel ? (4) Whether I had not been at the witches' dance with other sorcerers ? (5) Where I was born and who my parents were ? (6) Where I had sojourned before I came to the camp before Magdeburg ? and (7) Where and to what end I had learned women's work such as washing, baking, cooking, and also lute-playing ? Thereupon I would have told my whole story, that the circumstances of my strange adventures might explain all ; but the judge was not curious, only weary and peevish after his long march : so he desired only a round answer to each question ; and that I answered in the following words, out of which no one could yet learn aught that was exact or precise—as thus : (1) I had not been a student, but could read and write German. (2) I had been forced to wear a fool's coat because I had no other. (3) Because I was weary of the fool's coat and could come at no men's clothes. (4) I answered yes ; but had gone against my will and knew naught of witchcraft. (5) I was born in the Spessart and my parents were peasants. (6) With the Governor of Hanau and with a colonel of Croats, Corpes by name. (7) Among the Croats I had been forced against my will to learn cooking and the like : but lute-playing at Hanau because I had a liking thereto. So when my deposition was written out, " How canst thou deny," says he, " and say thou hast not studied, seeing that when thou didst pass for a fool, and the priest in the mass said ' Domine non sum dignus,' thou didst answer in Latin that he need not say that, for all knew it."

" Sir," said I, " others taught me that and persuaded me 'twas a prayer that one must use at mass, when our chaplain was saying it." " Yes, yes," said he, " I see thou art the very kind of fellow whose tongue must be loosed by the torture." Whereat I thought, " God help thee if thy tongue follow thy foolish head ! "

Early next morning came orders from the Judge-Advocate-General to our provost that he should keep me well in charge ; for he was minded as soon as the armies halted to examine me himself : in which case I must without doubt to the tor- ture, had not God ordered it otherwise. In my bonds I thought ever of my pastor at Hanau and old Herzbruder that was dead, how both had foretold how it would fare with me if I were rid of my fool's coat again.

Chap. xxvii : HOW THE PROVOST FARED IN THE BATTLE OF WITTSTOCK

THE same evening, and when we had hardly as yet pitched our tents, I was brought to the Judge-Advocate-General, who had before him my deposi- tion and also writing materials ; and he began to examine me more closely. But I, on the other part, told my story even as it had happened to me, yet was not believed, nor could the judge be sure whether he had a fool or a hard-bitten knave before him, so pat did question and answer fall and so strange was the whole history. He bade me take a pen and write, to see what I could do, and moreover to see if my handwriting was known, or if it had any marks in it that a man could recognise. I took pen and paper as handily as one that had been daily used to employ the same, and asked what I should write. The Judge-Advocate-General, who was perhaps vexed because my examination had prolonged itself far into the night, answered me thus : " What ! " says he, " write down ' Thy mother the whore.' "

Those words I did write down, and when they were read out they did but make my case worse,* for the Advocate-General said he was now well assured that I was a rogue. Then he asked the provost, had they searched me and found any writings upon me ? The provost answered him no ; for how could they search a man that had been brought to them naked ? But it availed nought ! The provost must search me in the presence of all, and as he did that diligently (O ill-luck !) there he found my two asses' ears with the ducats in them bound round my arms. Then said they : " What need we any further witness ? This traitor hath without doubt undertaken some great plot, for why else should any honest man disguise himself in a fool's raiment, or a man conceal himself in woman's garments ? And how could any suppose that a man would carry on him so great a quantity of money, unless it were that he intended to do some great deed therewith ? " For said they, did he not himself confess he had learned lute-playing under the cunningest soldier in the world, the commandant of Hanau ? " Gentlemen," says they, " what think you he did not learn among those sharp-witted Hessians ? The shortest way is to have him to the torture and then to the stake : seeing he hath in any case been in the company of sorcerers and therefore deserveth no better."

How I felt at that time any man can judge for himself ; for I knew I was innocent and had strong trust in God : yet I could see my danger and lamented the loss of my fair ducats, which the Judge-Advocate-General had put in his own pocket. But before they could proceed to extremities with me Banér's folk fell upon ours : at the first the two

* He wrote the words down, as he was told as if they meant the *judge's* mother.

armies fought for the best position, and then secondly for the heavy artillery, which our people lost forthwith. Our provost kept pretty far behind the line of battle with his helpers and his prisoners, yet were we so close to our brigade that we could tell each man by his clothing from behind; and when a Swedish squadron attacked ours we were in danger of our lives as much as the fighters, for in a moment the air was so full of singing bullets that it seemed a volley had been fired in our honour. At that the timid ducked their heads, as they would have crept into themselves: but they that had courage and had been present at such sport before let the balls pass over their heads quite unconcerned. In the fighting itself every man sought to prevent his own death with the cutting down of the nearest that encountered him: and the terrible noise of the guns, the rattle of the harness, the crash of the pikes, and the cries both of the wounded and the attackers made up, together with the trumpets, drums and fifes, a horrible music. There could one see nought but thick smoke and dust, which seemed as it would conceal the fearful sight of the wounded and dead: in the midst of it could be heard the pitiful outcries of the dying and the cheers of them that were yet full of spirit: the very horses seemed as if they were more and more vigorous to defend their masters, so furious did they shew themselves in the performance of that duty which they were compelled to do. Some of them one could see falling dead under their masters, full of wounds which they had undeservedly received for the reward of their faithful services: others for the same cause fell upon their riders, and thus in their death had the honour of being borne by those they had in life been forced to bear: others, again, being rid of the valiant burden that had guided them, fled from mankind in their fury and madness, and sought again their first freedom in the open field. The earth, whose custom it is to cover the dead, was there itself covered with them, and those variously distinguished: for here lay heads that had lost their natural owners, and there bodies that lacked their heads: some had their bowels hanging out in most ghastly and pitiful fashion, and others had their heads cleft and their brains scattered: there one could see how lifeless bodies were deprived of their blood while the living were covered with the blood of others;

here lay arms shot off, on which the fingers still moved, as if they would yet be fighting ; and elsewhere rascals were in full flight that had shed no drop of blood : there lay severed legs, which though delivered from the burden of the body, yet were far heavier than they had been before : there could one see crippled soldiers begging for death, and on the contrary others beseeching quarter and the sparing of their lives. In a word, 'twas naught but a miserable and pitiful sight. The Swedish conquerors drove our people from their position, which they had defended with such ill luck, and were scattered everywhere in pursuit. At which turn of things my provost, with us his prisoners, also took to flight, though we had deserved no enmity from the conquerors by reason of our resistance : but while the provost was threatening of us with death and so compelling us to go with him, young Herzbruder galloped up with five other horsemen and saluted him with a pistol and, "Lookye, old dog," says he, "is it the time now to breed young puppies ? Now will I pay thee for thy pains."

But the shot harmed the provost as little as if it had struck an anvil. So "Beest thou of that kidney," said Herzbruder, "yet I will not have come to do thee a courtesy in vain : die thou must even if thy soul were grown into thy body." And with that he compelled a musqueteer of the provost's own guard, if he would himself have quarter, to cut him down with an axe. And so that provost got his reward : but I being known by Herzbruder, he bade them free me from my fetters and bonds, set me on a horse, and charged his servant to bring me to a place of safety.

Chap. xxviii : OF A GREAT BATTLE WHEREIN THE CONQUEROR IS CAPTURED IN THE HOUR OF TRIUMPH

BUT even then, while my rescuer's servant conveyed me out of danger, his own master was, by reason of his greed of honour and of gain, carried so far afield that he in his turn was taken prisoner. So when the conquerors were dividing of the spoil and burying their dead, and Herzbruder was a-missing, his captain received as his inheritance me with his servant and his horses : whereby I must submit to be ranked as a horse-boy, and in exchange for that received nought, save only these promises : namely, that if I carried myself well and could grow a little older, he would mount me : that is, make a trooper of me : and with that I must be content.

But presently thereafter my captain was appointed lieutenant-colonel, and I discharged the same office for him that David did for Saul, for when we were in quarters I played the lute for him, and when we were on the march I must wear his cuirass after him, which was a sore burden to me : and although these arms were devised to protect their wearers against the buffets of the enemy, I found it the contrary, for mine own young which I hatched pursued me with the more security under the protection of those same arms : under the breastplate they had their free quarters, pastime, and playground, so that it seemed I wore the harness not for my protection but for theirs, for I could not reach them with my arms and could do no harm among them.* I busied myself with the planning of all manner of campaigns against them, to destroy this invincible Armada : yet had I neither time nor opportunity to drive them out by fire, (as is done in ovens) nor by water, nor by poison—though well I knew what quicksilver would do. Much less had I the opportunity to be rid of them by a change of raiment or a clean shirt, but must carry them with me and give them my body and blood to feed upon. And when they so tormented and bit me under the harness, I whipped out a pistol as if I would exchange shots with them : yet did only take out the ramrod and therewith drive them from their banquet. At last I discovered a plan, to wind a bit of fur round the ramrod and so make a pretty bird-lime for them : and when I could be at them under the harness with this louse-angler, I fished them out in dozens from their dens, and murdered them : but it availed me little.

Now it happened that my lieutenant-colonel was ordered to make an expedition into Westphalia with a strong detachment ; and if he had been as strong in cavalry as I was in my private garrison he would have terrified the whole world :

* The cuirass would be well lined to prevent chafing.

but as 'twas not so he must needs go warily, and for that reason also hide in the Gemmer Mark (a wood so called between Soest and Ham). Now even then I had come to a crisis with my friends : for they tormented me so with their excavations that I feared they might effect a lodgment between flesh and skin. Let no man wonder that the Brasilians do devour their lice, for mere rage and revenge, because they so torment them. At last I could bear my torment no longer, but when the troopers were busy—some feeding, some sleeping, and some keeping guard—I crept a little aside under a tree to wage war with mine enemies : to that end I took off mine armour (though others be wont to put it on when they fight) and began such a killing and murdering that my two swords, which were my thumbnails, dripped with blood and hung full of dead bodies, or rather empty skins : and all such as I could not slay I banished forthwith, and suffered them to take their walks under that same tree.

Now whenever this encounter comes into my remembrance forthwith my skin doth prick me everywhere, as if I were but now in the midst of the battle. 'Tis true I doubted for a while whether I should so revenge myself on mine own blood, and specially against such true servants that would suffer themselves to be hanged with me—yea, and broken on the wheel with me, and on whom, by reason of their numbers, I had often lain softly in the open air on the hardest of earth. But I went on so furiously in my tyrannical ways that I did not even mark how the Imperialists were at blows with my lieutenant-colonel, till at last they came to me, terrified my poor lice, and took me myself prisoner. Nor had they any respect for my manhood, by the power of which I had just before slain my thousands, and even surpassed the fame of the tailor that killed " seven at a blow." I fell to the share of a dragoon, and the best booty he got from me was my lieutenant-colonel's cuirass, and that he sold at a fair price to the commandant at Soest, where he was quartered. So he was in the course of this war my sixth master : for I must serve him as his foot-boy.

Chap. xxix: HOW A NOTABLY PIOUS SOLDIER FARED IN PARADISE, AND HOW THE HUNTSMAN FILLED HIS PLACE

NOW unless our hostess had been content to have herself and her whole house possessed by my army, 'twas certain she must be rid of them. And that she did, short and sharp, for she put my rags into the oven and burned them out as clean as an old tobacco-pipe, so that I lived again as 'twere in a rose-garden freed from my vermin : yea, and none can believe how good it was for me to be free from that torment wherein I had sat for months as in an ant's nest. But in recompense for that I had a new plague to encounter : namely, that my new master was one of those strange soldiers that do think to get to heaven : he was contented with his pay and never harmed a child. His whole fortune consisted in what he could earn by standing sentry and what he could save from his weekly pay ; and that, poor as it was, he valued above all the pearls of the Orient : each sixpence he got he sewed into his breeches, and that he might have more of such sixpences I and his horse must starve : I must break my teeth upon dry Pumpernickel, and nourish myself with water, or at best with small beer, and that was a poor affair for me— inasmuch as my throat was raw from the dry black bread and my whole body wasted away. If I would eat I must needs steal, and even that with such secrecy that my master could by no manner of means be brought to book. As for him, gallows and torture, headsmen and their helpers—yea, and surgeons too—were but superfluous. Sutlers and hawkers too must soon have beat a retreat from him : for his thoughts were far from eating and drinking, gaming and quarrelling : but when he was ordered out for a convoy or an expedition of any sort where pay was, there he would loiter and dawdle away his time. Yea, I believe truly if this good old dragoon had not possessed these soldierly virtues of loitering, he would never have got me : for in that case he would have followed my lieutenant-colonel at the double. I could count on no cast clothes from him : for he himself went in such rags as did beforetime my hermit in the woods. His whole harness and saddle were scarce worth three-halfpence, and his horse so staggering for hunger that neither Swede nor Hessian needed to fear his attack.

All these fair qualities did move his captain to send him to Paradise—which was a monastery so called—on protection-duty : not indeed as if he were of much avail for that purpose, but that he might grow fat and buy himself a new nag : and most of all because the nuns had asked for a pious and con-scientious and peaceable fellow for their guard. And so he rode thither and I behind him : for he had but one horse : and " Zounds ; " says he, " Simbrecht ; (for he could never frame to pronounce my name aright) when we come to Paradise we will take our fill." And I answered him : " Yes," said I, " the name is a good omen : God grant it that the place be like its name ! " " Yes, yes," says he, for he under-stood me not, " if we can get two ohms of the good West-phalian beer every day we shall not fare ill. Look to thyself : for I will now have a fine new cloak made, and thou canst have the old one : 'twill make a brave new coat for thee."

Well might he call it the old one : for I believe it could well remember the Battle of Pavia,* so weather beaten and shabby was it : and with the giving of it he did me but little kindness.

Paradise we found as we would have it and still better . in place of angels we found fair maidens, who so entertained us with food and drink that presently I came again to my former fatness : the strongest beer we had, the best West-phalian hams and smoked sausages and savoury and delicate meat, boiled in salt water and eaten cold. There too I learned to spread black bread a finger thick with salt butter, and put cheese on that so that it might slip down better : and when I could have a knuckle of mutton garnished with garlic and a good tankard of beer beside it, then would I refresh body and soul and forget all my past sufferings. In a word, this Paradise pleased me as much as if it had been the true Paradise : no other care had I except that I knew 'twould not always last, and I must fare forth again in my rags.

But even as misfortune ever came to me in abundance

* Some 120 years before.

when it once began to pursue me, so now it seemed to me that good fortune would run it hard : for when my master would send me to Soest to fetch his baggage thence, I found on the road a pack, and in the same some ells of scarlet cloth cut for a cloak, and red silk also for the lining. That I took with me, and at Soest I exchanged it with a clothier for common green woollen cloth fit for a coat and trappings, with the condition he should make such a coat and provide me also with a new hat : and inasmuch as I grievously needed also a new pair of shoes and a shirt, I gave the huckster the silver buttons and the lace that belonged to the cloak, for which he procured for me all that I wanted, and turned me out brand-new. So I returned to Paradise to my master, who was mightily incensed that I had not brought my findings to him : yea, he talked of trouncings, and for a trifle, an he had not been shamed and had the coat fitted him, would have stript it off me for to wear it himself. But to my thinking I had done a good piece of trading.

But now must the miserly fellow be ashamed that his lad went better clothed than he : therefore he rides to Soest, borrows money from his captain and equips himself in the finest style, with the promise to repay all out of his weekly protection-pay : and that he carefully did. He had indeed himself means to pay that and more also, but was too sly to touch his stores : for had he done that his malingering was at an end, wherein he hoped to abide softly that winter through, and some other naked fellow had been put in his place : but now the captain must perforce leave him where he lay, or he would not recover his money he had lent. Thence forward we lived the laziest life in the world, wherein skittles was our chief exercise : when I had groomed my dragoon's horse, fed and given him to drink, then I played the gentleman and went a-walking.

The convent was safeguarded also by our opponents the Hessians with a musqueteer from Lippstadt : the same was by trade a furrier, and for that reason not only a master-singer but also a first-rate fencer, and lest he should forget his art he daily exercised himself with me in all weapons, in which I became so expert that I was not afraid to challenge him whenever he would. My old dragoon, in place of fencing

with him, would play at skittles, and that for no other wager
but who should drink most beer at dinner : and so whoever
lost the convent paid.

This convent had its own game-preserves and therefore
its own huntsman, and inasmuch as I also was clad in green
I joined myself to him, and from him in that autumn and
winter I learned all his arts, and especially all that concerns
catching of small game. For that cause, and because also
the name Simplicissimus was somewhat uncommon and for
the common folk easily forgotten or hard to pronounce, every
one called me the "little huntsman": and meanwhile I
learned to know every way and path, and that knowledge
I made good use of thereafter. But when by reason of ill
weather I could not take my walks abroad in the wood, then
I read all manner of books which the bailiff of the convent
lent me. And so soon as the good nuns knew that, besides
my good voice, I could also play a little on the lute and the
harpsichord, then did they give more heed to me, and because
there was added to these qualities a prettily proportioned
body and a handsome face enough, therefore they deemed
all my manners and customs, my doings and my ways, to be
the ways of nobility : and so became I all unexpectedly a
much-loved gentleman, of whom one could but wonder that
he should serve so scurvy a dragoon.

But when I had spent the winter in the midst of such
pleasures, my master was discharged : which vexed him so
much (by reason of the good living he was to lose) that he fell
sick, and inasmuch as that was aggravated by a violent fever
(and likewise the old wounds that he had got in the wars in
his lifetime helped the mischief), he had but short shrift, for
in three weeks I had somewhat to bury, but this epitaph I
wrote for him :

"Old Miserly lies here, a soldier brave and good,
Who all his lifetime through shed ne'er a drop of blood."

By right and custom the captain could take and inherit
the man's horse and musquet and the general all else that
he left : but since I was a lively, well-set-up lad, and gave
hopes that in time I should not fear any man, it was offered
me to take all, if only I would take the place of my dead

master. And that I undertook the more readily because I knew my master had left a pretty number of ducats sewn into his old breeches, which he had raked together in his lifetime : and when in the process of things I must give in my name—namely, Simplicius Simplicissimus—and the musterclerk (which was named Cyriack) could not write it down aright, says he, " There is no devil in hell with such a name." Thereon I asked him quickly, " Was there one there named Cyriack ? " and clever as he thought himself, that he would not answer : and that pleased my captain so that from thenceforward he thought well of me.

Chap. xxx : HOW THE HUNTSMAN CARRIED HIM-
SELF WHEN HE BEGAN TO LEARN THE
TRADE OF WAR : WHEREFROM A YOUNG
SOLDIER MAY LEARN SOMEWHAT

NOW the commandant in Soest needed a lad in his stables, of the kind that I seemed to him to be, and for that reason he was not pleased well that I had turned soldier, but would try to have me yet : to that end he made a pretence of my youth and that I could not yet pass for a man : and having set this forth to my master, he sends to me and says he, " Harkye, little huntsman, thou shalt be my servant." So I asked what would my duties be : to which he answered I should help to tend his horses. " No, sir," quoth I, " we are not for one another : I would rather have a master in whose service the horses should tend me : but seeing that I can find none such, I will sooner remain a soldier." " Thy beard," says he, " is yet too small." " No, no," said I, " I will wager I can encounter any man of eighty years : a beard never yet killed a man, or goats would be in high esteem." " Oho ! " says he, " if thy courage be as high as thy wit, I will let thee pass for a soldier." I answered, " That can be tried upon the next occasion," and therewithal I gave him to understand I would not be used as a groom. So he left me as I was, and said the proof of the pudding was in the eating.

So now I betook myself to my old dragoon's old breeches,

and having dissected them, I recovered out of their entrails a good soldier's horse and the best musquet I could find : and all must for me be as bright as looking-glass. Then I bought a new suit of green clothes : for this name of the " huntsman " suited well with my fancy : and my old suit I gave to my lad ; for 'twas too small for me. And so could I ride on mine own account like a young nobleman, and thought no small beer of myself. Yea, I made so bold as to deck my hat with a great plume like an officer : and with that I raised up for myself enviers and mislikers : and betwixt them and me were presently hot words and at last even buffets. Yet hardly had I proved to one or two that same science which I had learned in Paradise of the good furrier, when behold, not only would all leave me in peace but would have my friendship moreover. Besides all this, I was ever ready to give my service for all expeditions on foot or on horseback : for I was a good rider and quicker on foot than most, and when it came to dealing with the enemy I must charge forward as for mere pleasure and ever be in the front rank. So was I in brief time known both among friends and foes, and so famous that both parties thought much of me, seeing that the most dangerous attacks were entrusted to me to carry out, and to that end whole detachments put under my command. And now I began to steal like any Bohemian, and if I made any capture of value, I would give my officers so rich a share thereof that 'twas allowed me to play my tricks on forbidden ground, for whatever I did I was supported. General Count Götz had left remaining in Westphalia three enemy's garrisons —to wit, in Dorsten, in Lippstadt, and in Coesfeld : and all these three I mightily plagued ! for I was before their gates, now here, now there, one day here and one day there, no less, and snapped up many a good prize, and because I ever escaped the folk came to believe of me I could make myself invisible and was as good as iron or steel. So now was I feared like the plague itself, so that thirty men of the enemy would not be shamed to flee before me if they did but know I was in their neighbourhood with fifteen. And at last it came to this : that where a contribution must be levied from a place, I was the man for that : and my plunder from that became as great as my fame. Mine officers and comrades loved their little huntsman : the chief partisans of the opposite side were terrified, and by fear and love I kept the countrymen on my side : for I knew how to punish my opposers, and them that did me the smallest service richly to repay : insomuch that I spent wellnigh the half of my booty in paying of my spies. And for that reason there went no reconnaissance, no convoy, no expedition out from the adversary whose departure was not made known to me : whereupon I laid my plans and founded my projects, and because I commonly brought the same to good effect by the help of good luck, all were astonished : and that chiefly at my youthful age : so that even many officers and good soldiers of the other party much desired to see me. To this must be added that I ever shewed myself courteous to my prisoners, so that they often cost me more than my booty was worth, and whensoever I could shew a courtesy to any of the adversary, and specially to any officer, without injury to my duty and to my allegiance to my master, I neglected it not. And by such behaviour I had surely been presently forwarded to the rank of officer, had not my youth hindered that : for whosoever, at the age wherein I then was, would be an ensign, must be of noble birth : besides, my captain could not promote me ; for there were no vacancies in his own company and he would not let me go to another : for so would he have lost in me a milch-cow and more too. So must I be and remain a corporal. Yet this honour, which I had gained over the heads of old soldiers, though 'twas but a small thing, yet this and the praise which daily I received were to me as spurs to urge me on to better things. And day and night I dreamed only of fresh plans to make myself greater : nay, I could not sleep by reason of such foolish phantasies. And because I saw that I wanted an opportunity to shew the courage which I felt in me, it vexed me that I could not every day have the chance to meet the adversary in arms and try the result. So then I wished the Trojan war back again, or such a siege as was at Ostende,* and fool as I was, I never thought that a pitcher goes to the well till it breaks : and that also is true of a young soldier and a foolish, when he hath but money and luck and courage : thereupon follow haughtiness and pride : and by

* Besieged by the Spaniards from 1601 to 1604.

reason of that pride I hired, in place of one foot-boy, two serving-men, whom I equipped well and horsed them well, and so gained the envy of all the officers.

Chap. xxxi : HOW THE DEVIL STOLE THE PARSON'S BACON AND HOW THE HUNTSMAN CAUGHT HIMSELF

NOW must I tell you a story or two of things that happened to me before I left the dragoons : and though they are trifling, yet are they amusing to be heard : for I undertook not only great things, but despised not also small affairs, if only I could be assured that thereby I should get reputation among the people.

Now my captain was ordered, with fifty odd men on foot, to Schloss Recklinghausen, and there to carry out a certain design : and as we thought that before the plan could be carried out we had best hide ourselves a day or two in the woods, each took with him provision for a week. But inasmuch as the rich convoy we waited for came not at the appointed time, our food gave out : and we dared not to steal, for so had we betrayed ourselves and caused our plan to come to nothing : and so hunger pressed us sore : moreover, I had in that quarter no good friends (as elsewhere) to bring me and my men food in secret. And therefore must we devise other means to line our bellies if we would not go home empty. My comrade, a journeyman Latinist who had but lately run from school and enlisted, sighed in vain for the barley soup which beforetime his parents had served up for his delight, and which he had despised and left untasted : and as he thought on those meals of old, so he remembered his school satchel, beside which he had eaten them.

" Ah, brother ; " says he to me, " is't not a shame that I have not learned arts enough to fill my belly now. Brother, I know, *re vera*, if I could but get to the parson in that village, 'twould provide me with an excellent *convivium*." So I pondered on that word awhile and considered our condition, and because they that knew the country might not leave the

ambush (for they had surely been recognised) while those
that were unknown to the people knew of no chance to steal
or buy in secret, I founded my plan on our student and laid
the thing before our captain. And though 'twas dangerous
for him also, yet was his trust in me so great, and our plight
so evil, that he consented. So I changed clothes with another
man, and with my student I shogged off to the said village
and that by a wide circuit, though it lay but half an hour from
us : and coming thither we forthwith knew the house next
the church to be the priest's abode ; for 'twas built town-
fashion and abutted on the wall that surrounded the whole
glebe. Now I had already taught my comrade what he should
say : for he had yet his worn-out old student's cloak on him :
but I gave myself out for a journeyman painter, as thinking
I could not well be called upon to exercise that art in the
village ; for farmers do not often have their houses decorated.

The good divine was civil, and when my comrade had
made him a deep Latin reverence and told lies in great abundance to him, as how the soldiers had plundered him on his road
and robbed him of all his journey-money, he offered him a
piece of bread and butter and a draught of beer. But I made
as though I belonged not to him, and said I would eat a snack
in the inn and then call for him, that we might ere the day
was spent come somewhat further on our way together. And
to the inn I went, yet more to espy what I could fetch away
that night than to appease mine hunger, and had also the luck
on the way to find a peasant plastering up of his oven, in which
he had great loaves of rye-bread, that should sit there and
bake for four-and-twenty hours. With the innkeeper I did
little business : for now I knew where bread was to be had :
yet brought a few loaves of white bread for our captain, and
when I came to the parsonage to warn my comrade to go, he
had already had his fill, and had told the priest I was a painter
and was minded to journey to Holland, there to perfect my
art. So the good man bade me welcome and begged me to
go into the church with him, for he would shew me some
pieces there that needed repair. And not to spoil the play, I
must follow. So he took me through the kitchen, and as he
opened the lock in the strong oaken door that led to the
churchyard, O mirum ! there I saw that the black heaven

above was dark with lutes, flutes, and fiddles, meaning the hams, smoked sausages, and sides of bacon that hung in the chimney; at which I looked with content, for it seemed as if they smiled at me, and I wished, but in vain, to have them for my comrades in the wood: yet they were so obstinate as to hang where they were. Then pondered I upon the means how I could couple them with the said oven full of bread, yet could not easily devise such, for, as aforesaid, the parson's yard was walled round and all windows sufficiently guarded with iron bars. Furthermore there lay two monstrous great dogs in the courtyard which, as I feared, would of a surety not sleep by night if any would steal that whereon 'twas the reward of their faithful guardianship to feed by day. So now when we came into the church and talked of the pictures, and the priest would hire me to mend this and that, and I sought for excuses and pleaded my journey, says the sacristan or bellringer, "Fellow," says he, "I take thee rather for a runaway soldier than a painter." To such rough talk I was no longer used, yet must put up with it: still I shook my head a little and answered him, "Fellow, give me but a brush and colours, and in a wink I will have thee painted for the fool thou art." Whereat the priest laughed, yet said to us both, 'twas not fitting to wrangle in so holy a place: with that I perceived he believed us both, both me and my student; so he gave us yet another draught and let us go. But my heart I left behind among the smoked sausages.

Before nightfall we came to our companions, where I took my clothes and arms again, told the captain my story, and chose out six stout fellows to bring the bread home. At midnight we came to the village and took the bread out of the oven: for we had a man among us that could charm dogs; and when we were to pass by the parsonage, I found it not in my heart to go further without bacon. In a word, I stood still and considered deeply whether 'twere not possible to come into the priest's kitchen, yet could find no other way but the chimney, which for this turn must be my door. The bread and our arms we took into the churchyard and into the bone-house, and fetched a ladder and rope from a shed close by. Now I could go up and down chimneys as well as any chimney-sweep (for that I had learned in my youth in the hollow trees), so on to the roof I climbed with one other, which roof was covered with a double ceiling and a hollow between, and therefore convenient for my purpose. So I twisted my long hair into a bunch on my head, and lowered myself down with an end of the rope to my beloved bacon, and fastened one ham after another and one flitch after another to the rope which my comrade on the roof most regularly hauled up and gave to the others to carry to the bonehouse. But alack and well-a-day ! Even as I shut my shop and would out again a rafter broke under me, and poor Simplicissimus tumbled down and the miserable huntsman found himself caught as in a mouse-trap : 'tis true, my comrades on the roof let down the rope to draw me up : but it broke before they could lift me from the ground. And, " Now huntsman," thought I, " thou must abide a hunt in which thy hide will be as torn as was Actaeon's," for the priest was awakened by my fall and bade his cook forthwith to kindle a light : who came in her nightdress into the kitchen with her gown hanging on her shoulders and stood so near me that she almost touched me : then she took up an ember, held the light to it, and began to blow : yet I blew harder, which so affrighted the good creature that she let both fire and candle fall and ran to her master. So I gained time to consider by what means I could help myself out : yet found I none.

Now my comrades gave me to understand through the chimney they would break the house open and have me forth : that would I not have, but bade them to look to their arms and leave only my especial comrade on the roof, and wait to see if I could not get away without noise and disturbance, lest our ambush should be frustrated : but if it could not be so, then might they do their best. Meanwhile the good priest himself struck a light ; while his cook told him a fearful spectre was in the kitchen who had two heads (for she had seen my hair in a bunch on my head and had mistook it for a second head). All this I heard, and accordingly smeared my face and arms with my hands, which were full of ashes, soot, and cinders, so vilely that without question I no longer could be likened to an angel, as those holy maidens in Paradise had likened me : and that same sacristan, had he but seen me, would have granted me this, that I was a quick painter. And now I began to rattle round in the kitchen in fearful wise, and to throw the pots and pans about : and the kettle-ring coming to my hand, I hung it round my neck, and the fire-hook I kept in my hand to defend myself in case of need.

All which dismayed not that good priest : for he came in procession with his cook, who bore two wax-lights in her hands and a holy-water stoup on her arm, he himself being vested in his surplice and stole, with the sprinkler in one hand and a book in the other, out of which he began to exorcise me and to ask who I was and what I did there. So as he took me to be the devil, I thought 'twas but fair I should play the devil's part as the Father of Lies, and so answered, " I am the Devil, and will wring thy neck and thy cook's too." Yet he went on with his conjuring and bade me take note I had no concern with him nor his cook ; yea, and commanded me under the most solemn adjuration that I should depart to the place whence I had come. To which I answered with a horrible voice, that 'twas impossible even if I would. Mean-while my comrade on the roof, which was an arch-rogue and knew his Latin well, had his part to play : for when he heard what time of day 'twas in the kitchen, he hooted like an owl, he barked like a dog, he neighed like a horse, he bleated like a goat, he brayed like an ass, and made himself heard down the chimney like a whole crew of cats bucking in February, and then again like a clucking hen : for the fellow could imitate any beast's cry and, when he would, could howl as naturally as if a whole pack of wolves were there. And this terrified the priest and his cook more than anything : yet was my conscience sore to suffer myself to be abjured as the devil ; for he truly took me for such as having read or heard that the devil loved to appear clad in green.

Now in the midst of these doubts, which troubled both parties alike, I was aware by good luck that the key in the lock of the door that led to the churchyard was not turned, but only the bolt shot : so I speedily drew it back and whipped out of the door into the churchyard, where I found my com-rades standing with their musquets cocked, and left the parson to conjure devils as long as he would. So when my comrade had brought my hat down from the roof, and we had packed up our provands, we went off to our fellows, having no further business in the village save that we should have returned the borrowed ladder and rope to their owners.

With our stolen food the whole party refreshed themselves, and all had cause enough to laugh over my adventure : only the student could not stomach it that I should rob the priest that had so nobly filled his belly, yea, he swore loud and long he would fain pay him for his bacon, had he but the means at hand ; and yet ate of it as heartily as if he were hired for the business. So we lay in our ambush two days longer and waited for the convoy we had so long looked for ; where we lost no single man in the attack, yet captured over thirty prisoners and as splendid booty as ever I did help to divide : and I had a double share because I had done best : and that was three fine Friesland stallions laden with as much merchandise as we could carry off in our haste ; and had we had time to examine the booty and to bring it to a place of safety, each for his own part would have been rich enough : but we had to leave more on the spot than we bore off, for we must hurry away with all speed, taking what we could carry : and for greater safety we betook ourselves to Rehnen, and there we baited and shared the booty : for there lay our main body.

And there I thought again on the priest, whose bacon I had stolen : and now may the reader think what a misguided, wanton, and overweening spirit was mine, when it was not enough for me to have robbed and terrified that pious man, but I must claim honour for it. To that end I took a sapphire set in a gold ring, which I had picked up on that same plundering expedition, and sent it from Rehnen to my priest by a sure hand with this letter : " Reverend Sir,—Had I but in these last days had aught in the wood to eat and so to live, I had had no cause to steal your reverence's bacon, in which matter 'tis likely you were terrified. I swear by all that is holy that such affright was against my will, and so the more do I hope for forgiveness. As concerning the bacon itself, 'tis but just it should be paid for, and therefore in place of money I send this present ring, given by those for whose behoof your goods must needs be taken, and beg your rever-

ence will be pleased to accept the same : and add thereto that he will always find on all occasions an obedient and faithful servant in him whom his sacristan took to be no painter and who is otherwise known as ' The Huntsman.' "

But to the peasant whose oven they had emptied, the party sent out of the general booty sixteen rix-dollars : for I had taught them that in such wise they must bring the country-folk on their side, seeing that such could often help a party out of great difficulties or betray such another party and bring all to the gallows. From Rehnen we marched to Münster and thence to Ham, and so home to Soest to our headquarters, where I after some days received an answer from his reverence, as follows : " Noble Huntsman,—If he from whom you stole the bacon had known that you would appear to him in devilish guise, he had not so often wished to behold the notorious huntsman. But even as the borrowed meat and bread have been far too dearly paid for, so also is the fright inflicted the easier to forgive, especially because 'twas caused (against his will) by so famous a person, who is hereby forgiven, with the request that he will once more visit without fear him who fears not to conjure the devil.— Vale."

And so did I everywhere, and gained much fame : yea, and the more I gave away and spent, the more the booty flowed in, and I conceived that I had laid out that ring well, though 'twas worth some hundred rix-dollars. And so ends this second book.

BOOK III

Chap. i: HOW THE HUNTSMAN WENT TOO FAR TO THE LEFT HAND

THE gentle reader will have understood by the fore going book how ambitious I had become in Soest, and that I had sought and found honour, fame, and favour in deeds which in others had deserved punishment. And now will I tell how through my folly I let myself be further led astray, and so lived in constant danger of life and limb ; for I was so busied to gain honour and fame that I could not sleep by reason of it, and being full of such fancies, and lying awake many a night to devise new plots and plans, I had many wondrous conceits. In this wise I contrived a kind of shoes that a man could put on hind part before, so that the heel came under his toes : and of these at mine own cost I caused thirty different pairs to be made, and when I had given these out to my fellows and with them went on a foray, 'twas clean impossible to follow our tracks : for now would we wear these, and now again our right shoes on our feet, and the others in our knapsacks. So that if a man came to a place where I had bidden them change shoes, 'twas for all the world, by the tracks, as if two parties had met together there and together had vanished away. But if I kept these new invented shoes on throughout, it seemed as I had gone thither whence in truth I had come, or had come from the place to which I now went. And besides this, my tracks were at all times confused, as in a maze, so that they who should pursue or seek news of me from the foot-prints could never come at me. Often I was close by a party of the enemy who were minded to seek me far away : and still more often miles away from some thicket which they had surrounded, and were searching in hopes to find me. And as I managed with my parties on foot, so did I also when we were on horseback : for to me 'twas simple enough to dismount at cross-roads and forked ways and there have the horses' shoes set on hind part before. But the common tricks that soldiers use, being weak in numbers, to appear from the tracks to be strong, or being strong to appear weak, these were for me so common and I held them so cheap that I care not to tell of them. Moreover, I devised an instrument wherewith if 'twas calm weather I could by night hear a trumpet blow three hours' march away, could hear a horse neigh or a dog bark at two hours' distance, and hear men's talk at three miles ; which art I kept secret, and gained thereby great respect, for it seemed to all incredible. Yet by day was this instrument, which I commonly kept with a perspective-glass in my breeches pouch, not so useful, even though 'twas in a quiet and lonely place : for with it one could not choose but hear every sound made by horses and cattle, yea, the smallest bird in the air and the frog in the water in all the country round, and all this could be as plainly heard as if one were in the midst of a market among men and beasts where all do make such noise that for the crying of one a man cannot understand another. 'Tis true I know well there are folk who to this day will not believe this : but believe it or not, 'tis but the truth. With this instrument I can by night know any man that talks but so loud as his custom is, by his voice, though he be as far from me as where with a good perspective-glass one could by day know him by his clothes. Yet can I blame no one if he believe not what I here write, for none of those would believe me which saw with their own eyes how I used the said instrument, and would say to them, " I hear cavalry, for the horses are shod," or " I hear peasants coming, for the horses are unshod," or " I hear waggoners, but 'tis only peasants ; for I know them by their talk." " Here come musqueteers, and so many, for I hear the rattling of their bandoliers." " There is a village near by, for I hear the cocks crow and the dogs bark." " There goes a herd of cattle ; for I hear sheep bleat and cows low and pigs grunt " ; and so forth. Mine own comrades at first would hold this but for vain boasting, and when they found that all I said proved true in fact, then all must be witchcraft, and what I said must have been told to me by the devil and his dam. And so I believe will the gentle reader also think. Nevertheless by such means did I often escape the adversary when he had news of me and came to capture me : and I deem that if I had published this discovery 'twould since have become common, for it would be of great service in war and notably in sieges. But I return to my history.

If I was not needed for a foray, I would go a-stealing, and then were neither horses, cows, pigs, nor sheep safe from me that I could find for miles round : for I had a contrivance to put boots or shoes on the horses and cattle till I came to a frequented road, where none could trace them : and then I would shoe the horses hind part before, or if 'twas cows and oxen I put shoes on them which to that end I had caused to be made, and so brought them to a safe place. And the big fat swine-gentry, which by reason of laziness care not to travel by night, these I devised a masterly trick to bring away, however much they might grunt and refuse. For I made a savoury brew with meal and water and soaked a sponge in it : this I fastened to a strong cord, and let them for whom I angled swallow that sponge full of the broth, but kept the cord in my hand, whereupon without further parley they went contentedly with me and paid their score with hams and sausages. And all I brought home I faithfully shared both with the officers and my comrades : and so I got leave to fare forth again, and when my thefts were spied upon and betrayed, they helped me finely through. For the rest, I deemed myself far too good to steal from poor men, or rob hen-roosts and filch such small deer. And with all this I began by little and little to lead an epicurish life in regard of eating and drinking : for now I had forgot my hermit's teaching and had none to guide my youth or to whom I might look up : for my officers shared with me and caroused with me, and they that should have warned and chastised me rather enticed me to all vices. By this means I became so godless and wicked that no villainy was too great for me to compass. But at last I was secretly envied, specially by my comrades, as having a luckier hand at thieving than any other, and also by my officers because I cut such a figure, was lucky in forays, and made for myself a greater name and reputation than they themselves had. In a word, I am well assured one party or the other would have sacrificed me had I not spent so much.

Chap. ii : HOW THE HUNTSMAN OF SOEST DID RID
HIMSELF OF THE HUNTSMAN OF WESEL

NOW as I was living in this fashion, and busied with this, namely, to have me certain devil-masks made and grisly raiment thereto appertaining with cloven hoofs, by which means to terrify our foes, and specially to take their goods from our friends unbeknown (for which the affair of the bacon-stealing gave me the first hint), I had news that a fellow was at Wesel, which was a renowned partisan, went clad in green, and under my name practised divers rapes and robberies here and there in the land, but chiefly among our supporters, so that well-founded plaints against me were raised, and I must have paid for it smartly, had I not clearly shewn that at the very time he played these and other like tricks in my name I was elsewhere. Now this I would not pardon him, much less suffer him longer to use my name, to plunder in my shape and so bring me to shame. So with the knowledge of the commandant at Soest I sent him an invitation to the open field with swords or pistols. But as he had no heart to appear, I let it be known I would be revenged on him, even though it were in the very quarters of the commandant at Wesel, who had failed to punish him. Yea, I said openly if I found him on a foray I would treat him as an enemy. And that determined me to let my masks alone with which I had planned to do great things, to cut my green livery in pieces, and to burn it publicly in Soest in front of my quarters, to say nothing of all my clothing and horse harness, which were worth well over a hundred ducats : yea, and in my wrath I swore that the next that should call me huntsman must either kill me or die by my hand, should it cost me my life : nor would I ever again lead a party (for I was not bound to do so, being no officer) till I had avenged myself on my counterfeit at Wesel. So I kept myself to myself and did no more any exploits, save that I did my duty as sentry wheresoever I might be ordered to go, and that I performed as any malingerer might, and as sleepily as might well be. And this thing became known in the neighbourhood, and the advance-parties of the enemy became so bold and assured at this that they every day would bivouac close to our pickets : and that at last I could endure no longer. Yet what plagued me most of all was this : that this huntsman of Wesel went ever on his old way, giving himself out for me and under that name getting plunder enough and to spare.

Meanwhile, while all thought I had laid myself to sleep on a bearskin and should not soon rise from it, I was inquiring of the ways and works of my counterfeit at Wesel, and found that he not only imitated me in name and clothing, but was also used to steal by night whenever he could find a chance : so I woke up again unexpectedly and laid my plans accordingly. Now I had by little and little trained my two servants like watch-dogs, and they were so true to me that each at need would have run through fire for me, for with me they had good food and drink and gained plenty of booty. One of these I sent to mine enemy at Wesel, to pretend that because I, that had been his master, was now begun to live like any idler and had sworn never again to ride on a raid, he cared not to stay longer with me, but was come to serve him, since 'twas he that had put on the huntsman's dress in his master's stead, and carried himself like a proper soldier : and he knew, said he, all highways and byways in the country, and could lay many a plan for him to gain good booty. My good simple fool believed it all, and let himself be persuaded to take the fellow into his service. So on a certain night he went with him and his comrade to a sheep-fold to fetch away a few fat wethers : but there was I and Jump-i'-th'-field my other servant already in waiting, and had bribed the shepherd to fasten up his dogs and to suffer the new-comers to burrow their way into the shed unhindered ; for I would say grace for them over their mutton. So when they had made a hole through the wall, the huntsman of Wesel would have it that my servant should slip in first : " But," says he, " No, for there might well be one on the watch that should deal me one on the head : I see plainly ye know not how to go a-mousing : one must first explore " ; and therewith drew his sword and hung his hat on the point, and pushing it through the hole again and again, " So," says he, " We shall find out if the good man be at home or not." This ended, the huntsman of Wesel was the first to creep through. And with that Jump-i'-th'-field had him by the arm which held his sword, and asked, would he cry for quarter ? That his fellow heard and would have run for it : but I, who knew not which was the huntsman, and was swifter of foot than he, overtook him in a few paces : so I asked him, " Of what party ? " Says he, " Of the emperor's." I asked, " What regiment ? I am of the emperor's side : 'tis a rogue that denies his master ! " He answered, " We are of the dragoons of Soest, and are come to fetch a couple of sheep : I hope, brother, if ye be of the emperor's party too, ye will let us pass." I answered, " Who are ye, then, from Soest ? " Says he, " My comrade in the shed is the huntsman." " Then are ye rogues," said I, " or why do ye plunder your own quarters ? The huntsman of Soest is no such fool as to let himself be taken in a sheep-fold." " Nay, from Wesel I should have said," says he : but while we thus disputed together came my servant and Jump-i'-th'-field to us with my adversary : and, " Lookye," says I, " Is it thus we come together, thou honourable rascal, thou ? Were it not that I respect the emperor's arms which thou hast undertaken to bear against the enemy, I would incontinently send a ball through thy head : till now I have been the huntsman of Soest, and thee I count for a rogue unless thou take one of these swords here present and measurest the other with me soldier-fashion." And with that my servant (who, like Jump-i'-th'-field, had on horrible devil's apparel with goat's horns) laid a couple of swords at our feet which I had brought from Soest, and gave the huntsman of Wesel the choice, to take which he would : whereat the poor huntsman was so dismayed that it fared with him as with me at Hanau when I spoiled the dance : he and his comrade trembled like wet dogs, fell on their knees, and begged for pardon. But Jump-i'-th'-field growled out, as 'twere from the inside of a hollow pot, " Nay, ye must fight, or I will break the neck of ye." " O honourable sir devil," says the huntsman, " I came not here to fight : oh, deliver me from this, master devil, and I will do what thou wilt." So as he talked thus wildly, my servant put one sword in his hand and gave me the other : yet he trembled so sore he could not hold it. Now the moon was bright, and the shepherd and his men could see and hear all from out their hut : so I called to him to come, that I might have a witness of this bargain : but when he came, he made as though he saw not the two in devils' disguise, and said, what cause had I to bicker so long with these two fellows in his sheep-fold : if I had aught to settle with them, I might do it elsewhere : for our business concerned him not at all : he paid his " Conterbission " regularly every month, and hoped, therefore, he might live in peace with his sheep. To the two fellows he said, why did they so suffer one man to plague them, and did not knock me on the head at once. " Why," said I, " thou rascal, they would have stolen thy sheep." " Then let the devil wring their necks for them," says the peasant, and away he went. With that I would come to the fighting again : but my poor huntsman could, for sheer terror, no longer keep his feet, so that I pitied him : yea, he and his comrade uttered such piteous plaints that, in a word, I forgave and pardoned him all. But Jump-i'-th'-field would not so be satisfied, but scratched the huntsman so grievously in the face that he looked as he had been at dinner with the cats, and with this poor revenge I must be content. So the huntsman vanished from Wesel, for he was sore shamed : inasmuch as his comrade declared everywhere, and confirmed it with horrible oaths, that I had in real truth two devils in the flesh that waited on me ; and so was I more feared, and contrariwise less loved.

Chap. iii : HOW THE GREAT GOD JUPITER WAS CAPTURED AND HOW HE REVEALED THE COUNSELS OF THE GODS

OF that I was soon aware : and therefore did I do away my godless way of life and give myself over to religion and good living. 'Tis true I would ride on forays as before, yet now I shewed myself so courteous and kindly towards friend and foe, that all I had to deal with deemed it must be a different man from him they had heard of. Nay, more, I made an end of my superfluous expense, and got together many bright ducats and jewels which I hid here and there in hollow trees in the country round Soest ; for so the well-known fortune-teller in that town advised me, and told me likewise I had more enemies in Soest and in mine own regiment than outside the town and in the enemy's garrisons : and these, said she, were all plotting against me and my money. And when 'twas noised in this place or that, that the huntsman was off and away, presently I was all unexpectedly at the elbow of them that so flattered themselves, and before one village was rightly certain that I had done mischief in another, itself found that I was close at hand : for I was everywhere like a whirlwind, now here now there : so that I was more talked of than ever, and others gave themselves out to be me.

Now it happened that I lay with twenty-five musquets not far from Dorsten and waited for a convoy that should come to the town : and as was my wont, I stood sentry myself as being near the enemy. To me there came a man all alone, very well dressed and flourishing a cane he had in his hand in strange wise : nor could I understand aught he said but this, " Once for all will I punish the world, that will not render me divine honours." From that I guessed this might be some mighty prince that went thus disguised to find out his subjects' ways and works, and now proposed duly to punish the same, as not having found them to his liking. So I thought, " If this man be of the opposite party, it means a good ransom ; but if not, thou canst treat him so courteously and so charm away his heart that he shall be profitable to thee all thy life long."

With that I leapt out upon him, presented my gun at him at full-cock, and says I, " Your worship will please to walk before me into yonder wood if he will not be treated as an enemy." So he answered very gravely, " To such treatment my likes are not accustomed " : but I pushed him very politely along and, " Your honour," said I, " will not for once refuse to bow to the necessities of the times." So when I had brought him safely to my people in the wood and had set my sentries again, I asked him who he was : to which he answered very haughtily I need not ask that, for I knew already he was a great god. I thought he might perhaps know me, and might be a nobleman of Soest that thus spoke to rally me ; for 'tis the custom to jeer at the people of Soest about their great idol with the golden apron : but soon I was aware that instead of a prince I had caught a madman, one that had studied too much and gone mad over poetry : for when he grew a little more acquainted with me he told me plainly he was the great god Jupiter himself.

Now did I heartily wish I had never made this capture : but since I had my fool, there I must needs keep him till we should depart : so, as the time otherwise would have been tedious, I thought I would humour the fellow and make his gifts of use to me ; so I said to him, " Now, worshipful Jove, how comes it that thy high divinity thus leaves his heavenly throne and descends to earth ? Forgive, O Jupiter, my question, which thou mightest deem one of curiosity : for we be also akin to the heavenly gods and nought but wood-spirits, born of fauns and nymphs, to whom this secret shall ever remain a secret." " I swear to thee by the Styx," answered Jupiter, " thou shouldst not know a word of the secret wert thou not so like to my cup-bearer Ganymede, even wert thou Paris's own son : but for his sake I communicate to thee this, that a great outcry concerning the sins of the world is come up to me through the clouds : upon which 'twas decided in the council of all the gods that I could justly destroy all the world with a flood : but inasmuch as I have always had a special favour to the human race, and moreover at all times shew kindness rather than severity, I am now wandering around to learn for myself the ways and works of men : and though I find all worse than I expected, yet am I not minded to destroy all men at once and without distinction, but to punish only those that deserve punishment and thereafter to bend the remainder to my will."

I must needs laugh, yet checked myself, and said, " Alas, Jupiter, thy toil and trouble will be, I fear, all in vain unless thou punish the world with water, as before, or with fire : for if thou sendest a war, thither run together all vile and abandoned rogues that do but torment peaceable and pious men. An thou sendest a famine, 'tis but a godsend for the usurers, for then is their corn most valuable : and if thou sendest a pestilence, then the greedy and all the rest of mankind do find their account, for then do they inherit much.

So must thou destroy the whole world root and branch, if thou wilt punish at all."

Chap. iv: *OF THE GERMAN HERO THAT SHALL CONQUER THE WHOLE WORLD AND BRING PEACE TO ALL NATIONS*

SO Jupiter answered, " Thou speakest of the matter like a mere man, as if thou didst not know that 'tis possible for us gods so to manage things that only the wicked shall be punished and the good saved : I will raise up a German hero that shall accomplish all with the edge of the sword ; he shall destroy all evil men and preserve and exalt the righteous." " Yea," said I, " but such a hero must needs have soldiers, and where soldiers are there is war, and where war is there must the innocent suffer as well as the guilty." " Oho ; " says Jupiter, " be ye earthly gods minded like earthly men, that ye can understand so little ? For I will send such a hero that he shall have need of no soldiers and yet shall reform the whole world ; at his birth I will grant to him a body well formed and stronger than had ever Hercules, adorned to the full with princeliness, wisdom, and understanding : to this shall Venus add so comely a face that he shall excel Narcissus, Adonis, and even my Ganymede : and she shall grant to him, besides his other fine parts, dignity, charm, and presence excelling all, and so make him beloved by all the world, for which cause I will look more kindly upon it in the hour of his birth. Mercury, too, shall endow him with incomparable cleverness, and the inconstant moon shall be to him not harmful but useful, for she shall implant in him an invincible swiftness : Pallas Athene shall rear him on Parnassus, and Vulcan shall, under the influence of Mars, forge for him his weapons, and specially a sword with which he shall conquer the whole world and make an end of all the godless, without the help of a single man as a soldier : for he shall need no assistance. Every town shall tremble at his coming, and every fortress otherwise unconquerable he shall have in his power in the first quarter of an hour : in a word, he shall have the rule over the greatest potentates of the world, and so nobly bear sway over earth and sea that both gods and men shall rejoice thereat."

"Yea," said I, "but how can the destruction of all the godless and rule over the whole world be accomplished without specially great power and a strong arm ? O Jupiter, I tell thee plainly I can understand these things less than any mere mortal man." " At that," says Jupiter, " I marvel not : for thou knowest not what power my hero's sword will have ; Vulcan shall make it of the same materials of which he doth forge my thunderbolts, and so direct its virtues that my hero, if he do but draw it and wave it in the air, can cut off the heads of a whole armada, though they be hidden behind a mountain or be a whole Swiss mile distant from him, and so the poor devils shall lie there without heads before they know what has befallen them. And when he shall begin his trium phal progress and shall come before a town or a fortress, then shall he use Tamburlaine's vein, and for a sign that he is there for peace and for the furthering of all good shall shew a white flag : then if they come forth to him and are content, 'tis well : if not, then will he draw his sword, and by its virtue, as before described, will hew off the heads of all enchanters and sorceresses throughout the town, and then raise a red flag : then if they be still obstinate, he shall destroy all murderers, usurers, thieves, rogues, adulterers, whores, and knaves in the said manner, and then hoist a black flag : whereupon if those that yet remain in the town refuse to come to him and humbly submit, then shall he destroy the whole town as a stiff necked and disobedient folk : yet shall he only execute them that have hindered the others, and been the cause that the people would not submit. So shall he go from country to country, and give each town the country that lies around it to rule in peace, and from each town in all Germany choose out two of the wisest and learnedest men to form his parliament, shall reconcile the towns with each other for ever, shall do away all villenage, and also all tolls, excises, interest, taxes, and octrois throughout Germany, and take such order that none shall ever again hear of forced work, watch-duties, contributions, benevolences, war-taxes, and other burdens of the people, but that men shall live happier than in the Elysian fields. And then," says Jupiter, " will I often assemble all

Olympus and come down to visit the Germans, to delight myself among their vines and fig-trees : and there will I set Helicon on their borders and establish the Muses anew thereon : Germany will I bless with all plenty, yea, more than Arabia Felix, Mesopotamia, and the land of Damascus : then will I forswear the Greek language, and only speak German ; and, in a word, shew myself so good a German that in the end I shall grant to them, as once I did to the Romans, the rule over all the earth."

" But," said I, " great Jupiter, what will princes and lords say to this, if this future hero so violently take from them their rights and hand them over to the towns ? Will they not resist with force, or at least protest against it before gods and men ? "

" The hero," answered Jupiter, " will trouble himself little on that score : he will divide all the great into three classes : them which have lived wickedly and set an evil example he will punish together with the commons, for no earthly power can withstand his sword : to the rest he will give the choice whether to stay in the land or not. They that love their fatherland and abide must live like the commons, but the German people's way of living shall then be more plentiful and comfortable than is now the life and household of a king ; yea, they shall be one and all like Fabricius, that would not share King Pyrrhus his kingdom because he loved his country and honour and virtue too much : and so much for the second class. But as to the third, which will still be lords and rulers, them will he lead through Hungary and Italy into Moldavia, Wallachia, into Macedonia, Thrace and Greece, yea, over the Hellespont into Asia, and conquer these lands for them, give them as helpers all them that live by war in all Germany, and make them all kings. Then will he take Constantinople in one day, and lay the heads of all Turks that will not be converted and become obedient before their feet : then will he again set up the Roman Empire, and so betake himself again to Germany, and with his lords of Parliament (whom, as I have said, he shall choose in pairs from every city in Germany, and name them the chiefs and fathers of his German Fatherland) build a city in the midst of Germany that shall be far greater than Manoah* in America, and richer than was

* A kind of Eldorado.

Jerusalem in Solomon's time, whose walls shall be as high as the mountains of Tirol and its ditches as broad as the sea between Spain and Africa. And there will he build a temple entirely of diamonds, rubies, emeralds, and sapphires, and in the treasury that he shall there build will he gather together rarities from the whole world out of the gifts that the kings in China and in Persia, the great Mogul in the East Indies, the great Khan of Tartary, Prester John in Africa, and the great Czar in Muscovy will send to him. Yea, the Turkish emperor would be yet more ready to serve him if it were not that my hero will have taken his empire from him and given it as a fief to the Roman emperor."

Then I asked my friend Jupiter what in such case would become of the Christian kings. So he answered, " Those of England, Sweden, and Denmark (because they are of German race and descent), and those of Spain, France, and Portugal (because the Germans of old conquered and ruled in those lands), shall receive their crowns, kingdoms, and incorporated lands in fee as fiefs of the German nation, and then will there be, as in Augustus's time, a perpetual peace between all nations."

Chap. v : HOW HE SHALL RECONCILE ALL RE-LIGIONS AND CAST THEM IN THE SAME MOULD

NOW Jump-i'-th'-field, who also listened to us, had wellnigh enraged Jupiter and spoiled the whole affair ; for said he, " Yea, yea ; and then 'twill be in Germany as in fairyland, where it rains muscatels and nought else, and where twopenny pies grow in the night like mushrooms : and I too shall have to eat with both cheeks full at once like a thresher, and drink myself blind with Malvoisie." " Yea, truly," said Jupiter, " and that the more because I will curse thee with the undying hunger of Erysichthon, for methinks thou art one of them that do deride my majesty," and to me said he, " I deemed I was among wood-spirits only : but meseems I have chanced upon a Momus or a Zoilus, the most envious creatures in the world. Is one to reveal to such traitors the decrees of heaven and so to cast pearls before swine ? " So I saw plainly he would not willingly brook laughter, and therefore kept down mine own as best I could, and " Most gracious Jupiter," said I, " thou wilt not, by reason of a rude forest-god's indiscretion, conceal from thy Ganymede how things are further to happen in Germany." " No, no," said he, " but I command this mocker, who is like to Theon, to bridle his evil tongue in future, lest I turn him to a stone as Mercury did Battus. But do thou confess to me thou art truly my Ganymede, and that my jealous Juno hath driven thee from heaven in my absence." So I promised to tell him all when I should have heard what I desired to know. Thereupon, " Dear Ganymede," says he, " for deny not that thou art he—in those days shall gold-making be as common in Germany as is pot-making now, and every horse-boy shall carry the philosophers' stone about with him." " Yea," said I, " but how can Germany be so long in peace with all these different religions ? Will not the opposing clergy urge on their flocks and so hatch another war ? " " No, no," says Jupiter, " my hero will know how to meet that difficulty cleverly, and before all things to unite all Christian religions in the world." " O wonderful," said I, " that were indeed a great work ! How could it come about ? " " I will with all my heart reveal it to thee," answered Jupiter, " for after my hero hath made peace for all mankind he will address all the heads of the Christian world both spiritual and temporal, in a most moving speech, and so excellently impress upon them their hitherto most pernicious divisions in belief, that of themselves they will desire a general reconciliation and give over to him the accomplishment of such according to his own great wisdom. Then will he gather together the most skilful, most learned, and most pious theologians of all religions and appoint for them a place, as did once Ptolemy for the seventy-two translators, in a cheerful and yet quiet spot, where one can consider weighty matters undisturbed, and there provide them all with meat and drink and all necessaries, and command them so soon as possible, and yet with the ripest and most careful consideration, first to lay aside the strifes that there be between their religions, and next to set down in writing and with full clearness the right, true, holy Christian religion in accordance with Holy Writ ; and with most ancient tradition, the recognised sense of the Fathers. At which time Pluto will sorely scratch his head as fearing the lessening of his kingdom : yea, and will devise all manner of plans and tricks to foist in an ' and,' and if not to stop the whole thing, yet at least to postpone it *sine die,* that is for ever. So will he hint to each theologian of his interest, his order, his peaceful life, his wife and child, and his privileges, and aught else that might sway his inclinations. But my brave hero also will not be idle : he will so long as this council shall last have all the bells in Christendom rung, and so call all Christian people to pray without ceasing to the Almighty, and to ask for the sending of the Spirit of Truth. And if he shall see that one or another doth allow himself to be tempted by Pluto, then will he plague the whole assembly with hunger as in a Roman conclave, and if they yet delay to complete so holy a work, then will he preach them all a sermon through the gallows, or shew them his wonderful sword, and so first with kindness, but at last with severity and threats, bring them to come to the business in hand, and no longer as before to befool the world with their stiff-necked false doctrines. So when unity is arrived at, then will he proclaim a great festival and declare to the whole world this purified religion ; and whosoever opposes it, him will he torment with pitch and sulphur or smear that heretic with box-grease and present him to Pluto as a New Year's gift. And now, dear Ganymede, thou knowest all thou didst desire to know : and now tell me in turn the reason why thou hast left heaven, where thou hast poured me so many a draught of nectar."

Chap. vi : HOW THE EMBASSY OF THE FLEAS FARED WITH JUPITER

NOW methought 'twas possible this fellow might be no such fool as he pretended, but might be serving me as I had served others in Hanau to escape from us the better : so I determined to put him in a passion, for in such plight it is easiest to know a real madman ; and says I, " The reason I am come down from heaven is that I missed thee there, and so took Daedalus's wings and flew down to earth to seek thee. But when I came to ask for thee I found thee in all places but of ill repute ; for Zoilus and Momus have throughout the world so slandered thee and all the other gods, and decried ye as wanton and stinking, that ye have lost all credit with mankind. Thyself, say they, beest a lousy, adulterous caperer after woman-kind ; how canst thou then, punish the world for such vices ? Vulcan they say is but a poltroon that let pass Mars's adultery without proper revenge ; and how can that halting cuckold forge any weapons of note ? Venus, too, is for her unchastity the most infamous baggage in the world : and how can she endow another with grace and favour ? Mars they say is but a murderer and a robber ; Apollo a shameless lecher ; Mercury an idle chatterer, thief and pander ; Priapus filth ; Hercules a brainsick ruffian ; and, in a word, the whole crew of the gods so ill famed that they should of right be lodged nowhere but in Augeas's stable, which even without them stinks in the nostrils of all the world."

" Aha ; " says Jupiter, " and who would wonder if I laid aside my graciousness and punished these wretched slanderers and blasphemous liars with thunder and lightning ? How thinkest thou, my true and beloved Ganymede, shall I curse these chatterers with eternal thirst like Tantalus, or hang them up with that loose talker Daphitas on Mount Thorax, or grind them with Anaxarchus in a mortar, or set them in Phalaris's red-hot bull of Agrigent ? Nay, nay, Ganymede : all these plagues and punishments together are too little : I will fill Pandora's box anew and empty it upon the rogues' heads : then Nemesis shall wake the furies and send them at their heels, and Hercules shall borrow Cerberus from Pluto and hunt those wicked knaves with him like wolves, and when I have in this wise chased and tormented them enough, then will I bind them fast with Hesiod and Homer to a pillar in hell and there have them chastised for ever without pity by the Furies."

Now while Jupiter thus spake he began to make a hunt for the fleas he had upon him : for these, as one might perceive, did plague him sore. And as he did so he cried, " Away with ye, ye little tormenters ; I swear to ye by Styx ye shall

never have that, that ye so earnestly desire." So I asked
him what he meant by such words. He answered, the nation
of the fleas, as soon as they learned he was come on earth,
had sent their ambassadors to compliment him : and there
had complained to him that, though he had assigned to
them the dogs' coats as a dwelling, yet on account of certain
properties common to women, some poor souls went astray
and trespassed on the ladies' furs ; and such poor wandering
creatures were by the women evil entreated, caught, and not
only murdered, but first so miserably martyred and crushed
between their fingers that it might move the heart of a stone.
" Yea," said Jupiter further, " they did present their case to
me so movingly and piteously that I must needs have sympathy with them and so promised them help, yet on condition
I should first hear the women ; to that they objected that
if 'twas allowed to the women to plead their cause and to
oppose them, they knew well they with their poisonous
tongues would either impose upon my goodness and loving-
kindness, and outcry the fleas themselves, or by their sweet
words and their beauty would befool me and lead me astray
to a wrong judgment. But if I must allow the women to
hunt, catch, and with the hunters' privilege to slay them in
their preserves, then their petition was that they might in
future be executed in honourable wise, and either cut down
with a pole-axe like oxen or snared like game, and no longer
to be so scandalously crushed between the fingers and so
broken on the wheel, by which means their own limbs were
made instruments of torture. " Gentlemen," said I, " ye
must be greatly tormented when they thus tyrannise over
ye." " Yea, truly," said they, " they be so envious of us.
Is it right ? Can they not suffer us in their territories ? for
many of them so cleanse their lap-dogs with brushes, combs,
soap and lye, and other like things, that we are compelled
to leave our fatherland and to seek other dwellings." Thereupon I allowed them to lodge with me and to make my person
feel their presence, their ways and works, that I might judge
accordingly : and then the rascally crew began so to plague
me that, as ye have seen, I must again be rid of them. I will
give them a privilege, but only this, that the women may
squeeze them and crush them as much as they will : and if

I catch any so pestilent a customer I will deal with him no better.

Chap. vii : HOW THE HUNTSMAN AGAIN SECURED HONOUR AND BOOTY

NOW might we not laugh as heartily as we would both because we must keep quiet and because this good fool liked it not : wherefore Jump-i'-th'-field came nigh to burst. And just then our look-out man that we had posted in a tree called to us that he saw somewhat coming afar off. So I climbed the tree myself, and saw through my perspective-glass it must be the carriers for whom we lay in wait : they had no one on foot, but some thirty odd troopers for escort, and so I might easily judge they would not go through the wood wherein we lay, but would do their best to keep the open, and there we should have no advantage over them, though there was even there an awkward piece of road that led through the clearing some six hundred paces from us, and three hundred paces from the end of the wood or hill. Now it vexed me to have lain there so long for nought, or at best to have captured only a fool ; and so I quickly laid me another plan and that turned out well. For from our place of ambush there ran a brook in a cleft of the ground, which it was easy to ride along, down to the level country : the mouth of this I occupied with twenty men, took my post with them, and bade Jump-i'-th'-field stay in the place where we had been posted to advantage, and ordered each one of my fellows, when the escort should come, that each should aim at his man, and commanded also that some should shoot and some should hold their fire for a reserve. Some old veterans perceived what I intended and how I guessed that the escort would come that way, as having no cause for caution, and because certainly no peasant had been in such a place for a hundred years. But others that believed I could bewitch (for at that time I was in great reputation on that account) thought I would conjure the enemy into our hands. Yet here I needed no devil's arts, only my Jump-i'-th'-field ; for even as the escort, riding pretty close together, was just about to pass by us, he began at my order to bellow most horribly like an ox, and to neigh like a horse ; till the whole wood echoed therewith and any man would have sworn there were horses and cattle there. So when the escort heard that they thought to gain booty and to snap up somewhat, which yet was hard to find in such a country so laid waste. So altogether they rode so hard and disorderly into our ambush as if each would be the first to get the hardest blow, and this made them ride so close that in the first salute we gave them thirteen saddles were emptied, and some that fell were crushed under the horses' hoofs. Then came Jump-i'-th'-field leaping down the ravine and crying, " Huntsman here ! " At this the fellows were yet more terrified and so dismayed that they would ride neither backward, forward nor sideways, but leapt down and tried to escape on foot. Yet I had them all seventeen prisoners with the lieutenant that had commanded them, and then attacked the waggons, where I unharnessed four-and-twenty horses, and yet got only a few bales of silk and holland : for I dared not spare the time to plunder the dead, far less to search the waggons well, for the waggoners were up and away on the horses as soon as the action began, and so might I be botrayed at Dorsten, and caught again on the way back. So when we had packed up our plunder comes Jupiter from the wood and cried to us, " Would his Ganymede desert him ? " I answered him, yes, if he would not grant the fleas the privilege they demanded. " Sooner," says he, " would I see them all lying in hell-fires." At that I must needs laugh, and because in any case I had horses to spare I had him set on one : yet as he could ride no better than a tailor, I must have him bound upon his horse : and then he told us our skirmish had reminded him of that of the Lapithae and the centaurs at Pirithous' wedding. So when all was over and we galloping away with our prisoners as if we were pursued, the lieutenant we had captured began to consider what a fault he had committed, as having delivered so bold a troop of riders into the hand of the enemy and given over thirteen brave fellows to be butchered, and so, being desperate, he refused the quarter I had given him, and would fain have compelled me to have him shot ; for he thought that not only would this mistake turn to his great shame, and he be answerable, but also would hinder his advancement, even if it came not to this, that he must pay for his error with his head. So I talked with him and shewed him that with many a good soldier inconstant fortune had played her tricks ; yet had I never seen any one that therefore had been driven desperate, and that so to act were a sign of faint-heartedness : for brave soldiers were ever devising how to make up for losses sustained ; nor should he ever bring me to break my plighted word or to commit so shameful a deed against all righteousness and against the custom and tradition of honourable soldiers. When he saw I would not do it he began to revile me in the hope to move me to anger, and said I had not fought with him honestly and openly, but like a rogue and a footpad, and had stolen the lives of his soldiers like a thief : and at this his own fellows that we had captured were mightily afraid, and mine so wroth that they would have riddled him like a sieve if I had allowed it ; and I had enough to do to prevent it. Yet I was in no wise moved at his talk, but called both friend and foe to witness of what happened, and had him bound and guarded as a madman, but promised him so soon as we came to our camp, and if my officers permitted, to equip him with mine own horses and weapons, of which he should have the choice, and prove to him in open field, with sword and pistol, that 'twas allowed in war to use craft against the adversary : and asked him why he had not stayed with the waggons, which he was ordered to do ; or, if he must needs see what was in the wood, why he had not made a proper reconnaissance, which had been better for him than now to begin to play fool's tricks to which no one would take heed. Herein both friend and foe approved me right, and said that among a hundred partisans they had never met one that would not for such words of reviling have not only shot the lieutenant dead, but would have sent all the prisoners to the grave after him.

So next morning I brought my prisoners and plunder safely to Soest, and gained more honour and fame from this foray than ever before : for each one said, " This will prove another young John de Werth* " ; which tickled me greatly. Yet would not the commandant permit me to exchange shots or

* The famous cavalry commander of the Imperialists.

to fight with the lieutenant : for he said I had twice overcome
him. And the more my triumphs thus increased the more
grew the envy of those that in any case would have grudged
me my luck.

Chap. viii : HOW HE FOUND THE DEVIL IN THE
TROUGH, AND HOW JUMP-I'-TH'-FIELD
GOT FINE HORSES

NOW I could by no means be rid of my Jupiter :
for the commandant would have none of him,
as a pigeon not worth the plucking, but said he
made me a free gift of him. So now I had a fool
of mine own and needed to buy none, though a year before
I must needs allow others to treat me as such. So wondrous
is fortune and so changeable the times ! Even now had the
lice troubled me, and now had I the very god of fleas in my
power ; half a year before was I serving a miserable dragoon
as page, and now I had command of two servants that called
me master ; and so I reflected at times that nothing is so
certain in this world as its uncertainty. And so must I fear
if ever Fortune should let loose her hornets upon me it would
altogether overwhelm my present happiness.

Now just then Count von der Wahl, as colonel in command
of the Westphalian circle, was collecting troops from all the
garrisons to make a cavalry expedition through the bishopric
of Münster towards the Vecht, Meppen, Lingen and such
places, but specially to drive off two companies of Hessian
troopers in the bishopric of Paderborn that lay two miles
from the city and had there done our people much damage.
So was I ordered out with our dragoons, and when a few
troops had been collected at Ham we beat up the quarters
of the said troopers, which were but an ill-protected village,
till the rest of our people came. They tried to escape, but
we drove them back into their nest, and offered them to let
them go without horse or weapons but with the clothes on
their backs ; to this they would not agree, but would defend
themselves with their carbines like musqueteers. So it came
to that, that in the same night I must try what luck I had in
storming, for the dragoons led the way ; and my luck was

so good that I, together with Jump-i'-th'-field, was among the first to come into the town, and that without hurt, and we soon cleared the streets ; for all that bore arms were cut down, and the citizens had no stomach for fighting ; so we entered the houses. Then said Jump-i'-th'-field, we should choose a house before which a big heap of dung stood, for in such the rich curmudgeons were wont to dwell, with whom commonly officers were billeted : on such a one we seized, and there Jump-i'-th'-field would first visit the stable and I the house, on the condition each should share with the other whatever he could lay hands on. So then each lit his torch, and I called to the master of the house but had no answer, for all had hid themselves, but came upon a room wherein was nought but an empty bed and a covered kneading-trough. This I knocked open in hopes to find somewhat valuable, but as I raised the cover a coal-black thing rose up against me which I took for Lucifer himself. Nay, I can swear I was never in my life so terrified as I was then, when I so unawares beheld this black devil. " May all the powers of hell take thee," I cried in my fear, and raised my hatchet wherewith I had broke open the trough, yet had not the heart to split the creature's skull : so down he knelt, raised his hands to me, and says he, " O massa, I beg by de good God, gib me my life." With that I first knew 'twas no devil, for he spake of God and begged for his life ; so I bade him get out of his trough : and that he did as naked as God made him. Then I cut a piece of my torch off for him to light me, the which he did obediently, and brought me to a little room wherein I found the master of the house, who, together with his people, was looking on at this merry sight, and begged with trembling for mercy. And that he easily came by, for in any case we might not harm the burghers, and besides he handed me over the baggage of the Hessian captain, among which was a fairly well-furnished, locked portmanteau, telling me the said captain and all his people, save one servant and the negro now present, were gone to their posts to defend themselves. Meanwhile Jump-i'-th'-field had made prize of the said servant and six fine saddle-horses in the stable : these we brought into the house, barred the doors, and bade the negro to put on his clothes ; and told the burgher what story he should tell to his captain. But when the gate was opened and the posts occupied, and our general of ordnance, Count von der Wahl, was admitted, he lodged his staff in the very house where we were. So in dark night we must needs seek other quarters ; and these we found with our comrades who had come in with the storming-parties : with them we made merry and spent the rest of the night in eating and drinking, when Jump-i'-th'-field and I had divided our booty. For my share I received the negro and the two best horses, of which one was a Spanish one, on which any soldier might meet his enemy, and with this thereafter I made no small show; but out of the portmanteau I got divers costly rings, and in a golden case set with rubies the Prince of Orange's portrait (for all the rest I left to Jump-i'-th'-field), so that the whole, it I had desired to give it away, would with the horses have stood me in 200 ducats : since for the negro, that was the poorest part of my booty, the Master-General of Ordnance to whom I presented him gave me two dozen thalers.

Thence we marched quickly to the Ems, yet accomplished but little : and as it happened that we came near Recklinghausen, I took leave, together with Jump-i'-th'-field, to speak with my pastor from whom I had stolen the bacon. With him I made merry and told him the negro had made me feel the same terror which he and his cook had felt, and presented him, moreover, with a fine striking watch for a friendly remembrance, which I had had out of the captain's portmanteau : and so did I take care to make friends in all places of them that would otherwise have had cause to hate me.

Chap. ix: OF AN UNEQUAL COMBAT IN WHICH THE WEAKEST WINS THE DAY AND THE CONQUEROR IS CAPTURED

BUT with my good fortune my pride so increased that in the end it could bring me nothing but a fall. For as we were encamped some half-hour from Rehnen, I had leave to go into the town with my dear comrade, there to have those arms furbished up which we had just received. And as it was our intent to be right merry with each other, we turned in to the best inn, and had minstrels sent for, to play our wine and beer down our throat. So we fell to drinking and roaring; and no sport was wanting, which could make the money fly: nay, I invited also lads from other regiments to be my guests, and so carried myself as a young prince who has command of land and folk and great sums to spend by the year. And thus we fared better than was pleasing to a company of troopers who sat there also at table, but with no such mad tricks as we. So, being angry, they began to jest upon us, "How comes it," said they to one another, "that these prop-hoppers* " (for they took us for musqueteers, seeing that no animal in the world is more like a musqueteer than is a dragoon, and if a dragoon fall from his horse he rises up a musqueteer) "can make such a show with their halfpence?" "Yonder lad," answered another, "is surely some straw-squire whose mother hath sent him the milk-pence, and those he now spends upon his comrades, that some time they may pull him out of the mud or through a ditch." With which words they aimed at me, for they took me for a young nobleman. Of such talk the maid that waited brought me private news: yet since I heard it not myself, I could do no more than fill a great beer-glass with wine and let it go round to the health of all good musqueteers, and at every round made such a hubbub that none could hear himself speak. And this vexed them yet more, so that they said aloud, "What in the devil's name have these prop-hoppers for an easy life of it!" Whereupon Jump-i'-th'-field answered, "And what matters that to the bootblacks?" This passed well enough; for he looked so big and held so fierce and threatening a carriage that no one cared to give him the rub. Yet he must again fall foul of them, and this time of a fellow of some consideration, who answered, "Ay, and if these loiterers could not so swagger here on their own dung-hill (for he thought we lay there in garrison, because our clothes seemed not so weather-beaten as those of the poor musqueteers who must lie day and night in open field), where could they show themselves? Who knows not that any of them in the battlefield is as surely the booty of the troopers as is the pigeon of the hawk?" But

* The musqueteer supported his piece on a prop or stake.

I answered him, " It is our business to take cities and fortresses, whereas ye troopers, if ye come but to the poorest
rat's-nest of a town, can there drive no dog out of his den.
Why may we not then have your good leave to make merry in
that which is more ours than yours ? "

The trooper answered, " Him who is master in the field
the fortresses must follow after : and that we troopers are
masters in the field is proved by this : that I for myself not
only fear not three such babes as thee, musquet and all, but
could stick a couple such in my hat-band, and then ask the
third where there were more to be found. And if I now sat
by thee," said he with scorn, " I would bestow on my young
squire a couple of buffets to prove the truth of this."

" Yea," said I, " and though I have as good a pair of
pistols as thou, notwithstanding I am no trooper, but only
a bastard between such and the musqueteers, yet, look you,
even a child hath heart enough to shew himself alone in open
field against such a bully on horseback as thou art, and
against all thine armoury."

" Aha ; thou swaggerer," said the fellow, " I hold thee
for a rascal if thou make not good thy words forthwith as
becomes an honourable nobleman "

So I threw him my glove and, " See then," said I, " if I get
this not from thee in fair field with my musquet only and on
foot, so hast thou right and good leave to hold and to reproach
me for such a one as thy presumption has even now named me."

Then we paid the reckoning and the trooper made ready
his carbine and pistols, and I my musquet : and as he rode
away with his comrades to the place agreed upon he told my
comrade Jump-i'-th'-field he might order my grave. So he
answered him he had better give it in charge to one of his
own fellows that he might order such for him. Yet thereafter
he rebuked me for my presumption, and said plainly he feared
I should now play my last tune. But I did but laugh, for I
had long since devised a plan how to encounter the best
mounted of troopers, if ever such an one should attack me
in the open field, though armed only with my musquet and
on foot. So when we came to the place where this beggar's
dance should be, I had my musquet already loaded with two
balls, and put in fresh priming and smeared the cover of the

pan with tallow as careful musqueteers be wont to do, to guard the touch-hole and powder in the pan from damp in rainy weather.

Before we engaged, our comrades on both sides agreed that we should fight in open field, and to that end that we should start, one from the East, the other from the West, in a fenced plot ; and thereafter each should do his best against the other as a soldier would do in face of the enemy ; and that no one should help either party before or during or after the fight, either to succour his comrade, or to avenge his death or hurt. So when they had thus engaged themselves with word and hand, I and my opposite gave each other our hand upon this, that each would forgive the other his death. In all which most unreasonable folly that ever a man of sense could entertain, each hoped to gain for his arm of the service the advantage, for all the world as if the entire honour and reputation of one or the other, depended upon the outcome of our devilish undertaking.

Now as I entered the stricken field at my appointed end with my match alight at both ends, and saw my adversary before my eyes, I made as if I shook out the old priming as I walked. Yet I did not so, but spread priming powder only on the cover of the pan, blew up my match, and passed my two fingers over the pan, as is the custom, and before I could see the white of the eyes of my opposite, who kept me well in sight, I took aim, and set fire to the false priming powder on the cover of the pan. Then the enemy, believing that my musquet had missed fire and that the touch-hole was stopped, rode straight down upon me pistol in hand, and all too anxious to pay me there and then for my presumption, but before he was aware I had the pan open and shut again, and gave him such a welcome that ball and fall came together.

Then I returned to my fellows, who received me with embraces ; but his comrades, freeing his foot from the stirrup, dealt with him and with us as honest fellows, for they returned me my glove with all praise. But even when I deemed my reputation to be at its height, came five-and-twenty musqueteers from Rehnen, who laid me and my comrades by the heels. Then presently I was clapped in chains and sent to headquarters, for all duels were forbidden on pain of death.

*Chap. x : HOW THE MASTER-GENERAL OF ORD-
NANCE GRANTED THE HUNTSMAN HIS
LIFE AND HELD OUT HOPES TO HIM OF
GREAT THINGS*

NOW as our General of Ordnance was wont to keep strict discipline, I looked to lose my head : yet had I hopes to escape, because I had at so early an age ever carried myself well against the enemy, and gained great name and fame for courage. Yet was this hope uncertain because, by reason of such things happening daily, 'twas necessary to make an example. Our men had but just beat up a dangerous nest of rats, and demanded a surrender, yet had received a denial ; for the enemy knew we had no heavy artillery. For that reason Count von der Wahl appeared with all our force before the said place, demanded a surrender once more by a trumpeter, and threatened to storm the town. Yet all he got thereby was the writing that here followeth :

" High and well-born Count, &c.,—From your Excellency's letter to me I understand what you suggest to me in the name of his Imperial Roman Majesty. Now your Excellency, with his great understanding, must be well aware how improper, nay unjustifiable, it were for a soldier to surrender a place like this to the adversary without especial necessity. For which reason your Excellency will not, I hope, blame me if I wait till his means of attack are sufficient. But if your Excellency have occasion to employ my small powers in any services but those touching my allegiance, I shall ever be,
    " Your Excellency's most obedient servant,
                                    " N. N."

Thereupon was much discussion in our camp about this place ; for to leave it alone was not to be thought on : to storm it without a breach would have cost much blood, and 'twould have been uncertain even then whether we should succeed or not : and if we had to fetch our heavy pieces and all their equipment from Münster and Ham, 'twould cost much time, trouble, and expense. So while great and small were hard at work a-reasoning, it came into my head that I should use this opportunity to get free : so I set all my wits to work, and reflected how one might cheat the enemy, seeing 'twas only the cannon that were wanted. And pretty soon I had devised a trick and let my lieutenant-colonel know I had plans by which the place could be secured without trouble and expense, if only I could be pardoned and set free. Yet some old and tried soldiers laughed and said, " Drowning men catch at straws ; and this good fellow thinks to talk himself out of gaol."

But the lieutenant-colonel himself, with others that knew me, listened to my words as to an article of belief ; wherefore he went himself to the Master-General of the Ordnance and laid before him my plan, with the recital, moreover, of many things that he could tell of me : and inasmuch as the Count had already heard of the Huntsman, he had me brought before him and for so long loosed from my bonds. He was set at table when I came, and my lieutenant-colonel told him how the spring before, having stood my first hour as sentry under St. James's Gate at Soest, a heavy rain with thunder and wind had suddenly come on, and when, each running from the fields and the gardens into the town, there was great press of foot and horse, I had had the wit to call out the guard, because in such a tumult a town was easiest to take. " At last," said the lieutenant-colonel further, " came an old woman dripping wet, and said even as she passed by the huntsman, ' Yea, I have felt this storm in my back for a fortnight.' So the huntsman, hearing this and having a rod in his hand, smote her with it over the shoulder, and says he, ' Thou old witch, couldst thou not let it loose before ; must thou wait till I stood sentry ? ' And when his officer rebuked him he answered, ' She is rightly served : the old carrion crow had heard a month ago how all were crying out for rain : why did she not let honest folk have it before ? It had been better for the barley and hops.' "

At this the general, though he was in general a stern man, laughed heartily ; but I thought, " If the colonel tell him of such fool's tricks, surely he will not have failed to speak of my other devices." So I was brought in, and when the general asked what was my plan I answered, " Gracious sir, although my fault and your Excellency's order and prohibition do both deny me my life, yet my most humble loyalty, which is due from me towards his Imperial Majesty, my most gracious Lord, even to the death, bids me so far as lies in my weak power yet do the enemy a damage, and further the interests and arms of his Majesty." So the general cut me short, and says he, " Didst thou not lately give me the negro ? " " Yea, gracious sir," said I. Then said he, " Well, thy zeal and loyalty might perhaps serve to spare thy life : but what plan hast thou to bring the enemy out of this place without great loss in time and men ? " So I answered, " Since the town cannot resist heavy artillery, my humble opinion is that the enemy would soon come to terms if he did but really believe we had such pieces." " That," said the general, " a fool could have told me ; but who will persuade them so to believe ? " Then I answered, " Thine own eyes ; I have examined their Mainguard with a perspective-glass and it can be easily deceived ; if we did but set a few baulks of timber, shaped like water-pipes, on waggons, and haul them into the field with many horses, they will certainly believe they are heavy pieces, specially if your Excellency will order works to be thrown up about the field as if to plant cannon there." " My dear little friend," answered the Count, " they be not children in the town : they will not believe this panto-mime, but will require to hear thy guns ; and if the trick fail," says he to the officers that stood around, " we shall be mocked of all the world." But I answered, " Gracious sir, an I can but have a pair of double musquets and a pretty large cask, I will make them to hear great guns : only beyond the sound there can be no further effect : but if against all expectation naught but mockery ensue, then shall I, the inventor, that must in any case die, take with me that mockery and purge it away with my life."

Yet the general liked it not, but my colonel persuaded him to it ; for he said I was in such cases so lucky that he doubted not this trick would succeed : so the Count ordered him to settle the matter as he thought it could best be done, and said to him in jest that the honour he should gain thereby should be reckoned to him alone.

So three such baulks were brought to hand, and before each were harnessed four-and-twenty horses, though two had been sufficient : and these towards evening we brought up in full sight of the foe : and meanwhile I had gotten me three double musquets and a great cask from a mansion near at hand, and set all in order as I would have it : and by night this was added to our fool's artillery. The double musquets I charged twice over and had them discharged through the said cask, of which the bottom had been knocked out, as if it was three trial shots being fired. Which sounded so thunderously that any man had sworn they were great serpents or demi-culverins. Our general must needs laugh at such trickery, and again offered the enemy terms, with the addition that if they did not agree that same evening it would not go so easily with them the next day. Thereupon hostages were exchanged and terms arranged, and the same night one gate of the town put into our hands, and this was well indeed for me : for the Count not only granted me my life that by his order I had forfeited, but set me free the same night and commanded the lieutenant-colonel in my presence to appoint me to the first ensigncy that should fall vacant : which was not to his taste (for he had cousins and kinsman many in waiting) that I should be promoted before them.

Chap. xi : CONTAINS ALL MANNER OF MATTERS OF LITTLE IMPORT AND GREAT IMAGINA-TION

ON this expedition nothing more of note happened to me : but when I came again to Soest I found the Hessians from Lippstadt had captured my servant that I had left to guard my baggage, together with one horse that was at pasture. From my servant the enemy learned of my ways and works, and therefore held me higher than before, as having been persuaded by common report I was but a sorcerer. He told them, moreover, he had been one of the devils that had so dismayed the Hunts-man of Wesel in the sheep-fold : which when the said hunts-man heard of, he was so shamed that he took to his heels again and fled from Lippstadt to the Hollanders. But it was my greatest good fortune that this servant of mine was taken, as will be seen in the sequel.

Now I began to behave myself somewhat more reputably than before, as having such fine hopes of presently being made ensign : so by degrees I joined company with officers and young noblemen that were eager for that office which I imagined I should soon get : for this reason these were my worst enemies, and yet gave themselves out to be my best friends : even the lieutenant-colonel was no longer so good to me ; for he had orders to promote me before his own kindred. My captain was my enemy because I made a better show in horses, clothing, and arms than he, and no longer spent so much on the old miser as before. He had rather have seen my head hewn off than an ensigncy promised me ; for he had thought to inherit my fine horses. In like manner my lieutenant hated me for a single word that I had lately without thought let slip : which came about thus : we two were on the last expedition ordered to a lonely post as vedettes : and as the turn to watch fell to me (which must be done lying down, besides that it was a pitch-dark night), the lieutenant comes to me creeping on his belly like a snake, and says he, " Sentry, dost thou mark aught ? " So I answered, " Yea, Herr Lieutenant." And " What ? what ? " says he. I answered, " I mark that your honour is afeared." And from thenceforward I had no more favour with him. Wherever the danger was greatest thither was I sent first of all : yea, he sought in all places and at all times to dust my jacket before I became ensign, and so could not defend myself. Nor were the sergeants less my enemies, because I was preferred to them all. And as to the privates, they too began to fail in their love and friendship to me, because it seemed I despised them, inasmuch as I no longer consorted specially with them but, as aforesaid, with greater Jacks, which loved me none the more.

But the worst was that no man told me how each was minded towards me, and so I could not perceive it, for many a one talked with me in friendliest wise that had sooner seen me dead. So I lived like a blind man in all security and became ever haughtier : and though I knew it vexed this one and that if I made a greater show than noblemen and officers of rank, yet I held not back. I feared not to wear a collar of sixty rix-dollars, red-scarlet hose, and white satin sleeves, trimmed all over with gold, which was at that time the dress of the highest officers : and therefore an eyesore to all. Yet was I a terrible young fool so to play the lord : for had I dealt otherwise and bestowed the money I so uselessly did hang upon my body in proper ways, I should have soon gained my ensigncy and also not have made so many enemies. Yet I stopped not here, but decked out my best horse, which Jump-i'-th'-field had gotten from the Hessian captain, with saddle, bridle, and arms in such fashion that when I was mounted one might well have taken me for another St. George. And nothing grieved me more than to know I was no nobleman, and so could not clothe my servant and my horse-boys in my livery. Yet, I thought, all things have their beginning ; if thou hast a coat-of-arms then canst thou have thine own livery ; and when thou art an ensign, thou must have a signet-ring, though thou art no nobleman. I was not long pregnant with these thoughts, but had a coat-of-arms devised for me by a herald, which was three red masks in a white field, and for a crest, a bust of a young jester in a calfskin with a pair of hare's ears, adorned with little balls in front : for I thought this suited best with my name, being called Simplicissimus. And so would I have the fool to remind me in my future high estate what manner of fellow I had been in Hanau, lest I should become too proud, for already I thought no small things of myself. And so was I properly the first of my name and race and escutcheon, and if any had jeered at me thereupon, I had without doubt presented him a sword or a pair of pistols. And though I had yet no thoughts of womenkind, yet all the same I went with the young nobles when they visited young ladies, of whom there were many in the town, to let myself be seen and to make a show with my fine hair, clothes, and plumes. I must confess that for the sake of my figure I was preferred before all, yet must I all the same hear how the spoilt baggages compared me with a fair and well-cut statue in which, beside its beauty, was neither strength nor sap ; for that was all they desired in me : and except the lute-playing there was nothing I could do or perform to please them : for of love as yet I knew nothing. But when they that knew how to pay their court would gibe at me for my wooden behaviour and awkwardness, to make themselves more beloved and to show off their ready speech, then would I answer, 'twas enough for me if I could still find my pleasure in a bright sword or a good musquet, and the ladies held me right : and this angered the gentlemen so that they secretly swore to have my life, though there was none that had heart enough to challenge me or give me cause enough to challenge one of them, for which a couple of buffets or any insulting word had been sufficient ; and I gave every chance for this by my loose talk, from which the ladies argued I must be a lad of mettle, and said openly my figure and my noble heart could plead better with any lady than all the compliments that Cupid ever devised : and that made the rest angrier than ever.

Chap. xii : HOW FORTUNE UNEXPECTEDLY BE-
STOWED ON THE HUNTSMAN A NOBLE
PRESENT

I HAD two fine horses that were at that time all the joy I had in the world. Every day I rode them in the riding-school or else for amusement, if I had naught else to do ; not indeed that the horses had anything to learn, but I did it that people might see that the fine creatures belonged to me. And when I went pranking down a street, or rather the horse prancing under me, and the stupid multitude looking on and saying, " Look, 'tis the huntsman ! See what a fine horse ! Ah, what a handsome plume ! " or " Zounds ! what a fine fellow is this ! " I pricked up mine ears and was as pleased as if the Queen of Sheba had likened me to Solomon in all his glory. Yet, fool that I was, I heard not what perhaps at that time wise folk thought of me or mine enviers said of me : these last doubtless wished I might break my neck, since they could not do it for me : and others assuredly thought that if all men had their own I could not practise such foolish swaggering. In a word, the wisest must have held me without doubt for a young Colin Clout, whose pride would certainly not last long, because it stood upon a bad foundation and must be supported only by uncertain plunder. And if I must confess the truth, I must grant that these last judged not amiss, though then I understood it not, for 'twas this and only this with me : that I would have made his shirt warm for any man or adversary that had to deal with me, so that I might well have passed for a simple, good soldier though I was but a child. But 'twas this cause made me so great a man, that nowadays the veriest horse-boy can shoot the greatest hero in the world ; and had not gunpowder been invented I must have put my pride in my pocket.

Now 'twas my custom in these rides to examine all ways and paths, all ditches, marshes, thickets, hills and streams, make myself acquainted with them and fix them in my memory, so that if one ever had occasion to skirmish with the enemy I might employ the advantage of the place both for defence and offence. To this end I rode once not far from the town by an old ruin where formerly a house had stood. At the first sight I thought this were a fit place to lay an ambush or to retreat to, specially for us dragoons if we should be outnumbered and chased by cavalry. So I rode into the courtyard, whose walls were pretty well ruined, to see if at a pinch one could take refuge there on horseback and how one could defend it on foot. But when to this end I would view all exactly and sought to ride by the cellar, the walls of which were still standing, I could neither with kindness nor force bring my horse, which commonly feared nought, to go where I would. I spurred him till I was vexed, but it availed not : so I dismounted and led him by the bridle down the ruined steps which he had shied at, so that I should know how to act another time : but he backed as much as he could ; yet at length with gentle words and strokings I had him down, and while I patted and caressed him I found that he was sweating with fear, and ever staring into one corner of the cellar, into which he would by no means go, and in which I could see naught at which the most skittish beast could shy. But as I stood there full of wonder and looked upon my horse all a-tremble with fear, there came on me also such a terror that 'twas even as if I was dragged upwards by the hair and a bucket of cold water poured down my back ; yet could I see nothing ; but the horse acted more and more strangely, till I could fancy nothing else but that I was perhaps bewitched, horse and all, and should come by my end in that same cellar. So I would fain go back, but the horse would not follow, and thereat I grew more dismayed and so confused that in truth I knew not what I did. At last I took a pistol in my hand, and tied the horse to a strong elder-tree that grew in the cellar, intending to go forth and find people near by that could help to fetch the horse out ; but as I was about this it came into my head that perchance some treasure lay hid in this old ruin, which was therefore haunted. To this conceit I gave heed, and looked round more exactly. And just in the place to which my horse refused to go I was ware of a part of the wall, unlike the rest both in colour and masonry, and about the bigness of a common chamber-shutter. But when I would approach 'twas with me as before, namely, that my hair stood on end ; and this strengthened my belief that a treasure must there be hid.

Ten times, nay a hundred times, sooner would I have exchanged shots with an enemy than have found myself in such a terror. I was plagued and knew not by what : for I heard and saw naught. So I took the other pistol from the holster as meaning with it to go off and leave the horse, yet could I not again mount the steps, for as it seemed to me a strong draught of wind kept me back ; and now I felt my flesh creep indeed. At last it came into my mind to fire the pistols that the peasants that worked in the fields close by might run to the spot and help me with word and deed. And this I did because I neither knew nor could think of any other means to escape from this evil place of wonders : and I was so enraged, or rather so desperate (for I knew not myself how 'twas with me), that as I fired I aimed my pistols at the very place wherein I believed the cause of my plight lay, and with both balls I hit the before-mentioned piece of the wall so hard that they made a hole wherein a man could set both his fists. Now no sooner had I fired than my horse neighed and pricked up his ears, which heartily rejoiced me : I knew not whether 'twas because the goblin or spectre had vanished or because the poor beast was roused by the noise of fire-arms, but 'tis certain I plucked up heart again and went without hindrance or fear to the hole, which I had just opened by the shot ; and there I began to break down the wall completely, and found of silver, gold, and jewels so rich a treasure as would have kept me in comfort to this day, if I had but known how to keep it and dispose of it well. There were six dozen old French silver table-tankards, a great gold cup, some double tankards, four silver and one golden salt-cellar, one old French golden chain, and divers diamonds, rubies, emeralds, and sapphires set in rings and in other jewellery ; also a whole casquet full of pearls, but all spoiled or discoloured, and then in a mouldy leather bag eighty of the oldest Joachim dollars of fine silver, likewise 893 gold pieces with the French arms and an eagle, a coin which none could recognise, because, as folks said, no one could read the inscription. This money, with the rings and jewels, I strapped into my breeches-pockets, my boots and my holsters, and because I had no bag with me, since I had but ridden forth for pleasure, I cut the housing from my saddle, and into it I packed the silver vessels (for 'twas lined, and would serve me well as a sack), hung the golden chain round my neck, mounted my horse joyfully, and rode towards my quarters. But as I came out of the courtyard I was aware of two peasants, that would have run as soon as they saw me ; yet having six feet and level country I easily overtook them, and asked why they would have fled and were so terribly afeared. So they said they had thought I was the ghost that dwelt in that deserted court, and if any came too near to him was wont to mishandle them miserably. Then as I asked further of his ways, they told me that for fear of this monster 'twas often many years that no one came near that place, save some stranger that had lost his way and came thither by chance. The story went, they said, that an iron trough full of money lay within guarded by a black dog, and also a maiden that had a curse upon her ; and to follow the old story they had themselves heard from their grandsires, there should come into the land a stranger nobleman that knew neither his father nor mother, and should rescue the maiden, and open the trough with a key of fire, and carry off the hidden gold. And of such foolish fables they told me many more ; but because they are but ill to hear, I here cut them short for briefness. Thereafter I did ask them what they too had been about,

since at other times they dared not go into the ruin. They
answered they had heard a shot and a loud cry ; and had run
up to see what was to do. But when I told them 'twas I that
shot in the hope that people would come into the ruin, because
I too was pretty much afeared, but knew nought of any cry,
they answered, " There might be shots enough heard in that
castle before any of our neighbourhood would come thither ;
for in truth 'tis so ghostly beset that we had not believed my
lord if he had said he had been therein, an we had not ourselves
seen him ride out thence."

So then they would know many things of me, especially what
manner of place it was within and whether I had not seen the
damsel and the black dog sitting on the iron trough, so that
if I had desired to brag I could have put strange fancies into
their heads . but I said not the least word, not even that I
had gotten the costly treasure, but rode away to my quarters
and looked upon my find, which mightily delighted me.

Chap. xiii : OF SIMPLICISSIMUS' STRANGE FANCIES AND CASTLES IN THE AIR, AND HOW HE GUARDED HIS TREASURE

NOW they that know the worth of money, and there
fore take it for their god, have no little reason on
their side ; for if there be a man in the world that
hath experienced its powers and wellnigh divine
virtues, that man am I. For I know how a man fares that hath
a fair provision thereof ; yet have I never yet known how he
should feel that had never a farthing in his pouch. Yea, I could
even take upon me to prove that this same money possesses
all virtues and powers more than any precious stones ; for it
can drive away all melancholia like the diamond : it causeth
love and inclination to study, like the emerald (for so comes
it that commonly students have more money than poor folk's
children) : it taketh away fear and maketh man joyful and
happy like unto the ruby : 'tis often an hindrance to sleep,
like the garnet : on the other hand, it hath great power to
produce repose of mind and so sleep, like the jacinth : it
strengtheneth the heart and maketh a man jolly and com-

panionable, lively and kind, like the sapphire and amethyst : it driveth away bad dreams, giveth joy, sharpeneth the understanding, and if one have a plaint against another it gaineth him the victory, like the sardius (and in especial if the judge's palm be first well oiled therewith) : it quencheth unchaste desire, for by means of gold one can possess fair women : and in a word, 'tis not to be exprest what gold can do, as I have before set forth in my book intituled " Black and White," if any man know how rightly to use and employ this information. As to mine own money that I had then brought together, both with robbery and the finding of this treasure, it had a special power of its own : for first of all it made me prouder than I was before, so much so that it vexed me to the heart that I must still be called " Simplicissimus " only. It spoiled my sleep like the amethyst : for many a night I lay awake and did speculate how I could put it out to advantage and get more to put to it. Yea, and it made me a most perfect reckoner, for I must calculate what mine uncoined silver and gold might be worth, and adding this to that which I had borrowed here and there, and which yet was in my purse, I found without the precious stones a fine overplus. Yet did my money prove to me its inborn roguery and evil inclination to temptation, inasmuch as it did fully expound to me the proverb " He that hath much will ever have more," and made me so miserly that any man might well have hated me. From my money I got many foolish plans and strange fancies in my brain, and yet could follow out no conceit of all that I devised. At one time I thought I would leave the wars and betake myself somewhither and spend my days in fatness a-looking out of the window ; but quickly I did repent me of that, and in especial because I considered what a free life I now led and what hopes I had to becone a great Jack. And then my thought was this, " Up and away, Simplicissimus, and get thyself made a nobleman and raise thine own company of dragoons for the emperor at thine own cost : and presently thou art a perfected young lord that with the times can rise yet higher." Yet as soon as I reflected that this my greatness could be made small by any unlucky engagement, or be ended by a peace that should bring the war soon to a finish, I could not find this plan to my taste. So then I began to wish I had my full age as a man : for hadst thou that, said I to myself, thou couldst take a rich young wife, and so buy thee a nobleman's estate somewhere and lead a peaceful life. There would I betake myself to the rearing of cattle and enjoy my sufficiency to the full : yet as I knew I was too young for this, I must let that plan go by the board also.

Such and the like conceits had I many, till at last I resolved to give over my best effects to some man of substance in some safe town to keep, and to wait how fortune would further deal with me. Now at that time I had my Jupiter still with me : for indeed I could not be rid of him : and at times the man could talk most reasonably and for weeks together would be sane and sober : but above all things he held me dear for my goodness to him ; and seeing me in deep thought he says to me, " Dear son, give away your blood-money ; gold, silver, and all." " And why ? " said I, " dear Jupiter ? " " Oh," says he, " to get you friends and be rid of your useless cares." To which I answered, " I would fain have more of such." Then says he, " Get more : but in such fashion will ye never in your life have more friends nor more peace : leave it to old misers to be greedy, but do ye so behave as becomes a fine young lad : for ye shall sooner lack good friends than good money."

So I pondered on the matter, and found that Jupiter reasoned well of the case : yet greed had such hold on me that I could not resolve to give away aught. Yet I did at last present to the commandant a pair of silver-gilt double tankards and to my captain a couple of silver salt-cellars, by which I achieved nothing more than to make their mouths water for the rest : for these were rare pieces of antiquity. My true comrade Jump-i'-th'-field I rewarded with twelve rix-dollars ; who in return advised me I should either make away with my riches or else expect to fall into misfortune by their means : for, said he, it liked the officers not that a common soldier should have more money than they : and he himself had known this : that one comrade should secretly murder another for the sake of money : till now, said he, I had been able to keep secret what I had gotten in booty, for all believed I had spent it on clothes, horses, and arms : but now I could conceal nought nor make folks believe I had no secret store of money : for each one made out the treasure I had found to be greater than it was : and yet I spent not so much as before. Nor could he help but hear what rumours went about among the men : and were he in my place he would let wars be wars : would settle himself in safety somewhere, and let our Lord God rule the world as He will. But I answered, " Harkye, brother, how can I throw to the winds my hopes of an ensigncy ? " " Yea, yea," says Jump-i'-th'-field, " but devil take me if thou ever get thine ensigncy. The others that wait for it would help to break thy neck a thousand times over if they saw that such a post was vacant and thou to have it. Teach me not how to know salmon from trout, for my father was a fisherman ! And be not angry with me, brother, for I have seen how it fares in war longer than thou. Seest thou not how many a sergeant grows grey with his spontoon that deserved to have a company before many others. Thinkest thou they are not fellows that have some right to hope ? And indeed they have more right to such promotion than thou, as thou thyself must confess." Nor could I answer aught, for Jump-i'-th'-field did but speak the truth from an honest German heart, and flattered me not : yet must I bite my lip in secret : for I thought at that time mighty well of myself. Yet I weighed this speech and that of my Jupiter full carefully, and considered that I had no single natural-born friend that would help me in straits or would revenge my death open or secret. And I myself could see plain enough how it stood with me : yet neither my desire of honour nor of money would leave me : and still less my hope to become great, to leave the wars, and to be in peace ; nay, rather I held to my first plan ; and when a chance offered for Cologne, whither I, with some hundred dragoons was ordered to convoy certain carriers and waggons of merchandise from Münster, I packed up my treasure, took it with me, and gave it in charge to one of the first merchants of that city to be drawn out on production of an exact list of the things. Now it was seventy-four marks of uncoined silver, fifteen marks of gold, eighty Joachim dollars, and in a sealed casquet divers rings and jewels, which, with gold and precious stones, weighed eight and a half pounds in all, together with 893 ancient golden coins that were worth each a gold gulden and a half. With me I took my Jupiter, as he desired it, and had kinsfolk of repute in Cologne : to whom he boasted of the good turns I had done him and caused me to be received of them with great honour. Yet did he never cease to counsel me that I should bestow my money better and buy myself friends that would be of more service to me than money in my purse.

Chap. xiv : HOW THE HUNTSMAN WAS CAPTURED BY THE ENEMY

S O on the journey home I pondered much how I should carry myself in future, so that I might get the favour of all : for Jump-i'-th'-field had put a troublesome flea in my ear, and had made me to believe I was envied of all : and in truth 'twas no otherwise. And now came into my mind what the famous prophetess of Soest had once said,* and so I burdened myself with yet greater cares. Yet with these thoughts did I sharpen my wit, and perceived that a man that should live without cares would be dull as any beast. Then I considered for what reason one and the other might hate me, and how I might deal with each to have his goodwill again, yet most of all must I wonder how men could be so false and yet give me nought but good words whereas they loved me not. For that cause I determined to deal as others did, and to say what would please each, yea, to approach every man with respect though I felt it not : for most of all I felt 'twas mine own pride had burdened me with the most enemies. Therefore I held it needful to shew myself humble again, though I was not, and to consort again with common folk, but to approach my betters hat in hand and to refrain from all finery in dress till my rank should be bettered. From the merchant in Cologne I had drawn 100 dollars, to repay the same with interest when he should return my treasure : these hundred dollars I was minded to spend on the way for the behoof of the escort, as now perceiving that greed makes no friends, and therefore was resolved on this very journey to alter my ways and make a new beginning. Yet did I reckon without mine host ; for as we would pass through the duchy

* See chap. iii.

of Berg there waited for us in a post of vantage eighty musqueteers and fifty troopers, even when I was ordered forward
with four others and a corporal to ride in front and to spy
out the road. So the enemy kept quiet when we came into the
ambush and let us pass, lest if they had attacked us the convoy
should be warned before they came into the pass where they
were : but after us they sent a cornet and eight troopers that
kept us in sight till their people had attacked our escort itself,
and we turned round to protect the waggons : at which they
rode down upon us and asked, would we have quarter. Now
for my part I was well mounted : for I had my best horse under
me : yet would I not run, but rode up a little hillock to see if
honour was to be had by fighting. Yet I was presently aware,
by the noise of the volley that our people received, what
o'clock it was, and so disposed myself to flight. But the cornet
had thought of all, and already cut off our retreat, and as I
was preparing to cut my way through he once again offered
me quarter, for he thought me an officer. So I considered
that to make sure of one's life is better than an uncertain
hazard, and therefore asked, would he keep his promise of
quarter as an honest soldier : he answered, " Yes, honestly."
So I presented him my sword and rendered myself up a
prisoner. At once he asked me of what condition I was : for
he took me for a nobleman and therefore an officer. But when
I answered him, I was called the Huntsman of Soest, " Then
art thou lucky," says he, " that thou didst not fall into our
hands a month ago : for then could I have given thee no
quarter, since then thou wast commonly held among our
people for a declared sorcerer."

This cornet was a fine young cavalier and not more than
two years older than I, and was mightily proud to have the
honour of taking the famous huntsman : therefore he observed
the promised quarter very honourably and in Dutch fashion,
which is to take from the Spanish prisoners of war nothing
that they carry under their belt : nay, he did not even have
me searched ; but I had wit enough to take the money out of
my pockets and present it to him when they came to a division
of spoils ; and also I told the cornet secretly to look to it that
he got as his share my horse, saddle, and harness, for he would
find thirty ducats in the saddle, and the horse had hardly his

equal anywhere. And for this cause the cornet was as much my friend as if I had been his own brother : for at once he mounted my horse and set me on his own. But of the escort no more than six were dead, and thirteen prisoners, of whom eight were wounded : the rest fled and had not heart enough to retake the booty from the enemy in fair field, the which they could have done, as being all mounted men against infantry.

Now when the plunder and the prisoners had been shared, the Swedes and Hessians (for they were from different garrisons) separated the same evening. But the cornet kept me and the corporal, together with three other dragoons, as his share because he had captured us : and so were we brought to a fortress which lay but a few miles from our own garrison.* And inasmuch as I had raised plenty of smoke in that town before, my name was there well known and I myself more feared than loved. So when we had the place in sight the cornet sent a trooper in advance to announce his coming to the commandant, and to tell him how he had fared and who the prisoners were, whereat there was a concourse in the town that was not to be described, for each would fain see the huntsman. One said this of me, and another that ; and the sight was for all the world as if some great potentate had made his entry. But we prisoners were brought straight to the commandant, who was much amazed at my youth ; and asked, had I never served on the Swedish side, and of what country I was : and when I told him the truth he would know if I had no desire to serve again on their side. I answered him that in other respects 'twas to me indifferent : but that I had sworn an oath to the emperor and therefore methought 'twas my duty to keep such. Thereupon he ordered us to be taken to the prize-master, but allowed the cornet, at his request, to treat us as his guests, because I had before so treated mine own prisoners and among them his own brother. So when evening was come there was a gathering both of soldiers of fortune and cavaliers of birth at the cornet's quarters, who sent for me and the corporal : and there was I, to speak the truth, extraordinary courteously entreated by them. I made merry as if I had lost nothing, and carried myself as confidently

* viz. Lippstadt.

and open-hearted as I had been no prisoner in the hands of my enemy but among my best friends. Yet I shewed myself as modest as might be ; for I could well imagine that my behaviour would be noted to the commandant, which was so, as I afterwards learned.

Next day we prisoners, one after another, were brought before the regimental judge-advocate-general, who examined us, the corporal first, and me second. But as soon as I entered the room he was filled with wonder at my youth, and to cast it in my teeth, " My child," says he, " what have the Swedes done to thee that thou shouldst fight against them ? "

Now this angered me : for I had seen as young soldiers among them as I was : so I answered, " The Swedes had robbed me of my coral and bells and my baby's rattle, and I would have them back." And as I thus paid him back in his own coin, the officers that sat by him were shamed, insomuch that one of them began to say to him in Latin he should treat me seriously, for he could hear that it was no child that he had before him. In that I was ware that his name was Eusebius ; for the officer so addressed him. So presently when he had asked my name, and I had told him, " There is no devil in hell," says he, " that is called Simplicissimus." " Nay," answered I, " and 'tis like there is none named Eusebius." And so I paid him back like our old muster-clerk Cyriack ; yet this pleased not the officers, who bade me remember I was their prisoner, and was not brought there to pass jests. At this reproof I blushed not, but answered : inasmuch as they held me prisoner like a soldier, and would not let me run away like a child, I had taken care that they should not make sport with me as with a child : as I had been questioned, so had I answered and hoped I had done no wrong therein. So they asked me of my country and my family, but especially if I had never served on the Swedish side : item, how it was with the garrison of Soest : how strong it was, and all the rest. To all which I answered quick and short and well, and in respect of Soest and its garrison as much as I could confidently state : yet I might well keep silence concerning my life as a jester, for of this I was ashamed.

Chap. xv : ON WHAT CONDITION THE HUNTSMAN
WAS SET FREE

MEANWHILE 'twas known at Soest how it had
fared with the convoy, how I and the corporal
had been captured and whither we had been
taken ; and therefore next day came a drummer
to fetch us back : whereupon the corporal and the three
others were delivered up, together with a letter to the following purport (for the commandant sent it to me to read) :

" Monsieur, etc.,—By the bearer, your tambour, your
message hath been delivered : and in answer thereto I restore
herewith, in return for ransom received, the corporal and the
three other prisoners : but as concerns Simplicissimus, called
the Huntsman, the same cannot be allowed to return, as
having once served on this side. But if I can serve your
honour in any matters short of those touching my allegiance,
you have in me a willing servant, and as such I remain,
" Your honour's obedient servant,
" [DANIEL] DE S[AINT] A[NDRE]." *

Now this letter did not half please me, yet I must return
thanks to him for suffering me to see it. But when I asked to
speak with the commandant I received answer he would himself
send for me as soon as he had despatched the drummer, which
should be done next morning : till then I must be patient.

So when I had waited the appointed time, the commandant
sent for me, and that just at dinner-time, and then for the
first time the honour fell to me of sitting at table with him.
And so long as the meal lasted he drank to my health and said
no word, great or small, of the business he had with me ; nor
was it my part to begin. But the meal now ended and I being
somewhat fuddled, says he, " My friend the Huntsman, ye
will have understood from my letter under what pretext I
have kept ye here : and indeed I intend no wrong or anything
contrary to reason and the usage of war, for yourself have
confessed to me and the judge-advocate that you once served

* The initials only of the name are given in the original.

on our side in the main army, and therefore must resolve yourself to take service under my command. And in time, if ye behave yourself well, I will so advance you as ye could never have hoped for among the Imperials, otherwise ye must not take it ill if I send you to that lieutenant-colonel from whom the dragoons before captured you." To which I answered, " Worshipful colonel " (for at that time 'twas not the usage that soldiers of fortune were entitled " your honour " even though they were colonels), " I hope, since I am bound by oath neither to the crown of Sweden nor its confederates, and still less to that lieutenant-colonel, that I am therefore not bound to take service with the Swedes and so to break the oath which I swore to the emperor, and therefore beg the worshipful colonel with all humility to be good enough to relieve me from such a proposal." " How ? " says the colonel, " do ye despise the Swedish service ? I would have you to know ye are my prisoner, and sooner than let you go to Soest to do the enemy service I will bring you to another trial, or let you rot in prison." And so, said he, I might lay my account.

Truly at these words I was afeared, yet would not yet give in, but answered, God would protect me both from such despiteful treatment and from perjury : for the rest, I persisted in my humble hope that the colonel would, according to his known reputation, deal with me as with a soldier. " Yea," said he, " I know well how I could treat ye if I would be strict ; but be ye better advised, lest I find cause to shew you other countenance." And with that I was led back to the prison.

And now can any man easily guess that I slept not much that night, but had all manner of thoughts : and next morning came certain officers with the cornet that had taken me, under colour of passing the time, but in truth to tell me that the colonel was minded to have me tried as a sorcerer if I would not otherwise be content. So would they have terrified me, and found out what my powers were : yet as I had the comfort of a good conscience, I took all coolly and said but little, as seeing well that the colonel cared for nothing but this : that he would fain have me no more at Soest. And well might he suppose that if he once let me go I should not leave that place, where I hoped for promotion, and moreover had two fine horses there and other things of price. Next day he had me brought to him again and asked, had I resolved otherwise. So I answered, " Colonel, to this I am determined, that I will sooner die than be perjured. Yet if the worshipful colonel will set me free and be pleased not to call upon me to do any warlike service, then will I promise him with heart, mouth, and hand to bear and use no arms against the Swedes and Hessians for the space of six months."

To that he agreed at once, gave me his hand upon it, and forgave me my ransom ; further, he commanded his secretary to draw up an agreement to that effect in duplicate, which we both subscribed, wherein he promised me protection and all freedom so long as I should remain in the fortress entrusted to him. On the other hand, I bound myself to the two points above named, videlicet : that I, so long as I should sojourn in the said fortress, would neither undertake anything to the hurt of the garrison and its commander, nor would conceal aught that was intended to their prejudice and damage, but would much more further their profit and benefit, and prevent any damage to them to the best of my ability—yea, that if the place were attacked I should and would help to defend it.

Thereupon he kept me to dine with him again, and shewed me more honour than I could in all my lifetime have looked for from the Imperials : and so by little and little he won me over, till I would not have returned to Soest even if he had let me go thither and had accounted me free from my promise.

Chap. xvi : HOW SIMPLICISSIMUS BECAME A NOBLEMAN

WHEN a thing is to be, all things shape themselves to that end. Now did I conceive that fortune had taken me to husband, or at least bound herself so close to me that the most contrary happenings must turn out to my profit : as when I learned at the commandant's table that my servant with my two fine horses had come from Soest. But I knew not (what at last I found) that tricky Fortune hath the siren's art, who do shew themselves kindest to those to whom they wish most harm, and so doth raise a man the higher but for this end : to cast him down the deeper. Now this servant, which I had before captured from the Swedes, was beyond measure true to me, who had done him great kindnesses. He therefore had saddled my two horses and rode out a good way from Soest to meet the drummer that should bring me back, that not only I might not have to walk so far, but also that I might not have to return to Soest naked or in rags : for he conceived I had been stripped. So when he met the drummer and the rest of the prisoners there he had my best clothing in a pack. But when he saw me not, but understood I was kept back to take service with the adversary, he set spurs to his horse and says he, " Adieu, tambours, and you too, Corporal : where my master is there will I be also," so he escaped and came to me at the very time when the commandant had set me free and was shewing me such great honour : who there-upon bestowed my horses in an inn till I could find for myself a lodging to my liking, and called me fortunate by reason of my servant's faith, yet wondered that I, as a common dragoon, and so young to boot, should possess such fine horses and be so well equipped ; nay, when I had taken leave and would go to my inn he praised one horse so loudly that I marked well he would fain have bought him from me. Yet because from modesty he ventured not to make a bid, I said if I might beg for the honour of his keeping the horse it was at his service. But he refused roundly, more because I was fairly tipsy, and he would not have the reproach of talking a present out of a drunken man, who might thereafter repent of it, than because he would not fain have had that noble horse.

That night I did consider how I would order my life in time to come ; and did decide to remain for the six months even where I was, and so in peace to spend the winter which was now at hand, for which I knew I had money enough for my purposes, without breaking into my treasure at Cologne. " In so long a time," thought I, " thou wilt be full grown and come to thy full strength, and so canst thou next spring take the field with more boldness among the emperor's troops."

Early next morning I reviewed my saddle, which was far better lined than the one I had presented to the cornet : and later on I had my horse led to the colonel's quarters and told him : as I had determined to spend the six months in which 'twas forbidden me to fight, peaceably and under the colonel's protection, here, my horses were of no use to me, which yet 'twere pity should be spoiled, and therefore begged him that he would consent to grant this charger here present a place among his own horses, and accept the same from me as a mark of grateful acknowledgment of favours received, and that without scruple. The colonel returned me thanks with great civility and very courteous offers of service, and the same afternoon sent me by his steward one fat ox alive, two fat pigs, a hogshead of wine, two hogsheads of beer, twelve cords of firewood ; all which he caused to be brought to me in front of my new lodging, which I had even now hired for half a year, and sent a message : that as he saw I was to live with him, and could easily conceive that I was at first ill-provided with victual, he had therefore sent me for household use a draught of wine and a joint of meat, together with the fuel to cook the same : with this in addition, that whereinsoever he could help me he would not fail. For which I returned thanks as civilly as I could : presented the steward with two ducats, and begged him to commend me to his master.

So when I saw I had gained such credit with the colonel for my liberality, I thought to earn praise also among the common folk, that none should take me for a mere malingerer : to that end I had my servant called before me in presence of my landlord, and " Friend Nicolas," said I, " thou hast shewn me more faithfulness than any master can expect from his servant ; but now, when I know not how to make it up to thee, as having no master and no leave to fight, wherefrom I might gain booty enough to reward thee as I would fain do, and in respect also of the peaceful life which I do intend henceforth to live, and therefore do need no servitor, I herewith give thee as thy pay the other horse, with saddle, harness and pistols, with the request that thou wouldst be content for the present to seek another master. And if I hereafter can serve thee in any way, do thou not fail to ask me." With that he kissed my hands and for tears could not speak, but would by no means have the horse, but held it better I should turn it into money to use for my maintenance. Yet at last I persuaded him to take it, after I had promised to take him again into my service so soon as I should need a man. At this parting my landlord was so moved that his eyes also filled with tears : and as my servant exalted me among the soldiers for this action, so did my landlord among the citizens.

As to the commandant, he held me for so determined a fellow that he would have ventured to build upon my word, since I did not only truly keep the oath I had sworn to the emperor, but in order to keep that other promise, which I had made to himself, with great strictness had rid myself of my fine horses, my arms, and my most faithful servant.

Chap xvii : HOW THE HUNTSMAN DISPOSED HIM-SELF TO PASS HIS SIX MONTHS : AND ALSO SOMEWHAT OF THE PROPHETESS

I DO think there is no man in the world that hath not a bee in his bonnet, for we be all men of one mould and by mine own fruits I can mark how others ripen. Oh coxcomb ! say you ; if thou beest a fool, thinkest thou others must be too ? Nay, that were to say too much : but this I maintain, that one man can hide his folly better than another. Nor is a man a fool because he hath foolish fantasies, for in youth we do all have the like : and he that lets those fantasies run loose is held to be a fool because others keep the fool concealed, and others do but shew the half of him. They that keep such whims under altogether be but peevish fellows, but they that now and then allow them (as time affords an opportunity) to shew their ears and put their heads out of window to get air lest they be choked, these I hold for the best and wisest men. Mine own fantasies I let forth only too far, as seeing myself so free and well provided with money ; so that I took me a lad whom I clothed as a nobleman's page, and that in the most fantastic colours, to wit, light brown bordered with yellow, which must be my livery, for so I fancied it : and he must wait upon me as if I were a nobleman and not until just before a common dragoon ; yea, and half a year before a poor horse-boy.

Now this, the first folly I committed in this town, though 'twas pretty gross, yet was remarked by none, much less blamed. But why ? The world is so full of such fooleries that none marks them now, nor laughs at them, nor wonders at them, for all are used to them. And so was I held for a wise and good soldier, and not for a fool only fit for baby's shoes. Then I bargained with my landlord for the feeding of my page and myself, and gave him, as payment on account, what the commandant had presented to me, as far as concerns food and fuel : but for the drink my page must keep the key, for I was very willing to give of such to all that visited me. And since I was neither citizen nor soldier, and therefore had no equals that were bound to keep me company, I consorted with both sides, and therefore daily found comrades enough ; and these I sent not away dry. Among the citizens I had most friendship with the organist, for music I loved and, without bragging, had an excellent voice which I had no mind to let rust : this man taught me how to compose, and to play better upon that instrument, as also upon the harp : on the lute I was already a master ; so I got me one of mine own and daily diverted myself with it. And when I was tired of music I would send for that furrier that had instructed me in the use of all arms in Paradise, and with him exercised myself to be yet more perfect. Also I obtained leave from the commandant that one of his artillerymen should instruct me in gunnery and something of artillery-practice for a proper reward. For the rest, I kept myself quiet and retired, so that people wondered, seeing how I, that had been used to plunder and bloodshed, now sat always over my books like a student.

But my host was the commandant's spy and my keeper, for well I noted that he reported to him all my ways and works ; but that suited me well enough, for of warfare I had never a thought, and if there was talk of it I behaved myself as I had never been a soldier, and was only there to perform my daily exercises, of which I but now made mention. 'Tis true I wished my six months at an end : yet could no man guess which side I would then serve. As often as I waited on the colonel he would have me to dine with him : and then at times the converse was so arranged that my intention might be known therefrom : but ever I answered so discreetly that none could know what I did mean. So once when he said to me, " How is't with ye, Huntsman ? Will ye not yet turn Swede ? An ensign of mine is dead yesterday," I made answer, " Worshipful colonel, seeing that it is but decent for a woman not to marry at once again after her husband's death, should I not also wait my six months ? " In such fashion I escaped every time, and gained the colonel's good will more and more ; so much so that he allowed me to take my walks both inside and outside the fortress : yea, at last I might hunt the hares, partridges, and birds, which was not permitted to his own soldiers. Likewise did I fish in the Lippe, and was so lucky at that, that it seemed as if I could conjure both fish and cray-fish out of the water. For this I caused to be made a rough hunting-suit only, in which I crept by night into the territory of Soest and collected my hidden treasures from here and there, and brought them to the said fortress, and so behaved as if I would for ever dwell among the Swedes.

By the same way came the prophetess of Soest to me and said, " Lookye, my son, did I not counsel thee well before that thou shouldst hide thy money outside the town of Soest ? I do assure thee 'tis thy greater good luck to have been cap-tured : for hadst thou returned to Soest, certain fellows that had sworn thy death, because thou wast preferred to them among the women, would have murdered thee in thy hunting." So I asked, " How could any be jealous of me, that meddled with women not at all ? " " Oh," says she, " of that opinion that thou art now, wilt thou not long remain : or the women will drive thee out of the country with mockery and shame. Thou hast ever laughed at me when I foretold thee aught : wouldest thou once more refuse to believe me if I told thee more ? Dost thou not find in the place where thou art better friends than in Soest ? I do swear to thee they hold thee only too dear, and that such exceeding love will turn to thy harm, if thou submit not to it." So I answered her, if she truly knew so much as she gave out, she should reveal to me how it stood with my parents and whether I should ever in my life come to them again : she should not be so dark in her sayings, but out with it in good German. Thereupon she said I might ask after my parents when my foster-father should meet me unawares, and lead my wet-nurse's daughter by a string : with that she laughed loud, and at the end said, she had of her own accord told to me more than to others that had begged it of her.

But as I began to jest upon her she quickly took herself away, after I had presented her with a few thalers ; for I had more silver coin than I could easily carry, having at that time a pretty sum of money and many rings and jewels of great price : for before this, whenever I heard of precious stones among the soldiers, or found such on expeditions or elsewhere, I bought them, and that for less than half the money they were worth. Such treasures did always cry aloud to me to let them be seen in public : and I did willingly obey, for being of a pretty proud temper, I made a show with my wealth and feared not to let mine host see it, who made it out to others as greater than it was. And they did wonder whence I had gathered it all together, it being well known that I had made deposit at Cologne of the treasure I had found, for the cornet had read the merchant's receipt when he took me prisoner.

Chap. xviii : HOW THE HUNTSMAN WENT A WOOING, AND MADE A TRADE OF IT

MY intent to learn artillery practice and fencing in these six months was good, and that I knew : yet 'twas not enough to protect me from idleness, which is the root of many evils, and especially ill for me because I had no one to command me. 'Tis true I sat industriously over books of all sorts, from which I learned much good : but a few came into my hands which were as good for me as grass for a sick dog. The incomparable "Arcadia," from which I sought to learn eloquence, was the first book that led me aside from good stories to books of love and from true history to romances of chivalry. Such sort of books I collected wherever I could, and when I found one I ceased not till I had read it through, though I should sit day and night over it. But these taught me, instead of eloquence, to practise lechery. Yet was such desire at no time so violent and strong that one could, with Seneca, call it a divine frenzy or, as it is described in Thomas Thomai's " Forest Garden," a serious sickness. For where I took a fancy there I had what I desired easily and without great trouble : and so had I no cause to complain as other wooers and lechers have had, which are chock full of fantastic thoughts, troubles, desires, secret pangs, anger, jealousy, revenge, madness, tears, bragging, threats and numberless other follies, and for sheer impatience wish for death. For I had money and was not too careful of it, and besides I had a fine voice, which daily I exercised with all manner of instruments. Instead of shewing my bodily skill in the dance, which I did never love, I did display it in fencing, engaging with my furrier : moreover, I had a fine smooth face, and did practise myself in a certain gracious amiableness, so that the women, even those that I did not greatly seek after, did of themselves run after me, and that more than I desired.

About this time came Martinmas : then with us Germans begins the eating and swilling, and that feast is full conscientiously observed till Shrovetide : so was I invited to different houses, both among the officers and burghers, to help eat the Martinmas goose. So 'twas that on such occasions I made acquaintance with the ladies. For my lute and my songs made all to look my way, and when they so looked, then was I ready to add such charming looks and actions to my new love-songs (which I did myself compose) that many a fair maid was befooled, and ere she knew it was in love with me. Yet lest I should be held for a curmudgeon I gave likewise two banquets, one for the officers and one for the chief citizens, by which means I gained me favour of both parties and an entry to their houses ; for I spared no expense in my entertainment. But all this was but for the sake of the sweet maids, and though I did not at once find what I sought with each and every one (for some there were that could deny me), yet I went often to these also, that so they might bring them that did shew me more favour than becomes modest maidens into no suspicion, but might believe that I visited these last also only for the sake of conversation. And so separately I persuaded each one to believe this of the others, and to think she was the only one that enjoyed my love. Just six I had that loved me well and I them in return : yet none possessed my heart or me alone : in one 'twas but the black eyes that pleased me ; in another the golden hair ; in a third a winning sweetness ; and in the others was also somewhat that the rest had not. But if I, besides these, also visited others, 'twas either for the cause I mentioned or because their acquaintance was new and strange to me, and in any case I refused and despised nothing, as not purposing always to remain in the same place. My page, which was an archrogue, had enough to do with carrying of love-letters back and forth, and knew how to keep his mouth shut and my loose ways so secret from one and the other that nought was discovered : in reward for which he had from the baggages many presents, which yet cost me most, seeing that I spent a little fortune on them, and could well say, " What is won with the drum is lost with the fife." All the same, I kept my affairs so secret that not one man in a hundred would have taken me for a rake, save only the priest, from whom I borrowed not so many good books as formerly.

Chap. xix : BY WHAT MEANS THE HUNTSMAN MADE FRIENDS, AND HOW HE WAS MOVED BY A SERMON

WHEN Fortune will cast a man down, she raiseth him first to the heights, and the good God doth faithfully warn every man before his fall. Such a warning had I, but would have none of it. For I was stiffly persuaded of this, that my fortune was so firmly founded that no mishap could cast me down, because all, and specially the commandant himself, wished me well ; those that he valued I won over by all manner of respect : his trusted servants I brought over to my side by presents, and with them perhaps more than with mine equals I did drink " Brotherhood " and swore to them everlasting faith and friendship : so, too, the common citizens and soldiers loved me because I had a friendly word for all. " What a kindly man," said they often, " is the huntsman ; he will talk with a child in the street, and hath a quarrel with no man ! "

If I had shot a hare or a few partridges I would send them to the kitchen of those whose friendship I sought, and also invited myself as a guest ; at which time I would always have a sup of wine (which was in that place very dear) brought thither also : yea, I would so contrive it that the whole cost would fall upon me. And when at such banquets I fell in converse with any, I had praise for all save myself, and managed so to feign humility as I had never known pride. So because I thus gained favour of all, and all thought much of me, I never conceived that any misfortune could encounter me, especially since my purse was still pretty well filled. Often I went to the oldest priest of the town, who lent me many books from his library : and when I brought one back then would he discourse of all manner of matters with me, for we became so familiar together that one could easily bear with the other. So when not only the Martinmas goose and the feast of pudding-broth were gone and over, but also the Christmas holidays, I presented to him for the New Year a bottle of Strassburg Branntwein, the which he, after Westphalian use, liked to sip with sugar-candy, and thereafter came to visit him, even as he was a-reading my " Joseph the Chaste," which my host without my knowledge had lent him. I did blush that my work should fall into the hands of so learned a man, especially because men hold that one is best known by what he writes. But he would have me to sit by him and praised my invention, yet blamed me that I had lingered so long over the love-story of Zuleika (which was Potiphar's wife). " Out of the abundance of the heart the mouth speaketh," said he moreover, " and if my friend had not known how it fares with a wooer's heart he could never so well have treated of this woman's passion or in so lively fashion pictured it."

I answered that what I had written was not mine own invention but extracted from other books to give me some practice in writing. " Yes, yes," says he, " of course I am pleased to believe it : yet may you be sure I know more of your honour than he conceives." At these words I was dismayed and thought, " Hath a little bird told thee ? " But he, seeing how I changed colour, went on to say, " Ye are lively and young, idle and handsome. Ye do live a careless life, and as I hear in all luxury : therefore do I beseech you in the Lord and exhort you to consider in what an evil case you stand : beware of the beast with the long hair, if you have any care for your happiness and health. Ye may perhaps say, ' How concerneth it the priest what I do or not ? ' (' Rightly guessed,' said I to myself) or, ' What right hath he to command me ? ' 'Tis true I have but the care of souls : but, sir, be assured that your temporal good, as that of my benefactor, is for mere Christian love as precious as if ye were mine own son. 'Tis ever a pity, and never can ye answer such a charge before your heavenly Father if ye do bury the talent He hath entrusted to you and leave to go to ruin that noble understanding which I do perceive in this your writing. My faithful and fatherly advice would be, ye should employ your youth and your means, which ye now do waste in such purposeless wise, to study, that some day ye may be helpful to God and man and yourself ; and let war alone, in which, as I do hear, ye have so great a delight ; and before ye get a shrewd knock and find the truth of that saying, ' Young soldiers make old beggars.' " This predication I listened to with great impatience, for I was not used to hear the like : yet I shewed not how I felt, lest I should forfeit my reputation for politeness, but thanked him much for his straightforwardness and promised him to reflect upon his advice : yet thought I within myself, what did it concern the priest how I ordered my life ; for just then I was at the height of my good fortune, and I could not do without those pleasures of dalliance I had once enjoyed. So is it ever with such warnings, when youth is unaccustomed to bit and bridle, and gallops hard away to meet destruction.

Chap. xx : HOW HE GAVE THE FAITHFUL PRIEST OTHER FISH TO FRY, TO CAUSE HIM TO FORGET HIS OWN HOGGISH LIFE

YET was I not so drowned in lust nor so dull as not to take care to keep all men's affection so long as I was minded to sojourn in that fortress, that is, till winter was over. And I knew well what trouble it might breed for a man if he should earn the ill will of the clergy, they being folk that in all nations, no matter of what

religion they be, enjoy great credit ; so I put on my considering cap, and the very next day I betook myself hot-foot to the
said pastor, and told him in fine words such a heap of lies,
how I had resolved to follow his advice, that he, as I could
see from his carriage, was heartily rejoiced thereat.

"Yea," said I, "up till this time, yea and in Soest also,
there was wanting for me nothing but such an angelic counsellor as I have found in your reverence. Were but the winter
over, or at least the weather better, so that I could travel
hence ! " And thereafter I begged him to assist me with his
advice as to which University I should attend. To that he
answered, himself had studied in Leyden, but he would counsel
to go to Geneva, for by my speech I must be from the High
Germany. " Jesus Maria ! " said I, " Geneva is farther from
my home than Leyden." " Can I believe mine ears ? " says
he, " 'tis plain your honour is a Papist ! Great Heavens, how
am I deceived ! " " How so, Pastor ? " said I, " must I be a
Papist because I will not to Geneva ? " " Nay," says he,
" but ye do call upon the name of Mary ! " " How," said I,
" is't not well for a Christian to name the mother of his
Redeemer ? " " True," says he, " yet would I counsel your
honour and beg of him as earnestly as I can to give honour to
God only and further to tell me plainly to what religion he
belongs, for I doubt much if he be Evangelical (though I have
seen him every Sunday in my church), inasmuch as at this
last Christmastide he came not to the table of the Lord
neither here nor in the Lutheran church." " Nay," said I,
" but your reverence knows well that I am a Christian : were
I not, I had not been so oft at the preaching : but for the rest,
I must confess that I follow neither Peter nor Paul, but do
believe simply all that the twelve articles of the Christian faith
do contain : nor will I bind myself to either party till one
or the other shall bring me by sufficient proofs to believe that
he, rather than the other, doth possess the one true religion of
salvation." Thereupon, " Now," says he, " do I truly, and
that for the first time, understand that ye have a true soldier's
spirit, to risk your life here, there and everywhere, since ye
can so live from day to day without religion or worship and
can so risk your hope of eternal salvation ! Great heaven,"
says he, " how can a mortal man, that must hereafter be damned

or saved, so defy all ? Your honour," says he, " was brought up in Hanau : hath he learned there no better Christianity than this ? Tell me, why do ye not follow in the footsteps of your parents in the pure religion of Christ, or why will ye not betake yourself to this our belief, of which the foundations be so plain both in Holy Writ and nature that neither Papist nor Lutheran * can ever upset them."

" Your reverence," I answered, " so say all of their own religion : yet which am I to believe ? Think ye 'tis so light a matter for me to entrust my soul's salvation to any one party that doth revile the other two and accuse them of false doctrine ? I pray you to consider, with impartial eyes, what Conrad Vetter and Johannes Nas have written against Luther, and also Luther against the Pope, but most of all what Spangenberg hath written against Francis of Assisi, which for hundreds of years hath been held for a holy and God-like man, and all this in print. To which party shall I betake myself when each says of the other that 'tis unclean, unclean ? Doth your reverence think I am wrong if I stay awhile till I have got me more understanding and know black from white ? Would any man counsel me to plunge in like a fly into hot soup ? Nay, nay, your reverence cannot upon his conscience do that ! Without question one religion must be right and the other two wrong : and if I should betake myself to one without ripe reflection I might choose the wrong as easily as the right, and so repent of my choice for all eternity. I will sooner keep off the roads altogether than take the wrong one : besides, there be yet other religions besides these here in Europe, as those of the Armenians, the Abyssinians, the Greeks, the Georgians, and so forth, and whichsoever I do choose, then must I with my fellow believers deny all the rest. But if your reverence will but play the part of Ananias for me and open mine eyes, I will with thankfulness follow him and take up that religion to which he belongs."

Thereupon, " Your honour," says he, " is in a great error : but I pray God to enlighten him and help him forth of the slough ; to which end I will hereafter so prove to him the truth of our Confession that the gates of hell shall not prevail against it." I answered I would await such with great anxiety:

* The pastor was ' Reformed ' (i.e. Calvinist).

yet in my heart I thought, " If thou trouble me no more anent my lecheries, I will be content with thy belief."

And so can the reader judge what a godless, wicked rogue I then was : for I did but give the good pastor fruitless trouble, that he might leave me undisturbed in my vicious life, and thinks I, " Before thou art ready with thy proofs I shall belike be where the pepper * grows."

Chap. xxi : HOW SIMPLICISSIMUS ALL UNAWARES WAS MADE A MARRIED MAN

NOW over against my lodging there dwelt a lieutenant-colonel on half-pay, and the same had a very fair daughter of noble carriage, whose acquaintance I had long desired to make. And though at the first she seemed not such an one as I could love and no other and cleave to her for ever, yet I took many a walk for her sake, and wasted many a loving look ; who yet was so carefully guarded against me that never once could I come to speak with her as I would have wished, neither might boldly accost her : for I had no acquaintance with her parents, and indeed they seemed far too high placed for a lad of such low descent as I deemed myself to be. At the most I could approach her in the going in and out of church, and then would I take opportunity to draw near and with great passion would heave out a couple of sighs, wherein I was a master, though all from a feigned heart. All which she, on the other hand, received so coldly that I must well believe she was not to be fooled like any small burgher's daughter : and the more I thought how hard 'twould be for me to compass her love, the hotter grew my desire for her.

But the lucky star which first brought me to her was even that one which the scholars wear at a certain season, in everlasting remembrance of how the three wise men were by such a star led to Bethlehem, and I took it for a good omen that such a star led me to her dwelling also. For her father sending for me, " Monsieur," says he, " that position of

* I.e. at the Antipodes : " at the other end of the world."

neutrality which you do hold between citizens and soldiers is the cause why I have invited you hither : for I have need of an impartial witness in a matter which I have to settle between two parties." With that I thought he had some wondrous great undertaking in hand, for papers and pens lay on the table : so I tendered him my services for all honourable ends, adding thereto that I should hold it for a great honour indeed if I were fortunate enough to do him service to his liking. Yet was the business nothing more than this (as is the usage in many places), to set up a kingdom, being as 'twas the Eve of the Three Kings : and my part was to see that all was well and truly performed and the offices distributed by lot without respect of persons. And for this weighty concern (at which his secretary also was present) my colonel must have wine and confectionery served, for he was a doughty drinker and 'twas already past the time for supper. So then must the secretary write, and I read out the names, and the young lady draw the lots while her parents looked on : and how it all happened I know not, but so I made my first acquaintance in that house : and they complaining greatly how tedious were the winter nights, gave me to understand I should, to make them pass more easily, often visit them of evenings, for otherwise they had no great pastime : which was indeed the very thing I had of long time desired.

So from that time forward (though for a while I must be on my good behaviour with the damsel) I began to play a new part, dancing on the limed twig and nibbling at the fool's bait till both the maid and her parents must needs believe I had swallowed the hook, though as yet I had not (by a long score) any serious intent. I spent all my day in arraying myself for the night (as witches used to do) : and the morrow in poring over books of love, composing from them amorous letters to my mistress, as if I dwelt a hundred leagues off or saw her but once in many years ; so at last I was become a familiar of the house, and my suit not frowned upon by her parents : nay, 'twas even proposed I should teach the daughter to play the lute. So there I had free entrance, not only by night but by day also, so that I could now alter my tune and no longer sing

" On the bat's back do I fly after sunset merrily,"

but did write a pretty enough ditty, in the which I lauded my good fortune which had granted me, after so many happy evenings, so many joyous days also wherein I could feast mine eyes on the charms of my beloved and be refreshed thereby : yet in the same song did bemoan my hard fate that made my nights so miserable and granted me not that I should spend the night, like the day, in sweet enjoyment : which, though it seemed somewhat bold, I sang to my love with adoring sighs and an enchanting melody, wherein the lute also bore its part and with me besought the maid that she would lend her aid to make my nights as happy as my days. To all which I had but a cold response : for 'twas a prudent maid and could at will give me a fitting answer to all my feigned transports, though I might devise them never so wisely. Yet was I shy of saying aught of matrimony : and if such were touched on in conversation, then would I make my speech brief and comprest. Of that my damsel's married sister took note, and therefore barred all access for me to my mistress, so that we might not be so often together as before : for she perceived her sister was deep in love with me, and that the business would not in such fashion end well.

There is no need to recount all the follies of my courtship, seeing that the books of love are full of such. It shall suffice for the gentle reader to know that at last I was bold to kiss my mistress, and thereafter to engage in other dalliance : which much desired advances I pursued with all manner of incitements, till at length I was admitted by her at night and laid myself by her side as naturally as if I were her own. And here, as every man knoweth what on such a merry tide is wont to happen, the reader may well suppose that I dealt dishonourably with the maiden. But no ; for all my purpose was defeated, and I found such resistance as I had never thought to find in any woman : for her intent was only for honourable marriage, and though I promised all that and with the most solemn oaths, yet would she grant me nothing before wedlock but only this, to lie by her : and there at length, quite worn out with disgust, I fell asleep. But presently thereafter was I rudely awoke : for at four o'clock of the morning there stood my colonel before my bed, a pistol in one hand and a torch in the other, and " Croat," he cries to

his servant, that stood by him also with a drawn sword,
" Croat, go fetch the parson as quick as may be ! " But I
awaking and seeing in what danger I lay, " Alas," thought I,
" make thy peace with God before this man make an end of
thee ! " And 'twas all green and yellow before mine eyes, and
I knew not whether I should open them or not.

" Thou lewd fellow ! " says he to me, " must I find thee thus
shaming of mine house ? Should I do thee wrong if I break the
neck of thee and of this baggage that hath been thine whore ?
Ah, thou beast, how can I refrain myself that I tear not thy
heart from thy body and hew it in pieces and cast it for the
dogs to eat ? " And with that he gnashed with his teeth and
rolled his eyes like a wild beast, I knowing not what to say
and my bedfellow able to do naught but weep : yet at last
I came to myself somewhat, and would have pleaded our
innocence ; but he bid me hold my peace, and now began
upon fresh matter, to wit, how he had trusted me as a very
different man and how I had repaid his trust with the worst
treachery in the world : and thereafter came in his lady wife
and began another brand-new sermon, till I would sooner have
lain in a hedge of thorns : nay, I believe she had not stayed
her speech for two hours or more had not the Croat returned
with the parson.

Now before he came I tried once or twice to arise : but the
colonel, with a fierce aspect, bade me lie still : and so I
was taught how little courage a fellow hath that is
caught on an ill errand, and how it fares with the heart of
a thief that hath broken a house and is captured yet having
stolen nothing. For I remember the good old days when,
if such a colonel and two such Croats had fallen foul of me,
I had made shift to put all three to flight : but now there I
lay like any malingerer and had not the heart to use my
tongue, let alone my fists.

" See, master parson," quoth my colonel, " the fair sight
to which I must perforce invite you, to be a witness of my
shame "—and hardly had he said the word in his accustomed tone when he began again to yell hundred devils and
thousand curses, till I could understand nothing of what he
said save of breaking of necks and washing of hands in blood ;
for he foamed at the mouth like a wild boar and demeaned

himself as if in truth he would take leave of his senses : I thinking every moment, " Now will he send a ball through thy head." Yet the good parson did his best to hinder him from any rash deed whereof he might repent him afterwards : for " How now ; Master Colonel," says he, " how now ! Give your own sound reason room to act, and bethink you of the old saying that to what is done and cannot be undone it behoves to give the handsomest name : for this fine young couple (which can hardly be matched in the land) be not the first, nor will be the last, to be overcome by the invincible power of love. The fault which they have committed (for a fault we must needs call it) may by themselves be easily repaired. I cannot indeed approve this way of matching : yet have these young folks deserved neither gallows nor wheel, nor hath the Herr Colonel any shame to expect if he will but keep secret and forgive this fault, which otherwise no man hath knowledge of, and so give his consent to their marriage and allow such marriage to be confirmed by public ceremony in church."

" What ? " says the colonel, " am I, instead of punishing them, to come to them cap in hand and make them my compliments ? Sooner would I when the day comes have them trussed up together and drowned in the Lippe ; nay, ye shall wed them here and that at once, for to this end I had ye fetcht : else will I wring the necks of both like hens."

But as to me, my thought was, " What wilt thou do ? Wilt thou eat thy leek or die ? At least 'tis such a maid as thou needest not to be shamed of : and when thou thinkest of thine own lowly descent, say, art thou worthy to sit where she puts off her shoes ? " Yet loud and long I swore and asseverated we had wrought no dishonour with one another, but got only for answer, we should have so behaved that none could suspect evil of us, whereas by our way of dealing we could quiet no man's doubts. So were we married by the said clergyman, sitting up in bed, and the ceremony over, were forced to rise and to leave the house. But I, who had now recovered myself and felt a sword by my side, must crack my joke : and " Papa-in-law," says I, " I know not why ye should carry yourself thus scurvily : when other young folk be wedded their next of kin do bring them to their bed-chamber, but your worship after my wedding doth cast me forth, not only from my bed but from the house : and in place of such congratulation as he should give me on my marriage, doth grudge me even the sight of my good brother-in-law's face and my service to him. Verily if this fashion hold, there will be few friendships bred by weddings in this world."

*Chap. xxii : HOW SIMPLICISSIMUS HELD HIS WED-
DING-FEAST AND HOW HE PURPOSED TO
BEGIN HIS NEW LIFE*

THE people at my lodging were all astonished when I brought the young maid home with me, and yet more when they saw how unconcernedly she went to bed with me. For though this trick which had been played me stirred up great perplexity in my mind, yet was I not so foolish as to put my bride to shame. And so even while I had my dear in mine arms I had a thousand conceits in my head, how I should begin and end my behaviour in this matter. Now thought I, " Thou art rightly served " : and yet again I considered that I had met with the greatest disgrace in the world, which I could not in honour pass over without due revenge. But when I remembered me that such revenge must harm my father-in-law and also my gentle and innocent bride, then all my plans were naught. At one time I was so sore ashamed that I planned to shut myself up and let no man see me again, and again I reflected that that would be to commit the chief and greatest folly. At the last I concluded that I would before all things win my father-in-law's friendship again, and would so carry myself to all others as if nothing had happened untoward, and as if I had made all things ready for my wedding. For, said I to myself, " Seeing that this business hath had a strange beginning, thou must give it a like end : for should folk know thou wast trapped in thy marriage and wedded like a poor maiden to a rich old cripple, mockery only will be thy portion."

Being full of such thoughts, I rose betimes, though I had rather have lain longer. And first of all I sent to my brother-in-law who had married my wife's sister, and told him in a word how near akin to him I now was, and besought him to suffer his good wife to come and help to prepare somewhat wherewith I might entertain people at my wedding, and if he would be so good as to plead with our father and mother-in-law on my behalf, I would in the meantime busy myself to invite such guests as would promote a peace between me and him. The which he took upon him to do, and I betook myself to the commandant, to whom I told in merry fashion how quaint a device my father-in-law and I had hatched for making up of a match, which device was so swift of operation that I had in a single hour accomplished the betrothal, the wedding, and the bedding. But inasmuch as my father-in-law had grudged me the morning draught, I was minded instead thereof to bid certain honourable guests to the wedding-supper, to which also I respectfully begged to invite himself.

The commandant was fit to burst with laughter at my comical story, and because I saw him in merry mood I made yet more free, giving as my excuse that I could not well be reasonable at such a time, seeing that bridegrooms for full four weeks before and after their wedding were never in their sober senses : but whereas they could play the fool without attracting note and in their four weeks by degrees return to their senses, I had had the whole business of matrimony thrust upon me in a wink, and so must play my tricks all at once, so as thereafter to enact the sober married man more reasonably. Then he demanded me what of the dowry, and how much of the rhino my father-in-law had given for the wedding feast—for of that, said he, the old curmudgeon had plenty. So I answered him that our marriage settlement consisted but in one clause—viz., that his daughter and I should never come in his sight again. But forasmuch as there was neither notary nor witness present I hoped the clause might be revoked, and that the more so because all marriages should tend to the furthering of good fellowship. So with such merry quips, which no one at such a time would have looked for from me, I obtained that the commandant and my father-in-law, whom he undertook to persuade, would appear at my wedding-supper. He sent likewise a cask of wine and a buck to my kitchen : and I made preparation as if I were to entertain princes, and indeed brought together a noble company, which did not only make merry with one another, but in the face of all men did so reconcile my father and mother-in-law with me that they gave me more blessing that night than cursing the night before. And so 'twas noised all over the town that our wedding had been of intent so arranged, lest any ill-natured folk should play some jest upon us. And me this speedy settlement of things suited full well. For had I come to be married with my banns called beforehand, as is the usage, 'twas much to be feared there would have been some baggages that would have given a world of trouble by way of hindrance : for I had among the burghers' daughters a round half-dozen that knew me only too well.

The next day my father-in-law treated my wedding-guests, but not so well as I by far, being miserly. And then I must first say what profession I was minded to follow, and how I would maintain my household : wherein I was first aware that I had now lost my noble freedom and must live henceforth under orders. Yet I carried myself obediently and was beforehand in asking my dear father-in-law, as a prudent gentleman, for his advice, to digest and to follow it : which speech the commandant approved and said, " This being a brisk young soldier, it were great folly that in the present wars he should think to follow any but the soldier's trade : for 'tis far better to stable one's horse in another man's stall than to feed another's nag in one's own. And so far as I am concerned, I promise him a company whenever he will."

For this my father-in-law and I returned thanks, and I refused no more, but shewed the commandant the merchant's receipt, which had my treasure in keeping at Cologne. " And this," said I, " I must first fetch away before I take service with the Swedes : for should they learn that I served their enemies, they of Cologne would laugh me to scorn and keep my treasure, which is not of such a kind as one can easily find by the roadside." This they approved, and so 'twas concluded promised and resolved between us three I should within a few days betake myself to Cologne, possess myself of my treasure, and so return to the fortress and there take command of my company. Furthermore a day was named on which a company should be made over to my father-in-law, together with the commission of lieutenant-colonel in the commandant's regiment. For Count Götz lying in Westphalia with many Imperial troops and his headquarters at Dortmund, my commandant looked to be besieged next spring, and so was seeking to enlist good soldiers. Yet was this care of his in vain : for the said Count Götz was, by reason of the defeat of John de Werth in the Breisgau, forced to leave Westphalia that same spring and take the field against the Duke of Weimar on the Rhine.

Chap. xxiii : HOW SIMPLICISSIMUS CAME TO A CERTAIN TOWN (WHICH HE NAMETH FOR CONVENIENCE COLOGNE) TO FETCH HIS TREASURE

THINGS do happen in different fashions. To one man ill luck cometh by degrees and slowly: another it doth fall upon in a heap. So hardly had I spent a week in the wedded state with my dear wife, when I took leave of her and her friends in my huntsman's dress with my gun upon my shoulder ; and because all the roads were well known to me, I came luckily to my journey's end without danger threatening. Nay, I was seen of no man till I came to the turnpike in Deutz that lieth opposite Cologne on this side the Rhine. But I saw many, and specially a a peasant in the land of Berg, that reminded me much of my dad in the Spessart ; and his son was still more like the old Simplicissimus. For the lad was herding swine as I was passing by : and the swine, scenting me, began to grunt and the lad to curse : " Thunder and lightning strike them and the devil fly away with them too ! " That the maidservant heard, and cried to the lad not to curse or she would tell his father. The boy answered, she might kiss . . . and burn her mother too : But the peasant hearing it, runs out of the house with a whip and cries out, " Wait, thou anointed rascal, I will teach thee to curse ; strike thee blind and the devil take thy carcase " : and with that he caught him by the collar, whipped him like a dancing bear, and at every stroke, " Thou wicked boy," says he, " I'll teach thee to curse, devil take thee,

I'll kiss . . . for thee ; I'll teach thee to talk of burning thy mother." Which manner of correction did remind me naturally of me and my dad, and yet had I not such decency and piety as to thank God for bringing me out of such darkness and ignorance, and into greater knowledge and understanding. And how then could I expect that the good fortune which daily rained upon me should endure ?

So when I came to Cologne I took up my abode with my Jupiter, which was just then in his right mind. But when I told him wherefore I had come, he told me at once that he feared I should but thresh straw ; for the merchant to whom I had given my money to keep it had become bankrupt and had fled : 'tis true my property had been officially sealed up and the merchant himself cited to appear ; but 'twas greatly doubted if he would return, because he had taken with him all of value that could easily be carried ; and before the case could be settled much water might flow under the bridges. How pleasing this news was to me any man can easily judge. I swore like a trooper, but what availed that ? I did not get my property back so, and had no hope of ever doing so : besides, I had taken with me no more than ten thalers for the journey, and so could not stay so long as the matter required. Moreover, 'twas dangerous for me to tarry there ; for I had reason to fear that, as now being attached to an enemy's garrison, I might be found out, and so not only lose my goods but fall into a still worse plight. Yet for me to return with the matter unsettled, leave my property wilfully behind, and have naught to show but the way back instead of the way thither, seemed to me also unwise. At last I determined I would stay in Cologne till the case was settled, and let my wife know the reason of my delay : so I betook myself to an advocate, which was a notary and told him my case, begging him to help me with counsel and action, for a proper reward ; and if he hastened on the matter I would make him a good present besides the fixed fees. And as he hoped to get plenty out of me he received me willingly and undertook to board and lodge me : and thereupon next day he went with me to the officers whose business it is to settle bankrupts' affairs, and handed in a certified copy of the merchant's acknowledgment, and produced the original : to which the answer was, we must be patient till the full examination of the matter, inasmuch as the things of which the acknowledgment spoke were not all to be found.

So now I prepared myself for another long time of idleness, in which I wished to see somewhat of life in great cities. My host was, as I have said, a notary and advocate : besides which he had half a dozen lodgers, and kept always eight horses in his stable which he used to hire out to travellers : moreover he had both a German and an Italian groom, that could be used either for driving or riding and also tended the horses, so that with this threefold, or rather three-and-a-half-fold trade he not only earned a good living but also doubtless put by a good deal : for because no Jews be allowed in that town he found it easier to make money in all manner of ways. I did learn much in the time I was with him, and especially to know all sicknesses of all men, which is the chiefest art of the doctor of medicine. For they say if the doctor do but know the disease, then is the patient already half cured. Now 'twas my host that furnished the reason why I understood this science, for I began with him, and thereafter to examine the condition of other persons. And many a one I knew to be sick to death that knew not of his own sickness at all and that was held by his neighbours—yea, and by the doctors too—to be a hale and hearty man. So did I find people that were sick with evil temper, and when this disease attacked them their visages were changed like those of devils, they roared like lions, scratched like cats, laid about them like bears, bit like dogs, and to shew themselves even worse than savage animals they would throw about everything that they could get into their hands, like madmen. 'Tis said this disease ariseth from the gall ; but I do rather believe its origin is in this, that a fool hath a fool's pride : so if thou hear an angry man rage, especially about a small matter, be thou bold to believe that man hath more pride than sense. From this disease followeth endless mischance both for the patient and for others : for the patient, palsy, gout, and early death (and perhaps an eternal death also). Yet can we with a good conscience refuse to call such men patients, be they never so dangerously ill, for patience is what they most do lack. Some, too, I saw quite sick with envy, of whom 'tis said that they eat their own hearts out, because they do ever walk so pale and sad. And this disease do I hold to be the most dangerous, as coming directly from the devil himself, though yet it spring from mere good fortune which the sick man's enemy doth enjoy : and he that can quite cure such an one may wellnigh boast that he hath converted a lost sinner to the Christian belief, for this disease can infect no true Christians, which have a jealousy only of sin and vice. The gaming passion I hold likewise for a disease, not only because the name doth imply as much, but specially because they that are infected therewith are mad after the thing as if poisoned : it hath its rise from idleness and not from greed, as some do judge ; and if thou take away from a man the chances of lust and idleness, that sickness will of itself depart. Likewise I found that gluttony is a disease : and that it cometh from habit and not from overmuch wealth. Poverty is indeed a good protective against it, but 'tis not thereby cured, for I saw beggars that revelled and rich misers that starved. It doth bring its own remedy on its back with it, and that is called Want, if not of money yet of bodily health, so much so that these patients commonly must of themselves be healed when it comes to this, that either from poverty or from disease they can devour no more. As to pride, I took it for a kind of madness, having its rise in ignorance : for if a man do but know himself and remember whence he is and whither he goeth, 'tis clean impossible that he can go on in his foolish pride. When I do see a peacock or a turkey-cock strut and gobble, I must needs laugh like a fool that these unreasoning beasts can so cleverly mock at poor man in this his great malady : yet have I never been able to find a special remedy against it : for they that are sick of it are without humility, as little to be cured as other madmen. Yea, I deemed, too, that immoderate laughter must be a disease, for Philemon died of it and Democritus was till his end sick of it. And so nowadays do our women say they could laugh till they died. ' Tis said it hath its origin in the liver : but I do believe it cometh from immoderate folly, for much laughter is no sign of a reasonable man : nor is it needful to present a remedy for it, since 'tis not only a merry madness but often doth leave a man before he can well enjoy it. Nor less did I remark how curiosity is but a disease and one born in the female sex : 'tis little to outside view yet in truth most dangerous, seeing that we all must pay for our first mother's curiosity. Of the rest, as sloth, revenge, jealousy, presumption, the passions of love, and the like, I will for this turn say naught, since 'twas never my intent to write of such, but will return to mine host, which indeed gave me the hint to reflect upon such-like failings, seeing that he himself was utterly ruled and possessed by greed.

Chap. xxiv : HOW THE HUNTSMAN CAUGHT A HARE IN THE MIDDLE OF A TOWN

THE fellow had, as I have said, all manner of trades by which he scraped together money: he fed with his guests and not his guests with him, and he could have plentifully fed all his household with the money they brought him in, if the skinflint had so used it : but he fed us Swabian fashion and kept a mighty deal back. At the first I ate not with his guests but with his children and household, because I had little money with me : there were but little morsels, that were like Spanish fasting-food for my stomach, so long accustomed to the hearty Westphalian diet. No single good joint of meat did we ever get but only what had been carried away a week before from the students' table, pretty well hacked at by them, and now, by reason of age, as grey as Methuselah. Over this the hostess, who must do the cooking herself (for she would pay for no maid to help her), poured a black, sour kind of gravy and bedevilled it with pepper. Yet though the bones were sucked so dry that one could have made chessmen of them, yet were they not yet done with, but were put into a vessel kept for the purpose, and when our miser had a sufficient quantity, they must be chopped up fine and all the fat that remained boiled out of them. I know not whether this was used for seasoning soup or greasing shoes. But on feast-days, of which there happened more than enough, and which were all religiously observed (for therein was our host full of scruples), we had the run of our teeth on stinking herrings, salt cod, rotten stockfish, and other decayed marine creatures : for he bought all with regard to cheapness only,

and grudged not the trouble to go himself to the fish-market and to pick up what the fishmongers themselves were about to throw away. Our bread was commonly black and stale, our drink a thin, sour beer which wellnigh burst my belly, and yet must pass as fine old October. Besides all this, I learned from his German servant that in summer-time 'twas yet worse : for then the bread was mouldy, the meal full of maggots, and the best dishes were then a couple of radishes at dinner and a handful of salad at supper. So I asked him why did he stay with the old miser. He answered he was mostly travelling, and therefore must count more on the drink-money of travellers than on that mouldy old Jew, who he said would not even trust his wife and children with the cellar-key, for he grudged them even a drop of wine, and, in a word, was such a curmudgeon that his like would be hard to find ; what I had seen up till now, said he, was nothing : if I did but stay there for a while I should perceive that he was not ashamed to skin a flea for its fat. Once, said he, the old fellow had brought home six pounds of tripe or chitterlings and put it in his larder ; but to the great delight of his children the grating chanced to be open : so they tied a tablespoon to a stick and fished all the chitterlings out, which they then ate up half-cooked, in great haste, and gave out 'twas the cat had done it. That the old coal-counter would not believe, but caught the cat and weighed her, and found that, skin, hair and all, she weighed not so much as his chitterlings.

Now as the fellow was so shameless a cheat, I desired no longer to eat at his private table but at that of the before-mentioned students, however much it might cost : and there 'twas certainly more royal fare ; yet it availed me little, for all the dishes that were set before us were but half-cooked, which profited our host in two ways—first in fuel, which he thus saved, and secondly, because it spoiled our appetite : yea, methought he counted every mouthful we ate and scratched his head for vexation if ever we made a good meal. His wine, too, was well watered and not of a kind to aid diges-tion : and the cheese which was served at the end of every meal was hard as stone, and the Dutch butter so salt that none could eat more than half an ounce of it at breakfast; as for the fruit, it had to be carried to and fro till it was ripe and fit to eat ; and if any of us grumbled thereat, he would begin a terrible abusing of his wife loud enough for us to hear : but secretly gave her orders to go on in the same old way.

Once on a time one of his clients brought him a hare for a present : this did I see hang in his larder, and did think for once we might have game to our dinner : but the German servant said to me we need not lick our lips over that, for his master had so contracted with the boarders that he need not serve them such dainties ; I should go to the Old Market in the afternoon and there see if the thing were not there for sale. So I cut a bit out of the hare's ear, and as we sat at our mid-day meal and the host was not there, I told them how our skinflint had a hare for sale, of which I was minded to cheat him, if one of them would follow me ; for so should we not only have some pastime, but would get the hare too. Every one of them consented ; for they had long desired to play our host a trick of which he could not complain. So that afternoon we betook ourselves to the place which I had learned of from the servant, where our host was wont to stand if he gave a tradesman aught for sale, to watch what the buyer paid, lest he should be cheated of a farthing. There we found him in talk with some of the nobles. Now I had engaged a fellow to go to the higgler that should sell the hare and to say, " Friend, that hare is mine, and I claim it as stolen property : last night 'twas snatched out of my window, and if thou give it not up willingly, 'tis at thy risk and the risks of the costs in court." The huckster answered he must first inquire of the matter : for there stood the gentleman of repute that had given him the hare to sell ; and he could surely not have stolen it. So as they disputed, they gathered a crowd round them ; which when our miser was ware of and saw which way the cat jumped, he gave a wink to the higgler to let the hare go, for by reason of all his boarders he feared yet greater shame. But the fellow I had hired contrived very cleverly to shew every one present the piece of the ear and to fit it into the slit, so that all said he was right and voted him the hare. Meanwhile I drew near with my company, as if we had come by chance, and stood by the fellow that had the hare and began to bargain with him, and when we were agreed I presented the hare to mine host with the request he would have it served up at our table : but the fellow I had engaged with I paid, instead of money for the hare, the price of a couple of cans of beer. So our skinflint must accept the hare, though with no good will, and dared not say a word, at which we had cause enough to laugh : and had I meant to stay longer in his house, I would have shewn him a few more such tricks.

BOOK IV

Chap. i: *HOW AND FOR WHAT REASON THE HUNTSMAN WAS JOCKEYED AWAY INTO FRANCE*

IF you sharpen a razor too much you will notch the edge, and if you overbend the bow, at last 'twill break. The trick I played on my host with the hare was not enough for me, but I devised others to punish his insatiable greed. So did I teach the boarders to water the salted butter and so to get rid of the overplus salt ; yea, and to grate the hard cheese like the Parmesans and moisten it with wine, all which things were to the miser like stabs in his heart. Nay, by my conjuring tricks at table I drew the water out of the wine, and made a song in which I compared the skinflint to a sow, from which there was no good to be looked for till the butcher had her dead upon the trestles. And so I myself furnished the reason why he paid me, and that well, with the trick ye shall now hear : for 'twas not my business to play such pranks in his house.

The two young nobles that were his boarders received a letter of exchange, and the command to go into France and there to learn the language, just at a time when our host's German groom was on his travels and elsewhere, and to the Italian, said he, he dared not trust his horses to him to take into France, for he knew little of him and feared he might forget to come back, and so should he lose his horses : and therefore he begged of me to do him the greatest service in the world and to accompany those two noblemen with his horses as far as Paris, for in any case my suit could not be argued before four weeks were over ; and he for his part would, if I would give him full powers, so faithfully further my interests as if I were there in person present. The young noblemen besought me also to the same end, and mine own desire to see France counselled me thereto : for now could I do this without special expense, and otherwise must spend those four weeks in idleness and spend money too. So I took

239

to the road with my two noblemen, riding as their postilion ; and on the way there happened to me nothing of note. But when we came to Paris and there put up at the house of our host's correspondent, where also the young noblemen had their letter of exchamge honoured, the very next day not only was I with the horses arrested, but a fellow that gave out that my host owed him a sum of money seized upon the beasts, with the leave of the commissary of the Quartier, and sold them. The Lord only doth know what I said to all this : but there I sat like a graven image and could not help myself, far less devise how I could return along a road so long and at that time so dangerous. The two noblemen shewed me great sympathy, and therefore honourably gave me a larger gratification ; nor would they have me leave them before I should find either a good master or a good opportunity to return to Germany. So they hired them a lodging, and for some days I stayed with them to wait upon one of them, which by reason of the long journey, as being unused thereto, was indisposed. And as I shewed myself so polite to him he gave to me all the clothing he put off : for he would be clad in the newest mode. Their counsel was, I should stay a couple of years in Paris, and learn the language : for what I had to fetch from Cologne would not run away. So as I halted between two opinions and knew not what to do, the doctor which came every day to cure my sick nobleman heard me once play on the lute and sing a German ditty to it, which pleased him so that he offered me a good salary, together with board at his own table, if I would live with him and teach his two sons : for he knew better than I how my affairs stood and that I should not refuse a good master. Thus were we soon agreed, for both the noblemen furthered the business all they could, and greatly recommended me : yet would I not engage myself save from one quarter of a year to the next.

The doctor spoke German as well as I did and Italian like his mother tongue : and therefore I was the more pleased to take service with him : and as I sat at my last meal with my noblemen, he was there too, and there all manner of sad fancies came into my head : for I thought of my newly wedded wife, the ensigncy promised me, and my treasure at Cologne, all which I let myself so easily be persuaded to leave : and

as we came to speak of our former host I had a whim, and said I over the table, " Who knoweth whether, perhaps, our host have not of intention trepanned me hither that he may claim and keep my property at Cologne ? " The doctor answered it might very well be so, especial if he deemed me a fellow of no family. " Nay," said one of the nobles, " if our friend was sent here to the end he should stay here, 'twas done because he so plagued the host on account of his avarice." " Nay," said the sick man, " I believe there is another reason : for as I stood of late in my chamber I heard the host talk loud with his Italian man ; so I listened to hear what 'twas all about, and at last from the servant's broken German I understood that the huntsman had accused him to the man's wife of not tending the horses well : all which the jealous knave, by reason of the man's imperfect speech, understood wrongly and in a dishonourable way, and therefore told the Italian he need but wait, for the huntsman should presently be gone." Since then, too, he had looked askance upon his wife and grumbled at her more than before, which I had myself remarked in the fool. Then said the doctor, " From whatever cause 'twas done, I am content that matters have so turned out that he must remain here. But be not dismayed ; I will at the first good opportunity help you back to Germany. Only write ye to the man at Cologne to have a care of the money, or he will be called sharply to account. And this also doth raise suspicion in me that 'tis a plot—namely, that he that gave himself out for the creditor is a very good friend both of your host and of his correspondent here, and I do believe the bond, on which he seized and sold the horses, was brought here by yourself."

Chap. ii : HOW SIMPLICISSIMUS FOUND A BETTER HOST THAN BEFORE

SO Monsieur Canard (for so was my new master called) offered to help me in word and deed, that I might not lose my property at Cologne ; for he saw how much it troubled me. So as soon as he had me to his house, he begged I would tell him exactly how my affairs stood, that he might understand and so devise how I might best be helped. Thereupon I thought 'twould avail me little if I revealed mine own poor birth, and so gave out I was a poor German nobleman that had neither father nor mother, but only some kinsfolk in a fortress wherein was a Swedish garrison ; all which, said I, I had perforce concealed from my host at Cologne and my two noblemen, as being all of the emperor's party, that they might not confiscate my money as the enemy's property. My intention it was, said I, to write to the commandant of the said fortress, in whose regiment I had been promised an ensigncy, and not only inform him in what fashion I had been deluded hither but also to beg him to have the goodness to take possession of my property, and in the meantime, until I could find opportunity to return to my regiment, to put it at the disposition of my friends. This plan the good Canard thought good, and promised me to forward the letter to their proper place though it were in Mexico or even in China. Accordingly I prepared letters to my wife, to my father-in-law, and to the colonel S(aint) A(ndré), commandant in Lippstadt, to whom I addressed the whole packet, and enclosed the two others. The contents were : that I would present myself again as speedily as might be, if only I could get the means to perform so long a journey, and begged both my father-in-law and the colonel to do their best to endeavour to recover my property by military process before the grass was grown over it, and gave them a full list of the amounts in gold, silver, and jewels. All these letters I drew up in duplicate ; and one copy Monsieur Canard took charge of : the other copy I did entrust to the post, that if one copy should go astray, the other at least might arrive safely.

So now was I at ease in my mind again, and was the more able to teach my master's two sons, which were brought up like young princes : for because Monsieur Canard was rich, therefore was he beyond all measure proud, and must make a display ; the which disease he had taken from the great men, with whom he daily had to do, and aped their ways. His house was like a prince's court, of which it wanted nothing save that none ever called him " gracious sir," and his conceit was so great that he would treat a marquis, when such came to visit him, as no better than himself. He was ready to help poor folk, and would take no small fees, but forgave them the money that his name might be more renowned. And because I was ever desirous of knowledge, and because I knew that he made much show of my person when I followed him with his other servants on a visit to some great man, I would help him in his laboratory in the preparation of his medicines. Thus was I become well acquainted with him, and that the more because it ever pleased him to speak the German tongue : so once on a time I said to him, why did he not write himself down as " of " his nobleman's residence which he had newly bought near Paris for 20,000 crowns, and why he would make simple doctors of his sons and would have them to study so hard. Were it not better, since he himself had a title of nobility, to buy them offices, as did other chevaliers, and so bring them entirely into the class of nobles ? " Nay," he answered, " if I visit a prince, to me 'tis said, ' Master doctor, be seated,' but to a nobleman, ' Wait thy turn ! ' " So said I, " But doth the doctor not know that a physician hath three faces—the first, an angel's, when the sick man sees him first ; the second, God's own, when he can help the sick ; and the third, the devil's own, when a man is healed and can be rid of him ? And so this honour of which ye speak doth but last so long as the sick man is plagued in his belly : but when 'tis over and the grumbling past there hath the honour an end, and ' Master Doctor,' quoth'a, ' there is the door ! ' And so the nobleman hath more honour in standing than the doctor in sitting, namely, because he waiteth ever on his own prince and hath the honour never to leave his side. Did ye not of late, Master Doctor, take of a prince's excrement into your mouth to try the taste ? Now I do say, I would sooner stand and wait for ten years than meddle with another man's dung, yea, even though I was bidden to be seated on beds of roses." To that he answered, " That I need not to have done, but did it willingly, that the prince might see how desperate anxious I was to understand his condition, and so my fee might be greater : and why should I not meddle with another's dirt, that payeth me perhaps a hundred pistoles for it, and I pay him naught that must eat filth of another kind at my bidding ? Ye talk of the thing like a German : and were ye not a German I had said, ye talk like a fool."

With that saying I was content, for I saw he would presently

be angry, and to bring him again into a good humour I begged
him he would forgive my simplicity and began to talk of
pleasanter matters.

Chap. iii : HOW HE BECAME A STAGE PLAYER AND
GOT HIMSELF A NEW NAME

NOW as Monsieur Canard had more game to throw
away than many have to eat, which yet have their
own preserves, and thus more meat was sent to
him by way of present than he and all his people
could eat, so had he also daily many parasites, so that it
seemed as if he kept open house. And once on a time there
visited him the king's Master of the Ceremonies and other high
personages, for whom he prepared a princely collation, as
knowing well whom he needed to keep as his friends, namely,
those that were ever about the king or stood well with him :
and to shew them his great goodwill and give them every
pleasure, he begged that I would, to honour him and to please
the high personages present, let them hear a German song
sung to the lute. This I did willingly, being in the mood (for
commonly musicians be whimsical people), and so busied
myself to play my best, and did so please the company that
the Master of the Ceremonies said 'twas great pity I could not
speak French : for so could he commend me greatly to the
king and queen. But my master, that feared lest I might be
taken from his service, answered him, I was of noble birth
and thought not to sojourn long in France, and so could hardly
be used as a common musician. Thereupon the Master of the
Ceremonies said he had never in his life found united in one
person such rare beauty, so fine a voice, and such admirable
skill upon the lute : and presently, said he, a comedy was to
be played before the king at the Louvre : and could he but
have my services, he hoped to get great honour thereby.
This Monsieur Canard did interpret to me : and I answered,
if they would but tell me what person I was to represent and
what manner of songs I was to sing, I could learn both tune
and words by heart and sing them to my lute, even if they were
in the French tongue : for perhaps my understanding might

be as good as that of a schoolboy such as they commonly use for such parts, though these must first learn both words and actions by heart.

So when the Master of the Ceremonies saw me so willing, he would have me promise to come to him next day in the Louvre to try if I was fit for the part : and at the time appointed I was there. The tunes of the songs I had to sing I could play at once perfectly upon the lute ; for I had the notes before me : and thereafter I received the French words, to learn them by heart and likewise to pronounce them, all which were interpreted for me in German, that I might use the actions fitted to the songs. All this was easy enough to me, and I was ready before any could have expected it, and that so perfectly (as Monsieur Canard declared) that ninety-nine out of a hundred that heard me sing would have sworn I was a born Frenchman. And when we came together for the first rehearsal, I did behave myself so plaintively with my songs, tunes, and actions that all believed I had often played the part of Orpheus, which I must then represent, and shew myself vexed for the loss of my Eurydice. And in all my life I have never had so pleasant a day as that on which our comedy was played. Monsieur Canard gave me somewhat to make my voice clearer : but when he tried to improve my beauty with oleum talci and to powder my curly hair that shone so black he found he did but spoil all. So now was I crowned with a wreath of laurel and clad in an antique sea-green robe in which all could see my neck, the upper part of my breast, my arms above the elbow and my knees, all bare and naked. About it was wrapped a flesh-coloured cloak of taffety that was more like a flag than a cloak : and in this attire I languished over my Eurydice, called on Venus for help in a pretty song, and at last led off my bride : in all which action I did play my part excellently, and gazed upon my love with sighs and speaking eyes. But when I had lost my Eurydice, then did I put on a dress of black throughout, made like the other, from out of which my white skin shone like snow. In this did I lament my lost wife, and did conjure up the case so piteously that in the midst of my sad tunes and melodies the tears would burst forth and my weeping choked the passage of my song : yet did I play my part right well till I came before Pluto and Proserpina in hell. To them I represented in a most moving song their own love that they bore to each other, and begged them to judge thereby with what great grief I and my Eurydice must have parted, and prayed with the most piteous actions (and all the time I sang to my lute) they would give her leave to return to me : and when they had said me " Yes," I took my leave with a joyful song to them, and was clever enough so to change my face, my actions, and my voice to a joyful tune that all that saw me were astonished. But when I again lost my Eurydice all unexpectedly I did fancy to myself the greatest danger wherein a man could find himself, and thereupon became so pale as if I would faint away : for inasmuch as I was then alone upon the stage and all spectators looked on me, I played my part the more carefully and got therefrom the praise of having acted the best. Thereafter I set me on a rock and began to deplore the loss of my bride with piteous words and a most mournful melody, and to summon all creatures to weep with me : upon that, all manner of wild beasts and tame, mountains, trees, and the like flocked round me, so that in truth it seemed as if 'twere all so done in unnatural fashion by enchantment. Nor did I make any mistake at all till the end : but then when I had renounced the company of all women, had been murdered by the Bacchantes and cast into the water (which had been so prepared that one could see only my head, for the rest of my body was beneath the stage in perfect safety), where the dragon was to devour me, and the fellow that was inside the dragon to work it could not see my head and so did let the dragon's head wag about close to mine, this seemed to me so laughable that I could not choose but make a wry face, which the ladies that looked hard upon me failed not to perceive.

From this comedy I earned, besides the high praise that all gave me, not only an excellent reward, but I got me yet another nickname, for thenceforth the French would call me naught but " Beau Alman." And as 'twas then carnival-time, many such plays and ballets were represented, in all which I was employed : but at last I found I was envied by others because I mightily attracted the spectators, and in especial the women, to turn their eyes on me : so I made an end of it, and that particularly because I received much offence on one occasion, when, as I fought with Achelous for Dejanira, as Hercules, and almost naked, I was so grossly treated as is not usual in a stage-play.

By this means I became known to many high personages, and it seemed as if fortune would again shine upon me : for 'twas even offered me to enter the king's service, of which many a great Jack hath not the chance : yet I refused : but much time I spent with ladies of quality that would have me sing and play to them, for both my person and my playing pleased them. Nor will I deny that I gave myself up to the temptations of the Frenchwomen, that entertained me secretly and rewarded me with many gifts for my services, till in the end I was wearied of so vile and shameful a trade, and determined so to play the fool no longer.

NOTE.—The fourth and fifth chapters of the original edition are devoted to a prolix and tedious account of an adventure—if adventure it may be called—of the kind hinted at in the last sentence of the third chapter. It is absolutely without connection with Simplicissimus's career as an actor in the war ; has no interest as a picture of manners ; and finally, can be read much better in Bandello, from whose much livelier story (vol. iv, novel 25, of the complete editions) it is copied. It is therefore omitted here.

Chap. iv : HOW SIMPLICISSIMUS DEPARTED SE-CRETLY AND HOW HE BELIEVED HE HAD THE NEAPOLITAN DISEASE

BY this my occupation I gathered together so many gratifications both in money and in things of worth that I was troubled for their safety, and I wondered no longer that women do betake themselves to the stews and do make a trade of this same beastly and lewd pursuit ; since it is so profitable. But now I did begin to take this matter to heart, not indeed for any fear of God or prick of conscience, but because I dreaded that I might be caught in some such trick and paid according to my deserts

So now I planned to come back to Germany, and that the more so because the commandant at Lippstadt had written to me he had caught certain merchants of Cologne, whom he would not let go out of his hands till my goods were first delivered to him : item, that he still kept for me the ensigncy he had promised, and would expect me to take it up before the spring : for if I came not then he must bestow it upon another. And with his letter my wife sent me one also full of all loving assurances of her hope to have me back. (Had she but known how I had lived she had surely sent me a greeting of another sort.)

Now could I well conceive 'twould be hard to have my congé from Monsieur Canard, and so did I determine to depart secretly so soon as I could find opportunity : which (to my great misfortune) I found. For as I met on a time certain officers of the Duke of Weimar's army, I gave them to understand I was an ensign of the regiment of colonel S(aint) A(ndré) and had been a long time in Paris on mine own affairs, yet now was resolved to return to my regiment, and so begged they would take me as their travelling-companion on their journey back. So they told me the day of their departure and were right willing to take me with them : thereupon I bought me a nag and made my provision for the journey as secretly as I could, got together my money (which was in all some 500 doubloons, all which I had earned from those shameless women), and without asking leave of Monsieur Canard went off with them ; yet did I write to him, and did date the letter from Maestricht ; so as he might think I was gone to Cologne : in this I took leave of him, with the excuse that I could stay no longer when my business at home required my presence.

But two nights out from Paris 'twas with me as with one that hath the erysipelas, and my head did so ache that next morning I could not rise : and that in a poor village where I could have no doctor and, what was worse, none to wait upon me : for the officers rode on their way next morning and left me there, sick to death, as one that concerned them not : yet did they commend me and my horse to the host at their departure and left a message for the mayor of the place that he should have respect to me as an officer that served the king. So there I lay for a couple of days and knew naught of myself, but babbled like a fool. Then they fetched the priest to me : but he could get nothing reasonable from me : and since he saw he could not heal my soul he thought on means to help my body as far as might be, to which end he had me bled and a sudorific given me, and had me put into a warm bed to sweat. This served me so well that the same night I did know where I was and whence I had come and that I was sick. Next morning came the said priest to me again and found me desperate : for not only had my money all been stolen, but I did believe I had (saving your presence) the French disease : for I had deserved this more than my pistoles, and I was spotted over my whole body like a leopard : nor could I either walk or stand, or sit or lie : and now was my patience at an end : for though I could not well believe 'twas God had given me the gold I had lost, yet was I now so reckless that I saw 'twas the devil had stolen it from me ! Yea, and I behaved as if I were quite desperate, so that the good priest had much ado to comfort me, seeing that the shoe pinched me in two places.

" My friend," says he, " behave yourself like a reasonable man, even if ye cannot embrace your cross like a good Christian. What do ye ? Will ye with your money also lose your life and, what is more, your hopes of eternal salvation ? " So I answered I cared not for the money ; if I could but be rid of this accursed sickness or were at least in a place where I could be cured. " Ye must have patience," answered the priest, " as must the poor children of whom there lie in this place over fifty sick of this disease." So when I heard that children also were sick of it, I was straightway cheered, for I could not well suppose that such would catch that filthy disease : so I reached for my valise to see what might still be there : but save my linen there was naught there but a casket with a lady's portrait, set round with rubies, that one at Paris had presented to me. The portrait I took out and gave the rest to the priest with the request he would turn it into money in the next town, so that I might have somewhat to live upon. Of which the end was that I got scarce the third part of its worth, and since that lasted not long my nag must go too : all which barely kept me till the pock-holes began to dry and I to get better.

Chap. v : HOW SIMPLICISSIMUS PONDERED ON HIS PAST LIFE, AND HOW WITH THE WATER UP TO HIS MOUTH HE LEARNED TO SWIM

WHEREWITHAL a man sinneth, therewith is he wont to be punished. This smallpox did so handle me that thenceforward I needed not to fear the women. I got such holes in my face that I looked like a barn-floor whereon they have threshed peas : yea, I became so foul of aspect that my fine curls in which so many women had been tangled were shamed of me and left their home : in place of which I got others that were so like a hog's bristles that I must needs wear a wig, and even as outwardly no beauty remained to me, so also my sweet voice departed—for I had had my throat full of sores. Mine eyes, that heretofore none ever found to lack the fire of love enough to kindle any heart, were now as red and watery as those of any old wife of eighty years that hath the spleen. And above all I was in a foreign land, knew neither dog nor man that would treat me fairly, was ignorant of their language, and had no money left.

So now I first began to reflect, and to lament the noble opportunities which had aforetime been granted to me for the furthering of my fortunes, which yet I had so wantonly let go by. I looked back and marked how my extraordinary luck in war and my treasure-trove had been naught but a cause and preparation for my ill fortune, which had never been able to cast me so far down had it not by a false countenance first raised me so high. Yea, I found that the good things that had happened to me, and which I had accounted truly good, had been truly bad, and had brought me to the depth of misery. Now was there no longer a hermit to deal so faithfully with me, no Colonel Ramsay to rescue me in my need, no priest to give me good advice ; and, in a word, no one man that would do me a good turn : but when my money was gone I was told to be off and find a place elsewhere, and might, like the prodigal son, be glad to herd with the swine.

So now first I bethought me of that priest's good advice, that counselled I should employ my youth and my wealth for study : but 'twas too late to shut the stable-door now that the horse was stolen. O swift and miserable change ! Four weeks ago I was a fellow to move princes to wonder, to charm women, and that made the people believe me a masterpiece of nature, yea an angel, but now so wretched that the very dogs did bark at me. I bethought me a thousand times what I must do : for the host turned me from the door so soon as I could pay no more. Gladly would I have enlisted, but no recruiting officer would take me as a soldier, for I looked like a scarecrow : work could I not, for I was still too weak, and besides used to no handicraft. Nothing did comfort me more than that 'twas now summer coming, and I could at a pinch lodge behind any hedge, for none would suffer me in any house. I had my fine apparel still, that I had had made for my journey, besides a valise full of costly linen that none would buy from me as fearing I might saddle him also with the disease. This I set on my shoulder, my sword in my hand and the road under my feet, which led me to a little town that even possessed an apothecary's shop. Into this I went, and bade him make me an ointment to do away the pock-marks on my face, and because I had no money I gave him a fine soft shirt ; for he was not so nice as the other fools that would take no clothes of me. For, I thought, if thou art but rid of these vile spots, 'twill soon better thy case for thee.

Yea, and I took the more heart because the apothecary assured me that in a week one would see little except the deep scars that the sores had eaten in my face. 'Twas market-day there, and there too was a tooth-drawer that earned much money, in return for which he was always ready with his ribald jests for the crowd. " O fool," says I to myself, " why dost thou not also set up such a trade ? Beest thou so long with Monsieur Canard, and hast not learned enough to deceive a simple peasant and get thy victuals ? Then must thou be a poor creature indeed."

Chap. vi : *HOW HE BECAME A VAGABOND QUACK*
AND A CHEAT

NOW at that time was I as hungry as a hunter : for my belly was not to be appeased ; and yet I had naught in my poke save a single golden ring with a diamond that was worth some twenty crowns. This I sold for twelve : and because I could plainly see these would last but for a time if I could earn nothing besides, I determined to turn doctor. So I bought me the materials for an electuary and made it up : likewise out of herbs, roots, butter, and aromatic oils a green salve for all wounds, wherewith one might have cured a galled horse : also out of calamine, gravel, crab's-eyes, emery, and pumice-stone a powder to make the teeth white : furthermore a blue tincture out of lye, copper, sal ammoniac and camphor, to cure scurvy, toothache, and eye-ache. Likewise I got me a number of little boxes of tin and wood to put my wares in ; and to make a reputable show I had me a bill composed and printed in French, on which could be read for what purpose each of these remedies was fitted. And in three days I was ended with my task, and had scarce spent three crowns on my drugs and gallipots when I left the town. So I packed all up and determined to walk from one village to another as far as Alsace and to dispose of my wares on the way, and thereafter, if opportunity offered, to get to the Rhine at Strassburg to betake myself with the traders to Cologne, and from there to make my way to my wife. Which design was good, but the plan failed altogether.

Now the first time I took my stand before a church with my wares and offered them my gain was small indeed, for I was far too shamefaced, and neither would my talk nor my bragging patter run well : and from that I saw at once I must go another way to work if I would gain money. So I went with my trumpery into the inn, and at dinner I learned from the host that in the afternoon all manner of folk would come together under the lime-tree before his house. And there he said I might sell something, if only my wares were good : but there were so many rogues in the land that people were mightily chary of their money unless they had real proof before their eyes that the medicine was truly good.

So when I found where the shoe pinched I got me a half-wineglass full of strong Strassburg Branntwein, and caught a kind of toad called Reling or Möhmlein, that in spring and summer sits in dirty pools and croaks, gold colour or nearly salmon colour with black spots on its belly, most hateful to see. Such an one I put in a wineglass with water and set it by my wares on a table under the lime-tree. And when the people began to gather together and stood round me, some thought I would, with the tongs that I had borrowed form the hostess, pull out teeth. But I began thus : " My masters and goot frients (for I could still speak but little French), I be no tooths-cracker, only I haf goot watter for ze eye, zat make all ze running go way from ze red eye." " Yea," says one, " that can one see by thine own eyes, that be like to two will-o'-the-wisps." " And zat is true," says I, " but if I had not ze watter sure I were quite blint : besides, I sell not ze watter. Ze elegtuary and ze powder for ze white tooths and ze wound-salve, zese will I sell, but ze watter I gif avay mit dem ! For I be no quack nor no cheater : I do sell mine elegtuary : and when I haf tried it, if it blease you not you needs not to puy it."

So I bade one of them that stood by to choose any one of my boxes of electuary, out of which I made a pill as large as a pea, and put it into my Branntwein, which the people took for water, and there pounded it up and then picked up the toad with the tongs out of the water-glass and said, " See, my goot frients, if this fenomous worm do drink mine elegtuary wizout dying, so is ze ting no goot, and zenn puy it not." With that I put the poor toad, that had been born in water and could bear no other element or liquor, into the Branntwein, and held it covered in with a paper so that he could not leap out : which began to struggle and to wriggle, yea, to do worse than if I had thrown him upon red-hot coals, for the Branntwein was much too strong for him : and after a short time he died and stretched out his four legs. At that the peasants opened their mouths and their purses too when they saw so plain a proof with their own eyes : for now they believed there could be no better electuary on earth than mine, and

I had enough to do to wrap up the stuff in the printed papers and take money for it.

For some of them did buy three, four, five, six times so much, that they might at need be provided with so sure an antidote against poison : yea, they bought also for their friends and kinsfolk that dwelt in other places, so that from this foolery (though 'twas no market-day) I gained by the evening ten crowns, and still kept more than the half of my wares. The same night I betook myself to another village, as fearing lest some peasant should be so curious as to put a toad in water to try the virtue of my electuary, and if it should fail my back should suffer for it.

But to shew the excellence of my antidote in another way, I made me, of meal, saffron, and galls, a yellow arsenic, and of meal and vitriol a sublimate of mercury ; and when I would show the effect of it I had ready two like glasses of fresh water on the table, whereof one was pretty strongly mixed with aqua fortis : into this I stirred a little of my electuary and dropped in as much of my two poisons as was needed : then was one water, that had no electuary (but also no aqua fortis) in it, as black as ink, while the other, by reason of the aqua fortis, remained as it was. " Aha," said they all, " see, that is truly a marvellous electuary for so little money ! " And then when I poured both together again the whole was clear once more : at that the good peasants dragged out their purses and bought of me : which not only helped my hungry belly, but also I could take horse again, earned much money on the way, and so came safely to the German border.

And so, my dear country-folks, put not your faith in quacks : or ye will be deceived by them, since they seek not your health but your wealth.

Chap. vii: HOW THE DOCTOR WAS FITTED WITH A MUSQUET UNDER CAPTAIN CURMUDGEON

NOW as I passed through Lorraine, my wares gave out, and because I must avoid garrison-towns I had no chance to get more : so must I devise another plan till I could make electuary again.

So I bought me two measures of Branntwein and coloured it with saffron, and sold it in half-ounce glasses to the people as a gold water of great price, good against fever, and so my two measures brought me in thirty gulden. But my little glasses running short, and I hearing of a glass-maker that dwelt in the county of Fleckenstein, I betook myself thither to equip myself afresh, but seeking for by-paths was by chance caught by a picket from Philippsburg that was quartered in the castle of Wagelnburg, and so lost all that I had wrung out of the people by my cheats on the journey ; and because the peasant that went with me to shew the way told the fellows I was a doctor, as a doctor I must willy-nilly be taken to Philippsburg. There was I examined and spared not to say who I was in truth ; which they believed not, but would make more of me than I could well be : for I should and must remain a doctor. Then must I swear I belonged to the Emperor's dragoons in Soest and declare on my oath all that had happened to me from then to now and what I now intended. " But," said they, " the Emperor had need of soldiers as much at Philippsburg as at Soest : and so would they give me entertainment, till I had good opportunity to come to my regiment : but if this plan was not to my taste, I might content myself to remain in prison and be treated as a doctor till I should be released ; for as a doctor I had been taken."

So I came down from a horse to a donkey, and must become a musqueteer against my will : which vexed me mightily, for want was master there, and the rations terrible small : I say not to no purpose " terrible " for I was terrified every morning when I received mine : for I knew I must make that suffice for the whole day which I could have made away with at a meal without trouble. And to tell truth 'tis a poor creature, a musqueteer, that must so pass his life in a garrison, and make dry bread suffice him—yea, and not half enough of that : for he is naught else than a prisoner that prolongs his miserable life with the bread and water of tribulation : nay, a prisoner hath the better lot, for he needs neither to watch, nor to go the rounds, nor stand sentry, but lies at rest and has as much hope as any such poor garrison-soldier in time at length to get out of his prison. 'Tis true there were some that bettered their condition, and that in divers ways, but none that pleased me and seemed to me a reputable way to gain my food. For some in this miserable plight took to themselves wives (yea, the most vile women at need) for no other cause than to be kept by the said women's work, either with sewing, washing and spinning, or with selling of old clothes and higgling, or even with stealing : there was a she-ensign among the women that drew her pay as a corporal : another was a midwife, and so earned many a good meal for herself and her husband : another could starch and wash : others laundered for the unmarried soldiers and officers shirts, stockings, sleeping-breeches and I know not what else, from which they had each her special name. Others did sell tobacco and provide pipes for the fellows that had need of them : others dealt in Branntwein : another was a seamstress, and could do all manner of embroidery and cut patterns to earn money : another gained a livelihood from the fields only ; in winter she gathered snails, in spring salad-herbs, in summer she took birds'-nests, and in autumn she would gather fruit of all kinds : a few carried wood for sale like asses, and others traded with this and that. Yet to gain my support in such a way was not for me : for I had a wife already. Other fellows did gain a livelihood by play, for at that they were better than sharpers and could get their simple comrades' money from them with false dice : but such a profession I loathed. Others toiled like beasts of burden at the ramparts ; but for that I was too lazy : and some knew and could practise a trade, but I, poor creature, had learned none such : 'tis true if any had had need of a musician I could have filled the place well, but that land of hunger was content with drums and fifes. Some stood sentry for others and night and day came never off duty, but I would sooner starve than so torment my body : some got them booty by expeditions : but I was not even trusted to go outside the gates : others could go a-mousing better than any cat, but such a trade I hated worse than the plague. In a word, wherever I turned, I could hit on no way to fill my belly. Yet what vexed me most of all was this, that I must needs endure all manner of gibes when my comrades said, " What, thou a doctor, and hast no art but to starve ? "

At length did hunger force me to inveigle a few fine carp

out of the town ditch up to me on the wall : but as soon as the colonel was ware of it I must ride the torture-horse for it, and was forbidden on pain of death to exercise that art further. At the last others' misfortune proved my good luck. For having cured a few patients of jaundice and two of fever (all which must have had a particular belief in me), it was allowed me to go out of the fortress on the pretence of collecting roots and herbs for my medicines : instead of which I did set snares for hares and had the luck to catch two the first night : these I brought to the colonel, and so got not only a thaler as a present, but also leave to go out and catch hares whensoever I was not on duty. Now because the country was waste and no man there to catch the beasts, which had therefore mightily multiplied, there came grist to my mill again, insomuch that it seemed as if it rained hares, or as if I could charm them into my snares. So when the officers saw they could trust me I was allowed to go out on plundering parties : and there I began again my life as at Soest, save that I might no longer lead and command such parties as heretofore in Westphalia ; for for that 'twas needful to know all highways and byways and to be well acquainted with the Rhine stream.

Chap. viii : HOW SIMPLICISSIMUS ENDURED A CHEERLESS BATH IN THE RHINE

YET must I tell you of a couple of adventures before I say how I was again freed from my musquet, and one in truth of great danger to life and limb, the other only of danger to the soul, wherein I did obstinately persist : for I will conceal my vices no more than my virtues, in order that not only may my story be complete, but also that the untravelled reader may learn what strange blades there be in this world.

As I said at the end of the last chapter, I might now go out with foraging-parties, which in garrison towns is not granted to every loose customer, but only to good soldiers. So once on a time nineteen of us together went up to the Rhine to lie in wait for a ship of Basel that was given out to carry secretly officers and goods of the Duke of Weimar's army. So above

Ottenheim we got us a fishing-boat wherein to cross over and post ourselves on an eyot that lay handy to compel all ships that drew near to come to land, to which end ten of us were safely ferried over by the fisherman. But when one of us that could at other times row well was fetching over the remaining nine, of whom I was one, the skiff suddenly capsized and in a twinkling we lay together in the Rhine. I cared not much for the others, but thought of myself. But though I strained to the utmost and used all the arts of a good swimmer, yet the stream played with me as with a ball, tossing me about, sometimes over, sometimes under. I fought so manfully that I often came up to get breath ; but had it been colder, I had never been able to hold out so long and to escape with my life. Often did I try to win to the bank, but the eddies hindered me, tossing me from one side to another : and though 'twas but a short time before I came opposite Goldscheur, it seemed to me so long that I despaired of my life. But when I had passed that village and had made sure I must pass under the Strassburg Rhine-bridge dead or alive, I was ware of a great tree whose branches stretched into the river not far from me. To this the stream flowed straight and strong : for which cause I put forth all the strength I had left to get to the tree, wherein I was most lucky, so that by the help both of the water and my own pains I found myself astride upon the biggest branch, which at first I had taken for a tree : which same was yet so beaten by waves and whirlpools that it kept bobbing up and down without ceasing, and so shook up my belly that I wellnigh spewed up lungs and liver. Hardly could I keep my hold, for all things danced strangely before my eyes. And fain would I have slipped into the water again, yet found I was not man enough to endure even the hundredth part of such labour as I had so far accomplished. So must I stick there and hope for an uncertain deliverance, which God must send me if I was to get off alive. But in this respect my conscience gave me but cold comfort, bidding me remember that I had so wantonly rejected such gracious help a year or two before ; yet did I hope for the best, and began to pray as piously as I had been reared in a cloister, determining to live more cleanly in future ; yea, and made divers vows. Thus did I renounce the soldier's life and forswore plundering for ever, did throw my cartridge-box and knapsack from me, and naught would suffice me but to become a hermit again and do penance for my sins, and be thankful to God's mercy for my hoped-for deliverance till the end of my days, and when I had spent two or three hours upon the branch between hope and fear there came down the Rhine that very ship for which I was to help lie in wait. So I lifted up my voice piteously and screamed for help in the name of God and the last Judgment, and because they must needs pass close to me, and therefore the more clearly see my wretched plight, all in the ship were moved to pity, so that they put to land to devise how best to help me. And because, by reason of the many eddies that were all round me (being caused by the roots and branches of the tree), it was not possible to swim out to me without risk of life nor to come to me with any vessel, small or great, my helping needed much thought : and how I fared in mind meanwhile is easy to guess. At last they sent two fellows into the river above me with a boat, that let a rope float down to me and kept one end of it themselves. The other end I with great trouble did secure, and bound it round my body as well as I could, so that I was drawn up by it into the boat like a fish on a line and so brought into the ship.

So now when I had in this fashion escaped death, I had done well to fall on my knees on the bank and thank God's goodness for my deliverance, and moreover then begin to amend my life as I had vowed and promised in my deadly need. But far from it. For when they asked me who I was and how I had come into this peril I began so to lie to the people that it might have made the heavens turn black : for I thought, if thou sayst thou wast minded to help plunder them, they will cast thee into the Rhine again. So I gave myself out for a banished organist, and said that as I would to Strassburg to seek a place as schoolmaster or the like on the upper Rhine, a party had captured me and stripped me and thrown me into the Rhine, which brought me to that same tree. And as I contrived to trick out these my lies finely, and also strength-ened them with oaths, I was believed, and all kindness shewn me in the matter of food and drink to refresh me, of which I had great need indeed.

At the custom-house at Strassburg most did land, and I with them, giving them all thanks ; and among them I was ware of a young merchant whose face and gait and actions gave me to understand that I had seen him before : yet could I not remember where, but perceived by his speech that 'twas that very same cornet that had once made me prisoner : and now could I not conceive how from so fine a young soldier he had been turned into a merchant, specially since he was a gentleman born. Yea, my curiosity to know if my eyes and ears deceived me or not urged me to go to him and say, " Monsieur Schönstein, is it you or not ? " to which he answered, " I am no Herr von Schönstein but a simple trader." " And I too," says I, " was never a huntsman of Soest but an organist, or rather a land-tramping beggar." And " O brother ! " he answered, " what the devil trade art thou of ? whither art thou bound ? " " Brother," said I, " if thou beest chosen by heaven to help preserve my life, as hath now happened for the second time, then 'tis certain that my destiny requires that I should not be far from thee."

Then did we embrace as two true friends, that had aforetime promised to love one another to the death. I must to his quarters and tell him all that had befallen me since I had left Lippstadt for Cologne to fetch my treasure, nor did I conceal from him how I had intended to lay wait for their ship with a party, and how we had fared therein. And he on his part confided to me how he had been sent by the Hessian General Staff to Duke Bernhard of Weimar on business of the greatest import concerning the conduct of the war : to bring reports and to confer with him on future plans and campaigns, all which he had accomplished and was now on his way back in the disguise of a merchant, as I could see. By the way also he told me that my bride at his departure was expecting child-bed, and had been well entreated by her parents and kinsfolk, and furthermore that the colonel still kept the ensigncy for me. Yet he jested at me by reason of my pock-marked face, and would have it that neither my wife nor the other women of Lippstadt would take me for the Huntsman. So we agreed I should lodge with him and on this opportunity return to Lippstadt which was what I most desired. And because I had naught but rags upon me he lent me some trifle in money, wherewith I equipped myself like to an apprentice-lad.

But as 'tis said, " What will be, must be," that I now found true : for as we sailed down the river and the ship was examined at Rheinhausen, the Philippsburgers knew me again, seized me and carried me off to Philippsburg, where I had to play the musqueteer as before : all which angered my friend the cornet as much as myself : for now must we separate : and he could not much take my part, for he had enough to do to get through himself.

Chap. ix : WHEREFORE CLERGYMEN SHOULD NEVER EAT HARES THAT HAVE BEEN TAKEN IN A SNARE

NOW hath the gentle reader heard in what danger of life I put myself. But as concerns the danger of my soul 'tis to be understood that as a musqueteer I became a right desperate fellow, that cared naught for God and His word. No wickedness was for me too great : and all the goodnesses and loving kindnesses that I had ever received from God quite forgotten ; and so I cared neither for this world nor the next but lived like a beast. None would have believed that I had been brought up with a pious hermit : seldom I went to church and never to confess : and because I cared so little for my own soul's health, therefore I troubled my fellow-men yet more. Where I could cheat a man I failed not to do it, yea I prided myself upon it, so that none came off scot-free from his dealings with me. From this I often got me a whipping, and still more often the torture-horse ; yea, I was often threatened with the strappado and the gibbet : but naught availed : I went on in my godless career till it seemed I would play the desperado and run post-haste to hell. And though I did no deed evil enough to forfeit my life, yet was I so reckless that, save for sorcerers and sodomites, no worse man could be found.

Of this our regiment's chaplain was ware, and being a right zealous saver of souls, at Eastertide he sent for me to know why I had not been at Confession and Holy Communion. But

I treated his many faithful warnings as I had done those of the good pastor at Lippstadt, so that the good man could make naught of me. So when it seemed as if Christ and His Baptism were lost in me, at the end says he, " O miserable man : I had believed that thou didst err through ignorance : now know I that thou goest on in thy sins from pure wickedness and of malice aforethought. Who, thinkest thou, can feel compassion for thy poor soul and its damnation ? For my part, I protest before God and the world that I am free of guilt as to that damnation ; for I have done, and would have gone on to do without wearying, all that was necessary to further thy salvation. But henceforward 'twill not be my duty to do more than that to provide thy body, when thy poor soul shall leave it in such a desperate state, shall be conveyed to no dedicated place there to be buried with other departed pious Christians, but to the carrion-pit with the carcases of dead beasts, or to that place where are bestowed other God-forgotten and desperate men." Yet this severe threatening bore as little fruit as the earlier warnings, and that for this reason only, that I was shamed to confess. O fool that I was ! For often I would tell of my knaves' tricks in great company and would lie to make them seem the greater ; yet now, when I should be converted and confess my sins to a single man, and him standing in God's place, to receive absolution, then was I as a stock or a stone. I say the truth : I was stockish ; and stockish I remained : for I answered, " I do serve the Emperor as a soldier : and if I die as a soldier, 'twill be no wonder if I, like other soldiers (which cannot always be buried in holy ground, but must be content to lie anywhere on the field in ditches or in the maw of wolf and raven), must make shift outside the churchyard."

And so I left the priest, which for his holy zeal for souls had no more return from me than that once I refused him a hare, which he urgently begged from me, on the pretence that since it had hanged itself in a noose and so taken its own life, therefore as a self-murderer it might not be buried in a holy place.

Chap. x : *HOW SIMPLICISSIMUS WAS ALL UNEX-*
PECTEDLY QUIT OF HIS MUSQUET

SO were things no better with me, but the longer the
worse. Once did the colonel say to me he would
discharge me for a rogue, since I would do no good.
But because I knew he meant it not, I said 'twas
easy enough, if only he would dismiss the hangman too,
to bear me company. So he let it pass, for well could he
conceive that I should hold it for no punishment but for a
favour if he would let me go : and against my will I must
remain a musqueteer and starve till the summer. But the
nearer Count von Götz came with his army, the nearer came
also my deliverance : for when that general had his headquarters at Bruchsal, my friend Herzbruder, that I had so
faithfully helped with my money in the camp before Magdeburg, was sent by the staff on certain business to our fortress,
where all shewed him great honour. I was even then sentry
before the colonel's quarters, and though he wore a coat of
black velvet, yet I knew him at first sight, yet had not the
heart to speak to him at once, as fearing lest, after the way
of the world, he should be ashamed of me or would not know
me, for by his clothes he was now of high rank and I but a
lousy musqueteer. But so soon as I was relieved I asked of
his servants his name and rank, to be assured that I did
not address another in his place, and yet I had not the
courage to speak to him, but wrote this billet to him and
caused it to be handed to him in the morning by his chamberlain.

" Monsieur, etc.,—If it should please my worshipful master
by his high influence to deliver one whom he once by his
bravery saved from bonds and fetters on the field of Wittstock, from the most miserable condition in the world, into
which he hath been tossed like a ball by unkind fortune,
'twould cost him little pains and he would for ever oblige
one, in any case his faithful servant but now the most wretched
and deserted of men.—S. SIMPLICISSIMUS."

No sooner had he read this than he had me to him and "Fellow countryman," says he, "where is the man that gave thee this?" "Sir," I answered, "he is a captive in this fortress." "Well," says he, "now go to him and say I would deliver him an he had the halter round his neck." "Sir," said I, "'twill not need so much trouble, for I am poor Simplicissimus himself, come not only to give thanks for his rescue at Wittstock, but also to beg to be freed from the musquet which I have been forced against my will to carry." But he suffered me not to make an end, but by embracing me shewed me how ready he was to help me : in a word, he did all that one faithful friend can do for another ; and before he asked me how I came into the fortress and to such a service, he sent his servant to the Jew to buy me a horse and clothing. And meanwhile I told him how it had fared with me since his father had died before Magdeburg, and when he heard I was the Huntsman of Soest (whose many famous exploits he had heard of) he lamented that he had not known such before, for so could he well have helped me to a company. So when the Jew came with a whole burden of soldiers' clothes, he chose out the best for me, bade me clothe myself, and so took me with him to the colonel. And to him, "Sir," says he, "I have in your garrison found this good fellow here present, to whom I am so much bounden that I cannot leave him in this low estate even if his good qualities deserved no better : and therefore I beg the colonel to do me this favour, and either to give him a better place or to allow me to take him with me and to further his promotion in the army, for which perhaps the colonel has no great opportunity here." At that the colonel crossed himself for sheer wonder to hear any man praise me ; and says he, "Your honour will forgive me if I say it is his part to try whether I am willing to serve him so far as his deserts do require : and so far as that goes, let him demand aught else that lies in my power and he shall understand my willingness by my actions. But as to this fellow, he is, according to his own showing, no soldier of mine, but belongs to a regiment of dragoons, and is besides so pestilent a companion that since he hath been here he hath given more work to my provost than a whole company, so that I must needs believe no water will ever drown him." So he ended with a laugh and wished me luck.

But for Herzbruder this was not enough, but he further begged the colonel not to refuse to invite me to his table, which favour he also obtained : and this he did to the end that he might tell the colonel in my presence what he only knew of me by hearsay in Westphalia from the Count von der Wahl and the commandant of Soest, all which actions he so praised that all must hold me for a good soldier. And I too carried myself so modestly that the colonel and his people that had known me before could but believe that with my new clothes I had become a new man. Moreover, when the colonel would know how I had gotten the name of doctor, I told them the whole story of my journey from Paris to Philippsburg and how many peasants I had cheated to fill my belly : at which they laughed heartily. And in the end I confessed openly it had been my intention so to vex and weary him, the colonel, with all manner of tricks, that he must at last turn me out of the garrison, if he would live at peace from all the complaints that I caused him. Thereupon he told of many rogueries I had committed while in the garrison, for example, how I had boiled up beans, poured grease over them, and sold the whole for pure grease ; also sand for salt, filling the sacks with sand below and salt above ; and again, how I had made a fool of one here and another there, and had made a jest of every man, so that during the whole meal they spoke only of me. Yet had I not had such a friend at court these same acts would have been held deserving of severe punishment. And so I drew my conclusion how 'twould go at court if a rogue should gain a prince's favour.

Our meal ended, we found the Jew had no horse which would serve Herzbruder for me : but as he stood in such esteem that the colonel could hardly afford to lose his good word, therefore he presented us with one from his own stable, saddle and bridle and all, on which my lord Simplicissimus was set and with his friend Herzbruder rode joyfully forth from the fortress. And some of my comrades did cry, " Good luck, brother, good luck," but others from envy, " The longer the halter the greater the luck."

Chap. xi : DISCOURSES OF THE ORDER OF THE MARAUDER BROTHERS

NOW on the way Herzbruder agreed with me that I should give myself out for his cousin that I might receive greater respect : and he for his part would get me a horse and a servant and send me to the regiment of Neuneck, wherein I could serve as a volunteer till an officer's place should fall vacant in the army, to which he could help me. And so in a wink I became a fellow that looked like a good soldier : but in that summer I did no great deeds, save that I helped to steal a few cattle here and there in the Black Forest and made myself well acquainted with the Breisgau and Alsace. For the rest, I had scant luck, for when my servant and his horse had been captured by the Weimar troops at Kenzingen I must needs work the other harder, and in the end so ride him to death that I was fain to join the order of the " Merode-brüder." My friend Herzbruder indeed would willingly have equipped me again : but seeing that I had so soon got rid of the first two horses, he held back, and thought to let me kick my heels till I had learned more foresight : nor did I desire it, for I found in my new companions so pleasant a society that till winter quarters should come I wished for no better employ.

Now must I tell you somewhat of these Merode brothers, for without doubt there be some, and specially those that be ignorant of war, that know not who these people be. And so have I never found any writer that hath included in his work an account of their manners, customs, rights, and privileges : besides which 'tis well worth while that not only the generals of these days but also the peasants should know what this brotherhood is. And first as concerns their name, I do hope 'twill be no disgrace to that honourable cavalier in whose service they got that name, or I could not so openly tack it on to any man. For I once saw a kind of shoe that had in place of eyelet-holes twisted cords, that a man might more easily stamp through the mud : and these were called Mansfeld's shoes because his troops first devised them. Yet should any call Count Mansfeld himself " Cobbler " on that account, I would count him for a fool. And so must you understand this name, that will last as long as Germans do make war : and this was the beginning of it : when this gentleman (Merode) first brought a newly raised regiment to the army his recruits proved as weak and crazy in body as the Bretons,* so that they could not endure the marching and other fatigues to which a soldier must submit in the field, for which reason their brigade soon became so weak that it could hardly protect the colours, and wherever you found one or more sick and lame in the market-place or in houses, and behind fences and hedges, and asked, " Of what regiment ? " the answer was wellnigh always " Of Merode."

Hence it arose that at length all that, whether sick or sound, wounded or not, were found straggling off the line of march or else did not have their quarters in the field with their own regiment, were called " Merode-brothers," just as before they were known as " swine-catchers " and " bee-taylors " : for they be like to the drones in the beehives which when they have lost their sting can work no more nor make honey, but only eat. If a trooper lose his horse or a musqueteer his health, or his wife and child fall ill and must stay behind, at once you have a pair and a half of Merode-brothers, a crew that can be compared with none but gipsies, for not only do they straggle round the army in front, in the flanks, in the middle, as it pleases them, but also they be like the gipsies in manners and customs. For you can see them huddled together (like partridges in winter) behind the hedges in the shade or, if the season require it, in the sun, or else lying round a fire smoking tobacco and idling, while the good soldier meanwhile must endure with the colours heat, thirst, hunger, and all manner of misery. Here again goes a pack of them pilfering alongside the line of march, while many a poor soldier is ready to sink under the weight of his arms. They plunder all they can find before, behind, and beside the army : and what they cannot consume that they spoil, so that the regiments, when they come to their quarters or into camp, do often find not even a good draught of water ;

* Referring to a body of Breton troops sent by Richelieu to help Guébriant. They turned out worthless.

and when they are strictly forced to stay with the baggage-train, you will often find this greater in number than the army itself. And though they do march together and lodge together, fight and make common cause, yet have they no captain to order them, no Feldwebel nor sergeant to dust their jackets, no corporal to rouse them up, no drummer to summon them to picket or bivouac duty, and, in a word, no one to bring them into the line of battle like an adjutant nor to assign them their lodgings like a quartermaster, but they live like noblemen. Howbeit whenever a commissariat-officer comes, they are the first to claim their share, undeserved though it be. Yet are the Provost-marshal and his fellows their greatest plague, being such as at times, when they play their tricks too scurvily, do set iron bracelets on their hands and feet, or even adorn them with a hempen collar and hang them up by their precious necks. They keep no watch, they dig no trenches, they serve on no forlorn hope, and they will never fight in line of battle, yet they be well nourished and fed. But what damage the general, the peasant, and the whole army, in which many such companions are to be found, do suffer, is not to be described. The basest of horse-boys, that doth naught but forage, is worth to the general more than one thousand such, that do make a trade of such foraging and lie at ease without excuse upon their bear-skins,* till they be taken off by the adversary or be rapped over the fingers when they do meddle with the peasants. So is the army weakened and the enemy strengthened : and even if a scurvy rogue of this kind (I mean not the poor sick man, but the riders without horses that for sheer neglect do let their horses perish, and betake themselves to the brotherhood to save their skins) do so pass the summer, yet all the use one can have of him is to equip him again for the winter at great cost that he may have somewhat to lose in the next campaign. 'Twere well to couple such together like greyhounds and teach them to make war in garrison towns, or even make them toil in chains in the galleys, if they will not serve on foot in the field till they can get a horse again. I say naught here of the many villages

* " Bearskinner " was the troopers' name for a malingerer. It was taken from a very old legend.

that, by chance or by malice, have been burned down by them ; how many of their own comrades they entice away, plunder, rob, and even murder, nor how many a spy can be concealed among them if he know but enough to give the name of a regiment and a company in the army. To this honourable brotherhood I now must belong, and so remained till the day before the Battle of Wittenweier, at which time our headquarters were at Schüttern : for going then with my comrades into the county of Geroldseck to steal cows and oxen I was taken prisoner by the troops of Weimar, that knew far better how to treat us, for they made us take musquets and distributed us in different regiments : and so I came into Hattstein's regiment.

Chap. xii : OF A DESPERATE FIGHT FOR LIFE IN WHICH EACH PARTY DOTH YET ESCAPE DEATH

NOW could I well understand I was born but for misfortune, for some weeks before the engagement happened I heard some lower officers of Götz's army that talked of our war : and says one, "Without a battle will this summer not pass : and if we win, in the next winter we shall surely take Freiburg and the Forest-towns : but if we earn a defeat we shall earn winter quarters too." Upon this prophecy I laid my plans and said to myself, " Now rejoice thee, Simplicissimus, for next spring thou wilt drink good wine of the Lake and the Neckar and wilt enjoy all that the troops of Weimar can win." Yet therein I was mightily deceived, for being now of those troops myself, I was predestinated to help lay siege to Breisach, for that siege was fully set afoot presently after the Battle of Wittenweier, and there must I, like other musqueteers, watch and dig trenches day and night, and gained naught thereby save that I learnt how to assail a fortress by approaches, to which matter I had paid but scant attention in the camp before Magdeburg. For the rest, I was but lousily provided for, for two or three must lodge together, our purses were empty, and so were wine, beer, and meat a rarity. Apples, with half as much bread as I could eat, were my finest dainties. And 'twas hard for me to bear this when I reflected on the fleshpots of Egypt, that is, on the Westphalian hams and sausages of Lippstadt. Yet did I think but little on my wife, and when I did so I did but plague myself with the thought that she might be untrue to me. At last was I so impatient that I declared to my captain how my affairs stood and wrote by the post to Lippstadt, and so heard from Colonel Saint André and my father-in-law that they had, by letters to the Duke of Weimar, secured that my captain should let me go with a pass.

So about a week or four days before Christmas I marched away with a good musquet on my shoulder from the camp down through the Breisgau, being minded at this same Christmas-tide to receive at Strassburg twenty thalers sent to me by my brother-in-law, and then to betake myself down the Rhine with the traders, since now there were no Emperor's garrisons on the road. But when I was now past Endingen and came to a lonely house, a shot was fired at me so close that the ball grazed the rim of my hat, and forthwith there sprang out upon me a strong, broad-shouldered fellow, crying to me to lay down my gun. So I answered, " By God, my friend, not to please thee," and therewith cocked my piece. Thereupon he whipped out a monstrous thing that was more like to a headsman's sword than a rapier, and rushed upon me : and now that I saw his true intent I pulled the trigger and hit him so fair on the forehead that he reeled, and at last fell. So to take my advantage of this I quickly wrested his sword out of his hand and would have run him through with it, but it would not pierce him ; and then suddenly he sprang to his feet and seized me by the hair and I him, but his sword I had thrown away. So upon that we began such a serious game together as plainly shewed the bitter rage of each against the other, and yet could neither be the other's master : now was I on top, and now he, and for a moment both on our feet, which lasted not long, for each would have the other's life. But as the blood gushed out in streams from my nose and mouth I spat it into mine enemy's face, since he so greatly desired it : and that served me well, for it hindered him from seeing. And so we hauled each other about in the snow for more than an hour, till we were so weary that to all appearance the weakness of one could not, with fists alone, have overcome the weariness of the other ; nor could either have compassed the death of the other of his own strength and without weapon. Yet the art of wrestling, wherein I had often exercised myself at Lippstadt, now served me well, or I had doubtless paid the penalty : for my enemy was stronger than I, and moreover proof against steel. So when we had wearied us wellnigh to death says he at last, " Brother, hold, I cry you mercy."

So says I, " Nay, thou hadst best have let me pass at the first." " And what profit hast thou if I die ? " quoth he. " Yea," said I, " and what profit hadst thou had if thou hadst shot me dead, seeing that I have not a penny in my pocket ? " On that he begged my pardon, and I granted it, and suffered him to stand up after he had sworn to me solemnly that he would not only keep the peace but would be my faithful friend and servant. Yet had I neither believed nor trusted him had I then known of the villainies he had already wrought. But when we were on our feet we shook hands upon this, that what had happened should be forgotten, and each wondered that he had found his master in the other ; for he supposed that I was clad in the same rogue's hide as him-self : and that I suffered him to believe, lest when he had gotten his gun again he should once more attack me. He had from my bullet a great bruise on his forehead, and I too had lost much blood. Yet both were sorest about our necks, which were so twisted that neither could hold his head upright.

But as it drew towards evening, and my adversary told me that till I came to the Kinzig I should meet neither dog nor cat, still less a man, whereas he had in a lonely hut not far from the road a good piece of meat and a draught of the best, I let myself be persuaded and went with him, he protesting with sighs all the way how it grieved him to have done me a hurt.

Chap. xiii : HOW OLIVER CONCEIVED THAT HE COULD EXCUSE HIS BRIGAND'S TRICKS

A DETERMINED soldier whose business it is to hold his life cheap and to adventure it easily, is but a stupid creature. Out of a thousand fellows you could hardly have found one that would have gone as a guest to an unknown place with one that had even now tried to murder him. On the way I asked him which army he was of. So he said, he served no prince but was his own master, and asked of what party I was. I answered I had served the Duke of Weimar but had now my discharge, and was minded to betake myself home. Then he asked my name, and when I said " Simplicius " he turned him round (for I made him walk before me because I trusted him not) and looked me straight in the face. " Is not thy name also Simplicissimus ? " quoth he. " Yea," says I, " he is a rogue that denies his own name : and who art thou ? " " Why, brother," he answered, " I am Oliver, whom thou wilt surely remember before Magdeburg." With that he cast away his gun and fell on his knees to beg for my pardon that he had meant to do me an ill turn, saying he could well conceive he could have no better friend in the world than he would find in me, since according to old Herzbruder's prophecy I was so bravely to avenge his death. And I for my part did wonder at so strange a meeting, but he said, " This is nothing new : mountain and valley can never meet, but what is truly strange is this, that I from a secretary have become a footpad and thou from a fool a brave soldier. Be ye sure, brother, that if there were ten thousand like us, we could relieve Breisach to-morrow and in the end make ourselves masters of the whole world."

With such talk we came at nightfall to a little remote labourer's cottage : and though such boasting pleased me not, yet I said " Yea," chiefly because his rogue's temper was well known to me, and though I trusted him not at all, yet went I with him in the said house, in which a peasant was even then lighting a fire : to him said Oliver, " Hast thou aught ready cooked ? " " Nay," said the peasant, " but I have still the cold leg of veal that I brought from Waldkirch." " Well then," said Oliver, " go bring it here and likewise the little cask of wine." So when the peasant was gone, " Brother," said I (for so I called him to be safer with him), " thou hast a willing host." " Oh, devil thank the rogue," says he, " I do keep his wife and child for him and also he doth earn good booty for himself ; for I do leave for him all the clothes that I capture, for him to turn to his own profit." So I asked where he kept his wife and child ; to which Oliver answered, he had them in safety in Freiburg, where he visited them twice a week, and brought him from thence his food, as well as powder and shot. And further he told me he had long prac- tised this freebooter's trade, and that it profited him more than to serve any lord : nor did he think to give it up till he had properly filled his purse. " Brother," says I, " thou livest in a dangerous estate, and if thou art caught in such a villainy, how thinkest thou 'twould fare with thee ?." " Aha," says he, " I perceive thou art still the old Simplicissimus : I know well that he that would win must stake somewhat : but remember that their lordships * of Nuremberg hang no man till they catch him." So I answered, " Yea, but put the case, brother, that thou art not caught, which is yet but un- likely, since the pitcher that goes often to the well must break at last, yet is such a life as thou leadest the most shameful in the world, so that I scarce can believe thou canst desire to die in it ? "

" What ? " says he, " the most shameful ? My brave Simplicissimus, I assure thee that robbery is the most noble exercise that one in these days can find in the world. Tell me how many kingdoms and principalities be there that have not been stolen by violence and so taken. Or is it ever counted for evil of a king or prince in the whole world that he enjoys the revenues of his lands, which commonly have been gained by his forefathers with violence and conquest ? Yea, what could be named more noble than the trade that I now follow ? I well perceive that thou wouldst fain preach me a sermon showing how many have been hanged, drawn, and quartered

* The allusion is to the escape of the robber-knight, Eppelin von Gailingen, from the Castle of Nuremberg.

for murder and robbery : but that I know already, for so the laws do command : yet wilt thou see none but poor and miserable thieves so put to death, as they indeed deserve for undertaking this noble craft, which is reserved for men of high parts and capacity. But when hast thou ever seen a person of quality punished by justice for that he has oppressed his people too much ? Yea, and more than that, when is the usurer punished, that yet doth pursue this noble trade in secret, and that too under the cloak of Christian love ? Why, then, should I be punishable, I that practise it openly without concealment or hypocrisy ? My good Simplicissimus, thou hast never read thy Machiavel. I am a man of honest mood, and do follow this manner of life openly and without shame. I do fight and do adventure my life upon it like the heroes of old, and do know that such trades, and likewise he that follows them, stand ever in peril : but since I do adventure my life thereupon, it doth follow without contradiction that 'tis but just and fair I should be allowed to follow my trade."

To that I answered, " Whether robbery and theft be allowed to thee or not, yet do I know that this is against the order of nature, that will not have it so that any man should do to another what he would not have done to himself. And this is wrong, too, as against the laws of this world, which ordain that thieves shall be hanged and robbers beheaded and murderers broken on the wheel : and lastly, 'tis also against the laws of God, which is the chiefest point of all : for He doth leave no sin unpunished." " Yea," said Oliver, " 'tis as I said : thou art still the same old Simplicissimus that hath not yet studied his Machiavel : but if I could but set up a monarchy in this fashion, then would I fain see who would preach to me against it."

And so had we disputed longer : but then came the peasant with meat and drink, and so we sat together and appeased our hunger, of which I at least had much need.

Chap. xiv: HOW OLIVER EXPLAINED HERZBRUDER'S
PROPHECY TO HIS OWN PROFIT, AND SO
CAME TO LOVE HIS WORST ENEMY

OUR food was white bread and a cold leg of veal.
And moreover we had a good sup of wine and a
warm room. "Aha! Simplicissimus," said Oliver,
"'tis better here than in the trenches before Breisach." "True," said I, "if one could enjoy such a life with
safety and a good conscience." At that he laughed loud, and
says he, "Yea, are the poor devils in the trenches safer than
we, that must every moment expect a sally of the garrison?
My good Simplicissimus, I do plainly see that, though thou
hast cast aside thy fool's cap, thou hast kept thy fool's head,
that cannot understand what is good and what is bad. And
if thou wert any but that same Simplicissimus that after
Herzbruder's prophecy must avenge my death, I would make
thee to confess that I do lead a nobler life than any baron."
With that I did think, "How will it go now? Thou must
devise another manner of speech, or this barbarous creature
with the help of his peasant may well make an end of thee."
So says I, "Who did ever hear at any time that the scholar
should know more than the master? And so, brother, if
thou hast so happy a life as thou dost pretend, give me a share
in thy good luck, for of good luck I have great need."

To which Oliver answered, "Brother, be thou assured that
I love thee as mine own self, and that the affront I put upon
thee to-day doth pain me more than the bullet wherewith thou
didst wound my forehead, when thou didst so defend thyself
as should any proper man of courage. Therefore why should
I deny thee anything? If it please thee, stay thou here with
me: I will provide for thee as for myself. Or if thou hast no
desire to stay with me, then will I give thee a good purse of
money and go with thee whithersoever thou wilt. And that
thou mayest believe that these words do come from my heart,
I will tell thee the reason wherefore I do hold thee in such
esteem: thou dost know how rightly old Herzbruder did hit
it off with his prophecies: and look you, that same did so
prophesy to me when we lay before Magdeburg, saying,

' Oliver, look upon our fool as thou wilt, yet will he astonish thee by his courage, and play thee the worst tricks thou hast ever known, for which thou shalt give him good cause at a time when ye know not one another. Yet will he not only spare thy life when it is in his hands, but after a long time he will come to the place where thou art to be slain : and there will he avenge thy death.' And for the sake of this prophecy, my dear Simplicissimus, am I ready to share with thee the very heart in my breast. For already is a part of that prophecy fulfilled, seeing that I gave thee good reason to shoot me in the head like a valiant soldier and to take my sword from me (which no other hath ever done) and to grant me my life, when I lay under thee and was choking in blood : and so I doubt not that the rest of the prophecy which concerns my life shall be fulfilled. And from this matter of the revenge I must conclude, brother, that thou art my true friend, for an thou wert not, thou wouldest not take upon thee to avenge me. And now thou hast the innermost thoughts of my heart : so now do thou tell me what thou art minded to do." Upon that I thought, " The devil trust thee, for I do not : if I take money from thee for the journey I may well be the first whom thou slayest : and if I stay with thee I must expect some time to be hanged with thee." So I determined I would befool him, tarrying with him till I could find opportunity to be quit of him : and so I said if he would suffer me I would stay with him a day or a week to see if I could accustom myself to his manner of life : and if it pleased me he should find in me a true friend and a good soldier : and if it pleased me not, we could at any time part in peace. And on that he drank to my health, yet I trusted him not, and feigned to be drunken before I was so, to see if he would be at me when I could not defend myself.

Meanwhile the fleas did mightily plague me, whereof I had brought good store from Breisach : for when it grew warm they were no longer content to remain in my rags but walked abroad to take their pleasure. Of that Oliver was aware, and asked me had I lice ? To which I answered, " Yea, indeed, and more than I can hope to have ducats in my life." " Say not so," said Oliver, " for if thou wilt abide with me thou canst earn more ducats than thou hast lice now." I answered,

" 'Tis as impossible as that I can be quit of my lice." " Yea,"
says he, " but both are possible " : and with that he commanded the peasant to fetch me a suit that lay in a hollow tree
near the house ; which was a grey hat, a cape of elk-skin, a
pair of scarlet breeches, and a grey coat : and shoes and
stockings would he give me next day. So as I saw him so
generous I trusted him somewhat better than before, and
went to bed content.

*Chap. xv : HOW SIMPLICISSIMUS THOUGHT MORE
PIOUSLY WHEN HE WENT A-PLUNDERING
THAN DID OLIVER WHEN HE WENT TO
CHURCH*

SO the next morning, as day began to break, says
Oliver, " Up, Simplicissimus ; we will fare forth in
God's name to see what we can come by." "Good
Lord," thought I, " must I then in thy holy name go
a-thieving ? " I that aforetime when I left my good hermit
could not hear without marvelling when one man said to
another, " Come, brother, we will in God's name take off a
cup of wine together " ? for that I counted a double sin, that
a man should be drunken, and drunken in God's name. " My
heavenly Father," thought I, " how am I changed since
then ! My faithful Lord, what will at last become of me if
I turn not ? Oh ! check thou my course, that will assuredly
bring me to hell if I repent not."

So speaking and so thinking did I follow Oliver to a village
wherein was no living creature : and there to have a better
view we did go up into the church steeple : there had he in
hiding the shoes and stockings that he had promised me the
night before, and moreover two loaves of bread, some pieces
of dried meat, and a barrel half full of wine, which would
have easily afforded him provision for a week. So while I
was putting on what he gave me he told me here was the
place where he was wont to wait when he hoped for good
booty, to which end he had so well provisioned himself, and,
in a word, told me he had several such places, provided with
meat and drink, so that if he could not find a friend at home

in one place he might catch him elsewhere. For this must I praise his prudence, yet gave him to understand that 'twas not well so to misuse a place that was dedicated to God's service. " What," says he, " misuse ? The churches them- selves if they could speak would confess that what I do in them is naught in comparison with the sins that have afore- time been committed in them. How many a man and how many a woman, thinkst thou, have come into this church since it was built, on pretence of serving God, but truly only to shew their new clothes, their fine figure, and all their bravery ! Here cometh one into church like a peacock and putteth himself so before the altar as he would pray the very feet off the saints' images ! And there standeth another in a corner to sigh like the publican in the temple, which sighs be yet only for his mistress on whose face he feedeth his eyes, yea, for whose sake he is come thither. Another cometh to the church with a packet of papers like one that gathereth contributions for a fire, yet more to put his debtors in mind than to pray : and an he had not known those debtors would be in the church he had sat at home over his ledgers. Yea, it doth happen often that when our masters will give notice of aught to a parish, it must be done of a Sunday in the church, for which reason many a farmer doth fear the church more than any poor sinner doth fear the judge and jury. And thinkest thou not there be many buried in churches that have deserved sword, gallows, fire, and wheel ? Many a man could not have brought his lecherous intent to a good end had not the church helped him. Is a bargain to be driven or a loan to be granted, 'tis done at the church door. Many a usurer there is that can spare no time in the week to reckon up his rogueries, that can sit in church of a Sunday and devise how to practise fresh villainies. Yea, here they sit during mass and sermon to argue and talk as if the Church were built for such purpose only : and there be matters talked of that in private houses none would speak about. Some do sit and snore as if they had hired the place to sleep in : and some do naught but gossip of others and do whisper, ' How well did the pastor touch up this one or that one in his sermon ! ' and others do give heed to the discourse but for this reason only ! not to be bettered by it, but that they may carp at and blame their minister if he do but stumble once at a word (as they understand the matter). And here will I say naught of the stories I have read of amorous intercourse that hath its beginning and end in a church ; for I could not now remember all I could tell thee of that. Yet canst thou see how men do not only defile churches with their vices while they live but do fill them with their vanity and folly after they be dead. Go thou now into a church, and there by the gravestones and epitaphs thou wilt see how they that the worms have long ago devoured do yet boast themselves : look thou up and there wilt thou see more shields and helmets, and swords and banners, and boots and spurs than in many an armoury : so that 'tis no wonder that in this war the peasants have fought for their own in churches as if 'twere in fortresses. And why, then, should it not be allowed to me—to me, I say, as a soldier—to ply my trade in a church, whereas aforetime two holy fathers did for the mere sake of precedence cause such a blood-bath in a church * that 'twas more like to a slaughter-house than a holy place ? Yea, I would not so act if any did come here to do God's service ; for I am but of the lay people : yet they, that were clergymen, respected not the high majesty of the emperor himself. And why should it be forbidden to me to earn my living by the church when so many do so earn it ? And is it just that so many a rich man can for a fee be buried in the church to bear witness of his own pride and his friends' pride, while yet the poor man (that may have been as good a Christian as he and perchance a better), that can pay naught, must be buried in a corner without ? 'Tis as a man looks upon it : had I but known that thou wouldst scruple so to lay wait in a church I had devised another answer for thee : but in the meanwhile have thou patience till I can persuade thee to a better mind."

Now would I fain have answered Oliver that they were but lewd fellows that did dishonour the churches as did he, and that they would yet have their reward. Yet as I trusted him not, and had already once quarrelled with him, I let it pass. Thereafter he asked me to tell him how it had fared

* In 1063 the retainers of the Bishop of Hildesheim and the Abbot of Fulda fought in church at Goslar, and much bloodshed ensued.

with me since we parted before Wittstock, and moreover why I had had the jester's clothes on when I came into the camp before Magdeburg. Yet as my throat did mightily pain me, I did excuse myself and prayed him he would tell me the story of his life, that perchance might have strange happenings in it. To that did he agree, and began in this manner to tell me of his wicked life.

Chap. xvi : OF OLIVER'S DESCENT, AND HOW HE BEHAVED IN HIS YOUTH, AND SPECIALLY AT SCHOOL

"MY father," said Oliver, "was born not far from Aachen town of poor parents, for which reason he must in his youth take service with a rich trader that dealt in copper wares : and there did he carry himself so well that his master had him taught to write, read, and reckon, and set him over his whole household as did Potiphar Joseph. And that was well for both parties, for the merchant's wealth grew more and more through my father's zeal and prudence, and my father became prouder and prouder through his prosperity, so that he grew ashamed of his parents and despised them, of which they complained, yet to no purpose. So when he was five-and-twenty years of age, then died the merchant, and left an aged widow and one daughter, which last had played the fool and was not barren : but her child soon followed his grandfather. Thereupon my father, when he saw her at once fatherless and childless but not moneyless, cared not at all that she could wear no maiden's garland again, but began to pay her court, the which her mother well allowed, not only because her daughter might so recover her reputation but also because my father possessed all knowledge of the business and in especial could well wield the Jews' Spear.* And so by this marriage was my father in a moment a rich man and I his son and heir, whom for his wealth's sake he caused to be tenderly brought up : so was I kept in clothes like a young nobleman, in food like a

* Act as a usurer or cheat.

baron, and in attendance like a count, for all which I had more to thank copper and calamine than silver and gold.

" So before I reached my seventh year I had given good proof of what I was to be, for the nettle that is to be stings early : no roguery was too bad for me, and where I could play any man a trick I failed not to do so, for neither father nor mother punished me for it. I tramped with young rascals like myself through thick and thin in the streets and was already bold enough to fight boys stronger than myself : and did I get beat, my foolish parents would say, ' How now ? Is a great fellow like that to beat a mere child ? ' But if I won (for I would scratch and bite and throw stones), then said they, ' Our little Oliver will turn out a fine fellow.' And with that my indolence grew : for praying I was yet too young : and if I did curse like a trooper, 'twas said I knew not what I said. So I became worse and worse till I was sent to school : and there I did carry out what other wicked lads do mostly think of, yet dare not practise. And if I spoiled or tore my books, my mother would buy me others lest my miserly father should be wroth. My schoolmaster did I plague most, for he might not deal with me hardly, receiving many presents from my parents, whose foolish love to me was well known to him. In summer would I catch crickets and bring them secretly into the schoolroom, where they did play a merry tune. In winter would I steal snuff and scatter it in that place where 'tis the custom to whip the boys. And so if any stiff-necked scholar should struggle my powder would fly about and cause an agreeable pastime : for then must all sneeze together.

" So now I deemed myself too great a man for small roguery, but all my striving was for higher things. Often would I steal from one and put what I had stolen in another's pouch to earn him stripes, and with these tricks was I so sly that I was scarce ever caught. And of the wars we waged (wherein I was commonly colonel) and the blows I received —for I had ever a scratched face and a head full of bruises— I need not to speak : for every man doth know how boys do behave : and so from what I have said canst thou easily guess how in other respects I spent my youth."

Chap. xvii : HOW HE STUDIED AT LIÈGE, AND
HOW HE THERE DEMEANED HIMSELF

"NOW the more my father's riches increased, the more flatterers and parasites he had round him, all which did praise my fine capacities for study, but said no word of all my other faults or at least would excuse them, seeing well that any that did not so could never stand well with my father and mother. And so had they more pleasure in their son than ever had a tomtit that has reared a young cuckoo. So they hired for me a special tutor, and sent me with him to Liège, more to learn foreign tongues than to study : for I was to be no theologian, but a trader. He, moreover, had his orders not to be hard with me, lest that should breed in me a fearful and servile spirit. He was to allow me freely to consort with the students, lest I might become shamefaced, and must remember that 'twas to make, not a monk, but a man of the world of me, one that should know the difference between black and white.

" But my said tutor needed no such instruction, being of himself given to all manner of knaveries. And how could he forbid me such or rebuke me for my little faults when he himself committed greater ? To wine and women was he by nature most inclined, but I to wrestling and fighting : so did I prowl about the streets at night with him and his likes and learned of him in brief space more lechery than Latin. But as to my studies, therein I could rely on a good memory and a keen wit, and was therefore the more careless, but for the rest I was sunk in all manner of vice, roguery, and wantonness : and already was my conscience so wide that one could have driven a waggon and horses through it. I heeded nothing if I could but read Berni or Burchiello or Aretine during the sermon in church : nor did I hear any part of the service with greater joy than when 'twas said ' Ite missa est.'

" All which time I thought no little of myself but carried me right foppishly : every day was for me a feast-day, and because I behaved myself as a man of estate, and spent not only the great sums that my father sent me for my needs, but also my mother's plentiful pocket-money, therefore the women began to pay us court, but specially to my tutor. From these baggages I learned to wench and to game : how to quarrel, to wrestle, and to fight I knew well before, and my tutor in no wise forbade my debaucheries, since he himself was glad to take part in them. So for a year and a half did this monstrous fine life endure, till my father did hear of it from one that was his factor in Liège, with whom indeed we had at first lodged : this man received orders to keep a sharper eye upon us, to dismiss my tutor at once, to shorten my tether, and to examine into my expense more carefully. Which vexed us both mightily : and though he, my tutor, had now his congé, yet did we hold together, one way or the other, both by day and night : yet since we could no longer spend money as before, we did join ourselves to a rogue that robbed folks of their cloaks at night ; yea, or did drown them in the Meuse : and what we in this fashion earned with desperate peril of our lives, that we squandered with our whores, and let all studies go their way.

" So one might as we, after our custom, were prowling by night, to plunder students of their cloaks, we were overcome, my tutor run through the body, and I, with five others that were right rascals, caught and laid by the heels : and next day we being examined and I naming my father's factor, that was a man much respected, the same was sent for, questioned concerning me, and I on his surety set free, yet so that I must remain in his house in arrest till further order taken. Meanwhile was my tutor buried, the other five punished as rogues, robbers and murderers, and my father informed of my case : upon which he came himself with all haste to Liège, settled my business with money, preached me a sharp sermon, and shewed me what trouble and unhappiness I had caused him, yea, and told me it seemed as my mother would go desperate by reason of my ill conduct : and further threatened me, in case I did not behave better, he would disinherit me and send me packing to the devil. So I promised amendment and rode home with him : and so ended my studies."

Chap. xviii: OF THE HOMECOMING AND DEPAR-
TURE OF THIS WORSHIPFUL STUDENT,
AND HOW HE SOUGHT TO OBTAIN AD-
VANCEMENT IN THE WARS

"BUT when my father had me safely home, he
found I was in very truth spoiled. I had proved
no worshipful dominie as he had hoped, but a
quarreller and a braggart, that imagined he knew
everything. So hardly was I warm at home when he said
to me, ' Hearken, Oliver, I do see thine asses' ears a-growing
fast : thou beest a useless cumberer of the ground, a rogue
that will never be worth aught : to learn a trade art thou
too old : to serve a lord thou art too insolent, and to understand and follow my profession thou art but useless. Alas,
what have I accomplished with all the cost that I have
spent on thee ? For I did hope to have my joy in thee and
to make of thee a man : and now must I buy thee out of the
hangman's hand. Oh fie, for shame ! 'Twere best I should
set thee in a treadmill and let thee eat the bread of affliction
till some better luck arise for thee, when thou shalt have
purged thee of thine iniquities.'

"Now when I must day by day hear such lectures, at
the last was I out of all patience, and told my father roundly
I was not guilty of all, but he and my tutor, that led me
astray : and had he no joy of me, so was he rightly served,
that had given his parents no joy of him, but had let them
come to beggary and starvation. On that he reached for
a stick and would have paid me for my plain speaking,
swearing loud and long he would have me to the House of
Correction at Amsterdam. So away I went, and the same
night betook me to his newly bought farm, watched my
opportunity, and rode off to Cologne on the best horse I could
find in his stables.

"This horse did I sell, and forthwith lit upon even such
a crew of rogues and thieves as I had left at Liège. So at
play they did know me for what I was and I them, for both
did know so much. Straightway I was made one of their
brotherhood, and was their helper in their nightly excursions.

Yet when presently one of our band was caught in the Old Market as he would relieve a lady of quality of her heavy purse, and specially when I had seen him stand an hour in the pillory with an iron collar on, and, further, had seen one of his ears cut off and himself well whipped, that trade pleased me no more, but I enlisted as a soldier : for just then the colonel with whom we served before Magdeburg was a-recruiting. Meanwhile had my father learned where I was, and so did write to his factor he should inquire concerning me : which befell even then when I had drawn my first pay : and that the factor told my father, which gave orders that he should buy me out, cost it what it might : but when I heard that, I had fear of the House of Correction, and so would not be bought out. Through this was my colonel aware I was a rich merchant's son, and so fixed his price so high that my father left me as I was, intending to let me kick my heels awhile in the wars and so perchance come to a better mind.

" 'Twas not long before it happened that my colonel's writer died, in whose place he employed me, as thou knowest. And thereupon I began to have high thoughts, in hope to rise from one rank to another, and so in the end to become a general. From our secretary I did learn how to carry myself, and my intent to grow to a great man caused me to behave myself as a man of honour and repute, and no longer, as of old time, to play rogues' tricks. Yet had I no luck till our secretary died, and then methought, ' Thou must see to it that thou hast his place.' And all I could I spent : for when my mother heard I had begun to do well she ever sent me moneys. Yet because young Herzbruder was beloved by our colonel and was preferred to me, I purposed to have him out of the way, specially because I was sure the colonel would give him the secretary's place. And at the delaying of the promotion which I so much desired I was so impatient that I had me made bullet proof by our Provost, so to fight with Herzbruder and settle matters by the sword : yet could I not civilly come at him. Yea, and our Provost warned me from my purpose and said, ' Even if thou makest him a sacrifice, yet will it do thee more harm than good, for thou wilt but have murdered the colonel's favourite.'

"Yet did he advise me I should steal somewhat in Herzbruder's presence and give it to him : for so could he bring it about that he should lose the colonel's favour. To that I agreed, and stole the parcel-gilt cup at the colonel's christening-feast and gave it to the Provost, by means of which he rid me of young Herzbruder, as thou wilt surely remember, even then when he, by his sorcery, filled thy pockets with puppies."

Chap. xix : HOW SIMPLICISSIMUS FULFILLED HERZBRUDER'S PROPHECY TO OLIVER BEFORE YET EITHER KNEW THE OTHER

ALL was green and yellow before mine eyes when I must so hear from Oliver's own mouth how he had gone about with my best friend, and yet I could take no revenge : mine inclination thereto I must needs pocket up lest he should mark it : and so begged he should tell me how it had further fared with him before the battle at Wittstock. "Why, in that encounter," said Oliver, " I carried myself like no quill-driver that is set upon his inkstand, but like a good soldier, being well mounted and bullet-proof, and moreover being counted in no squadron : for so could I show my proper valour, as one that doth mean to rise higher by his sword or to die. So did I fly around our brigade like a whirlwind, both to exercise myself and to shew our men I was more fit for arms than for the pen. Yet all availed nothing, for the Swedes' luck prevailed, and I must share the ill-fortune of our folk and must accept that quarter which a little before I would have given to no man.

" So was I with the other prisoners put into a foot regiment, which same was presently sent away to Pomerania on furlough : where, since there were many raw recruits, and I had shown a very notable courage, I was promoted corporal. Yet I was minded to make no long stay there, but as soon as might be to return to the emperor's service, to which party I was ever most affected, and that although doubtless my advancement had been far quicker among the Swedes. And my escape I brought to pass thus. I was sent out with seven musqueteers to a neighbouring post to demand the contribution, which was in arrears : and so having got together some eight hundred gulden or more, I shewed my fellows the gold and caused their eyes to lust after it, so much so that we agreed to divide the same and so make our escape. This being settled, I did persuade three of them to help me to shoot the other four dead, and such being accomplished we divided the money, namely, 200 gulden to each : and with that we marched off to Westphalia. Yet on the way did I persuade one of the three to help me to knock the other two on the head ; and then when we two were to divide the spoil I did make an end with the last man, and so came by good luck safely with the money to Wesel, where I took up my quarters and made merry with my money.

" But when this was now nearly spent, and I still had my love of fine living, then did I hear of a certain young soldier of Soest and what fine booty he had gained, and what a name he had earned : and so was I heartened up to follow in his footsteps. And as they called him, by reason of his green clothing, the Huntsman, so did I have such green raiment made for myself, and under his name did so plunder and steal in his and our own quarters, and that with every circumstance of wanton mischief, that it came near to this, that foraging parties should be forbidden on both sides. He ('tis true) stayed at home, but when I still went on a-mousing in his name all I could, then did that same huntsman for that same reason challenge me. But the devil might fight with him : for, as 'twas told me, he had ever the devil in his jacket : and that devil had soon made an end of my wound-proof. Yet could I not escape his craft, for with the help of a servant of his did he beguile me with my comrade into a sheep-fold, and there would force me, in the presence of two living devils that were his seconders by his side, to fight with him by moonlight. Which when I refused, they did compel me to the most contemptible actions in the world, and that my comrade soon spread abroad : of which I was so shamed that I up and away to Lippstadt and there took service with the Hessians : yet there I remained not long, where none could trust me, but tramped away further to the Dutch. And there did I find, 'tis true, more punctual payment, but too slow a war for my humour : for there were we kept in like monks and must live as chastely as nuns.

" So since I could no more shew my face among either Imperials, Swedes or Hessians, had I been willing wantonly to run the risk, as having deserted from all three, and since I could now no longer stay with the Hollanders, having violently deflowered a maiden, which act seemed likely presently to bring about its results, I thought to take refuge with the Spaniards, in the hope to escape home from them and to see how my parents fared. Yet as I set about that plan I missed my points of the compass so foully that I fell among the Bavarians, with whom I marched among the Merodians, from Westphalia as far as the Breisgau, and earned me a living by dicing and stealing. When I had aught I spent my day on the gaming-ground and my night among the sutlers : had I naught, I stole what I could, and often in a day two or three horses, both from pasture and from stables, sold them, and gamed away what I got, and then at night I would burrow under the soldiers' tents and steal away their purses from under their very heads. Were we on the march I would keep a watchful eye on the portmantles that the women did carry behind them ; these would I cut away. And so I kept myself alive till the battle before Wittenweier, wherein I was made prisoner, once more thrust into a foot-regiment, and so made one of Weimar's soldiers. But the camp before Breisach liked me not, so I left it early and went off to forage for myself, as thou seest I do. And be thou well assured, brother, that already I have laid low many a proud fellow and have earned a noble stock of money : nor am I minded to cease till I see I can get no more. And now it doth come to thy turn to tell me of thy life and fortunes."

Chap. xx: HOW IT DOTH FARE WITH A MAN ON WHOM EVIL FORTUNE DOTH RAIN CATS AND DOGS

NOW when Oliver had ended his discourse, I could not enough admire the Providence of God. Now could I understand how the good God had not alone protected me like a father from this monster in Westphalia, but had, moreover, so brought it about that he should go in fear of me. Now could I see what a trick I had played on him, to which the old Herzbruder's prophecy did apply, yet which he himself expounded, as may be seen in the fourteenth chapter, in another way, and that to my great profit. For had this beast but known I was the Huntsman of Soest he had surely made me drink of the same cup I served to him before at the sheep-fold. I considered, moreover, how wisely and darkly Herzbruder had delivered his predictions, and thought in myself that, though his prophecies were wont commonly to turn out true, yet 'twould go hard and must happen strangely if I was to revenge the death of one that had deserved the wheel and the gallows : I found it also good for my health that I had not first told him of my life, for so had I told him the way how I before had disgraced him. And as I thought thereupon, I did mark in Oliver's face certain scratches that he had not at Magdeburg, and so did conceive that these scars were the tokens of Jump-i'-th'-field, when at that former time he, in the likeness of a devil, did thus scrabble his face, and so asked him whence he had those signs, adding thereto that, though he had told me his whole life, yet I must gather that he had left out the best part, since he had not yet told me who had so marked him.

" Ah, brother," answered he, " were I to tell all my tricks and rogueries the time would be too long both for you and me : yet to shew thee that I conceal from thee none of my adventures I will tell thee the truth of this, though methinks 'tis but a sorry story for me.

" I am fully assured that from my mother's womb I was predestined to a scratched face, for in my very childhood I was so treated by my schoolfellows when I wrangled with

them : and so likewise one of those devils that waited on the
Huntsman of Soest handled me so roughly that six weeks
long one could see the marks of his claws in my face : but the
scars thou seest in my face had another beginning, to wit
this. When I lay in winter quarters with the Swedes in
Pomerania, and had a fair mistress by me, mine host must
leave his bed, for us to lie there : but his cat that had been
used to sleep therein would come every night and plague us,
as one that could not so easily spare her wonted bed-place as
her master and mistress had done : this did vex my wench
(that could at no time abide a cat) so sore that she did swear
loudly she would shew me no more favour till I had made
an end of this cat. So being desirous to have her society yet,
I devised how not only to please her but so to avenge myself
of the cat as to have sport therein. With that I packed the
beast in a bag, took my host's two great watch-dogs (which
at any time had no love for cats, but were familiar with me),
and the cat in the sack, to a broad and pleasant meadow,
and there thought to have my jest, for I deemed, since there
was no tree hard by for the cat to escape to, that the dogs
would chase her up and down for a while on the plain like a
hare, and so would afford me fine pastime. But zounds ; it
turned out for me not only dogs' luck, as people say, but cats'
luck (which sort of luck few can have known or 'twould
assuredly long ago have been made a proverb of), since the
cat, when I did open the bag, seeing only an open field and
on it her two fierce enemies, and nothing high whereto she
could escape, would not so easily take the field and so be torn
to pieces, but betook herself to mine own head as finding no
higher place, and as I sought to keep her away my hat fell off :
so the more I tried to pull her down, the deeper she stuck in
her claws so as to hold fast. Such a combat the dogs could
not endure to see, but joined the sport themselves, and
jumped up with open jaws in front, behind, and on either side
of me to come at the cat, which yet would not leave my head,
but maintained her place by fastening of her claws both in
my face and my head, as best she could. And if she missed
to give the dogs a pat with her glove of thorns, be sure she
missed not me : yet because she did sometimes strike the
dogs on the nose, therefore they busied themselves to bring

her down with their claws, and in so doing dealt me many a shrewd scratch in the face : yea, and if I with both hands strove to tear the cat from her place, then would she bite and scratch me to the best of her ability. And thus was I, both by the dogs and the cat at once so attacked, so mauled, and so terribly handled that I scarce looked like a man at all, and, what was worst of all, I must run the risk that if they so snapped at the cat they might by chance catch me by the ear or nose and bite it off. My collar and jerkin were so bloody that they were like to a smith's travise on St. Stephen's Day, when the horses are let blood ; nor could I devise any means to save myself from this torment, but at last must cast myself on the ground that the dogs might so seize the cat, unless I was willing to allow my poll to continue to be their battle-ground : 'tis true the dogs did then kill the cat, but I had by no means so noble sport from this as I had hoped, but only mockery and such a face as now thou seest before thee. At which I was so enraged that I shot both dogs dead, and did so bastinado my mistress that had given me cause for this fool's trick that she ran away from me, doubtless because she could no longer love so horrible a mask."

Chap. xxi : A BRIEF EXAMPLE OF THAT TRADE WHICH OLIVER FOLLOWED, WHEREIN HE WAS A MASTER AND SIMPLICISSIMUS SHOULD BE A PRENTICE

FAIN would I have laughed at this story of Oliver's, yet must show compassion only : and even as I began to tell him my history we saw a coach come up the road with two outriders. On that we came down from the church-tower and posted ourselves in a house that stood by the wayside and was very convenient for the way-laying of passengers. I must keep my loaded piece in reserve, but Oliver with one shot brought down at once one rider and his horse before they were ware of us : upon which the other forthwith fled : and while I, with my piece cocked, made the coachman halt and descend, Oliver leapt upon him and with his broad sword did cleave his head to the teeth, yea, and would thereafter have butchered the lady and the children that sat in the carriage and already looked more like dead folk than live ones : but I roundly said, that I would not have, but told him if he would do such a deed he must first slay me.

" Ah," says he, " thou foolish Simplicissimus, I had never believed thou wert so wicked a fellow as thou dost seem." " But brother," said I, " what hast thou against these innocents ? an they were men that could defend themselves 'twere another story." " How," he answered : " cook your eggs and there will be no chickens hatched. I know these young cockatrices well : their father the major is a proper skinflint, and the worst jacket-duster in the world."

And with such words he would have gone on to slay them : yet I restrained him so long that in the end I softened him : and 'twas a major's wife, her maids, and three fair children, for whom it grieved me much : these we shut up in a cellar that they might not too soon betray us, in which they had nothing to eat but fruit and turnips till they might chance to be released by some one : thereafter we plundered the coach, and rode off with seven fine horses into the wood where it was thickest.

So when we had tied them up and I had looked round me a little I was ware of a fellow that stood stock-still by a tree not far off : him I pointed out to Oliver and said 'twere well to be on our guard. " Why, thou fool," said he, " 'tis a Jew that I did tie up there : but the rogue is long ago frozen and dead." So he goes up to him and chucks him under the chin, and says he, " Aha ; thou dog, thou didst bring me many a fair ducat " : and as he so shook his chin there rolled out of his mouth a few doubloons that the poor rogue had rescued even in the hour of death. At that Oliver put his hand in his mouth and brought out twelve doubloons and a ruby of great price, and says he, " This booty have I to thank thee for, Simplicissimus "; and with that gave me the ruby, took the gold himself, and went off to fetch the peasant, bidding me in the meanwhile to stay by the horses and beware lest the dead Jew should bite me, whereby he meant I had no such courage as himself.

But he being gone to fetch his peasant, I had heavy thoughts, and did consider in what a dangerous state I now lived. And first I thought I would mount one of the horses and escape : yet did I fear lest Oliver should catch me in the act and shoot me ; for I had my suspicion that he did but try my good faith for this once, and so stood near by to watch me. Again I thought to run away on foot, but then must fear, even if I should give Oliver the slip, that I should not escape from the peasants of the Black Forest, which were then famous for the knocking of soldiers on the head. "And suppose," said I, "thou takest all the horses with thee, so that Oliver shall have no means to pursue thee, yet if thou be caught by the troops of Weimar, thou wilt as a convicted murderer be broken on the wheel." In a word, I could devise no safe means for my flight, and chiefly because I was there in a desolate forest where I knew neither highway nor by-way : and besides all that my conscience was now awake and did torment me, because I had stopped the coach and had been the cause that the driver had so miserably lost his life, and both the ladies with the innocent children had been laid fast in the cellar, wherein perchance, like this Jew, they must perish and die. Then again I would comfort me on the score of mine innocence, as being compelled against my will : yet there contrariwise my conscience answered me, I had long before deserved for my rogueries to fall into the hands of justice in the company of this arch-murderer, and so receive my due reward, and perhaps, methought, just Heaven had so provided that I should even so be brought to book. At the last I began to hope for better things and besought God's goodness to help me forth from this plight, and being in so pious a mood I said to myself, "Thou fool, thou art neither imprisoned nor fettered : the whole wide world stands open before thee : hast thou not horses enough to take to flight ? or, if thou wilt not ride, yet are thy feet swift enough to save thee."

But as I thus plagued and tormented myself and yet could come to no plan, came Oliver back with our peasant, which guided us with the horses to another farm, where we did bait and, taking turn by turn, did each get two hours' sleep. After midnight we rode on, and about noon came to the uttermost boundary of the Switzers, where Oliver was well known, and had us nobly entertained : and while we made merry the host sends for a couple of Jews, that bought the horses from us at half their price. And all was so plainly and clearly settled that there was little need of parley. For the Jews' chief question was, were the horses from the emperor's side or the Swedes' : and thereupon hearing they were from Weimar's army, " Then," said they, " must we ride them not to Basel but into Swabia to the Bavarians." At which close acquaintance and familiarity I must needs wonder.

So we feasted like princes, and heartily did I enjoy the good forest-trout and the savoury crayfish. And when 'twas evening we took to the road again, loading our peasant with baked meats and other victual like a pack-horse : with all which we came the next day to a lonesome farm, where we were friendly welcomed and entertained, and by reason of ill weather stayed two days : thereafter through woods and by-ways we came to that very hut whither Oliver did take me when first he had me to his companion.

Chap. xxii : HOW OLIVER BIT THE DUST AND TOOK SIX GOOD MEN WITH HIM

SO as we sat down to refresh our bodies and to rest, Oliver sent the peasant out to buy food and also powder and shot. He being gone, he takes off his coat and says he, " Brother, I can no longer carry this devils' money about with me alone " : and with that unbound a pair of bags like sausages that he wore on his naked body, threw them on the table, and went on, " Of these thou must take care till I come to my holidays and we both have enough, for the accursed stuff hath worked sores upon my body, so that I can no longer carry it." I answered, " Brother, hadst thou as little as I, 'twould not gall thee." But he cut me short. " How," says he, " what is mine is also thine ; and what we do further win shall be fairly shared." So I took up the two sausages and found they were indeed mighty heavy, being gold pieces only. Then I told him 'twas all ill-packed, and an he would, I would so sew the money in that it should not vex him half so much in the carrying. And when he agreed to this he had me with him to a hollow tree wherein he had scissors, needles, and thread : and there I made for him and me a pair of knapsacks out of a pair of breeches, and many a fine red penny I sewed therein. So having put the same on under our shirts, 'twas as if we had golden armour behind and before, by means of which we were become, if not proof against bullets, yet against swords. Then did I wonder why he kept no silver coin : to which he answered he had more than a thousand thalers lying in a tree from which he allowed the peasant to buy victuals, and never asked for a reckoning, as not greatly valuing such trash.

This done and the money packed, away we went to our hut, and there cooked our food and warmed ourselves by the stove all night. And thither at one o'clock of the day, when we did least expect it, came six musqueteers with a corporal to our hut with their pieces ready and their matches burning, who burst in the door and cried to us to surrender. But Oliver (that, like me, had ever his loaded piece lying by him and his sharp sword also, and then sat behind the table, and I by the stove behind the door) answered them with a couple of musquet-balls, wherewith he brought two to the ground, while I with a like shot slew one and wounded the fourth. Then Oliver whipped out his terrible sword (that could cut hairs asunder and might well be compared to Caliburn, the sword of King Arthur of England) and therewith he clove the fifth man from the shoulder to the belly, so that his bowels gushed out and he himself fell down beside them in gruesome fashion. And meanwhile I knocked the sixth man on the head with the butt-end of my piece, so that he fell lifeless : but Oliver got even such a blow from the seventh, and that with such force that his brains flew out, and I in turn dealt him that did that such a crack that he must needs join his comrades on the dead muster-roll. So when the one that I had shot at and wounded was ware of such cuffs and saw that I made for him with the butt of my piece also, he threw away his gun and began to run as if the devil was at his heels. Yet all this fight lasted no longer than one could say a paternoster, in which brief space seven brave soldiers did bite the dust.

Now when I thus found myself master of the field, I examined Oliver to see if he had a breath left in him, but finding him quite dead, methought 'twas folly to leave so much money on a corpse that could not need it, and so I stripped him of his golden fleece that I had made but yesterday and hung it round my neck with the other. And having broken mine own gun, I took Oliver's musquet and sharp battle-sword to myself, wherewith I provided me against all chances, and so away I went and that by the road by which I knew our peasant must return : and sitting down by the wayside I waited for him and further considered what I should now do.

Chap. xxiii : HOW SIMPLICISSIMUS BECAME A RICH MAN AND HERZBRUDER FELL INTO GREAT MISERY

NOW I sat but half an hour in thought when there comes to me our peasant puffing like a bear, and, running with all his might, was not ware of me till I had him fast : and "Why so fast ? " says I, " what news ? " " Quick," he answered, " away with ye ! for here cometh a corporal with six musqueteers that are to seize you and Oliver and bring you to Liechteneck dead or alive : they took me and would have it I should lead them to you : yet am I luckily escaped and come hither to warn ye."

" O villain," thought I, " thou hast betrayed us to get Oliver's money that lieth in the tree." Yet of this I let him mark nothing (for I would have him to shew me the way), but told him both Oliver and they that should take him were dead : which when he would not believe, I was good enough to go with him that he might see the miserable sight of the seven bodies, and says I, " The seventh of them that should take us I let go : and would to God I could bring these to life again, for I would not fail to do it."

At that the peasant was amazed with fear and asked, " What plan have ye now ? " " Why," quoth I, " the plan is already resolved on : for I give thee the choice of three things : either lead me by safe by-ways through the wood to Villingen, or shew me Oliver's money that lieth in the tree, or die here and keep these dead men company : an thou bringest me to Villingen thou hast Oliver's money for thyself alone : if thou wilt shew it me I will share it with thee : but if thou wilt do neither, I shoot thee dead and go my way."

Then would he fain have made off, but feared the musquet, and so fell on his knees and offered to guide me through the wood. So we started in haste and walked the whole of that day and the next night, which was by great good luck a very bright one, without food or drink or rest of any kind, till towards daybreak we saw the town of Villingen lie before us, and there I let my peasant go. And what supported us in this long journey was : for the peasant the fear of death and for me the desire to escape, myself and my money ; yea, I do wellnigh believe that gold lendeth a man strength : for though I carried a heavy enough load of it yet I felt no especial weariness.

I held it for a lucky omen that even as I came to the gates of Villingen they were being opened, where the officer of the watch examined me ; and hearing that I gave myself out to be a volunteer trooper of that regiment to which Herzbruder had appointed me when he released me from my musquet at Philippsburg, and also said that I had escaped from Weimar's camp before Breisach, by whose men I had been captured at Wittenweier and made to serve among them, and that I now desired to come to my regiment among the Bavarians, he gave me in charge of a musqueteer, who led me to the commandant. The same was yet asleep, for he had spent half the night awake about his affairs, so that I must wait a full hour and a half before his quarters, and because the folk just then came from early mass I had a crowd of citizens and soldiers around me that would all know how matters stood before Breisach : at which clamour the commandant awoke and without further delay had me brought to him.

Then began he to examine me, and I said even as I did at the gate. Whereupon he asked me of certain particularities of the siege and so forth, and at that I confessed all ; namely, how I had spent some few days with a fellow that had also escaped, and with him had attacked and plundered a coach, with intent to get so much booty from Weimar's people that we could get us horses, and so properly equipped could come to our regiments again ; but yesterday we had been attacked unawares by a corporal and six other fellows that would have taken us, whereby my comrade had been left dead on the field with six of the enemy, while the seventh as well as I had escaped : but he to his own party. But of the rest, namely, how I would have come to my wife at Lippstadt, and how I had two such well-stuffed breast and back-plates, of that I said no word, and made no scruple to conceal it, for what did it concern him ? Nor did he ask me of it at all, but much more was amazed and would hardly believe that Oliver and I had killed six men and put the seventh to flight, even though my comrade had paid with his life. So as we talked there was occasion to speak of Oliver's wonderful sword that I had by my side : which pleased him so well that if I would part civilly from him and get a pass I must hand it over to him in return for another that he gave me. And in truth it was a fine and beautiful blade, with a perpetual calendar engraved thereupon, nor shall any persuade me 'twas not forged by Vulcan *in hora Martis*, and altogether so prepared as is told of that sword in the Heldenbuch, by which all other swords are cleft asunder and the most courageous and lion-hearted foes are put to flight like fearful hares. So when he had dismissed me and commanded to give me a pass I went the nearest way to an inn, and knew not whether I should first eat or sleep : for I needed both. Yet would I sooner appease my belly, and so commanded meat and drink, and considered how I should lay my plans to come in safety to my wife at Lippstadt with my money ; for I was as little minded to go to my regiment as to break my neck.

But while I so speculated and mused of one and another cunning device, there limped into the room a fellow with a stick in his hand, his head bound up, one arm in a sling, and clothes so poor that I would have given him not a penny for them : and so soon as the drawer was ware of him he would have cast him forth, for he smelt vilely and was so full of lice that a man could have garrisoned the whole Swabian *

---

* He may possibly mean the three old fortifications of which ruins still remain : Schwaben-, Schweden-, and Alexander-schanze ; all of which are close to his favourite spa at Griesbach.

heath with them. Yet he prayed he might but be allowed to warm himself, which yet was not granted. But I taking pity on him and interceding for him, with difficulty he was let to come to the stove : and there he looked upon me, as I thought, with a curious longing and a great attention to my drinking, and uttered many sighs. So when the drawer went to fetch me a dish of meat, he came to me at my table and held out an earthen penny-pot, so that I might well understand what he would have : so I took the can and filled up his little pot for him before he asked. But " O friend," says he, " for Herzbruder's sake give me somewhat to eat also." Which when he said it cut me to the heart ; for well I saw it was Herzbruder himself. Then had I nearly swooned to see him in so evil a plight, yet I recovered myself and fell upon his neck and set him by me, where the tears did gush from our eyes : his for joy and mine for pity.

Chap. xxiv : OF THE MANNER IN WHICH HERZ-BRUDER FELL INTO SUCH EVIL PLIGHT

NOW by reason of the suddenness of this our meeting we could neither eat nor drink, but only ask one of the other how it had fared with each since we had last met. Yet as the host and the drawer went ever in and out, we could have no private discourse : and the host marvelling that I could suffer so lousy a companion by me, I told him that in time of war such was the custom among good soldiers that were comrades : and when I understood further how Herzbruder had till now been in the Spital, and there had been supported by alms, and his wounds but sorrily bound up, I hired of the host a separate chamber, put Herzbruder to bed, and sent for the best surgeon I could find, besides a tailor and a sempstress to clothe him and to rid him of his lice : and having in my purse those same doubloons that Oliver had fetched out of the dead Jew's mouth, I cast them on the table, and says I to Herzbruder, in the host's hearing, " See, brother ; there is my money : that will I spend on thee and consume with thee."

So with that the host entertained us nobly : but to the surgeon I showed the ruby that had belonged to the said Jew, and was worth some 20 thalers, and told him that as I purposed to spend such small moneys as I had for our food and for the clothing of my comrade, therefore I would give him that ring if he would quickly and thoroughly cure my said comrade, with which he was content, and bestowed his best care upon that cure. And so I tended Herzbruder like my second self, and caused a modest suit of grey cloth to be made for him. But first I went to the commandant for my pass, and told him how I had met a comrade sorely wounded : for him I would wait till he was sound, for were I to leave him behind me I could not answer for it to my regiment : which intention the commandant approved and allowed me to stay as long as I listed, with the further offer that when my comrade could follow me he would provide us both with sufficient passes.

Then, coming back to Herzbruder and sitting by his bed alone, I begged him he would freely tell me how he had come into so evil a plight : for I thought he might perchance have been driven from his former place for weighty reasons or for some fault, and so degraded and brought to his present evil case. But " Brother," said he, " thou knowest that I was the Count of Götz his factotum and dearest intimate friend : on t'other hand thou knowest well how evil an end this last campaign hath come to under his generalship and command, wherein we not only lost the Battle of Wittenweier, but did also fail to raise the siege of Breisach. Seeing, then, that on this account all manner of rumours be afloat, and that most unfair ones, and in especial now that the said count is cited to Vienna to justify himself, therefore for fear and shame I do willingly live in this humble plight, and often do wish either to die in this misery or at least so long to lie concealed till the said Count shall have proved his innocence : for so far as I know he was at all times true to the Roman emperor : and that in this set year he hath had no good luck is, in my opinion, more to be ascribed to the Providence of God (who giveth victory to whom He will) than to the Count his neglectfulness.

" Now when we were to relieve Breisach and I saw that on

our side all was done so sleepily, I armed mine own self and
marched forth with the rest upon the bridge of boats as if I
in person were to finish the business ; which was neither my
profession nor my duty : yet I did it for an example to others,
because we had accomplished so little that summer then past.
But luck or ill-luck would so have it that I, being among the
first to sally forth, was also among the first to look the enemy
in the face upon the bridge, where was a sharp encounter, and
as I had been foremost in attack, so when we gave way before
the furious charge of the French I was the last to retreat, and
so fell into the enemy's hands : and there did I receive a
bullet in the right arm and another in the leg, so that I could
neither run nor hold a sword : and as the straitness of the
place and the desperateness of the action allowed no talk of
giving or taking of quarter, I got me a crack on the head
which brought me to the ground, and there, being finely clad,
I was by some stripped and in the confusion thrown into the
Rhine for dead : in which sore strait I called to God for help
and left myself to His good pleasure ; and while I offered up
my prayers I found His help at hand : for the Rhine did cast
me up on land where I did staunch my wounds with moss :
and though in so doing I was nigh frozen, yet I found in me a
special strength to creep from thence (for God helped me) so
that I, though miserably wounded, came to certain Merode-
brothers * and soldiers' wives, that one and all had compassion on me though they knew me not : yet all already
despaired of the relief of that fortress ; and that did hurt me
more than all my wounds : but they refreshed and clothed
me by their fire, and before I could even bandage up my
wounds I must behold how our people prepared for a shameful
retreat and gave up our cause as lost : which caused me
dreadful pain : and for that reason I resolved to make myself
known to none, and so not to make myself a mark for mockery :
wherefore I joined myself to certain wounded men of our army
that had their own surgeon with them : to him I gave a
golden cross that I still had about my neck, for which he
bound up my wounds so as to last till now. And in such poor
plight, my good Simplicissimus, have I made shift so far, and
am minded to reveal to no man who I am till I see how the

* See chap. xi. above.

Count of Götz his affair will turn out. And now that I see thy goodness and faith, it breedeth in me great comfort that the good God hath not forsaken me : for this very morning, when I came from early mass and saw thee stand before the commandant's quarters, I did fancy that God had sent thee to me in shape of an angel to help me in my need."

So I did comfort him as best I could, and secretly told him I had yet more money than those doubloons that he had seen ; and that all was at his service. Therewith I also told him of Oliver's end, and how I had perforce avenged his death, which so enlivened his spirits that it also helped his body, in such wise that every day he grew better of his wounds.

BOOK V

Chap. i : HOW SIMPLICISSIMUS TURNED PALMER
AND WENT ON A PILGRIMAGE WITH
HERZBRUDER

NOW Herzbruder being wholly restored and healed
of his wounds, he told me in secret he had in his
greatest need made a vow to go on a pilgrimage to
Einsiedeln. And since in any case he was now so
near to Switzerland, he would perform the same though he
must beg his way thither. This was pleasant hearing for me :
so I offered him my money and my company, yea, and would
buy a couple of nags to do the journey upon, not indeed for
the reason that religion urged me thereto, but rather to see
the Confederates' country as the one land wherein sacred
peace yet flourished. So I rejoiced much to have the opportunity to serve Herzbruder on such a journey, seeing that I
loved him almost more than myself. Yet he refused both my
help and my company with the excuse that his pilgrimage
must be performed on foot and with peas in his shoes : and
should I be in his company not only should I hinder him in
his pious thoughts, but should also bring on myself great
discomfort by reason of his slow going. All which he said to
be rid of me, because he did scruple on so holy a journey to
spend money that had been gained by robbery and murder :
besides, he would not put me to too great expense, and said
openly that I had already done more for him than I owed
him or he could hope to repay : upon which we fell into a
friendly dispute, which same was so pleasant a quarrel that
I have never heard the like, for we talked of nothing but this,
that each one said he had not yet done for his fellow so much
as one friend should for another, nay, was yet far from making
up for the benefits he had received. Yet all this would not
move him to take me for a companion, till I perceived that
he had a disgust both at Oliver's money and mine own godless
life : therefore I made shift with a lie and persuaded him
that my intent to reform my life did move me to go to

Einsiedeln : and should he hinder me from so good a work, and I thereupon should die, he should hardly answer for it : by which I persuaded him to suffer me to visit that holy place with him, especially since I (though 'twas all lies) made an appearance of great penitence for my wicked life, and moreover did persuade him I had laid on myself a penance to go to Einsiedeln on peas even as he. But this quarrel was scarce over ere we fell into another, for Herzbruder was too full of scruples : and hardly would he suffer me to use the commandant's pass, because 'twas made out for me to go to my regiment.

"How now ! " said he, " is it not our intent to better our lives and to go to Einsiedeln ? And now see, in Heaven's name wilt thou make a beginning with deceit and blind men's eyes with falsehood ? ' He that denieth Me before the world him will I deny before My heavenly Father,' saith Christ. What faint-hearted cowards be we ! If all Christ's martyrs and confessors had done the same there would be few saints in heaven. Let us go in God's name and under His protection whither our holy intent and desires lead us, and let God contrive for us the rest : for so will He bring us in safety where our souls shall find peace." But when I set before him how man should not tempt God, but suit himself to the times, and use such means as could not be done without, and specially because to go on pilgrimage was an unwonted thing for the Soldatesca, so that if we revealed our purpose we should be accounted rather deserters than pilgrims, which might bring us great trouble and danger : and chiefly how the holy apostle St. Paul, to whom we could not compare ourselves, had wonderfully suited himself to the times and needs of this world, at the last he consented that I should get a pass to go to my regiment. With this we passed out of the town at the shutting of the gates, with a trusty guide, as we would go to Rotweil ; but turned off short by a by-way and came the same night over the Switzers' boundary and next morning to a village, where we equipped ourselves with long black cloaks, pilgrims' staves, and rosaries, and sent our guide home with a good wage.

And here in comparison with other German lands the country seemed to me as strange as if I had been in Brazil or China.

I saw how the people did trade and traffic in peace, how the stalls were full of cattle and the farmyards crowded with fowls, geese, and ducks, the roads were used in safety by travellers, and the inns were full of people making merry. There was no fear of an enemy, no dread of plundering, and no terror of losing goods and life and limb ; each man lived under his own vine and fig-tree, and that moreover (in comparison with other German lands) in joy and delight, so that I held this land for an earthly Paradise, though by nature it seemed rough as might be. So it came about that all along the road I did but gape at this and that, whereas Herzbruder was praying on his rosary, for which I earned many a reproof from him ; for he would have it I should pray without ceasing, to which I could not accustom myself.

But at Zürich he found me out and told me the truth as tartly as might be. For having rested the night at Schaff-hausen, where the peas did mightily gall my feet, and I fearing to walk upon them next day, I had them boiled and put into my shoes again, and so came happily to Zürich, while he found himself in sorry plight, and said to me, " Brother, thou hast great favour of God, that notwithstanding the peas in thy shoes thou canst walk so well." " Yea," said I, " dear Herzbruder : but I did boil them, or I had not been able so far to walk upon them."

" God-a-mercy ! " says he, " what hast done ? Thou hadst better have put them out of thy shoes if thou didst but act a mockery with them. I fear me lest God punish thee and me alike. Take it not evil of me, brother, if I of brotherly love do tell in plain German what I have at heart, namely this, that I fear, unless thou dealest otherwise with God, thine eternal salvation standeth in jeopardy : I do assure thee, I love no man more than thee, yet I deny not that if thou betterest not thyself I must scruple to bear such love to thee further." At which I was struck so dumb with fear that I could not at all recover myself, but freely confessed to him I had put the peas in my shoes not for piety but to please him, that he might take me with him on his journey. " Ah, brother," quoth he, " I see thou art far from the way of salvation, peas or no peas : God give thee a better mind ; for without such cannot our friendship endure."

From that time forward I followed him sorrowfully as one going to the gallows ; for my conscience began to smite me ; and as I reflected on all manner of things, all the tricks I had played in my life did pass before mine eyes : and first I lamented that my lost innocence, that I had brought out from the forest and in the world had in so many ways forfeited ; and what increased my trouble was this, that Herzbruder spake now but little with me, and looked not upon me save with sighs, so that it seemed to me as he were certain of my damnation and lamented it.

Chap. ii : HOW SIMPLICISSIMUS, BEING TERRIFIED OF THE DEVIL, WAS CONVERTED

IN such fashion we came even to Einsiedeln, and so into the church even as the priest was casting out an evil spirit : which was to me a new and strange sight, wherefore I left Herzbruder to kneel and pray as much as he listed and went off from curiosity to see such a spectacle. But hardly had I drawn nigh when the evil spirit cried out of the poor man, " Oho ! rascal, doth ill-luck send thee hither ? I did think to find thee with Oliver in our hellish abode when I should return, and now I see thou art to be found here. Thou adulterous, murderous whoremonger, canst thou think to escape us ? O ye priests, have naught to do with him : he is a worse hypocrite and liar than I : he doth but mock and make a jest of God and religion." Thereupon the exorcist commanded the spirit to be silent, for none would believe him as being an arch-liar.

" Yes, yes," he answered, " ask this runagate monk's companion and he can well tell you that this atheist is not afraid to boil the peas upon which he vowed to travel hither." Upon which I knew not whether I stood on my head or my heels, hearing all this and all men staring upon me : but the priest rebuked the spirit and bade him be silent : yet would not that day cast him out. In the meanwhile came Herzbruder, even as I looked for very terror more like a dead than a live man, and between hope and fear knew not what to be at. So he comforted me as best he could, assuring the bystanders, and especially the good fathers, that in my life I had never been a monk, but certainly a soldier that perhaps might have done more evil than good : and added, the devil was a liar and had made the story of the peas much worse than it really was. Yet was I so confounded in spirit that 'twas with me even as if I already felt the pains of hell, so that the priests had much ado to comfort me : yea, they bade me go to confession and communion, but the spirit cried again out of the man possessed, " Yes, yes : he will make a fine confession, that knoweth not even what confession is : and indeed what would ye have of him ? for he is of a heretic mind and belongeth to us : yea, his parents were more of Anabaptists than Calvinists. . . ." But at that the exorcist again commanded the spirit to hold his peace and said to him, " So will it grieve thee the more if this poor lost sheep be snatched out of thy jaws and gathered into the fold of Christ " : at which the spirit began to roar so fearfully that 'twas terrible to hear : yet in that grisly song I found my greatest comfort ; for I thought if I could not again enjoy God's favour the devil would not take it so ill.

Now although I was then in no wise prepared for confession, and though in my lifetime it had never come into my thoughts, but I had always for mere shame feared it as the devil fears holy water, yet at that moment I felt in me such repentance for my sins and such a desire to do penance and to lead a better life that forthwith I asked for a confessor ; at which sudden conversion and amendment of life Herzbruder rejoiced greatly ; for he had perceived and well knew that so far I had belonged to no religion. Thereafter I openly professed myself of the Catholic Church, went to confession and to mass after absolution received, with all which I felt so light and easy at my heart that 'tis not to be expressed : and what is most marvellous is this, that the devil in the possessed man henceforward left me in peace, whereas before my confession and absolution he cast up against me certain knaveries I had committed, with such particularities as he had been ordained for naught else but to point out my sins : yet the hearers believed him not, as being a liar, especially since my honourable pilgrim's dress shewed me in another light.

In this gracious place we abode fourteen days, and there

I thanked God for my conversion, and marked the miracles that were there done : all which did incite me to some show of piety and godliness. Yet did the same last but as long as it might : for even as my conversion took its beginning, not from love of God but from dread and fear of damnation, so did I by degrees become lukewarm and slothful, because I little by little forgot the terror that the Evil One had struck into me. So when we had sufficiently viewed the relics of the saints, the vestments, and other remarkable things of the abbey, we betook ourselves to Baden, there to spend the winter.

Chap. iii : HOW THE TWO FRIENDS SPENT THE WINTER

THERE did I hire a cheerful parlour and a chamber for us, such as the visitors to the baths do commonly use to have, especially in summer : which be mostly rich Switzers that do resort here more to pass the time and make a show than to take baths for any disease. So also I bargained for our food, and Herzbruder, seeing how princely I began, counselled me frugality, and reminded me of the long hard winter that we had yet to pass, for he dreamt not that my money would hold out so long ; and I should need all I had, he said, for the spring when we should depart : for much money was soon spent if one ever took from it and never added to it : 'twas blown away like smoke and was certain never to return, etc. At such loyal counsel I could no longer conceal from Herzbruder how rich my treasury was, and how I was minded to spend it for the good of both of us, since its extraction and growth were so unholy that I could not think to buy lands with it ; and even if I were not minded to spend it so as to maintain so my best friend on earth, yet it were but right that he, Herzbruder, should enjoy Oliver's money in revenge for the insult he had before received from him before Magdeburg. And when I knew myself to be in all safety, I drew off my two shoulder-bags, divided the ducats and pistoles, and said to Herzbruder he might dispose of this money at will, and spend and disburse it as he would, so that it might best profit us both.

When he saw, besides the greatness of my faith in him, how much the money was, with which I, without him, could have been a pretty rich man, " Brother," says he, " since I have known thee thou hast done naught but shew thy constant love and truth to meward. But tell me, how thinkest thou that I can ever repay thee ? I speak not of the money, for this perchance might in time be repaid, but of thy love and faith, and especially of the exceeding trust thou hast in me, which is not to be estimated. In a word, brother, thy noble soul doth make me thy slave, and the favour thou shewest me is more easy to admire than to repay. O honest Simplicissimus, into whose mind it never entereth (even in these godless days in which the world is full of knavery) to think how poor, needy Herzbruder might with this fair stock of money make off and in his place leave thee in want ! Of a surety, brother, this proof of true friendship bindeth me more to thee than if a rich lord should give me thousands. Only I beg thee, my brother, remain master guardian and steward of thine own money. For me 'tis enough that thou art my friend."

To this I answered, " What strange discourses be these, my honoured Herzbruder ? Ye give me to understand ye are much bounden to me, and yet will ye not see to it that I spend not my money vainly and to your damage and mine ! " And so we disputed with one another childishly enough, because each was drunken with love of the other · thus was Herzbruder made at once my steward, my treasurer, my servant, and my master : and in our time of leisure he told me of his life and by what means he was known and promoted by Count Götz, whereupon I told him how I had fared since his father (of pious memory) died : for until then we had never had so much time. But when he heard I had a young wife in Lippstadt, he did reprove me that I had not repaired to her rather than with him to Switzerland, for that had been more fitting, and was my duty moreover : and when I would excuse myself, that I could not find it in my heart to leave him, my best friend, in misery, he persuaded me to write to my wife and tell her of my condition, with the promise to visit her as soon as might be : to that I did add excuses for my long absence, namely, all manner of contrarious happenings, though greatly I had desired to be with her long ere now.

Meanwhile Herzbruder, learning from the public prints that it stood well with General Count Götz, and that in particular he would succeed in his vindication before his Imperial Majesty, would be set free, and even again receive command of an army, sent an account of how he stood to that general at Vienna, and wrote also to the Bavarian army on the score of his baggage that he had there : yea, and began to hope his fortunes would again flourish. Upon which we concluded to part in the spring, he going to the said count, and I to my wife at Lippstadt : yet not to pass the winter in idleness we did learn from an engineer to make more fortifications on paper than the kings of France and Spain together could build : so too I made acquaintance with certain lachymists that, because they saw I had money at my back, would teach me to make gold, an I would but bear the expense of it : yea, and I do believe they had persuaded me thereto had not Herzbruder given them their congé, saying that he that possessed such an art would not need to go about like a beggar, nor to ask others for money.

But though Herzbruder did receive from Vienna a gracious answer from the said count and fine promises, I heard no single word from Lippstadt, though on several post-days I did write in duplicate. Which put me in ill humour and was the cause that that spring I went not to Westphalia, but obtained from Herzbruder that he should take me with him to Vienna and let me share in his hoped-for good fortune. So with my money we equipped ourselves like two cavaliers, both in clothing, horses, servants, and arms, and travelled by Constance to Ulm, where we embarked upon the Danube, and from thence in eight days came safely to Vienna.

Chap. iv : IN WHAT MANNER SIMPLICISSIMUS AND HERZBRUDER WENT TO THE WARS AGAIN AND RETURNED THENCE

THINGS be strangely ordered in this changeful world ; 'Tis said he that should know all things would soon be rich : but I say he that always could seize his opportunity would soon be great and powerful. For many a skinflint or cheeseparer (both which honourable titles are given to misers) gets rich enough by knowing and using some knack of gain : yet is he not therefore great, but is and remaineth always of less estimation than when he was poor : but he that can make himself great and powerful, him riches follow after close. So did luck, that is wont to give power and riches, look on me favourably for once, and gave me when I had been some eight days in Vienna opportunity in hand to mount upon the rungs of fame without hindrance : yet I did it not. And why ? I hold 'twas because my fate had willed for me another road, namely, that along which my foolishness did lead me.

For the Count von der Wahl, under whose command I had before made myself famous in Westphalia, was even then in Vienna when I came thither with Herzbruder : which last was at a banquet when divers Imperialist councillors of war were present with the Count of Götz and others, where the talk was of all manner of strange fellows, soldiers of different qualities, and famous partisans : and there was mention made of the huntsman of Soest, and such famous exploits of him told that some wondered at the youth of the fellow and lamented that the crafty Hessian colonel Saint André had hung a weight round his neck so that he must either lay aside the sword or serve under Swedish colours : for the said Count von der Wahl had found out all the trick which the same colonel had played me at Lippstadt. Herzbruder, that was there present and would fain have forwarded my interest, asked for indulgence and leave to speak, and said he knew that huntsman of Soest better than any man in the world, which was not only a good soldier that feared not the smell of powder, but also a good rider, a perfected fencer, an excellent professor of musquetry and artillery, and besides all this one that would yield place to no engineer in the world : that he had left not only his wife (that had been so shamefully imposed upon him), but all that he had at Lippstadt, and again sought the emperor's service, and so had in the last campaign served under the Count of Götz, and being then taken by the troops of Weimar and desiring to return to the Imperialists, had with his comrade slain a corporal and six musqueteers that had pursued them and would bring them back, and had earned rich booty thereby, and so had come with him to Vienna with intent to offer his service once more against his Imperial Majesty's enemies, provided only he could have such terms as suited him : for as a common soldier he would serve no more.

By this time the worshipful company were so flustered with good liquor that they must satisfy their curiosity to see the huntsman : to which end Herzbruder was sent to fetch me in a coach : who on the way instructed me how I should carry myself among these persons of quality, since my fortune in time to come depended on this. So when I came to them, at first I answered all questions very short and sententiously, so that they began to admire me as one who said nothing that had not a prudent meaning : in a word, I so presented myself that I pleased all, besides this, that I had from Count von der Wahl the reputation of a good soldier. But with all this I got drunk, and well can I believe that in that condition I proved to all how little I had been at court. And this was the end of it all : that a colonel of foot promised me a company in his regiment, which I refused not : for I thought, " To be a captain is indeed no trifle." Yet Herzbruder next day rebuked me for my folly, and said, had I but held out longer I had risen to high rank.

So was I presented to a company as their captain, which company, although with me 'twas in respect of officers fully staffed, yet counted no more than seven privates that could stand sentry. Besides, my under-officers were such old cripples that I must needs scratch my head when I looked upon them. And so it came about that in the next engagement, which happened not long after, I was with them miserably beaten : in which affair Count von Götz lost his life and Herzbruder his testicles, which were shot away : and I had my share in the leg though 'twas but a trifling wound. Whereupon we betook ourselves to Vienna, there to be cured, and also because we had there left all our property. But besides these wounds, which were soon healed, there appeared in Herzbruder other evil symptoms which the doctors could not at first recognise, for he was paralysed in all his extremities like a choleric person whom his gall doth plague, to which complexion he was no more given than to anger. Nevertheless he was counselled to take the waters, and to that end the Griesbach in the Black Forest was commended to him. And so doth fortune suddenly change. For Herzbruder just before had been minded to marry a young lady of quality, and to that end to get him made a Freiherr and me a nobleman : but now must he make other plans ; for having lost that by which he had meant to propagate his family, and being, moreover, threatened with a tedious sickness ensuing upon that loss, in which he would have need of good friends, he made his will, and appointed me heir of all his property, the more so because he saw how for his sake I cast my fortune to the winds and gave up my command, that I might bear him company to the Spa and there wait on him till he should recover his health.

Chap. v : *HOW SIMPLICISSIMUS RODE COURIER AND IN THE LIKENESS OF MERCURY LEARNED FROM JOVE WHAT HIS DESIGN WAS AS REGARDS WAR AND PEACE*

SO as soon as Herzbruder could ride we despatched our money (for now we had but one purse in common) by way of banker's draft to Basel, equipped ourselves with horses and servants, and made our way up the Danube to Ulm and thence to the Spa before mentioned, for now 'twas May and pleasant travelling. There did we hire a lodging : but I rid to Strassburg, not only to receive in part our money which we had conveyed thither by way of Basel, but also to inquire for the medicos of experience that should prescribe for Herzbruder recipes and the manner of his taking the baths. These came to me, and were of opinion that Herzbruder had indeed been poisoned, yet was the poison not strong enough to kill him off-hand, and therefore it had made its way into his limbs, from whence it must be evacuated by drugs, antidotes and sweating-baths, which cure would last some eight weeks or so. At that Herzbruder remembered at once when and by whom that poison had been given him ; namely, by them that would have had his place in the army : and when he further learned from the physicians that his cure needed no spa, then was he assured the field-surgeon had by his enemies been bribed to send him so far away : yet did he resolve to complete his cure there at the spa, for 'twas not only a healthy air but also there was cheerful company among the bathing-guests.

This time would I not waste : for I had a desire to see my wife once more : and since Herzbruder needed me not greatly, I did open to him my project, which he did praise, and advised me I should visit her, giving me also certain trinkets of price which I should on his behalf present to her, and therewith beg her pardon for that he had been the cause why I had not before sought her out. With that I rode to Strassburg, and not only provided myself with moneys but inquired also how I might prosecute my journey in the safest way : whereupon I found 'twas not to be accomplished by a horseman riding alone ; for the roads were made unsafe by the parties sent out from so many garrisons of the two contending armies. So I got me a pass for a post-rider of Strassburg, and drew up certain letters to my wife, her sisters, and her parents, as I would send him with them to Lippstadt : yet feigned to be of a different mind, took back the pass from the messenger, sent back my horse and servant, and disguised myself in a red and white livery : in that I journeyed by ship to Cologne, which was at that time neutral between the two parties.

And first I must go to visit my Jupiter, that had aforetime appointed me his Ganymede, to ask how it fared with the property I had left there : but him I found quite brain-sick again and full of anger against the human race. " O Mercury," says he, as soon as he saw me, " what news from Münster ? Do men conceive they can make peace without my good will ? Nay, never ! they did have peace. Why kept they it not ? Was not vice everywhere triumphant when they provoked me to send them war ? And how have they deserved that I should give them peace again ? Have they since been converted ? Are they not become worse, and do they not run into war as to a festival ? Or have they perchance repented them by reason of the famine that I sent among them, whereof so many thousands died of hunger ? Or hath the grievous pestilence terrified them to better their ways, whereby so many millions were cut off ? Nay, nay, Mercurius, they that remain, that did see these dreadful sufferings with their own eyes, have not only not repented, but be grown worse than ever they were. And if they have not been turned by so many sore plagues, nor have ceased to live in godless wise in the midst of such trial and tribulation, what will they do if I should grant them again the delights of golden peace? Then must I fear lest, as once did the giants, so they now should try to storm my heaven. But such overweening I will check in good time and leave them to perish in their war." But I knowing how one must go about with this god if one would make him hear reason, "Oh, great god," says I, "all the world doth sigh for peace and promise great amendment: why wilt thou then continue to refuse them such?" "Yea," answered Jupiter, "doubtless they sigh: yet not for my sake but their own: not that each may praise God under his own vine and fig-tree, but that they may enjoy the fruit thereof in peace and delight. Of late I asked of a scurvy tailor, should I give him peace? He gave me answer, 'twas the same to him, that must ply his needle as well in peace as in war: and the like answer I got from a brazier, which said if he could get no bells to found in peace time, yet in time of war he had enough to do with cannon and mortars So likewise, a smith replied to me and said, ' Though I have no ploughs and hay-carts to mend in war-time, yet have I so many war horses and army waggons to deal with that I can well afford to do without peace.' Lookye then, dear Mercurius, why should I grant them peace? True there be some that do desire it, yet only as I say, for their belly's sake and their pleasure: contrari-wise there be others that will still have war, not because 'tis my will, but because 'tis for their profit. And just as the masons and carpenters desire peace, to earn money by the building again of ruined houses, so others that be not sure of earning a living by their handicraft in time of peace do hope for the continuing of war, wherein they can steal."

Now when I found my Jupiter so to go about with these matters, I could well conceive that he, with so confused a mind, could give me little account of mine own, and so I made not my business known to him, but took the bull by the horns, and away by by-paths well known to me, to Lippstadt, where I inquired for my father-in-law as I were a messenger from foreign parts, and learned at once that he, with his wife, had quitted this world six months before, and secondly, that my dear wife, having been delivered of a man-child, that was now with her sister, had in like manner straightway, after her lying-in, quitted this mortal scene. Upon that I delivered to my brother-in-law the writings which I had before addressed to my father-in-law, to my wife, and to him, my wife's brother. Who would have entertained me himself, to learn from me, as from a messenger, how it fared with Simplicissimus and of what rank he was now. In the end mine own sister-in-law did at length converse with me, I telling of myself all the good I knew ; for my pock-pitted face had so marred and changed me that no man could know me more, save Herr von Schönstein : and he, as my true friend, did hold his tongue. But I telling her at length how Herr Simplicissimus had many fine horses and servants and rode abroad in a black-velvet coat all trimmed with gold, " Yea," said she, " I did ever believe he was of no such low descent as he gave himself out to be : the commandant of this place did ever persuade my late parents, with great assurances, that they had made a good match with him for my sister, which had ever been a virtuous maiden : yet of all that I myself could never look for a good ending. Nevertheless did he content himself and resolve to take upon him either Swedish or Hessian service in the garrison here : and to that end would he fetch hither his goods that he had left at Cologne : which turned out ill, and he himself was by clean roguery spirited away into France, leaving my sister, that had had him to husband but for four weeks, yea, and a half-dozen of citizens' daughters likewise, with child by him ; all which one after another, and my sister last of all, were brought to bed of boys. So since my father and mother were dead, and I and my husband without hope of children, we did adopt my sister's child to be the heir of all our property, and with the help of the commandant here did get possession of his father's money at Cologne ; which same might be reckoned at three thousand gulden ; and so the young lad when he shall come of age shall have no cause to count himself among the paupers. Yea, I and my husband do love the child so much that we would not yield him up to his own father though he came in person to fetch him away : moreover, he is the comeliest of all his half-brothers, and so like to his father as he had been cut out on his very pattern : and I know if my brother-in-law did but hear what a fair son he hath he would not delay to come hither were it but to see the little sweetheart."

The like talk my sister-in-law held, by which I might well perceive her love to my child, which now ran about in his first breeches, and rejoiced mine heart : and with that I brought out the trinkets that Herzbruder had given me to present on his behalf to my wife : which, said I, Master Simplicissimus had given me to deliver to his wife for a salutation : who being dead, I accounted it fair to leave the same for his child : all which my brother-in-law and his wife received with joy, and were convinced thereby that I had no want of means, but must indeed be a fellow of a different sort from that which they had fancied me to be. So now I pressed for leave to be gone, and having obtained such, I begged in the name of Simplicissimus to kiss Simplicissimus the younger, that I might tell the same to his father for a token. And this being done with the goodwill of my sister-in-law, my nose and the child's began at once and together to bleed, till I thought my heart would break : yet did I hide my feelings, and that none might have time to mark the cause of this sympathy, I took myself off at once, and after fourteen days of much trouble and danger came again to the spa in beggar's garb : for on the way I had been plundered and stripped.

Chap. vi : *A STORY OF A TRICK THAT SIMPLI-CISSIMUS PLAYED AT THE SPA*

SO being returned, I found Herzbruder rather worse than better, though the doctors and apothecaries had plucked him cleaner than any pigeon : nay, more : he seemed to me now to be childish, nor could he walk straight. I did hearten him up as best I could, but his was an ill plight ; himself perceiving well by his loss of strength that he could not last long ; and his chief comfort was this, that I should be by his side when he should close his eyes. Contrariwise I was merry, and sought my pleasure where I thought to find it : though in such wise that Herzbruder lacked none of my care. Yet because I knew myself now for a widower, the fine weather and my young blood enticed me to wantonness, whereunto I did fully give myself over ; for the fear that had possessed me at Einsiedeln I had now quite forgot. Now there was at the spa a fair lady * that gave herself out to be a person of quality, yet was to my thinking more " mobilis " than " nobilis " : to this man-trap did I pay my constant court as to one that seemed a bona roba, and in brief space of time did obtain not only free entry to her but also all such favours as I could desire. Yet had I from the first a disgust at her lightness, and so did devise how I might in all courtesy be rid of her : for methought she had her eye more on my purse than on me for a bridegroom : yea, and did persecute me with hot and wanton glances and the like tokens of her burning love wheresoever I might be, till I must be shamed both for her sake and mine own.

At that time there was at the baths a rich Switzer of quality : from whom was stolen not only his money, but his wife's jewellery, which was of gold, silver, pearls, and precious stones. And since 'tis as grievous to lose such things as 'tis hard to get them, therefore the said Switzer would move heaven and earth to come by them again, and did even send for the famous devil-driver of the Goatskin,† which did so plague the thief by his charms that he must needs restore the stolen goods to their proper place : for which the wizard earned ten rix-dollars.

With this enchanter I had fain conversed : but, as I then conceived, it could not be, without lessening of my dignity (for at that time I thought no small beer of myself). So I did engage my servant to be drunk with him that same night (having learned he was a toper of the first quality) to see if by such means I could have his acquaintance : for so many strange things were told to me of him that I could not believe till I had heard them from himself. To that end did I disguise myself as a strolling quack, and sat down by him at table to

* This was " Courage," the heroine of some of Grimmelshausen's later romances.

† Unknown.

see if he could guess or the devil could tell him who I was: yet could I mark no such knowledge in him, but he would drink and drink, taking me for that which my raiment proclaimed me, yea, and drank some few glasses to my health, yet shewed more respect to my knave than to me. For to him he told in all confidence that if he that had robbed the Switzer had thrown but the smallest part thereof into running water and so shared the booty with the devil, it had been impossible either to name the thief or to get back the goods.

To all these silly conceits I listened, and wondered how the father of deceits and lies can by so small a thing bring men into his clutches. I could easily conceive that this was a clause in our enchanter's indenture with the devil, and perceive how such a trick could not help the thief if only another exorcist were fetched in to detect the theft, in whose compact this condition was not to be found: and so charged my knave, that could steal better than any gipsy, to make the man drunk and then steal his ten rix-dollars, and presently thereafter to cast a couple of batzen into the river Rench. This he did with all diligence, and when the witch-doctor next morning missed his money, he betook himself to a thicket by the bank of the Rench, doubtless to confer with his familiar spirit: by whom he was so ill-handled that he came off with a face all bruised and scratched: whereat I felt such pity for the poor old rogue that I gave him back his money and sent him a message that, since he now could see what a traitorous, evil spirit the devil was, he might renounce his service and company, and turn to God again: which warning brought me but little profit, for presently my two fair horses sickened and died by witchcraft; and what else could I expect? for I lived like Epicurus in his stye and never did commend my goods to God's care: why, therefore, should the wizard not be able to revenge himself on me?

Chap. vii : HOW HERZBRUDER DIED AND HOW SIMPLICISSIMUS AGAIN FELL TO WANTON COURSES

WITH the spa I was the more pleased the longer I stayed, for not only did the guests increase daily, but the place and the manner of life also delighted me hugely. I joined acquaintance with the merriest that resorted thither and did begin to learn courtesy and compliment, wherewith I had till then troubled myself but little : and so was counted as of the nobility, my people calling me ever " noble captain " ; for no mere soldier of fortune did ever gain so high a post at that age at which I still was. So with these rich fops I made, and they with me, not acquaintance only but sworn friendship ; and pastime, play, eating, and drinking were all my work and care, which robbed me of many a fair ducat without my much perceiving or marking of it : for my purse was yet fairly heavy with Oliver's legacy.

Meanwhile things went from bad to worse with Herzbruder, till at last he must pay the debt of nature, all doctors and physicians now deserting him on whom they had fattened so long. So he confirmed once more his last will and testament and made me heir of all he had to receive from his late father's property. And in return I gave him a noble funeral and sent his servants on their way with mourning and money withal.

Yet his disease heartily vexed me, and especially because he had been poisoned : and though I could not change that, yet it changed me : for now I eschewed all company and sought only for solitude to give a hearing to my sad thoughts : to which end I would hide myself in some thicket and there would muse, not only upon what a friend I had lost, but also how I should never in my life find such another one. At times I would lay all manner of plans for my future life and yet could resolve on none : now I thought I would to the wars again : and then bethought me how even the poorest peasant in this land was better off than any colonel : for into those mountains came never a foraging party. Yea, I could well fancy what an army would find to do there in ravaging of the country, seeing that all the farmhouses were well kept, as if in peace-time, and all the stalls full of cattle, while in many a village of Germany in the plains neither dog nor cat could be found. So as I delighted myself with hearing of the sweet song of birds, and did fancifully conceive how the nightingale should by her dulcet song silence all other birds and force them to listen either from shame or to steal somewhat of her pleasant strains, there came to the opposite bank of the stream a beauty, that did move me more, because she wore but the habit of a peasant girl, than could any fine demoiselle have done ; which took a basket from her head wherein she had a pack of fresh butter, to sell at the spa : this did she cool in the water that it might not melt by reason of the great heat, and meanwhile, sitting down upon the grass, did throw aside her kerchief and her peasant hat and wipe the sweat from her face, so that I could exactly observe her and feed my curious eyes upon her : and truly methought I had never seen a fairer form in my life : for the mould of her figure seemed perfect and without blemish, her arms and hands white as snow, her face fresh and sweet, but her black eyes full of fire and amorous looks. So as she was packing of her butter up again I cried across to her, " Ah, maiden, 'tis true ye have cooled your butter in the water with your fair hands, yet with your bright eyes have ye set my heart afire." But she no sooner saw and heard me but away she ran as if she were pursued, without answering me a word, and so left me possessed with all the follies wherewith fantastic lovers are wont to be tormented.

But my desire to be further illumined by this sun left me not in peace in the solitude I had chosen, but caused me to care no more for the song of the nightingale than for the howl of a wolf : therefore I made my way to the spa, and did send my page in front to accost the pretty butter-seller and to bargain with her till I should come : so he did his best, and I, when I came, did mine also : but found a heart of stone, and such coldness as I had never thought to find in any peasant-girl, which made me yet more in love, especially since I, that had been much a scholar in such schools, might well judge by such a carriage she would not easily be befooled.

And now should I have had either a great enemy or a great

friend : either an enemy to think of and devise evil against, and so to forget my fool's love, or a friend that should give me other counsel and warn me from the folly I proposed. But alas ! I had naught but my money, which did but dazzle me, and my blind desires which led me astray, I giving them the rein, and mine own impudence, that ruined me and brought me to disaster. Fool that I was, I should have judged by our clothes, as by an evil omen, that her love would work me woe. For I having lost Herzbruder and the girl her parents, we were both dressed in mourning clothes when we first met : and so what joy could our love portend ? In a word, I was properly caught in a fool's snare, and therefore as blind and without reason as the boy Cupid himself : and because I had no hope otherwise to satisfy my bestial desires, I did determine to marry her.

" For how ! " thought I, " thou beest by descent but a peasant's brat and wilt never in thy life keep thy castle : and this fair champaign is a noble land, that throughout this grisly war hath, in comparison with other parts, maintained itself in peace and prosperity : besides, thou hast gold enough to buy thee even the best farm in this countryside : and now shalt thou marry with this honest peasant-girl and get thee a lord's reputation among the country-folk. And where couldst find a cheerfuller dwelling-place than near the spa, where thou canst, by reason of the coming and going of the guests, see a new world every six weeks, and so conceive how the great world doth change from one age to another ? "

Such and a thousand like plans I made, till at length I sought my sweetheart in marriage and (yet not without pains) did obtain her consent.

Chap. viii : HOW SIMPLICISSIMUS FOUND HIS SECOND MARRIAGE TURN OUT, AND HOW HE MET WITH HIS DAD AND LEARNED WHO HIS PARENTS HAD BEEN

SO I made fine preparation for the wedding : for all seemed rose-colour to me. Not only did I buy up the whole farm whereon my bride had been born, but began also a fine new building besides, as if I would rather keep court than keep house : and before the wedding was over I had already more than thirty head of cattle on the farm ; for so many could it maintain all the year round : in a word, I had the best of everything and such fine household plenishing as only folly like mine could devise. But soon I must whistle to a different tune, for I found my bride too knowing ; and now, all too late, was I ware of the cause why she had been so loath to take me : and what vexed me most was that I could tell to no man my silly plight. I knew well enough that 'twas reasonable I must pay the piper ; yet the knowledge made me not more patient, still less better in life ; nay, rather I thought to betray the traitress, and so began to go a-grazing where I could find pasture : which kept me rather in good company at the spa than at home, and for a year at least I left my housekeeping to take care of itself. And for her part my wife was as slovenly as I : an ox that I had had slaughtered for household use she salted in baskets like pork, and when she was to prepare a sucking-pig for me she tried to pluck it like a fowl : yea, she would cook crayfish with a roasting-jack and trout on a spit : from which examples a man may judge what manner of housewife I found her : and withal she would drink freely of the good wine and share it with her good friends : and that was a sign of my coming disasters.

Now it fell out that as I was walking down the valley with some fops of the spa to visit a company at the lower baths, there met us an old peasant with a goat on a string, that he wished to sell, and because methought I had seen him before, I asked whence he came with his goat. At which he doffed his cap and " Your worship," says he, " that I may not tell you." " How," said I, " surely thou hast not stolen the beast ? " " Nay," answered the peasant, " but I bring him from a village there in the valley, the which I may not mention to your worship in the presence of a goat " * which caused my company to laugh, and because I changed colour they deemed I was vexed or ashamed that the peasant did answer me so neatly. Yet my thoughts were otherwise, for by the great wart that this peasant had, like an unicorn, in the middle of his forehead, I was assured 'twas my dad from the Spessart,

* The jest is now unintelligible.

and so would first play the conjurer before I would make myself known and delight him with so fine a son as my clothes shewed me to be. So I said to him, " Good father, is not your home in the Spessart ? " " Yes, your worship," says he. " Then," said I, " did ye not some eighteen year agone have your house and farm plundered and burnt by the troopers ? " " Yea, God-a-mercy," quoth the peasant, " yet 'tis not so long ago " : but I asked him further, " Did ye not, then, have two children, a grown daughter and a young lad that kept your sheep ? " " Nay, your worship," says my dad, " the daughter was my child but not the boy : yet would I bring him up as mine own." And by that I understood I was no son of this rough yokel : and that in part rejoiced me yet again troubled me, for I thought now I must be some bastard or foundling, and therefore asked my dad how he had come by the said boy or what reason he had had to rear him as his own. " Ah," says he, " I had strange luck with him : by war I got him and by war I lost him."

But now being afeard lest some fact should come to light that would disgrace my birth, I turned the discourse upon the goat again and asked if he had sold it to the hostess for cooking, which would seem strange to me as knowing that her guests used not to eat old goat's flesh. But " Nay, your worship," quoth the peasant, " the hostess hath goats enow and will pay naught for such : I do bring her for the countess that is at the spa to bathe. For Doctor Busybody hath ordered certain herbs for this goat to eat : and the milk that she gives therefrom the doctor taketh to make a medicine for the countess, that is to drink the milk and so be cured : for they say the countess hath no stomach, and if the goat help her 'twill do more than the doctor and all his sawbones together." While he thus talked I considered how I might have further speech with him, and so offered him for the goat a dollar more than the doctor or the countess would give : to which he readily agreed (for small gain will easily turn folk), yet on condition he should first tell the countess that I had bid a thaler more : and if she would give as much she should have the preference : if not, he would bring me the goat and would in the evening let me know how the business stood. With that my dad went his way and I, with my company, ours :

yet could I and would I not stay longer with them, but turned me back and went where I found my dad again : who still had his goat, for others would not give him so much as I : which, for so rich people, did amaze me, yet made me not more niggardly : for I took him to my new-bought farm and paid him for his goat, and when I had him half-foxed I asked of him whence came the lad to him of whom we spoke to-day. "Ah, your worship," says he, "the Mansfeld war brought him to me and the Nördlingen battle took him away again." "And that," quoth I, "must be a merry story," and so I begged him, since we had naught else to talk of, to tell it me to pass the time.

With that he began, and says he, "When Mansfeld * lost the battle at Höchst, his people were scattered abroad as not knowing whither to flee : of whom many came into the Spessart, seeking woods wherein to hide them : but though they had escaped death on the plains they found it in the hills : for since both parties thought it their right to plunder and murder one another on our lands, we peasants would have a finger in their pie too. So 'twas but seldom that a farmer would go into his woods without a musquet, for we could not bide at home with our hoes and ploughs. And in this wild business did I light upon a fair young lady mounted on a goodly horse, in a savage and lonesome wood, yet not far from my farm : and just before, I had heard shots fired : and at first I took her for a man, for she rode like such : yet when I saw her raise hands and eyes to heaven and in a pitiful voice, though in a strange tongue, cry aloud to God, I lowered my gun, with which I would have fired upon her, and uncocked it ; for her cries and actions did well assure me 'twas a woman, and one in trouble withal. So we drew near to each other, and when she saw me, ' Ah,' says she, ' if ye be a Christian and an honest man, I pray you for God and His mercy, yea, and for that Last Judgment before which we must all give account of our deeds and misdeeds, to bring me to some married woman that with God's help may deliver me of my burden ! ' Which words, as being of such import, together with the gentle speech and the troubled, yet fair and kind face

* It was really Christian of Brunswick, marching to join Mansfeld.

of the poor lady, did compel me to such pity that I took her horse by the bridle and led her over bush and brier to the thickest part of the wood whither I had brought my wife, my child, my people, and my cattle for refuge : and there within half an hour was she delivered of that young boy of whom we did discourse to-day."

With that my dad finished his story and his glass : for I was no niggard of my wine for him : and when he had emptied it I asked him how it fared thereafter with the lady : to which he answered thus : " When she was delivered she begged me to be godfather, and to bring the child to baptism as soon as might be, and told me her own and her husband's name that they might be written in the book of Christenings : and then did she open her wallet wherein she had full costly trinkets, and of these gave so many to me, to my wife and child, my maid-servant and to another woman that was by, that we might well be content with her : but even while she did this, and told us of her husband, she died under our hands, having first commended the child to us. But since the tumult in the land was then so great that none could abide in his own house, we had much trouble to come by a clergyman that should baptize the child and attend the funeral. Yet both being done, 'twas commanded me by our burgomaster and our priest that I should rear the child till 'twas grown, and for my trouble and cost should keep all the lady's property save a few rosaries and precious stones and jewellery, which I should keep for the child. So my wife did nourish the babe with goat's milk, and we loved the lad, and did think when he should be grown up to give him our daughter to wife : but after the battle at Nördlingen did I lose both boy and girl and all that I possessed."

" Now," says I to my dad, " ye have told me a pretty tale enough and yet forgot the best part : for ye have not told me the name of the lady or her husband or the child." " Your honour," he answered, " I thought not ye desired to know it : but the lady's name was Susanna Ramsay : her husband was Captain Sternfels, of Fuchsheim, and because my name was Melchior did I have the child baptized Melchior Sternfels, of Fuchsheim, and so inscribed in the book."

Now from that I knew clearly that I was the true-born son

of my hermit and of Governor Ramsay's sister ; but alas ! far too late, for my parents were both dead, and of my uncle Ramsay could I learn nothing save that the Hanauers had rid themselves of him and his Swedish garrison, whereat he had gone crazy for rage and vexation. But I treated my godfather well with wine, and next day had his wife fetcht likewise : yet when I declared myself to them, would they not believe it, till I did shew them a black and hairy mole I had upon my breast.

Chap. ix : IN WHAT MANNER THE PAINS OF CHILD-
BIRTH CAME UPON HIM, AND HOW HE
BECAME A WIDOWER

NOT long after this I did take my godfather with me, and ride into the Spessart to get certain news and certificate of my descent and noble birth ; which I gat without difficulty from the book of baptisms and my godfather's witness : and presently thereafter visited the priest that had dwelt at Hanau and had taken care of me : which gave me a writing to declare where my late father had died, and that I had abode with him to his death and thereafter for a long time with Master Ramsay, the commandant at Hanau, under the name of Simplicissimus : yea, I had an instrument containing my whole history drawn up by a notary out of the mouth of witnesses ; for I thought, " Who knoweth when thou wilt have need of it ? " And this journey did cost me 400 thalers, for on my return I was captured by a party, dismounted, and plundered so that I and my dad or godfather came off naked and hardly with our lives.

Meanwhile things went ill at home : for as soon as my wife knew her husband was a nobleman she not only did play the great lady, but did neglect all housekeeping ; which I bore in silence because she was big with child : moreover, misfortune came on my cattle and robbed me of my chiefest and best : all which 'twould have been possible to endure, but O Gemini ! misfortunes came not singly : for even then while my wife was delivered, the maid was brought to bed likewise : and the child she bore was indeed like to me, but that which my wife had was so like to the farm-servant as it had been cut on the pattern of his face. Nay, more! for the lady of whom I writ above did in the same night cause one to be laid at my door with notice in writing that I was the father: and so did I get a family of three at once, and could not but expect that others would creep out of every corner, which caused me not a few grey hairs. But so will it fare with whoever doth follow his own bestial lusts in such a godless and wicked way of life as I had led.

And now what to do! I must have the baptism and be soundly punished by the magistrate: and the government being then Swedish, and I an old soldier of the emperor, the score was the heavier to pay: all which was but the preface to my complete ruination the second time. And although all these manifold disasters did greatly trouble me, yet my wife contrariwise took all lightly; yea, did mock at me day and night about the fine treasure that had been laid at my door and for which I had paid so dearly: yet had she but known how 'twas with me and the maid she would have plagued me yet worse: but that good creature was so complacent as to let herself be persuaded with as much money as I should other ways have been fined for her sake, to swear her child to a fop that had at times visited me the year before and had been at the wedding, but whom otherwise she knew not. Yet must she go a-packing, for my wife did suspect what I thought of her and the farm-servant, yet dared not hint thereat: for else had I proved to her that I could not at once be with her and with the maid. Yet all the while I was tormented with the thought that I must rear a child for my servant, and mine own sons should not be my heirs, and yet must I hold my peace and be glad that none else knew of it: and with such thoughts did I daily torment myself, while my wife revelled every hour in wine; for since our marriage she had so used herself to the bottle that 'twas seldom away from her mouth, and she herself scarce went to bed any night but half-drunk: by which means she robbed her child of its nourishment and so inflamed her inward parts that soon after they fell out, and so made me a widower the second time, which went so to my heart that I wellnigh laughed myself into a sickness.

Chap. x : RELATION OF CERTAIN PEASANTS CON-CERNING THE WONDERFUL MUMMELSEE

SO now did I find myself restored to mine ancient freedom, but with a purse pretty well emptied of gold, and yet a great household overburdened with cattle and servants. Therefore I took my foster-father Melchior to be as my father, and my foster-mother, his wife, to be my mother, and young bastard Simplicissimus that had been laid at my door I made my heir, and handed over to these two old people house and farm, together with all my property save a few yellow-boys and jewels that I had saved and kept hidden to meet extreme need : for now had I conceived such a loathing for the company and society of all women that I had determined, having fared so ill with them, never to marry again. So this old couple, which in matters rustic could hardly meet their likes for skill, presently arranged my housekeeping in different fashion. For they got rid of such cattle and servants as were of no use, and in their place had for the farm such as would bring profit. So my old dad and my mammy bade me be of good cheer, and promised if I would let them manage all to keep me ever a good horse in the stable and myself so well furnished that I could now and then drink my measure of wine with any honest companion. And presently I was ware of what manner of people now managed my estate : for my foster-father with the labourers tilled the ground, and bargained for cattle and wood and resin sharper than any Jew, while his wife gave herself to cattle-breeding and contrived to save the milk-penny and keep it better than ten such wives as I had had. In such wise my farmyard was in short space furnished with all needful implements and cattle small and great, so that soon 'twas esteemed one of the best in that country-side : and I meanwhile took my walks abroad and gave myself up to contemplations, for when I saw how my foster-mother earned more by her bees alone, in wax and honey, than my wife had gained from cattle, swine, and all the rest together, I could well conceive that in other matters she would not be caught napping.

Now it happened on a time that I took my walk in the spa, more for the sake of a draught of fresh water than, according to my former usage, to make acquaintance with the fops : for I had begun to imitate the thriftiness of my parents, who counselled me I should not much consort with folk that so wantonly wasted their own and their father's goods. Yet I joined myself to a company of men of moderate rank who even then were in discourse concerning a strange matter, namely, of the Mummelsee, which said they was bottomless, and which was situate on one of the highest mountains near by : and they had sent for several old peasants and would have them to tell all that one and the other had heard of this wondrous lake, to whose stories I hearkened with great delight, though I held them all to be as vain fables as be some of Plinius's tales.

For one said if any man should tie up an odd number of things such as peas or pebbles, or what not, in a kerchief, and let it down into the water, presently the number would be even. And if one should drop in an even number, at once it became odd. Others, and indeed the most part, declared, and confirmed what they said by examples, that if a man should throw in one or more stones, however fair the skies might be till then, at once there would arise a terrible storm with fearful rain, hail and hurricane. From that they came to all manner of strange histories that had happened there, and what wondrous appearances of earth- and water-spirits had there been seen and how they had talked with mankind. One told how on a time, as certain herdsmen were keeping cattle by the lake, there arose a brown ox out of the water that mixed with the other cattle, but there followed him a little mannikin to drive him back into the lake ; who would not obey till the little man had sworn that if he did not come back he should suffer all the ills of human kind. At which words ox and man again sank into the lake. Another said it happened at a time when the lake was frozen over that a peasant, with his oxen and sundry trunks of trees, such as we hew planks out of, passed over the lake without harm ; but when his dog would follow him the ice broke, and so the poor beast fell in and was never seen again. And yet another swore 'twas solemn truth that a huntsman following in the track of game was passing by the lake, and there saw a water-spirit sitting with a whole lapful of coined money and playing therewith ; at whom when he would have shot, the spirit sank into the water, and cried, " Hadst thou but prayed me to help thee in thy trade, I would have made thee and thine rich for life."

Such and the like tales, which seemed to me all as fables with which we do amuse our children, did I hearken to, and never deemed it possible that there could be such a bottomless lake upon a high mountain. But there were other peasants, and those old and credible men, that affirmed that within their own and their father's memory high and princely persons had journeyed to behold the said lake, and that a reigning Duke of Würtemberg had caused a raft to be made, and had put out into the lake thereupon to sound its depth : but that after the measures had already let down nine thread-cables (which is a measure of length better understanded of the peasants' wives of the Black Forest than of me or any other geometer) with a sinking-lead, and yet had found no bottom, the raft, contrary to the nature of wood, began to sink, so that they that were upon it must perforce give up their purpose and make all haste to land, and so to this day can be seen the fragments of the raft on the shore of the lake, with the arms of Würtemberg and other matters carved upon the wood for a memorial of this history. Others called many witnesses to prove that a certain archduke of Austria had desired to drain the lake, but was by many dissuaded and at the petition of the people of the land the plan given up, for fear lest the whole country might be drowned and destroyed. Furthermore, the said noble princes had caused barrels full of trout to be put into the lake ; all which in less than an hour died before their eyes and floated away through the outlet of the lake, notwithstanding that the stream that flows under the mountain on which the lake lies and through the valley that takes its name therefrom produces by nature such fish, and that the outlet of the lake is into the said stream.

Chap. xi : *OF THE MARVELLOUS THANKSGIVING*
OF A PATIENT, AND OF THE HOLY
THOUGHTS THEREBY AWAKENED IN
SIMPLICISSIMUS

THESE last did so affirm what they said that I now began almost entirely to believe them, and they did so move my curiosity that I determined to visit this wondrous lake. But of those that with me had listened to the whole story one judged one way and another another, from which sufficiently appeared their different and contradictory ways of thinking. For my part I said the German name Mummelsee * sufficiently declared that there was about the thing, as about a masquerade, some disguise, so that none might fathom either its nature or its depth, which had never yet been discovered, though such high personages had attempted it. And with that I betook me to the same place where a year before I had seen my departed wife for the first time and drank in the sweet poison of love. And there I laid myself down on the green grass in the shade, yet took no heed as I had done before to what the nightingales did sing, but rather pondered on the changes I had suffered since then. I represented to myself how in that very place I had begun to be in place of a free man a slave of love, and how since then I had become from an officer a peasant, from a rich peasant a poor nobleman, from a Simplicissimus a Melchior, from a widower a husband, from a husband a cuckold, and from a cuckold a widower again ; moreover, from a peasant's brat I had proved to be the son of a good soldier, and yet again the son of my old dad. Then again I reflected how fate had robbed me of my Herzbruder, and in his place had provided me with two old married folk. I thought of the godly life and decease of my father ; the piteous death of my mother ; and, further, of the manifold changes which I had undergone in my lifetime, till I could no longer refrain myself from tears. And even while I reflected how much good money I in my lifetime had possessed and squandered away, and began to lament there-

* " Goblin " or rather " bogey " lake.

fore, there came two good soakers or wine-bibbers on whom the gout had fastened in their limbs, whereby they were crippled and needed both the baths and to drink the waters : these set themselves down by me, for 'twas a fair place to rest, and each bewailed to the other his sad case as thinking that they were alone. So said the one, " My doctor hath sent me here either as one of whose healing he despaired or else as one that with others might help him to repay my host here for the keg of butter he sent him : I would I had either never seen him in my life or else that he had at the first sent me to the spa, for so should I either have more money than now or else be sounder, for the waters suit my case right well." And " Ah " says the other, " I thank my God that He hath given me no more money to spare than what I have, for had my doctor known that I had more behind he had never counselled me to come to the spa ; but I must have shared all between him and his apothecaries, that for this cause do oil his palms year by year—yea, even though I should have died and perished in the meanwhile. These greedy fellows send not men like us to so healthful a place till they be well assured they can help us no more, or else find us pigeons they can pluck no longer : and if the truth must be confessed, he that once deals with them, and of whom they know that he has money, must pay them only to this end, that they keep him sick." And much more evil had these two to say of their doctors, but I care not to tell it all : otherwise might the gentlemen of that profession take it amiss and some time or other give me a dose that should purge my soul out of my body. Nay, I do but mention it for this cause, because this second patient, in giving thanks to God that He had given him no more wealth, so comforted me that I banished clean out of my mind all vexations and heavy thoughts that had assailed me on the score of money : and I did resolve to strive no more for honour nor gold nor for aught else that the world loveth. Yea, I determined to be a philosopher and to devote myself to a godly life, and in especial to lament mine own impenitence and to endeavour myself, like my dear departed father, to ascend to the highest degree of piety.

*Chap. xii : HOW SIMPLICISSIMUS JOURNEYED
WITH THE SYLPHS TO THE CENTRE OF
THE EARTH*

NOW this desire to visit the Mummelsee increased
with me when I learned from my foster-father
that he had been there and knew the way thither ;
but when he heard that I likewise would go, "And
what will ye gain," says he, " by going thither ? My son
with his old dad will see naught else but the picture of a pond
lying in the midst of a great wood, and when he hath paid
for his present taste with sore distaste, he will have naught
but repentance and weary feet (for a man can hardly come
to the place by riding) and the way back instead of the way
thither. Nor should ever any man have had me to go thither
had I not been forced to flee there when Doctor Daniel (by
which he meant Duc d'Anguin *) marched with his troops
down through the country to Philippsburg." Yet my curiosity
would not be turned aside by his dissuasion, but I got me a
fellow that should guide me thither ; so my father, seeing
my fixed intent, said, since the oat-crop was gathered in, and
there was neither hoeing nor reaping to be done on the farm,
he would even go with me and shew the way. For he loved
me so that he would fain not let me out of his sight, and since
all the people of the country believed I was his true-born son,
he was proud of me ; and so behaved to me and to all others
as a poor man might well do in respect of a son whom good
fortune, without his own help and assistance, had turned into
a fine gentleman.

So together we set off over hill and dale and came to the
Mummelsee ; and that before we had gone six hours, for my
dad was as lively as a cricket and as good a traveller as any
young man. And there we consumed what meat and drink
we had brought with us, for the long journey and the high
mountain on which the lake lieth had made us both hungry
and thirsty. So having refreshed ourselves I did inspect the
lake, and found lying in it certain hewn timbers which my dad

* D'Enghien.

and I took to be the remains of the Würtemberg raft : and I by geometry took or estimated the length and breadth of the water (for 'twas far too wearisome to go round the lake and measure it by paces or feet), and entered the dimensions, by means of the scale of reduction, in my tablets. And having done this, the sky being completely clear and the air windless and calm, I must needs try what truth was in the legend that a storm would arise if any should throw a stone into the lake ; having already found those stories I had heard, how the lake would suffer no trout to live in it, to be true, by reason of the mineral taste of the waters. So to make trial of this, I walked along the lake to the left, where the water, which elsewhere is as clear as a crystal, doth begin, by reason of the monstrous depth, to shew as black as coal, and therefore is so dreadful of appearance that the mere look of it doth terrify. And there I began to cast in stones as great as I could carry ; my foster-father or dad not only refusing to help me, but warning and begging me to give over, as much as in him lay : but I went busily on with my work, and such stones as by reason of their size and weight I could not carry, I rolled down till I had cast more than thirty such into the lake. Then began the sky to be covered with black clouds, in which terrible thundering was heard, so that my dad, which stood on the other side of the lake by the outlet, lamenting over my work, cried out to me that I should escape, lest we be caught by the rain and the dreadful storm, or even a worse mishap chance to us. But in despite of all I answered him, " Father, I will stay and await the end even though it rained pitch-forks." " Yea, yea," answered he, " ye act like all madcap boys, that care not if the world perish."

But I, while I listened to his scolding, turned not mine eyes away from the depths of the lake, expecting to see certain bladders or bubbles rising up from the bottom, as is wont to happen when stones are thrown into deep water whether still or running. Yet saw I naught of the kind, but was ware of certain creatures floating far down in the depths, which in form reminded me of frogs, and flitted about like sparks from a mounting rocket which in the air doth work its full effect : and as they came nearer and nearer to me they seemed to grow larger and more like to the human form : at which at first great wonder took hold of me, and at last, when I saw them hard by me, a great fear and trembling. " Ah," said I then to myself in my terror and wonder, and yet so loud that my dad, that stood beyond the lake, could hear me, though the noise of the thunder was dreadful, " how great are the wondrous works of the Creator ! yea, even in the womb of the earth and the depths of the waters ! " And scarce had I said these words when one of these sylphs appeared upon the waters and answered me, " Aha, and thou dost acknowledge that before thou hast seen aught thereof : what wouldst say if thou wert for once in the Centrum Terrae and beheldest our dwelling which thy curiosity hath disturbed ? "

Meanwhile there rose up here and there more of such water-spirits, like diving birds, all looking upon me and bringing up again the stones I had cast in, which amazed me much. And the first and chiefest among them, whose raiment shone like pure gold and silver, cast to me a shining stone of the bigness of a pigeon's egg and green and transparent as an emerald, with these words : " Take thou this trinket, that thou mayst have somewhat to report of us and of our lake." But scarce had I picked it up and pocketed it when it seemed to me the air would choke or drown me, so that I could not stand upright but rolled about like a ball of yarn, and at last fell into the lake. Yet no sooner was I in the water than I recovered, and through the virtue of the stone I had upon me could breathe in water instead of air : yea, I could with small effort float in the lake as well as could the water-spirits, yea, and with them descended into the depths ; which reminded me of nothing so much as of a flock of birds that so descend in circles from the upper air to light upon the ground.

But my dad having beheld this marvel in part (namely, so much of it as was done above the water), made off from the lake and home again as if his head were on fire. And there he told the whole history ; but especially how the water-spirits had brought back those stones that I had cast into the lake, in the midst of the thunderstorm, and had lain them where they came from, but in exchange had taken me down with them. So some believed him but most accounted it a fable. Others conceived that I had, like another Empedocles of Agrigentum (which cast himself into Mount Aetna that all might think, since he was nowhere to be found, that he was taken up to heaven), drowned myself in the lake, and charged my father to spread such tales about me to gain for me an immortal name : for, said they, it had long been marked by my melancholic humour that I was half-desperate.

Others would fain have believed, had they not known my strength of body, that my adopted father had himself murdered me to be rid of me (being a miserly old man) and so be master alone on my farm : so that at this time naught else but the Mummelsee and me and my departure and my foster-father could be talked of or discoursed on either at the spa or in the countryside.

Chaps. xiii–xvi contain merely a farrago of nonsense conveyed in conversations with the prince of the Mummelsee, who explains to Simplicissimus the construction of the "earth's crust " and the nature of sylphs, and in turn is treated by him to an account of earthly affairs, on which he makes the usual commonplace satirical remarks (see the Introduction).

Chap. xvii : HOW SIMPLICISSIMUS RETURNED FROM THE MIDDLE OF THE EARTH, AND OF HIS STRANGE FANCIES, HIS AIR-CASTLES, HIS CALCULATIONS : AND HOW HE RECKONED WITHOUT HIS HOST

MEANWHILE the time drew near that I should return home ; therefore the king bade me declare my wishes, whereby I understood he was minded to do me a favour. So I said, no greater kindness could be shewn me than to cause a real medicinal spring to rise on my farm. " And is that all ? " answered the king, " I had thought thou wouldst have taken with thee some of these great emeralds from the American Sea and have asked to bear them with thee back to earth. Now do I see that there is no greed among you Christians." Therewith he handed to me a stone of strange and glittering colours, and said, " Put this in thy pouch, and wheresoever thou layest it on the ground, there will it begin to seek the Centre of the

Earth again, and to pass through the most fitting mineralia, till it come back to us, and for our part we will send thee a noble mineral spring, that shall work thee such good and profit as thou hast deserved of us by thy declaration of the truth." So thereupon the prince of the Mummelsee took me again under his charge, and passed with me through the road and the lake by which we had come. And this way back seemed to me far longer than the way thither, so that I reckoned it at three thousand five hundred German-Swiss miles well measured ; but doubtless the cause that the time seemed so long to me was that I had no speech of my escort, save that I learned from them they were from three to five hundred years old and lived all this time without the least disease.

For the rest, I was in fancy so rich with my spring that all my wits and all my thoughts were busied with this, to wit, where I should plant it and how turn it to profit. And first I had my plans for the fine buildings that I must set up that the bathing-guests might be properly accommodated, and I for my part might gain great hire for lodgings. Then I devised already by what bribes I could persuade the doctors to prefer my new miraculous spa to all the others, yea, even to that of Schwalbach, and so procure for me a crowd of rich patients : in my fantasy I even levelled whole mountains lest they that came and went should find the way wearisome to travel : already I hired sharp-witted drawers, sparing cooks, careful chambermaids, watchful grooms, spruce intendants of the baths and springs, and already I thought of a place where in the midst of the wild mountains by my farm I might plant a fine level pleasure-garden, and there rear all manner of rare plants, that the bathing-guests and their wives that came from foreign parts might walk therein, where the sick might be cheered and the sound might be amused and exercised with all manner of sports and pastimes. Then must the doctors, for a reward, write me a noble treatise on my spring and set down on paper its healing qualities ; and this I would have printed with a fine plate wherein my farm should be depicted and a ground plan thereof given ; by reading which any absent patient might at once believe and hope himself in health again. Then would I have all my children fetched from Lippstadt, to have them taught all that was needful to know of my new watering-place; for 'twas my intent to scarify my guests' purses well though not their backs. With such rich fancies and overweening castles in the air I came again into the upper world, for this oft-mentioned prince brought me again to land from his Mummelsee with dry clothes; and there I must forthwith cast from me the talisman that he had at first given me when he fetched me away; else had I either been choked in the air or must have plunged my head under the water again, such was the effect of the said stone. Which being done, and he having taken it to him again, we commended each other to the protection of the most High, as men that should never meet again; so he with his people dived under and sank into his depths; but I with my stone which the king had given me went thence as full of joy as if I had fetched the golden fleece home from Colchis.

But alas! my joy, of which I vainly hoped for the everlasting continuance, endured not long, for hardly was I gone from that lake of wonders when I began to go astray in that monstrous wood, for I had not marked from what direction my dad had brought me to the lake. Yet I went some way on before I was aware of my mistake, ever making calculations how I could plant that noble spring on my farm, and build round it, and earn for myself a peaceful revenue as proprietor thereof. In this way I unawares strayed further and further from the place whither I desired to come and, worst of all, I found it not out till the sun was sinking and I was helpless. For there I stood in the midst of a wilderness like Simple Simon, without food or arms, of which I might well have need during the night that was coming on. Yet I found comfort in my stone that I had brought with me from the very bowels of the earth. " Patience, patience ! " said I to myself : " this will again repay thee for all sufferings undergone. All good things take time, and fine rewards be not won without great toil and labour : else would every fool need but to wipe his beard to get possession at will of even such a noble spring as thou hast in thy poke."

And having spoken thus I got with my new resolve new strength, so that I went forward with a bolder gait than hereto-

fore, although night now overtook me. The full moon indeed
shone on me brightly, but the tall fir-trees kept the light from
me more than the deep sea had done that very day ; yet I
made my way on, till about midnight I was ware of a fire
afar off, to which I straightway walked, and saw from a
distance that there were certain woodmen about it, resin-
gatherers ; and though such folk be not at all times to be
trusted yet my necessity compelled me and my own courage
urged me on to speak to them. So I came quietly behind them
and said, " Good night or good day or good morrow or good
even, gentlemen : for tell me what hour it is that I may know
how to greet ye." With that the whole six stood or sat there
all a-tremble with fear and knew not what to answer me. For
I, being of great stature and just at that time, by reason of
mourning for my late wife, being in black raiment ; and in
especial having a terrible cudgel in mine hand, on which I
leaned like a wild man of the woods, my figure seemed to them
dreadful. " How," says I, " will none answer me ? " Yet
they stayed yet a good while in amazement, till at last one
came to himself well enough to ask, " Who be the gentleman ? " By that I heard they must be of the Swabian
nation ; which men esteem as simple-minded yet with little
cause : so I said I was a travelling scholar, but newly come
from the Venusberg, where I had learned a heap of wondrous
arts. " Oho," quoth the eldest woodman, " Praise God ; for
now do I believe that I shall live to see peace again, because
the wandering scholars are on their travels anew ! "

Chap. xviii : *HOW SIMPLICISSIMUS WASTED HIS*
SPRING IN THE WRONG PLACE

IN this wise we came to converse with one another, and
I found so much courtesy among them that they invited
me to sit down and offered me a piece of black bread
and thin cow's milk cheese, both of which I did thank-
fully accept. At last they became so familiar with me that
they hinted I should, as a travelling scholar, tell their fortunes : and I, knowing somewhat of physiognomics and
palmistry, began to tell to one after the other such stuff

as I deemed would content them, that I might not lose credit with them ; for in spite of all I was not at my ease among these wild woodmen. Then would they learn curious arts from me : but I fobbed them off with promises for the next day, and desired they would suffer me to rest a little. And having so played the gipsy for them, I laid myself down a little apart, more to listen and to perceive how they were minded than as having any great desire to sleep (though my appetite thereto was not lacking) ; and the more I snored the more wakeful they appeared. So they put their heads together and began to dispute one against another who I might be : they held that I could be no soldier because I wore black clothing, nor no townsman-blade, that could so suddenly appear far from all men's dwellings in the Muckenloch (for so was the wood called) at so unwonted a time. At the last they resolved I must be a journeyman Latinist * that had lost his way, or, as I myself had declared, a travelling scholar, because I could so excellently tell fortunes. " Yea," says another, " yet he knew not all for that reason : 'tis some wandering soldier, maybe, that hath so disguised himself to spy out our cattle and the secret ways of the wood. Aha ! if we knew that we would so put him to sleep that he should forget ever to wake again." But another quickly took him up, that held the contrary and would have me to be somewhat else. Meanwhile I lay there and pricked up my ears and thought, " If these clodhoppers set upon me, two or three of them will need to bite the dust before they make an end of me." But while they took counsel and I tormented myself with fears, of a sudden I found myself lying in a pool of water. O horrors ! now was Troy lost and all my splendid plans gone to naught, for by the smell I perceived 'twas mine own mineral spring. With that, for very rage and despite, I fell into such a frenzy that I wellnigh had fallen on those six peasants and fought them all. " Ye godless rogues," says I to them, and therewith sprang up with my terrible cudgel, " by this spring that welleth forth where I have lain ye well may see who I am ; it were small wonder if I should so trounce ye all that the devil should fetch ye, because ye have dared to cherish such evil thoughts in your hearts," and thereto I added looks so threatening and

* A hedge schoolmaster.

341

terrible that all were afraid of me. Yet presently I came to myself and perceived what folly I committed. " Nay," thought I, " 'tis better to lose the spring than one's life, and that thou canst easily forfeit if thou attack these clowns." So I gave them fair words again, and before they could recollect themselves : " Arise," said I, " and taste of this noble spring which ye and all other woodmen and resin-gatherers will henceforth be able to enjoy in this wilderness through my help."

Now this my discourse they understood not, but looked one upon another like live stockfish till they saw me very soberly take the first draught out of my hat. Then one by one they arose from beside their fire, and looked upon this miracle and tasted the water ; but instead of being grateful to me as they should have been, they began to curse and said they would I had chanced on some other spot with my spring : for if their lord came to know of it, then must the whole district of Dornstett do forced-work to make a road thither, which would bring great hardship upon them. " But," says I, " on the contrary, ye will all have your profit therefrom : for ye can turn your fowls, your eggs, your butter, and your cattle and the rest more easily into money." " Nay, nay," said they, " the lord will put in an innkeeper that will take all the profit alone : and we must be his poor fools to keep road and path in trim for him, and earn no thanks thereby."

But at last they disagreed : for two were for keeping the spring and four demanded of me that I should take it away ; which, had it been in my power, I had willingly done whether it pleased them or teased them. So as day began to break, and I had no more to do there, but must rather take heed lest we came together by the ears, I said that unless they were minded that all the cows in that valley should give red milk as long as the spring flowed they must presently shew me the way to Seebach ; with which they were content, and to that end sent two of them with me ; for one had feared to go with me alone.

So I departed thence, and though the whole land there was barren and bore nothing but pine-cones, yet would I with a curse have made it yet poorer, for there I had lost all my hopes ; yet went I silently enough with my guides till I came to the top of the hill, where I could a little trace my way by the lie of the country. And there I said to them, " Now, my masters, ye can turn your new spring to fine profit if ye go forthwith and tell your lords of its coming up ; for that will bring ye a rich reward, seeing that the prince will surely build about it for the glory and gain of the country, and for the promotion of his own interest will have it made known to all the world." " Yea," said they, " fools should we be in truth so to bind rods for our own backs ; we had rather the devil would take thee and thy spring too : thou hast heard enough to know why we desire it not." " Ah, miscreants ! " quoth I, " should I not call ye disloyal rogues that depart so far from the ways of your pious forefathers, which were so true to their prince that he could boast that he might venture to lay his head upon the knees of any of his subjects and there sleep in safety. But ye blackcaps, to 'scape a trifling task for which ye would in time be recompensed and of which all your posterity would reap a rich reward, ye be so dishonest as to refuse to make known this healing spring, which were both to the profit of your worshipful prince and also to the welfare and health of many a sick man. What would it cost ye though each should do a few days' forced work to that end ? " " How," said they, " we would rather kill thee that thy spring might remain unknown." " Ye nightbirds," says I, " there must be more of ye for that," and therewith heaved up my cudgel and chased them to all the devils, and thereafter went my way down hill westwards and southwards, and so came after much toil and tumble about sunset to my farm, and found it true indeed what my dad had prophesied to me, namely, that I should get naught from this pilgrimage save weary legs and the way back for the way thither.

Chap. xix is an uninteresting excursus on certain communities of Anabaptists in Hungary.

*Chap. xx : TREATS OF A TRIFLING PROMENADE
FROM THE BLACK FOREST TO MOSCOW
IN RUSSIA*

THE same autumn there drew near to us French,
Swedish, and Hessian troops to refresh themselves
among us and to keep the Free City in the neighbourhood (which was built by an English king,*
and called after his name) blockaded, for which cause every
man gathered together his cattle and the best of his goods and
fled into the woods among the mountains. I too did as my
neighbours did and left my house pretty well empty, wherein
a Swedish colonel on half-pay was lodged. The same found
still remaining in my cabinet certain books, for in my haste
I could not bring all away ; and among others certain mathematical and geometrical essays, and also some on fortification,
wherewith our engineers be principally busied, and therefore
at once concluded that his quarters could belong to no common
peasant, and so began to inquire of my character and to court
my acquaintance, till by courteous offers and threats inter-
mingled he wrought me to it that I should visit him at mine
own farm, where he treated me very civilly and restrained
his people, that they should do my goods no unnecessary
damage or hurt. And by such friendly treatment he brought
it about that I told him of all my business, and in especial of
my family and descent. Thereat he wondered that I in the
midst of war could so dwell among peasants, and look on while
another tied his horse to my manger, whereas I with more
honour could tie mine own horse to another's : I should, said
he, gird on the sword again and not allow my gift which God
had bestowed on me to perish by the fireside, and behind the
plough ; for he knew, if I would enter the Swedish service,
my capacity and my knowledge of war would soon raise me
to high rank. This I treated but coldly, and told him advancement was ever far off if a man had no friends to take him by
the hand : whereto he replied that my good qualities would
soon procure me both friends and advancement ; nay, more :

* Offa. Offenburg.

344

he doubted not that I should find kinsmen at the Swedish headquarters, and those of some account, for there there were many Scottish noblemen and men of rank. Further, said he, a regiment had been promised to him himself by Torstensohn; which promise if it were kept (of which he doubted not) then would he at once make me his lieutenant-colonel. With such and the like words he made my mouth to water, and inasmuch as there were but now scanty hopes of peace, and for me to suffer further billeting of troops did but mean utter ruin, therefore I resolved to serve again, and promised the colonel to go with him if only he would keep his word and give me the post of lieutenant-colonel in the regiment he was to have.

And so the die was cast; and I sent for my dad or foster-father, which was still with my cattle at Bairischbrunn;* and to him and his wife I devised my farm as their own property; yet on condition that after his death my bastard Simplicissimus that had been laid at my door should inherit it with all appurtenances, since there were no heirs born in wedlock. Thereafter I fetched my horse and all the gold and trinkets I still had, and having settled all my affairs and taken order for the education of my said by-blow of a son, on a sudden the blockade I spoke of was raised, so that before we looked for it we must decamp and join the main army.

Under the colonel I served as a steward, and maintained him with his servants and horses and all his household by theft and robbery, which is called in soldiers' language foraging. But as to the promises of Torstensohn, of which he had talked so big at my farm, they were not so great by a good deal as he had given out, but as it seemed to me he was rather looked at askance. "Aha," says he to me, "some malicious dog hath slandered me at headquarters. Yet I shall not need to wait long": but when he suspected that I should not endure to tarry longer with him he forged letters as if he had to raise a fresh regiment in Livonia where his home was, and persuaded me to embark with him at Wismar and to sail thither. And there too we found naught, for not only had he no regiment to raise, but was besides a nobleman as poor as a church mouse: and what he had came from his wife. Yet though I had now been twice deceived

* Baiersbronn.

and had suffered myself to be enticed so far afield, yet I took the bait the third time ; for he shewed me writings he had received from Moscow, in which, as he professed, high commands in the army were offered him, for so he interpreted the said letters to me and boasted loudly of good and punctual pay : and seeing that he started off with his wife and child, I thought, surely he is on no wild-goose chase.

And so with high hopes I took the road with him, for otherwise I saw no means or opportunity to get back to Germany. But as soon as we came over the Russian frontier, and sundry discharged German soldiers met us, I began to be alarmed and said to my colonel, " What the devil do we here ? We leave the country where war is, and where there is peace and soldiers be of no account and disbanded, thither we come." Yet still he gave me fair words and said I should leave it to him ; he knew better what he was about than these fellows that were of no account.

But when we came in safety to the city of Moscow, I saw at once the game was up. 'Tis true my colonel conferred daily with great men, but far more with bishops than boyars, which seemed to me not so much grand as far too monkish, and aroused in me all manner of fancies and reflections, though I could not conceive what he aimed at : but in the end he revealed to me that war was over and that his conscience urged him on to embrace the Greek religion ; and that his sincere advice to me was, inasmuch as otherwise he could help me no more as he had promised, to follow his example : for his Majesty the Czar had already good accounts of my person and my great capabilities : and would be graciously pleased, if I would agree to the conditions, to endow me as a knight with a fine estate and many serfs ; which most gracious offer was not to be rejected, since for any man it was better to have in so great a monarch rather a gracious lord than an offended prince. At this I was much confounded, and knew not what to answer, for had I had the colonel in another place I would have answered him rather by deeds than words : but now I must play my cards otherwise, and consider the place where I was, and where I was like to a prisoner ; and therefore was silent a long time before I could resolve upon an answer. At length I said to him I had indeed come with the purpose to serve the Czar's Majesty as a soldier, to which he, the colonel, had persuaded me ; and if my services in war were not needed I could not help it ; far less could I lay it to the charge of the Czar that I had for his sake undertaken so long a journey in vain, for he had not written to me to come. But that his Majesty condescended so graciously to dispense his royal favour to me would be a thing for me rather to boast of before all the world than most humbly to accept it and to earn it, since I could not just now determine to alter my religion, and only wished I were dwelling again in my farm in the Black Forest and so causing no man concern or inconveniency. To which he replied, " Your honour may do as he pleases : only I had conceived that if God and good luck favoured him, he would do well to be thankful to both ; but if he will accept no help and refuses to live like a prince, at least I hope he will believe that I have spared no pains to help him to the best of my ability." Thereupon he made me a deep reverence, went his way, and left me in the lurch, not allowing me even to give him my company to the door.

So as I sat there all perplexed and reviewed my present condition I heard two Russian carriages before our lodging, and looking out of the window saw my good master colonel with his sons enter the one and his wife with her daughters the other. Which were the Czar's carriages and his livery, and divers priests there also which waited upon this honourable family and shewed them all kindness and good will.

Chap. xxi : HOW SIMPLICISSIMUS FURTHER FARED
IN MOSCOW

FROM this time I was watched, not openly indeed, but secretly, by certain soldiers of the Strelitz guard, and that without my knowledge ; and my colonel and his family never once came in my sight, so that I knew not what was become of him : and all this, as may easily be thought, brought in my head strange conceits and many grey hairs also. There I made the acquaintance of the Germans that dwell in Moscow, some as traders, some as mechanics, and to them lamented my plight and how I had

been deceived by guile ; who gave me comfort and direction
how I, with a fair opportunity, might return to Germany.
But so soon as they got wind of it that the Czar had determined
to keep me in the land and would force me to it, they all
became dumb towards me, yea, avoided my company, and
'twas hard for me even to find a shelter for my head. For I
had already devoured my horse, saddle and trappings and all,
and was now doling out one to-day and to-morrow another of
the ducats which I had wisely sewn into my clothes. At last
I began to turn into money my rings and trinkets, in the hope
to keep myself so until I could find a fair occasion to get back
to Germany. Meanwhile a quarter of a year was gone, after
which the said colonel, with all his household, was baptized
again and provided with a fine nobleman's estate and many
serfs.

At that time there went out a decree that both among
natives and foreigners no idlers should be allowed (and that
with heavy penalties) as those that took the bread out of the
mouth of the workers, and all strangers that would not work
must quit the country in a month and the town in four-and-
twenty hours. With that some fifty of us joined together with
intent to make our way, with God's help, through Podolia to
Germany ; yet were we not two hours gone from the town
when we were caught up by certain Russian troopers, on the
pretence that his Majesty was greatly displeased that we had
impudently dared to band together in such great numbers,
and to traverse his land at pleasure without passports, saying
further that his Majesty would not be going beyond his rights
in sending us all to Siberia for our insolent conduct. On the
way back I learned how my business stood : for the commander of the troop told me plainly, the Czar would not let
me forth of the country : and his sincere advice was that I
should obey his Majesty's most gracious will and join their
religion, and (as the colonel had done) not despise a fine
estate ; assuring me also that if I refused this and would not
live among them as a lord I must needs stay as a servant
against my will : nor must his Majesty be blamed that he would
not allow to depart from his country a man so skilful as the
before-mentioned colonel had reported me to be. Then did
I disparage mine own worth, and said the honourable colonel

must surely have ascribed to me more arts, virtues, and knowledge than I possessed : 'twas true indeed I had come into the land to serve his Majesty the Czar and the worshipful Russian people, even at the risk of my life, against their enemies : but to change my religion, to that I could not resolve me : yet so far as I could in any wise serve his Majesty without burdening my conscience, I would not fail to do my utmost endeavour.

Then was I set apart from the rest and lodged with a merchant, where I was openly watched, yet daily provisioned from the court with rich food and costly liquors, and also daily had visitors that talked with me and now and again would invite me as a guest. In especial there was one to whose charge I had without doubt been chiefly commended, a crafty man, that entertained me daily with friendly talk ; for now could I speak Russian pretty well. So he discoursed with me oftentimes of all manner of mechanic arts, as well as of engines of war and others, and of fortification and artillery practice. At last, after much beating about the bush to find out whether I would give in to his master's wishes, when he found there was no hope of my changing even in the least point, he begged that I would for the honour of the great Czar impart and communicate to their nation somewhat of my science : for his Majesty would requite my complaisance with high and royal favours. To which I answered, my desires had ever been to that end, most dutifully to serve the Czar, seeing that for this purpose I had come into his country, albeit I perceived that I was kept like a prisoner. But he replied, " Nay, nay, sir, ye be no prisoner, but his Majesty doth hold ye so dear that he cannot resolve to part with your person." So says I, " Wherefore then am I guarded ? " " Because," he answered, " his Majesty feareth lest any harm should happen to ye."

So now understanding my proposals, he said the Czar was graciously pleased to consider of digging for saltpetre in his own country and making of powder there ; but because there was no one in the land that could deal with the matter, I should do him an acceptable service if I would undertake the work : to that end I should be provided with men and means enough ready to hand, and he in his own person would most sincerely beg of me not to reject such a gracious proposal, seeing that they were already well assured that I had a full knowledge of such matters. To which I answered, " Sir, I say as I said before : if I can serve his Majesty in anything, provided only he will be graciously content to leave me undisturbed in my religion, I will not fail to do my best." Whereat the Russian, which was one of their chief magnates, was heartily glad and pledged me in drink deeper than ever a German.

Next day there came from the Czar two great nobles with an interpreter to make a final agreement with me, and presented me on behalf of the Czar with a costly Russian robe : and a few days after I began to seek for saltpetre and to instruct the Russians that had been assigned to me how to separate it from the earth and refine it ; and at the same time I drew up a plan of a powder-mill, and taught others to burn charcoal, so that in brief space we had ready a goodly amount both of musquet and ordnance powder ; for I had people enough, besides mine own servants that were to wait on me, or, to speak more truly, to keep watch and ward over me.

I being thus well started, there comes to me the beforementioned colonel in Russian clothes and nobly escorted by many servants ; without doubt by such a show of glory to persuade me to go over to that religion. But I knew well that the clothes came from the Czar his wardrobe, and were but lent him to make my mouth water : for 'tis the commonest of customs at the Russian court : and that the reader may understand how 'tis managed, I will give him an instance of mine own self. For once was I busied with taking order at the powder-mills (which I caused to be built on the river outside Moscow) as to what task one and the other of the people assigned to me should perform that day and the next, when of a sudden there was an alarm that the Tartars, 100,000 horse strong, were but four miles away plundering the country and advancing continually : so must I and my people needs betake ourselves to the palace, to be equipped out of the Czar's armoury and stables. And I for my part, in place of a cuirass, was clad in a quilted silk breastplate that would stop any arrow, but could not keep out any bullet : moreover boots and spurs and a princely head-dress with a heron plume, and a sabre that would split a hair, mounted with pure gold and studded with precious stones, were given to me, and of the Czar's horses such an one was put between my legs as I had never seen the like of in my life, far less ridden ; so I and my horses blazed with gold, silver, pearls and precious stones. I had a steel mace hanging by me that shone like a mirror, and was so well made and heavy that I had easily beaten to death any that I dealt a blow with it, so that the Czar himself could not ride into battle better equipped : and there followed me a white standard with a double eagle to which the people flocked from all sides and corners, so that before two hours were over we were forty thousand strong and after four hours nigh sixty thousand, with whom we marched against the Tartars ; and every quarter of an hour I had my orders from the Czar ; which yet were but this, that I should this day approve myself a soldier, having given myself out for one, that his Majesty might as such esteem and recognise me. So every moment our troop was increased with great and small soldiers and officers ; yet in all this haste could I discover none that should command the whole body, or array the battle. It needs not that I should tell all, for my story is not much concerned with this encounter. I will but say this only, that we came suddenly upon the Tartars in a valley or deep dip in the land, encumbered with tired horses and much booty, and least of all expecting us ; whom we attacked on all sides with such fury that at the very onset we scattered them. There at the first attack I called to my followers in the Russian speech, " Come now, let each do as I do ! " and that they all shouted to one another, while I with a loose rein charged at the enemy, and of the first I met, which was a Mirza or prince's son, I cleft the head in twain, so that his brains were left hanging on my steel mace. This heroical example did the Russians follow, so that the Tartars might not withstand their attack, but turned to a general flight, while I dealt like a madman, or rather like one that from desperation seeketh death and cannot find it, for I smote down all that came before me, Tartar and Russian alike ; and they that were commanded by the Czar to watch me followed me so hard that I had ever my back guarded. There was the air so full of arrows as it had been swarms of bees, of which my share was

one in the arm ; for I had turned back my sleeve that so
with less hindrance I might use my sword and came to cleave
and batter ; and until I received the wound my heart did
laugh within me at such bloodshed ; but when I saw mine
own blood flow, that laughter was turned into a mad fury.

So when these savage foes had been put to flight, it was
commanded me by divers nobles in the name of the Czar that
I should carry to their emperor the news how the Tartars
had been defeated : and at their bidding I rode back with some
hundred horsemen at my heels, with whom I rode through
the town to the Czar's palace, and was by all men received
with triumph and gratulation ; but so soon as I had made my
report of the battle (albeit the Czar had already news of all
that happened) I must again doff my princely apparel, which
was again stored away in the Czar his wardrobe, though both
it and the horse trappings were bespattered and befouled all
over with blood and so almost entirely ruinated ; whereas
I had thought, since I had borne myself so knightly in the
encounter, the clothes should at least have been left me,
together with the horse, for a reward. But from this I could
well judge how 'twas managed with the Russian robe of state
of which my colonel made use ; for 'tis all but lent finery
which, like all else in Russia, pertaineth to the Czar alone.

Chap. xxii : BY WHAT A SHORT AND MERRY ROAD HE CAME HOME TO HIS DAD

NOW as long as my wound was a-healing 'tis true
I was treated like a prince ; for I walked abroad
at all times clad in a furred gown of cloth of gold
lined with sables, though the wound was neither
mortal nor dangerous, and in all the days of my life I have
never tasted such rich foods as then ; but this was all their
reward I had for my labours, save the praise which the Czar
favoured me with, and this too was spoiled for me by the
envy of certain nobles. So now, being completely sound again,
was I sent down the Volga in a ship to Astrachan, to set up a
powder-mill there as in Moscow, for 'twas not possible for the
Czar to furnish these frontier fortresses from Moscow with

fresh and good powder, which must needs be carried by water and that with great risk. And this service I willingly undertook, for I had promises that the Czar, after the accomplishment of such business, would send me back to Holland, and that with a good reward in money proportionable to my services. But alas! when we think we stand safest and most certain in the hopes and conceits we have formed, there comes a wind unawares, and in a wink blows away all the flimsy stuff whereon we had founded our hopes so long.

Yet the Governor of Astrachan treated me like the Czar himself, and in brief space I had all on a good footing; his old ammunition which was quite spoiled and ruined and could do no harm to any, I refounded (as a tinker makes new tin spoons out of old ones), which was then a thing unheard of among the Russians; by reason of which and other arts of mine some held me to be a sorcerer, others a new saint or prophet, and others, again, for a second Empedocles or Gorgias Leontinus. But being hard at work and busied at night in a powder-mill outside the fortifications, I was in thievish wise captured and carried off by a horde of Tartars, which took me with others so far into their country that I not only could see the herb Borametz or sheep-plant growing but did even eat thereof: which is a most strange vegetable; for it is like a sheep to look upon, its wool can be spun and woven like natural sheep's wool, and its flesh is so like to mutton that even the wolves do love to eat thereof. But they that had captivated me did barter me away for certain wares of China to the Tartars of Nuichi, which again presented me as a rare gift to the King of Corea, with whom they had but then made a truce. And there was I highly valued, for there could none be found like me in the handling of sword and rapier; and there I taught the king how, with his piece over his shoulder and his back turned to the target, he could yet hit the bull's-eye; in reward for which at my humble petition he gave me my liberty again, and let me go by way of Japonia to the Portuguese of Macao, which made but small count of me. So I went about among them like a sheep that has strayed from the flock, till at last in marvellous fashion I was captured by Turkish corsairs, and by them, after they had dragged me about with them for a full year among strange foreign nations that do inhabit the isles of the East Indies, sold to certain merchants of Alexandria in Egypt. These carried me with their wares to Constantinople, and because the Turkish emperor was just then fitting out galleys against the Venetians and needed rowers, therefore must many Turkish merchants part with their Christian slaves (yet for ready payment), among whom I was one, as being a strong young fellow. And now must I learn to row ; which heavy task nevertheless endured not more than two months : for our galley was in the Levant right valiantly overcome by the Venetians, and I with all my companions freed from the power of the Turks : and the said galley being brought to Venice with rich booty and divers Turkish prisoners of high degree, I was set at liberty, as wishing to go to Rome and on pilgrimage to Loretto, to view those places and to thank God for my deliverance. To which end I easily obtained a passport, and moreover from several honourable persons, especially Germans, reasonable help in money, so that now I could provide me with a pilgrim's staff and enter on my journey.

So I betook me by the nearest way to Rome, where I fared right well, for both from great and small I got me much alms ; and tarrying there nigh six weeks, I took my way with other pilgrims, of whom some Germans, and especially certain Switzers, to Loretto : from whence I came over the Saint Gotthard Pass back through Switzerland to my dad, which had kept my farm for me ; and nothing remarkable did I bring home save a beard which I had grown in foreign parts.

Now had I been absent three years and some months, during which time I had fared over the most distant seas and seen all manner of peoples, but had commonly received from them more evil than good ; of which a whole book might be writ. And in the meanwhile the Westphalian treaty had been concluded, so that I could now live with my dad in peace and quiet : and him I left to manage and to keep house, but for myself I sat down to my books, which were now both my work and my delight.

*Chap. xxiii : IS VERY SHORT AND CONCERNETH
SIMPLICISSIMUS ALONE*

ONCE did I read how the oracle of Apollo gave as
answer to the Roman deputies, when they asked
what they must do to rule their subjects in peace,
this only, "Nosce teipsum," which signifieth, "Let
each man know himself." This caused me to reflect upon the
past and demand of myself an account of the life I had led,
for I had naught else to do. So said I to myself : " Thy
life hath been no life but a death, thy days a toilsome shadow,
thy years a troublous dream, thy pleasures grievous sins,
thy youth a fantasy, and thy happiness an alchemist's
treasure that is gone by the chimney and vanished ere thou
canst perceive it. Through many dangers thou hast followed
the wars, and in the same encountered much good and ill
luck : hast been now high, now low : now great, now small :
now rich, now poor : now merry, now sorry : now loved,
now hated : now honoured, now despised : but now, poor
soul, what hast thou gained from thy long pilgrimage ? This
hast thou gained . I am poor in goods, my heart is burdened
with cares, for all good purposes I am idle, lazy, and spoilt ;
and, worst of all, my conscience is heavy and vexed : but
thou, my soul, art overwhelmed with sin and grievously
defiled ; the body is weary, the understanding bemused ;
thine innocence is gone, the best years of youth are past, the
precious time lost : naught is there that gives me pleasure,
and withal I am an enemy to myself. But when I came, after
my sainted father's death, into the great world, then was
I simple-minded and pure, upright and honest, truthful,
humble, modest, temperate, chaste, shame-faced, pious and
religious, but soon became malicious, false, treacherous, proud,
restless, and above all altogether godless, all which vices I
did learn without a teacher. Mine honour have I guarded
not for its own sake, but for mine own exaltation. I took
note of time not to employ it well for mine own soul's welfare,
but for the profit of my body. My life have I often put in
jeopardy, and yet I have never busied myself to better it that
I might die blest and comforted ; for I looked only to the

present and to my temporal profit, and never once thought on the future, much less remembered that I must some time give an account before the face of God Almighty."

With such thoughts I tormented myself daily ; and just then there came into my hands certain writings of the Franciscan friar Quevara, of which I must here set down some ; for they were of such power as fully to disgust me with the world.

Chap. xxiv : WHY AND IN WHAT FASHION SIM-PLICISSIMUS LEFT THE WORLD AGAIN

The first part of the chapter is a fair translation, extending to many pages, of Quevara's somewhat trite reflections on the vanity of a worldly life. It is taken from Albertini's translation of a book called " Of the burden and annoyance of a courtier's life." 8vo. Amberg, 1599. The only part of the chapter which concerns the story is as follows.

ALL these words I pondered carefully and with continual thought, and they so pierced my heart that I left the world again and became a hermit. Fain would I have dwelt by my spring in the Muckenloch, but the peasants that dwelt near would not suffer it, though it had been for me a wilderness to my taste ; for they feared I should reveal the spring and so move their lord to force them to make highways and byways thither, especially now that peace was secured. So I betook myself to another wilderness and began again my old life in the Spessart ; but whether I shall, like my father of blessed memory, persevere therein to the end, I know not. God grant us all His grace that we may all alike obtain from Him what doth concern us most, namely, a happy

END

APPENDIX A

THE success of " Simplicissimus " induced Grimmelshausen to publish a " Continuatio " or sequel, which certainly does not seem to have been contemplated when he wrote the last chapter of the original work. It, as well as three lesser " continuations " which were published later, is entirely unworthy of the author, though all four seem to be genuine products of his pen. It is a string of allegories, ghost stories, fables, and monotonous chronicles of adventure, not redeemed from dulness by occasional gross filth. For one reason only it deserves our attention ; viz., the curious anticipation of the story of Robinson Crusoe which is contained in chapters xix to xxii. A subjoined " relation " of Jean Cornelissen of Harlem gives an account of his finding Simplicissimus and leaving him on his island well provided with necessaries : but this narrative is so overloaded with childish stories of the castaway's miraculous powers and performances that an abstract of it only is here given at the end.

From the middle of chapter xix to the end of chapter xxiii is fully translated.

CONTINUATION

Chap. xix : HOW SIMPLICISSIMUS AND A CARPENTER ESCAPED FROM A SHIPWRECK WITH THEIR LIVES AND WERE THEREAFTER PROVIDED WITH A LAND OF THEIR OWN

SO taking ship and coming from the Sinus Arabicus or Red Sea into the ocean, and having a fair wind, we held our course to pass by the Cape of Good Hope, and sailed for some weeks so happily that way that we could have desired no other weather : but when we deemed that we were now over against the isle of Madagascar there suddenly arose such a hurricane that we had scarce time to take in sail. And the storm increasing, we must needs cut down the mast and leave the ship to the mercy of the waves, which carried us up, as it were, to the clouds, and in a trice plunged us down again to the depths; all which lasted a full half-hour and taught us all to pray most piously. At length were we cast upon a sunken reef with such force that the ship with a terrible crack broke all in pieces, at which there arose a lamentable and piteous outcry. Then was the sea in a moment strown with chests, bales, and fragments of the ship, and then one could hear and see the unlucky folk, here and there, some on and some under the waves, clinging to anything that in such need came first within their grasp, and with dismal cries lamenting their ruin and commending of their souls to God. But I, with the ship's carpenter, lay upon a great timber of the vessel which had certain cross-pieces yet fast to it, to which we clung and spake to one another. And little by little the dreadful wind abated; the raging waves of the angry sea grew calmer and less; yet on the other hand there followed pitch-dark night with terrible rain, till it seemed as if we should be drowned from above in the midst of the sea. And this endured till midnight, by which time we had been in sore straits; but then was the sky clear again, so that we could see the stars, by which we perceived that the wind drove us more and more from the coast of Africa towards the open sea and the unknown land of Australia, which troubled us both greatly. Now towards daybreak it grew dark again, so that we could not see each other though we lay close at hand: and in this darkness and piteous plight we drove ever onward, till of a sudden we were aware that we were aground and stuck fast. So the carpenter, which had an axe hanging to his girdle, tried with it the depth of the water and found it on the one side of us not a foot deep, which heartily rejoiced us and gave us sure hope that God had in some way helped us to land, as we perceived by a sweet odour that we smelt as soon as we came to ourselves a little. Yet because 'twas dark and we both wearied out, and in especial looked presently for daylight, we had not courage enough to commit ourselves to the sea and make for land, notwithstanding we already thought to hear at a distance the song of divers birds, which indeed was so. But as soon as the blessed daylight shewed itself in the east, we saw through the dusk a small island overgrown with bushes lying close before us; whereupon we betook ourselves to the water on that side, which grew shallower and shallower till at length, with great joy, we came to dry land. So there we fell on our knees and kissed the ground, and thanked God above for His fatherly care in bringing of us to land; and in such fashion did I come to my island. As yet could we not know whether we were in an inhabited or an uninhabited land and whether on the mainland or an island : but this we marked at once, that it must be a right fertile soil ; for all was overgrown thick with shrubs and trees like a hemp-field, so that we could hardly come through it. But when it was now broad day, and we had made our way through the shrubs some quarter of an hour's march from the shore, we could not only find no trace of human dwelling, but moreover lighted here and there upon many strange birds that had no fear of us, but suffered us to take them with our hands, from all which we might judge we were on an uninhabited island, yet most fruitful. There did we find citrons, pomegranates, and cocoa-nuts, with which fruits we refreshed ourselves right well ; and when the sun rose we came to a plain covered with palm-trees, from which palm wine is made ; the which was but too pleasing to my comrade, who loved the same more than was good for him. So there we set ourselves down in the sun to dry our clothes, which we stripped off and to that end hung them on the trees, but for our own parts walked about in our shirts : and my carpenter cutting a palm-tree with his axe, found it was full of wine : yet had we no vessel to catch it in, and for our hats, we had lost them both in the shipwreck.

So the kindly sun having dried our clothes again, we put them on and climbed up the high, rocky mountain that lieth on the right hand towards the north between this plain and the sea, and looking about us found that we were on no mainland but on this island, which in circuit exceeded not an hour and a half's journey. And because we could see neither near nor far off any land but only sea and sky, we were both troubled, and lost all hope ever to see mankind again ; yet contrariwise it did comfort us that the goodness of God had brought us to this land both safe and most fruitful, and not to a place that belike would prove barren or inhabited of man-eaters. So we began to consider of our way to act ; and because we must live even as prisoners on this island with one another we did swear perpetual fidelity each to each.

Now on the said mountain there not only sat and flew many birds of divers kinds, but it was so full of nests with eggs that we could not sufficiently marvel thereat. Of these eggs we did eat some and took still more with us down the hill, on which we found the spring of sweet water which flows into the sea towards the east with such force that it might well turn a small mill-wheel ; at which we rejoiced anew and resolved to set up our abode beside the said spring. Yet for our new housekeeping we had no other furniture but an axe, a spoon, three knives, a prong or fork, and a pair of scissors : and nothing more. 'Tis true my comrade had some thirty ducats about him, but these we had gladly bartered for a tinder-box had we known where to buy one : for they were of no use to us at all ; yea, less than my powder-horn, which was still full of priming ; this did I dry, for it was all like a soft cake, in the sun, scattered some upon a stone, covered it with easy-burning stuff such as the moss and cotton which the cocoanut-trees furnished in plenty, and then drawing a knife sharply through the powder, kindled it, which rejoiced us as much as our rescue from the sea : and had we but had salt and bread and vessels to hold our drink we had esteemed ourselves the luckiest fellows in the world, though four-and-twenty hours before we might have been counted among the most miserable ; so good and faithful and merciful is God, to whom be glory for ever and ever, Amen.

Then we caught some birds forthwith, of which whole flocks flew about us, plucked, washed, and stuck them on a wooden spit, and so I began to turn the roast, while my comrade fetched me wood and prepared a shelter that, if it should come on to rain again, might protect us from the same, for these Indian rains in the parts towards Africa are wont to be very unhealthy ; but our lack of salt we supplied with lemon-juice to give a flavour to our food.

*Chap. xx : HOW THEY HIRED A FAIR COOK-MAID
AND BY GOD'S HELP WERE RID OF HER
AGAIN*

THIS was the first meal of which we partook upon
our island ; and having ended it, we had naught
else to do but gather dry wood to keep up our fire.
We would fain have explored the whole island at
once, but by reason of the fatigue we had passed through,
sleep so overpowered us that we must needs lie down to rest
and sleep till broad daylight. And finding it so, we walked
down the brook or glade as far as its mouth where it flows
into the sea, and saw with amazement how a great multitude
of fish of the size of middling salmon or large carp swam up
the little river into the fresh water, so that it seemed as a
great herd of swine were driven violently in ; and finding
also certain bananas and sweet potatoes, which be excellent
fruits, we said to each other we had surely found the Land of
Cocaigne or Monkeys' Paradise, (though no four-footed beast
there) if we had but company to help us to enjoy both the
fruitfulness of this noble island and also the plenty of birds
and fishes on it : yet could we find no single sign that ever
men had been there.

But as we began to take counsel how we should further
order our housekeeping and whence we might have vessels
wherein both to cook and to catch the juice from the palms
and let it ferment in its own fashion, that we might have the
full enjoyment of it, and as we walked on the shore in talk
of this, we saw far out at sea something that tossed about,
which we at a distance could not make out, though it seemed
bigger than it really was. For when it came near and was
driven ashore on the coast of the island it proved to be a
woman, half-dead, lying on a chest, and with both hands
fast clasped to the handles of it. Her for Christian charity
we drew to dry land ; and dreaming her to be a Christian
woman of Abyssinia both by her clothing and certain marks
she had on her face, we were the more busy to bring her to,
to which end (yet with all honesty, as becomes them that deal
with modest women in such a case) we set her on her head

till a good deal of water had run out of her, and albeit we had no cordial to revive her more than our citron-juice, yet we ceased not to press under her nose that spirituous liquor which is found at the very end of the lemon-peel and to shake and move her about, till at last she began to stir of herself and to speak in Portuguese : which as soon as my comrade heard, and as a lively colour began to shew itself in her face, he said to me, " This Abyssinian was once on our ship as maid to a Portuguese lady of quality ; for I knew them both well : they dwelt at Macao and were purposed to sail with us to the Isle of Annabon." And she, so soon as she heard him speak, shewed herself right glad, and called him by name, and told us not only of her whole journey, but how she was rejoiced both that he and she were still alive, as also that they had as old acquaintances met on dry land and out of all danger. At that my carpenter asked what manner of wares might be in the chest. To which she answered they were certain parcels of Chinese apparel with firearms and weapons, besides divers vessels of porcelain both small and great, that should have been sent by her master to a great prince in Portugal. At which news we rejoiced greatly, seeing that these were the things which we most needed. Then did she beg of us that we should shew her kindness and keep her with us : for she would gladly serve us in cooking, washing, and other duties of a maid and obey us as a slave, if we would but keep her under our protection and suffer her to partake with us of the sustenance which fortune and nature provided in that place.

So with great toil and trouble we dragged the chest to that place which we had chosen for our dwelling ; where we did open it, and found therein things so fitted to our needs that we could have desired nothing better for our then condition and for the use of our household. These goods we unpacked and dried them in the sun, in which business our new maid shewed herself diligent and serviceable ; and thereafter we began to slay, boil, and roast birds, and while my carpenter went to fetch palm-wine I climbed up the mountain to gather eggs for us, meaning to boil them hard and to use them in place of good bread. And as I went I considered with hearty gratitude the great gifts and goodness of God, that had with such fatherly kindness caused His Providence to watch over us and gave us the promise of further help. There did I fall upon my face, and stretching out my arms and lifting up my heart to God I prayed thus : " O heavenly Father of all mercies, now do I find indeed that Thou art more ready to give than we to ask ; yea, dearest Lord, Thou hast with the fulness of Thy divine riches supplied us more quickly and more plentifully than we poor creatures ever thought to ask of Thee at all. O faithful Father, may it please Thy infinite compassion to grant to us that we may never use these Thy gifts and favours otherwise than as is agreeable to thy Holy will and pleasure, and as may tend to the honour of Thy great and unspeakable Name, that we, with all the Elect, may ever praise, honour, and glorify Thee here on earth and hereafter in heaven for ever and for evermore." And with these and the like words, which flowed from the very depth of my soul, with hearty and true faith, I went on till I had gathered all the eggs we needed, and with them came back to our hut even as our supper stood excellently well served upon the chest we had that day fished out of the sea with our cook-maid, and which my comrade had made use of for a table.

Now while I was absent seeking for eggs, my comrade, which was a lad of some twenty odd years, I being now over forty, had struck a bargain with our maid that should be both for his ruin and mine ; for finding themselves alone in my absence, and talking together of old times and also of the fruitfulness and great delight of this blessed, yea more than fortunate isle, they had grown so familiar that they had begun to speak of a match between them, of which the pretended Abyssinian would not hear, unless 'twere agreed that my comrade the carpenter should make himself master of the island and rid them of me ; for, said she, it were impossible for them to dwell in peace in wedlock so long as an unmarried man lived by them.

" For bethink thyself," says she, " how would not suspicion and jealousy plague thee, if thou wert my husband, and yet the old fellow talking with me day by day, even if he should never think to make a cuckold of thee ! Nay, but I know a better plan : if I be to be married on this island, that well can feed a thousand or more persons to increase the human race, then let the old fellow marry me ; for were it so 'twere but a year to count on, or perhaps twelve or at most fourteen, in which time he and I might breed a daughter and marry her to thee, who would not then be of the age that the old man is now ; and in the meantime ye might cherish the certain hope that the one should be the other's father-in-law and the other his son-in-law, and so do away all evil suspicions and deliver me from all dangers which otherwise I might encounter with. Doubtless 'tis true that a young woman like me would sooner wed with a young man than an old : yet must we suit ourselves to the circumstance as our present plight doth require, to provide that I and she that may be born of me shall be in safety."

By this discourse, which lasted much longer and was more fully set forth than I have here described, and also by the beauty of the pretended Abyssinian (which in the light of the fire did shine more perfect than ever in my comrade's eyes) and by her lively actions, my good carpenter was so captivated and befooled that he was not ashamed to say he would sooner throw the old man (meaning me) into the sea and send the whole island to the devil than deliver over to him so fair a lady : and thereupon was the bargain I spoke of concluded between them, namely, that he should slay me with his axe from behind or in my sleep ; for he was afeared of my great strength of body, as well as of my staff, which he had himself fashioned for me as strong as a weaver's beam.*

So this compact being made, she shewed my comrade close to our dwelling a kind of fine potter's earth, of which she promised to make fine earthen vessels after the manner of the Indian women on the Guinea coast, and laid all manner of plans how she would maintain herself and her family on this island, rear them and provide for them a peaceful and sufficient livelihood, yea even to the hundredth generation : and could not boast enough of what profit she could make of the cocoanut-trees and the cotton which the same do bear or produce, out of which she would provide herself and all her children's children with clothing.

But I, poor wretch, came knowing no word of this foul

* Literally " a Bohemian ear-picker."

business, and sat down to enjoy what was yet before me, saying moreover, according to the worshipful Christian usage, the Benedicite ; yet no sooner had I made the sign of the Cross over the meats and over my companions at table and asked God's blessing, when our cookmaid vanished away with the chest and all that had been in it, and left behind her such an horrible stench that my comrade fainted clean away because of it.

Chap. xxi : HOW THEY THEREAFTER KEPT HOUSE TOGETHER AND HOW THEY SET TO WORK

HOW as soon as he was recovered and come to his senses, he knelt down before me and folded his hands, and for a full quarter of an hour continually said nothing but " Oh, my father ! O my brother ! O my father ! O my brother ! " and then began with the repeating of these words to weep so bitterly that for very sobbing he could utter no word that could be understood, until I conceived that by reason of the fear and the stench he had lost his reason. But when he would not cease this behaviour and continually besought my forgiveness, I answered him, " Dear friend, what have I to forgive thee that hast never harmed me in my life ? Do but tell me how I can help thee." " Nay," says he, " I seek for pardon ; for I have sinned against God and thee and myself " : and therewith began again his former lamentations, and went on so long that at last I said I knew no evil of him, and if he had done any such that weighed upon his conscience, I would not only from my heart forgive and condone anything that concerned myself, but also, so far as he might have sinned against God, would with him beseech the divine mercy for pardon. At which words he embraced my knees and kissed them, and looked upon me so sorrowfully that I was as one dumb, and could not conceive or guess what ailed the lad ; but when I had taken him to my arms and embraced him, begging him to tell me what troubled him and how I could help him, he confessed to me in every particular his discourse with the pretended Abyssinian, and the resolve he had formed in respect of me in despite of God and of Nature and of Christian love and of the laws of true friendship which we had solemnly sworn one to another : and this he did with such words and behaviour that from it his sincere repentance and contrite heart might easily be guessed and presumed.

So I comforted him as well as I could, and said : God had peradventure sent us this as a warning, that we might in time to come be better aware of the devil's snares and temptations and live in the constant fear of God : that he had of a surety cause enough to pray God heartily for forgiveness for his evil intent, yet even greater cause to thank Him for His goodness and mercy, seeing that He had in such fatherly wise plucked him forth from wicked Satan's traps and snares and so saved him from destruction now and eternally : and that we must perforce here walk more circumspectly than if we dwelt in the midst of the world among other men ; for should one or the other or both fall into temptation, there would be none at hand to help us but God Himself, whom we must therefore the more diligently keep before our eyes and without ceasing pray for His help and assistance.

By talk of such things he was, 'tis true, somewhat cheered, yet would not be altogether content, but humbly besought me to lay upon him a penance for his sin. So to raise up his prostrate spirit as far as might be, I said that he being a carpenter, and having yet his axe by him, should in the same place where we, as well as our hellish cookmaid, had come to land, set up a cross on the shore ; whereby he would not only perform a penance well pleasing to God, but also bring it to pass that in time to come the evil spirit, who doth ever fear the sign of Holy Cross, would not again so easily attack our island. He answered, " Not only a cross on the shore but two also on the mountain will I make ready and set up, if only, my father, I may again possess thy grace and favour and be assured of God's forgiveness." In which fervour he went away straightway and ceased not to toil till he had made ready three crosses, whereof we set up one on the sea-shore and the other two apart on the highest top of the hill, with the inscription that followeth :

" To the honour of God Almighty and in despite of the enemy of mankind, Simon Meron, of Lisbon in Portugal, with counsel and help of his faithful friend Simplicius Simplicissimus, a High German, did fashion and here set up this token of our Saviour's sufferings, for Jesus Christ His sake."

Thenceforward we began to live somewhat more religiously than before ; and in order to our reverencing and keeping of the Sabbath, I every day, in place of an almanack, cut a notch in a post and on Sundays a cross ; and then would we sit together and talk of holy and godly things ; and this fashion must I use because I had not yet invented anything to serve me in the stead of ink and paper, by means of which I might set down somewhat in writing to keep count of our life.

And now to end this chapter I must make mention of a strange adventure that did greatly terrify and distress us on the evening after our cook her vanishing ; for the first night we perceived it not, because sleep overpowered us at once by reason of fatigue and great weariness. And this was it. We having still before our eyes the thousand snares by which the accursed devil would have wrought our ruin in the form of the Abyssinian, could not sleep, but passed the time in watching, and indeed for the most part in prayer ; and so soon as it became a little dark we saw floating around us in the air an innumerable quantity of lights, which gave forth such a bright glow that we could discern the fruit on the trees from the leaves : this we deemed to be another invention of the enemy to torment us, and therefore kept still and quiet, but in the end found 'twas but a kind of firefly or glow-worm, as we call them in Germany, which are generated by a particular kind of rotten wood that is found in this island, and shine so bright that one can well use them in place of a lighted candle ; for I have written this book for the most part thus : and if they were as common in Europe, Asia, and Africa as they be here, the candle-sellers would do a poor trade.

Chap. xxii : FURTHER SEQUEL OF THE ABOVE STORY, AND HOW SIMON MERON LEFT THE ISLAND AND THIS LIFE, AND HOW SIMPLICISSIMUS REMAINED THE SOLE LORD OF THE ISLAND

AND now seeing we must perforce remain where we were, we began to order our housekeeping accordingly. So my comrade made out of a black wood that is almost like to iron mattocks and shovels for us both, with the help of which we first dug holes for the three crosses before mentioned, and secondly drew the sea-water into trenches, where, as I had seen at Alexandria in Egypt, it turned into salt ; and thirdly we began to make us a cheerful garden ; for we deemed that idleness would be for us the beginning of destruction ; fourthly, we dug another channel for the brook, into which we could at pleasure turn it off, and so leave the old river-bed dry, and take out as many fish and crayfish as we would with hands and feet dry : fifthly, we found near the said brook a most beautiful potter's clay : and though we had neither lathe nor wheel and, most of all, no borer or other instruments so as to make anything of the kind and so mould for ourselves vessels, and though we had never learned the craft, yet we devised a plan by which we got what we wanted ; for having kneaded and prepared the clay as it should be, we made rolls of it of the thickness and length of English tobacco-pipes, and these we stuck one upon another like a snail's shell and formed out of such whatever vessels we would, both great and small, pots and dishes, for cooking and drinking : and when our first baking of these prospered, we had no longer reason to complain of lack of anything ; 'tis true we had no bread ; but yet plenty of dried fish which we used in its stead. And in time our scheme for getting salt turned out well, so that now we had nothing to complain of but lived like the folk in the golden age of the world : and little by little we learned how with eggs, dried fish, and lemon peel, which two last we ground to a soft meal between two stones, and birds' fat, which we got from the birds called boobies and noddies, to bake savoury cakes in place of bread : likewise did my comrade devise how to draw off the palm-wine very cleverly into great pots and let it stand for a few days till it fermented ; and then would he drink of it till he reeled, and this at last he came to do every day, and God knoweth how I dissuaded him therefrom. For he said if 'twas allowed to stand longer 'twould turn to vinegar ; in which there was some truth ; yet I answered him, he should not at one time draw so much but only enough for our needs ; to which he replied that 'twas a sin to despise the gifts of God, and that the palm-trees must have a vein opened at proper times lest they should be choked with their own blood : and so must I give a loose rein to his appetites unless I would be told that I grudged him that of which we had plenty.

And so, as I have said, we lived like the first men in the golden age, when a bountiful heaven produced for them all good things from the earth without labour on their part ; but even as in this world there is no life so sweet and happy that is not at times made bitter by the gall of suffering, so happened it with us : for the richer we grew daily in larder and cellar, the more threadbare did our clothes from day to day become, till at last they rotted on our bodies. And 'twas well for us indeed that we thus far had had no winter ; no, not the slightest cold ; although by this time, when we began to go naked, we had by my notch-calendar spent more than a year and a half on the island, but all the year round 'twas such weather as is wont to be in Europe in May and June, save that about August and a little before it used to rain mighty hard and there were great thunderstorms : moreover from one solstice to another the days did not vary in length more than an hour and a quarter. But although we were alone upon the island, yet would we not go naked like brute beasts, but clothed as became honest Christians of Europe : and had we but had four-footed beasts it had been easy to help ourselves by using their hides for clothing ; for lack of which we skinned the birds we took, such as boobies and penguins and made clothes of this ; yet because for want of the needful tools and other material for the purpose we could not dress them so as to last, they became stiff and uneasy and fell away in pieces from our bodies before we were aware of it. 'Tis true the cocoanut-trees bore cotton enough for us, yet could we neither weave nor spin : but my comrade, that had been some years in India, shewed me on the leaves at the very tip a thing like a sharp thorn ; which if it be broken off and drawn along the stem of the leaf, as we do with the bean-pods called Faseoli to strip them of their rind, there will remain hanging on the said pointed thorn a string as long as the stem or the leaf is, so that one can use the same for needle and thread too ; and this provided me with opportunity to make for us breeches of those leaves and sew them together with the threads of their own growing.

But while we thus lived together, and had so improved our condition that we had no longer any cause to trouble for overwork, waste, want, or calamity, my comrade went on daily tippling at his palm-wine as he had begun, and now had made a habit of it, till at last he so inflamed his lungs and liver that, before I was rightly ware of it, he by his untimely death left me and the island and palm-wine and all. Him did I bury as well as I was able ; and as I pondered upon the uncertainty of human life and other the like matters, I wrote for him this epitaph that followeth :

" That I am buried here and not in ocean deep,
Nor in the flames of hell (from which may God us keep !)
The cause was this : three things did for my soul contend :
The first the raging sea : the next the infernal fiend.
These two did I escape by God His help and grace :
The third was wine of palms, which brought me to this place."

So I became lord of the whole island and began again a hermit's life, for which I had now not only opportunity more than enough but also a fixed desire and purpose thereto. 'Tis true I made all use of the good things and gifts of this place, with hearty thanks to God, whose goodness and might alone had so richly provided for me, but withal I was careful not to misuse this superfluity. And often did I wish that I had Christian men with me that elsewhere must suffer poverty and need, to profit with me by the gifts that God had given : but because I knew that for His Almighty power 'twas more than possible, if it were but His divine will, to bring thither more folk in easier and more miraculous fashion than I had been brought, it often gave me cause humbly to thank Him for His divine Providence in that He had in such fatherly wise cared for me more than many thousands of other men, and set me in a place so full of content and peace.

Chap. xxiii : IN WHICH THE HERMIT CONCLUDES HIS STORY AND THEREWITH ENDS THESE HIS SIX BOOKS

NOW had my comrade hardly been a week dead when I marked that my abode was haunted. " Yea, yea," I thought, " Simplicissimus, thou art now alone, and so 'twas to be expected that the evil one should endeavour to torment thee. Didst not look that that malicious spirit would make thy life hard for thee ? Yet why take count of him, when thou hast God to thy friend ? Thou needest but somewhat wherein to exercise thyself ; else wilt thou come to thy ruin from mere idleness and superfluity ; for besides him thou hast no enemy but thine own self and the plenty and pleasaunce of this island ; therefore make thy resolve to strive against him who in his own conceit is the strongest of all. For be he overcome by God his help, then shouldst thou, if God will, by His grace remain master of thyself."

And with these thoughts I went my way for a day or two, and they made of me a better and piouser man ; for I did prepare myself for that encounter which without doubt I must endure with the evil spirit ; yet herein did I for this time deceive myself ; for as on a certain evening I perceived a somewhat that could be heard, I went out of my hut, which stood close beneath a spur of that mountain, beneath which was the spring of that sweet water that floweth through the island into the sea ; and there saw I my comrade that scrabbled with his fingers in a cleft of the rock. Then may ye easily understand that I was afeard ; yet quickly I plucked up heart and commended myself to God's protection with the sign of Holy Cross, and thought, " This thing must be ; 'twere better to-day than to-morrow."

With that I went up to the spirit and used to him such

words as be customary in such a case. And then forthwith I understood that 'twas my deceased comrade, which in his lifetime had there concealed his ducats, as thinking that if, sooner or later, a ship should come to the island, he would recover them and take them away with him; yea, and he gave me to know that he had trusted more in this handful of money, whereby he hoped again to come to his home, than on God; for which cause he must now do penance by such unrest after his death, and moreover against his will be a cause of uneasiness to myself. So at his desire I took forth the money, yet held it as less than naught, as will the sooner be believed because I had nothing on which to employ it. And this was now the first affright that I had after I was left alone; yet afterwards was plagued by spirits of other sorts than this one; whereof I will say no more, but this only, that by God's help and grace I attained to this, that I found no single enemy more, save only mine own thoughts, which were oft troubled enough; for these go not scot-free before God, as men do vainly talk, but in His good time a reckoning must be paid for these also.

So that these might the less stain my soul with sins, I busied myself not only in the avoiding of that which profited naught, but did impose on myself a bodily task the which to perform with my customary prayer; for as man is born for work like the bird for flying, so on the other hand doth idleness inflict her sicknesses both on soul and body, and in the end, when we be least ware of it, eternal ruin. For this cause I planted me a garden, of which indeed I had less need than the waggon hath of a fifth wheel, seeing that the whole island might well be called one lovely pleasure-garden; so was my work of no other avail but that I brought this and that into completer order, albeit to many the natural disorder of the plants as they grew mingled together might appear more pleasing, and again that, as aforesaid, I shunned idleness. O how oft did I wish, when I had wearied out my body and must give it rest, that I had godly books wherein to comfort, to delight, and to edify myself! But such I could not come by. Yet as I had once read of a holy man that he said the whole wide world was to him one great book; wherein to recognise the wondrous works of God and to be cheered to praise Him, so I

thought to follow him therein, howbeit I was, so to speak,
no longer in the world. For that little island must be my
whole world, and in the same, every thing, yea, every tree,
an incitement to godliness and a reminder of such thoughts
as a good Christian should have. Thus, did I see a prickly
plant, forthwith I thought on Christ his crown of thorns ;
saw I an apple or a pomegranate, then I reflected on the fall
of our first parents and mourned therefore ; when I did draw
palm-wine from a tree, I fancied to myself how mercifully
my Redeemer had shed His blood for me on the tree of the
Holy Cross ; when I looked on sea or on mountain, then I
remembered this or that miracle which our Saviour had
wrought in such places ; and when I found one or more
stones that were convenient for casting, I had before mine
eyes the picture of the Jews that would have stoned Christ ;
and when I walked in my garden I thought on the prayer
of agony in Mount Olivet, or on the grave of Christ, and how
after His Resurrection He appeared to Mary Magdalene in
the garden. Such thoughts were my daily occupation ; never
did I eat but that I thought on the Last Supper, and never
cooked my food without the fire reminding me of the eternal
pains of hell.

At last I found that with Brazil-juice, of which there be
several sorts on this island, when mixed with lemon-juice, 'twas
easy to write on a kind of large palm-leaves ; which rejoiced
me greatly ; for now could I devise and write out prayers in
order ; yea, in the end, considering with hearty repentance
my whole life and my knavish tricks that I had committed
from my youth up, and how the merciful God, despite all such
gross sins, had not only thus far preserved me from everlasting damnation, but had given me time and opportunity
to better myself and to be converted, to beg His forgiveness
and to thank Him for His mercies, I did write down all that
had befallen me in this book made of the afore-mentioned
palm-leaves, and laid them together with my comrade's
ducats in this place, to the end that if at any time folk should
come hither, they might find such, and therefrom learn who
it was that before inhabited this island. And whoso shall
find this and read it, be it to-day or to-morrow, either before
or after my death, him I beg that if he meet therein with words

which be not becoming, for one that would do better, to speak, much less to write, he will not be angered thereat, but will consider that the telling of light actions and stories demands words fitting thereto ; and even as the house-leek cannot easily be soaked by any rain, that so a true and devout spirit cannot forthwith be infected, poisoned, and corrupted by any discourse, though it seem as wanton as you will. The honourably minded Christian reader will rather wonder, and praise the divine mercy, when he shall find that so knavish a companion as I have been yet hath had such grace of God as to resign the world and to live in such a condition that therein he hopeth to come to eternal glory and to attain to everlasting blessedness by the sufferings of his Redeemer, through a pious

END

APPENDIX B

ATTACHED to chap. xxiii is the " Relation of Jean Cornelissen of Harlem, a Dutch sea-captain, to his good friend German Schleifheim von Sulsfort concerning Simplicissimus."

Its contents are as follows :

On a voyage from the Moluccas to the Cape of Good Hope Cornelissen is separated by stress of weather from the fleet with which he had sailed. Having many of his crew sick, and no fresh water, he is delighted to discover Simplicissimus' isle. His men go ashore and find the hermit's dwelling, which, as the captain only afterwards learn they plunder, and generally behave brutally. Cornelissen finds the crosses and many pious inscriptions on trees, which prove to him that the unknown is a good Christian though probably a Papist. The crew track Simplicissimus to a vast cavern, on entering which their lights are miraculously extinguished. There is an earthquake, and the seamen who had taken part in the plundering of the hermit's dwelling are smitten with madness. Cornelissen, with the chaplain and officers, determines to find Simplicissimus at any cost. They penetrate the cave, but their lights also go out, and Simplicissimus addresses them from the darkness and remonstrates with them for their interference. The chaplain apologises, and asks how the madmen may be cured : he is told that they are to swallow the kernels of certain plums they had eaten. They offer to take him back to Europe, but he refuses. After making a bargain with them to secure his being left in peace, Simplicissimus shews himself surrounded with his glow-worms. He leads them out of the cave and shews them his ruined hut, and tells how his ducats and his book had been stolen. The madmen are brought to their senses again. Simplicissimus recovers his book, which he entrusts to Cornelissen, but again refuses to return to sinful Europe. They rebuild his hut for him, provide him with plenty of tools, a burning-glass, cotton clothing, and a pair of rabbits for breeding purposes : and so, their sick being all recovered, sail away and leave him there.

[A reference to the " Introduction " will show that this island adventure could have had no place in the Simplician cycle of romances ; unless we suppose, which is highly improbable, that the author meant it to be subsequent to the inn episode, in which Simplicissimus' family and friends all meet. Most likely we have here the latest addition, in point of composition, to the legend.]

[The following is given as a specimen of the nonsense of which the various continuations are made up.]

APPENDIX C

" *Continuatio*," *chap*. *xiii* : *HOW SIMPLICISSIMUS IN RETURN FOR A NIGHT'S LODGING, TAUGHT HIS HOST A CURIOUS ART*

NOW the evening before this I had lost a certain catalogue of those special arts which I had aforetime practised and written down that I might not forget them so easily : yet I depended not on this to remember how to perform them and with what helps. For example I do here set down the beginning of this list :

So to prepare matches or fuses that they shall give out no smell, seeing that by such smell musqueteers be often betrayed and their plans defeated.

To prepare match so that it will burn though it be wet.

To prepare powder so that it will not burn though red-hot steel be thrust therein : very useful for fortresses that must harbour much of so dangerous a guest.

To shoot men or birds with powder alone so that they shall lie as dead for a while and yet rise up again without harm.

To give a man double strength without the use of carbine-thistle or other such forbidden means.

If a sally from a fortress be checked, so to spike the enemy's guns in a moment that they must burst.

To spoil a man's gun so that it will scare all game to cover till it be again cleansed with a certain other substance.

To hit the bull's-eye in a target more quickly by laying the gun on the shoulder and firing backward, than if a man should take aim and fire in the accustomed way.

A special art to provide that no bullet may hit thee.

To prepare an instrument by means of which, specially on a still night, a man can in wondrous wise hear all that sounds or is spoken at an incredible distance (otherwise clean impossible and supernatural) ; very profitable for sentries and specially in sieges, etc. (bk. iii, chap. i).

In like manner were many arts described in the said catalogue which mine host had found and read : so he came to me himself into my chamber, shewed me the list, and asked whether 'twas possible that these things could be done by natural means ; for that could he scarce believe ; yet must confess that in his youth, when he served as a page in Italy with Field-marshal von Schauenburg, it was given out by some that the princes of Savoy were proof against bullets : which the said Field-marshal desired to make proof of in the person of Prince Thomas, whom he then kept besieged in a fortress ; for when on a time both sides had agreed on a truce for an hour to bury the dead and to confer together, he had commanded a corporal of his regiment, that was held to be the best marksman in the whole army, to take aim at the said prince while he should be standing on the parapet of the wall for a parley, and so soon as the hour agreed upon should end, to fire at him with his piece, with which he could put a lighted candle out at fifty paces : that this corporal had taken careful note of the time and kept the said prince under observation the whole time of the truce, and at the very moment when it ended with the first stroke of the hour, fired at him : yet had his piece, contrary to all belief, missed fire, and before the corporal could make ready again the prince was gone behind the parapet ; whereupon the corporal pointed out to the Field-marshal, who had likewise come to him on the trenches, a Switzer of the prince's guard, at whom he aimed and hit him in such fashion that he rolled over and over ; wherefrom it plainly appeared that there was something in the story that no prince of the house of Savoy could be hit or harmed. Yet whether this was brought about by such arts, or whether perchance the said princely house enjoyed a special grace from God, being, as 'twas said, sprung from the race of the royal prophet David, he knew not.

I answered, " I know not either, but this I do know of a surety, that the arts here specified be natural and no witchcraft." Which if he would not believe, let him but say which he held to be the most wonderful and impossible and I would at once to satisfy him (provided only that 'twas one that asked not long time but only such means as I had then at hand), make trial of it, for I must presently be a-foot and pursue my journey. At that he said this seemed to him the most impossible, that gunpowder should not burn if fire were put to it, unless one should first pour the powder into water , which if I could by natural means effect he would believe concerning all the other arts, though there were over sixty of them, what he might not see and before such trial could not believe. I answered, let him bring me quickly a charge of powder and also a certain substance which I had need of, and fire also, and presently he should see that the trick would hold. This being done, I caused him to follow my process and then set light to the powder : yet could he do no more than burn here and there a grain though he worked at it for a quarter of an hour, and accomplished no more than that he cooled a red-hot iron and quenched matches and lighted coals in the very powder itself. " Aha ! " says he, " the powder is bad." But I answered him in act, and without much ado, before he could count a score, so worked it that the powder blew up when he had scarce touched it with the fire.

377

[The following study appeared as the introduction to the Routledge and Dutton edition of THE ADVENTUROUS SIMPLICISSIMUS, published in 1924.]

APPENDIX D

THE course of German literature has been compared to a succession of hills and valleys, of which the most striking are the Golden Age of medieval poetry in the thirteenth century, the sterile period of the sixteenth and seventeenth centuries, and the zenith of German literature which was reached in the latter half of the eighteenth century. The thirteenth century saw the popular epic at its height with the composition of the *Nibelungenlied* and *Gudrun*, the masters of the Court Epic, Wolfram von Eschenbach and Gottfried von Strassburg, and the greatest of all the Minnesingers, Walther von der Vogelweide. During the eighteenth century rose the twin stars, Goethe and Schiller. Between these two epochs lies a period of gradual decadence, culminating in the seventeenth century, when German literature sank to its lowest ebb. It was the age which gave Shakespeare and Milton to England, and Corneille, Racine and Molière to France, but during the whole of the period, roughly from the death of Hans Sachs in 1576 to the publication of the first cantos of Klopstock's *Messias* in 1748, there is hardly anything in German literature which has any intrinsic worth, or other than historical interest, except a few hymns and those of the works of Grimmelshausen which are connected with the name of *Simplicissimus*. The *Nibelungenlied* and the Court Poetry were alike forgotten, and the essential characteristic of the writers of the seventeenth and early eighteenth centuries was their abject dependence on foreign models, at first the literature of Spain and later that of France. Even when Lessing, after a great effort, was successful in pointing out to the writers of Germany the way to better things, it was by showing them in the first place not only that the path to salvation lay through the rejection of French models, but further, that they must begin their education anew by turning to the literature of England, which would teach them more wholesome and fruitful principles than they could imbibe from France.

In England and Spain, literature had already drawn new strength from the Renaissance, without losing its own national characteristics, and was thus able to appeal not only to the educated classes, but to every rank of society. Italy and France had likewise a literature in the popular tongue which was appreciated by the ruling caste, but in Germany the state of affairs was very different. As far as literature was concerned, the national marrow appeared to have dried up. The reigning house of Austria, the traditional head of the " Holy Roman Empire of Germany Nationality," was completely estranged from German culture, and the Emperor Charles V declared that German was a language for horses. Even in the eighteenth century, Frederick the Great held the German language in contempt, and while he ignored Lessing, he bestowed his patronage on Voltaire. After the Renaissance, there was an unbridged gulf between the vernacular popular literature and the Latin literature of the scholars, which lasted well into the seventeenth century, for there was no mutual fusion of the popular literary elements with the new art form that had sprung from the humanistic movement. When literature took new shape, it was cultivated by scholars and intended to appeal only to the educated. For the common people there was a corrupted popular literature which did not fail to appear regularly at the Spring and Autumn fairs, and from which inspiration was later to be drawn by no less a person than Goethe.

The seventeenth century was a transition period, when the national consciousness was almost annihilated by the religious and political struggles which made Germany a cockpit for half the nations of Europe. The claim of Frederick the Elector Palatine to the throne of Bohemia was the initial episode of the Thirty Years' War, which began in 1618 as an internal conflict, developed into a European war, and was only concluded in 1648 by the Treaty of Westphalia. The combination of religious, political and feudal quarrels brought upon German soil ill-disciplined hordes of French, Walloon, Italian, Spanish, Swedish, Danish, and Croat mercenaries, to say nothing of Scotch and Irish soldiers of fortune, who fought for the most part not for any particular cause, but for the master who paid them. In consequence there was little restraint put upon looting and violence, and the soldier and citizen looked upon each other as natural enemies. The overrunning of the country with these foreign armies, the degeneration of social life to the verge of barbarity, even to cannibalism, and the decadence of literature to a mere means of frivolous amusement, present a picture of utter national degradation, which lasted far beyond the conclusion of peace. The ruin to which the country was brought may be judged by the fact that the population of the Empire sank during the period of the war from 16 million to 6 million, a diminution of about two-thirds. The startling transition to the Golden Age of German literature in the latter half of the eighteenth century, to the highest pinnacle it has ever reached before or since, is therefore perhaps the most amazing phenomenon in the whole of world literature. It is evident that some of the roots of the tree which put forth such magnificent blossoms must stretch back into the previous century, and though the trunk was dormant for so long, the roots continued to draw a nourishment, which was meagre, but sufficient to preserve the life-force in the midst of the foreign, parasitical growth by which it was threatened. Grimmelshausen, who did more than any other writer of the age to keep alive the national spirit in literature by fusing the popular and the learned elements, stands almost isolated, and his peculiar importance will best be understood by examining the state of the German novel before the publication of *Simplicissimus*.

The first novels in German literature were the long epic poems of the medieval Court poets, but the invention of printing gave an enormous impetus to the composition of stories in prose. The prose novel was at its origin dependent for its subject-matter on French sources, just as the medieval poets had borrowed their plots from the *troubadours*, and until the first half of the seventeenth century, the German novel-reading public was fed almost exclusively on translations and adaptations of foreign works. About the middle of the sixteenth century, the novelist Jörg Wickram, who was also a Meistersinger, wrote original novels, in which, to be sure, he exhibited no remarkable talent, but since he was not dependent on foreign sources for his subject-matter, he is looked upon as the father of the German novel. His attempts to found a novel of common life were unsuccessful, and were soon forgotten, for in the second half of the century there came from France the famous cycle of novels, or romances of chivalry, known as *Amadis of Gaul*.

Appendix

The first *Amadis* was Spanish, and was written in the second half of the fifteenth century by Garcia Ordoñez de Montalvo, who based his story on an older version which is now lost. He added adventures of Amadis' son, other Spanish authors continued the story with the adventures of further descendants, and Nicolas Herberay des Essarts translated the first eight books freely into French in the first half of the sixteenth century. Other Frenchmen continued to add to the stories, and in the year 1569 there began to appear free translations into German, which continued until the seventeenth century. In addition, the German public was supplied with novels of equally interminable length, manufactured on the same plan, and containing the same elements of pseudo-chivalry, marvellous adventures and erotic interludes as the originals.

When the readers tired of the impossible adventures of *Amadis* and the other romances of chivalry, it was again to foreign sources that the authors turned. The desire to escape into a world of dreams, which had already been noticeable in the popularity of the idealistic romances of chivalry, was now directed into another channel, that of the idealistic pastoral romance, which was just as pseudo-pastoral as the *Amadis* romances were pseudo-chivalrous. They were both aspects of the Golden Age for which humanity is always yearning. The *Arcadia* of the Italian Jacopo Sannazaro, at the beginning of the sixteenth century, became the model both for the Spaniard Montemayor's *Diana*, which appeared in 1545, and for Sir Philip Sidney's *Arcadia*, which appeared in 1590, after the author's death. Honoré d'Urfé's *L'Astrée*, the first and most famous of the French pastoral romances, appeared during 1610–27, and Sidney's novel was translated into German by Martin Opitz in 1629.

The pastoral romance, however, in its turn had to make way for a new form of novel, to which it was closely related. Chiefly through the influence of Martin Opitz, who translated in 1626 the allegorical political novel *Argenis*, written in Latin, of the Scotsman John Barclay, the heroic-gallant novel was introduced into Germany. *Argenis* describes under a thin veil the condition of France, torn by party quarrels, under the last of the Valois. This introduction of contemporary persons and politics, which was the outstanding feature of Barclay's *roman à clef*, was imitated in

Germany by authors who wrote romances full of similar
hidden allusions, but lacked the Scotsman's political judgment
and sense of balance. They also filled their novels with long
didactic disquisitions, without any attempt to adapt them
to the story, so that the sole reason for their insertion appears
to have been in order to exhibit the authors' more or less useless learning. Opitz's translation was of great importance for
the development of the German novel, and from now on the
divorce between the literature of the people and that of the
educated classes became more acute, since the novelists
were not only mostly of aristocratic birth, but they were
alienating themselves intentionally from the national,
popular tradition.

The heroic-gallant novel exhibits on the surface its descent
from the romance of chivalry, for although the magic equipment and fairy-tale atmosphere have disappeared, the chief
characters are still princes and princesses, and the adventures
they undergo are vastly estranged from the realm of probability. They are also indeed the same people we meet in
the pastoral romances. The only difference is in the setting.

The first original novelist after Jörg Wickram was Philipp
von Zesen, who, unlike any of his contemporaries, looked
upon his writing as a profession. The seventeenth century
regarded literature as a hobby, as an amusement for a man's
leisure hours, and Zesen's numerous frictions with his fellow-
authors may have owed much to his isolated position as a
professional novelist.

His first works were translations from the French, but he
soon commenced to write romances which were independent
of foreign sources, and his best-known works are *The Adriatic
Rosemund* (1645), *Assenat* (1670) and *Simson* (1679). They
are all of reasonable length but filled with irrelevant
exhibitions of the author's extremely varied knowledge,
though he did make some attempt to deal with psychological
problems. Zesen naturalised the heroic-gallant novel in
Germany, and it was not very long before the original works
of this type were more numerous than the translations and
adaptations. Andreas Heinrich Bucholtz published his
Herkules and Valiska in 1660, following it five years later
with *Herkuliskus and Herkuladisla,* and the most distinguished
of the fashionable novelists in point of rank was the Duke
Anton Ulrich of Brunswick-Lüneburg, whose *The Syrian*

Appendix

Aramena appeared in 1669–73 and *The Roman Octavia* in 1677. The heroic-gallant novel attained its highest development in the last quarter of the century with Heinrich Anshelm von Ziegler's *The Asiatic Banise* (1688) and Casper von Lohenstein's *Arminius and Thusnelda* (1689). Arminius, or Hermann, is the ancient hero of the Teutons, and Lohenstein is entitled to credit for choosing a protagonist from his country's past. In these last two novels, the type of the heroic romance is seen in its most characteristic form, and *The Asiatic Banise* was the most popular of all the fashionable novels of the seventeenth century. Perhaps the most striking evidence of the kind of public to which the novelists of the period wished to appeal, is afforded by the dedications, which are mostly to dukes and duchesses, kings and queens, emperors and empresses, and one novel is even dedicated to " all the princesses of the Holy Roman Empire."

In spite of all the pedantry and wearisome length of the seventeenth-century novel, one can yet divine the tortuous attempts to hammer out a new form of literary art. It has always been characteristic of the Germans to precede practice by theory. The theory and formalism of the first decades of the century demonstrate their anxiety to have a firm basis of rules on which to raise the literary edifice, but though it was during this period that the prose medium consolidated its hold in German literature, the main desire of the reading public was for entertainment, and interest was centred almost solely on the subject-matter. The form was unimportant, and since the supply of original works was not sufficient to satisfy the prevalent reading mania, there was all the time a continuous output of translations of heroic-gallant novels from the French.

Even in the previous century, however, there had already arisen in Spain a reaction against the exaggerated, marvellous adventures of impossibly ideal heroes and heroines. It was the Spaniards who gave Europe the original *Amadis*, but they redeemed their literary reputation by the invention of the picaresque novel, which soon became popular in Italy, France and Germany. In the year 1615; there appeared in Munich a translation of Mateo Aleman's *Guzman de Alfarache*, the original of which had been published at Madrid in 1599. The translation, or rather free adaptation, was by Aegidius Albertinus, the secretary of the Duke Maximilian of Bavaria, and about ten years later it was followed by a continuation from another hand, which had no connection whatever with the original, except the name. The alterations made by Aegidius Albertinus were not to the advantage of the book, for he left out parts of the narrative, in order to introduce tedious "discourses." The next Spanish picaresque novel to be introduced into Germany was *La vida de Lazarillo de Tormes* (1554), which, together with Cervantes' short story, *Rinconete y Cortadillo*, was translated and adapted by Nicolaus Ulenhart and published at Augsburg in 1617. Both the novel and the short story appeared in one volume. The *Justina* of Úbeda, which describes the career of a female vagabond, was translated from Spanish into Italian and, in 1626, from the Italian into German. There was also published in 1621 a translation of a part of *Don Quixote*, which is a satire on the absurd exaggerations of the romance of chivalry. A single episode had already been translated in 1617, but a complete version did not appear till much later. These translations and adaptations were soon followed by a mass of German romances of the same type.

In the picaresque novel, the adventures are transferred to a more probable plane. The knights and shepherds have given place to the rogue, who has to make his way through life by means of his wits, and the atmosphere is realistic. We descend among the people, and there is a connection between the heroes of the picaresque novel and those of the German popular literature. During the fifteenth and sixteenth centuries there appeared the folk-book of *Till Owlglass*, the rogue who lives by pretending to be a fool. Other popular figures were Doctor Faust, the Wandering Jew, and the people of Schilda, who were as stupid as our Wise Men of Gotham. These creations were, for the most part, genuinely German, and rooted in popular legend, so when the *picaro* was introduced from Spain, there was little difficulty in naturalising him in Germany. Johann Fischart had already adapted Rabelais' *Gargantua and Pantagruel* freely to the German genius and German conditions in his *Geschichtklitterung*. When Ulenhart translated Cervantes' *Rinconete*, he transferred the scene to Prague, and the chief of the band of rogues was the Zuckerbastel, of whom Grimmelshausen speaks at the beginning of *Simplicissimus*. Neither Wickram's attempt to found a national novel, nor the continued popularity of the folk-books, was able to stem the tide of foreign literature, and even the German picaresque novel did not owe its origin to the German national spirit. The Thirty Years' War, however, familiarised people with the living prototypes of the vagabond who was now finding his way into literature, and it remained for Grimmelshausen to transform this novel of adventure into a truly national novel. Of the mass of translations and imitations of the Spanish models which appeared during the seventeenth century, there is nothing to compare even remotely with *Simplicissimus*, which is the only German novel of the century that can be said to spring directly from the actual experience of the author, and to give a true and original picture of social conditions at the time of the Thirty Years' War.

There remains another form of literature to be mentioned, which is connected with one aspect of the picaresque novel. The *Sueños* of the Spaniard Francisco de Quevedo are satires in the form of dream-pictures, and they were translated into many languages, to be followed inevitably by adaptations and imitations. The satirist Hans Michael Moscherosch began to publish in Strassburg about the year 1640 *The Visions of Philander von Sittewald*, which is an attempt to adapt Quevedo's *Sueños* to German conditions. Moscherosch substituted for the Spanish conditions satirised by Quevedo, the even more undesirable and degenerate conditions of his own country, and it is perhaps significant that he is entirely lacking in the humour which is to be found in his Spanish model.

The title-page of *Simplicissimus* states that the story is by German Schleifheim von Sulsfort, but an advertisement to the reader, which was appended to the sixth book, says that it " is the work of Samuel Greiffenson von Hirschfeld, since I not only found it among his papers after his decease, but he himself also refers in this book to *The Chaste Joseph*, and in his *Satirical Pilgrim* he refers to this his *Simplicissimus*, which he wrote partly in his youth, when he was still a musketeer ; but from what cause he altered his name by transposing the letters, and put instead German Schleifheim von Sulsfort on the title, is unknown to me." The consequence of this statement was that for nearly two hundred years, the name of Samuel Greiffenson von Hirschfeld appeared in the literary histories as the author of *Simplicissimus* and other works. It was not until nearly the middle of last century that the name of the greatest German prose writer of his time was found to be Hans Jacob Christoffel von Grimmelshausen, who had a peculiar passion for publishing his books under pseudonyms, which are all more or less perfect anagrams of his real name. The complete list of his pseudonyms, in addition to the above two, is as follows ; some of them are spelt in a variety of ways :—

> Melchior Sternfels von Fugshaim,
> Philarchus Grossus von Trommenheim,
> Signeur Messmahl,
> Michael Regulin von Schmsdorf,
> Erich Stainfels von Grufensholm,
> Simon Lengfrisch von Hartenfels,
> Israel Fromschmidt von Hugenfels,

and the letters A c eee ff g hh ii ll mm nn oo rr sss t uu.

The reason for this hide-and-seek method of signing his books may have been the contempt in which the literature of the common people was held. In the few cases where Grimmelshausen published under his real name, the book in question was either a heroic-gallant novel of the type then in fashion, or a harmless political pamphlet which was not likely to call down on the head of the author the wrath of the powers that were. At the same time it is to be observed that the custom of writing under pseudonyms was not unusual at that time, and Grimmelshausen may merely have been amusing himself with the game of anonymity. There is a sonnet appended to his novel *Dietwald and Amelinde*, which shows that the authorship of *Simplicissimus* and other books was not an absolute secret, and in nearly all his writings he seems to have taken pains to hint in some manner or other at his real name.

The early part of Grimmelshausen's life is somewhat of a mystery. It is even uncertain whether he was born in 1624 or '25, as is generally assumed, or, according to the latest theory, in 1610. He refers to himself as " Geln-husanus," a citizen of Gelnhausen, in Hesse, so he was probably born either in that town or in the vicinity. His grandfather is said to have been a baker. It has been suggested that the family originally belonged to the nobility, and became impoverished in the fourteenth century, but there is hardly any evidence to support this view. Until the year 1639, all that we know for certain is that he was for at least four years on active service in the army. About this time he became secretary to Count von Schauenburg, the commandant of Offenburg, in Baden, and he appears to have kept his position until 1647 and perhaps later. In the following year he held a similar position in a regiment, where he saw more fighting, but it was not long before he returned to Offenburg, where he married Katharina Henninger on August the 30th, 1649, and again became secretary to the commandant. In the following year he went to live in Gaisbach, near Oberkirch, where he was still in the service of the Schauenburg family, for whom he seems to have performed various duties, including that of steward, and he also for a time acted as host to a tavern belonging to them. In the year 1667 he was appointed to the post of mayor in the village of Renchen, in the Black Forest, which belonged to the bishopric of Strassburg. Among his duties were those of magistrate and tax collector, but he appears to have enjoyed a considerable amount of leisure for his literary work. Seven years later, the district was invaded by the French, and Grimmelshausen's family was scattered. It is probable that he again joined the army, but we know nothing definite about his fate except for the entry in the parochial register at Renchen, which states that he died on August the 17th, 1676, and that though his sons were dispersed, they all returned to the house. *Anno 1676, Augusto 17. obiit in Domino Honestus et magno ingenio et eruditione Iohannes Christophorus von Grimmelshausen praetor huius loci, et quamuis ob tumultus belli nomen militiae dederit et pueri hinc inde dispersi fuerint, tamen hic casu omnes convenerunt, et parens Sacramento Eucharistiae pie munitus obiit et sepultus est, cuius anima requiescat in sancta pace.*

Grimmelshausen thus appears to have had a very adventurous youth, succeeded by a long period of sedentary work and leisure, when his duties were not too arduous to permit him to make up for his early lack of education by extensive reading, in addition to which his literary industry was considerable. He was self-taught, but to judge from the varied mass of scientific and literary allusions and quotations, which are scattered so profusely throughout his writings, it would be natural to assume that he had read widely not only in German, but also in French and Latin. He appears to know his Roman authors, and to have much more than a nodding acquaintance with jurisprudence, theology, astronomy and mathematics. He most probably, however, drew a great deal of his knowledge of this type from the collections of miscellaneous information which performed at that time the service of encyclopædias. He certainly possessed an excellent first-hand acquaintance with contemporary German literature, in addition to a vast stock of legendary lore. His works are a mine of information about the superstitions of the people and their social customs, and he must have travelled very extensively. According to the Latin entry by the pastor of Renchen in the parochial register, Grimmelshausen was regarded as a man of great intellect and erudition, and his position as mayor, or *Schultheiss*, naturally made him one of the most distinguished citizens of the place. He is thought in later years to have become converted to Catholicism, and he was certainly in the service of the Catholic Bishop of Strassburg, whose friendly attitude to the French invaders made things more difficult for Grimmelshausen when Renchen was overrun, for the Emperor relieved the Bishop's subjects of their oath of allegiance. Even this theory has little evidence to support it, however, and in spite of the numerous details concerning him which have been discovered in quite recent years, we are as much in the dark as ever with regard to the essential features of what was certainly an extremely varied and adventurous career. A considerable amount can be learned from his writings, because his vitally realistic style enabled him to pour out all the accumulated store of knowledge about countries and people, which his wars and travels had instilled into him. He was in touch with the actual world around him, and knew how to communicate his experience in literary form. He cannot be identified completely with his hero Simplicissimus, though there is not the slightest doubt that there is much in the novel which is of an autobiographical nature.

Grimmelshausen's first literary effort, a translation from the French, was followed within a period of about eighteen years by a score or so of other books in quick succession. The following is a detailed list, which is all the more

Appendix

important, as our knowledge of the actual facts of the author's life is so scanty :—

1659. *Der fliegende Wandersmann nach dem Mond, [The Flying Traveller in the Moon].* This is a translation of F. Baudoin's *L'homme dans la Lune,* which appeared in Paris in 1648. The French book is itself a translation of Francis Godwin's *The Man in the Moon, or a Discourse of a Voyage thither, by Domingo Gonsales,* published in London in 1638. The title sufficiently explains the contents of the volume. Among other peculiarities, the inhabitants of the moon have a habit of exchanging any moon-child, who exhibits a tendency to vice, for an earth-child, and that is supposed to have been the origin of the inhabitants of America. Some details of Godwin's book were imitated by Cyrano de Bergerac, from whom Swift derived valuable hints for Gulliver's voyage to Laputa.

1660. *Traumgeschicht von Dir und Mir, [Dream-story of You and Me],* and *Reise in die neue Oberwelt des Monds, [Journey to the New Upper-world of the Moon].* These are both satirical dream-pictures. In the former, Oliver Cromwell is mentioned as being still alive, so the story must have been written before 3rd September, 1658.

1666. *Der satyrische Pilgram, [The Satirical Pilgrim].* A satirical treatise in popular form, dealing among other things with God, money, dancing, women, wine, beauty, priests, poetry, love, tobacco, philosophy, beggars and war.

1667. *Der keusche Joseph, [The Chaste Joseph].* Deals with the biblical story of Joseph and Potiphar's wife. The later editions of this book contain the story of Joseph's servant, Musai, who is a sort of *picaro*.

1668. *Der abenteuerliche Simplicissimus, [The Adventurous Simplicissimus].* It is most probable that the first edition appeared in this year, though the earliest edition in existence bears the date 1669. The first edition contained five books, but as its popularity was very great, Grimmelshausen hurriedly wrote a sixth book, which appeared at first separately, in 1669, as *Continuation of the Adventurous Simplicissimus, or Conclusion of the Same,* and was then included in the same volume as the original work. This extra book is not included in the present edition, as it only disturbs the cohesion of the story by providing a new beginning and a new conclusion, and has no intrinsic merit in itself. It is interesting solely because it presents a picture of Simplicissimus cast away on a desert island, and is therefore an example of a " Robinsonade " some fifty years before the publication of Defoe's *Robinson Crusoe*, a book which called forth great enthusiasm and a correspondingly large number of imitations in Germany.

Two years later there appeared a first, second and third *Continuatio*, which are equally, if not even more worthless than the so-called sixth book ; they were most probably first printed in various almanacs published by Grimmelshausen.

Between 1670 and 1674 there appeared four more sequels, which, together with *Simplicissimus* and the *Continuations*, form what are known as the *Simplician Writings*. These sequels are *Trutz-Simplex : oder Lebensbeschreibung der Erzbetrügerin und Landstörzerin Courage*, [*Trutz-Simplex, or the Life of the Arch-Impostor and Adventuress Courage*], *Der seltsame Springinsfeld*, [*The Rare Jump-in-the-Field*], *Das wunderbarliche Vogelnest*, [*The Magic Bird's Nest*] and *Der ewigwährende Kalender*, [*The Everlasting Almanac*].*

1670.   *Simplicissimi wunderliche Gaukeltasche*, [*Simplicissimus' Singular Juggler's-Bag*]. A puzzle picture-book.

1670.   *Der erste Bärenhäuter*, [*The first Sluggard* or *Malingerer*]. This story gives the origin of the word *Bärenhäuter*. In the year 1396, a German soldier lost his way in a wood, when an evil spirit appeared to him and offered him a rich reward if he would enter his service. The soldier was first ordered to shoot a bear which just then came in sight, and then to promise to stand sentry for an hour at midnight during a period of seven years. During this time he was not to comb or cut either hair or beard, cut his nails, blow his nose, wash his hands, face or other part of his body ; he was to wear the skin of the bear he had just shot, instead of a cloak, use it instead of a bed and never say the Lord's Prayer. On account of this bear's skin (*Bärenhaut*), he was to be called Bärenhäuter. The soldier faithfully carried out his master's orders, and was rewarded eventually with a beautiful wife.

1670.   *Dietwald und Amelinde*. A romance, in the heroic-gallant manner, of two royal and virtuous lovers.

1670.   *Simplicianischer Zweiköpfiger Ratio status*, [*Simplician Two-headed Ratio Status*]. Disquisitions on the origin

* For contents of these sequels, see below, p. xxx.

and meaning of sovereignty. The idea is that the people should choose their own ruler, but the book is merely a compilation, based on other sources.

1672. *Das Ratstübel Plutonis, oder Kunst, reich zu werden,* [*The Council Chamber of Pluto,* or the Art of becoming rich*]. Simplicissimus, his father and mother, Courage, Springinsfeld and various other characters discuss the art of becoming rich.

1672. *Proximus und Lympida.* An historical novel of a similar type to *Dietwald and Amelinde.*

1672. *Die Verkehrte Welt,* [*The World turned topsy-turvy*]. The author descends to Hell, converses with the damned, and describes the conditions in the upper world ironically as being beyond reproach. A satire on Court life. The author had already employed the same idea in the Mummelsee episode in *Simplicissimus.*

1673. *Der deutsche Michel,* [*The German Michael*]. This is a nickname for the typical German, like the English " John Bull." The book deals in a popular manner with current abuses in the German language.

1673. *Simplicissimi Galgenmännlein,* [*Simplicissimus' Mandrake*]. Deals with the superstition concerning the root of the mandragora, which often has human shape, and is dug up at midnight at the foot of the gallows. It is engendered from the semen of a man who has been hanged, and possesses magic virtues.

1673. *Der Stolze Melcher,* [*Proud Melcher*]. The story of a peasant's son who goes to the War of 1672–78 between France and Holland and returns home in humble circumstances, thus giving his relations and neighbours an opportunity of expressing their views on the foolishness and frivolity of the younger generation.

Grimmelshausen's writings have been likened to an oasis in the desert. " The agony which I have had to endure in reading the works of Lohenstein, Ziegler and their contemporaries, in order to be able conscientiously to judge Grimmelshausen's relationship to the other German novelists of the seventeenth century, entitles me to employ such a strong expression. I know of no novelist of the seventeenth century in Germany, who can bear the remotest comparison with Grimmelshausen, and of all the literary romances of the seventeenth century, there is none which is so deeply

---

* Grimmelshausen exhibits his weakness in Latin by confusing *Pluto* with *Plutus*, and making *ratio* a masculine noun.

rooted in the life of the people as the *Simplician Writings.*"*
The heroic-gallant novelists scorned to draw their material
from contemporary life, and believed that distance of time
and place lent the enchantment which the educated reader
of the period found so necessary as an anodyne. In consequence, they have sunk into obscurity, and the one enduring
prose-work of the century, the first five books of *Simplicissimus*, on which the fame of Grimmelshausen rests, is
an unique contribution to contemporary sociological history.

The discursive title is at the same time a programme. The
story is to tell the life and adventures of an individual who
has seen, learned and done many strange things, and has
eventually decided voluntarily to quit the world of action
and experience for the tranquillity of a hermit's cell. It is
a novel of development, and although the attitude of the
hero is on the whole fairly passive, since he is influenced by
the situations in which he is placed, instead of moulding
them to his own ends, there is yet a satisfying external
unity, and there is sufficient of a psychological problem for
the novel to bear some slight comparison with the medieval
epic of *Parzival* by Wolfram von Eschenbach and the *Wilhelm
Meister* of Goethe. Parzival goes out into the world as an
innocent youth, a "guileless fool," who on his journey
through life has to solve the problem of adapting himself to
his worldly environment, without losing his vision of the
higher life and those spiritual ideals which are so hard to
reconcile with the practical necessities of material sur-
roundings. Wilhelm Meister also goes through a period of
apprenticeship and wandering, and succeeds eventually in
combining poetry and life, in reconciling the two aspects
of his double nature, the poet and the man of the world.
Simplicius starts life as an ignorant peasant lad, receives a
rather narrow, one-sided and superficial education from the
hermit and knows nothing of the realities of life until he
leaves his forest and arrives in Hanau. Before long, however,
he develops the ready, practical sense and adaptability,
which bring him fame and fortune as the huntsman of Soest.
After he has bought his farm in the Black Forest, his adventures
cease to be actual, and read more like those of Baron Mun-
chausen. The extraordinary episode of the Mummelsee, and

* F. Bobertag: *Über Grimmelshausens Simplicianische Schriften.*
[Breslau, 1874.]

his journey to Russia and back via Asia, are utterly out of harmony with the remainder of the story, and the final retreat to a hermit's cell, preceded by a lengthy farewell to the world, taken bodily from a work of the Spanish ascetic Antonius de Guevara, does not come as a natural consummation.

The most congenial feature in the character of Simplicius is the firm, enduring friendship that subsists between him and the younger Herzbruder. This friendship deserves to be cited as that of a new Damon and Pythias, for it could not be exceeded in disinterestedness on either side. In his affairs with women he is light-hearted in the extreme. He even seems to feel no compunction at leaving his wife in Lippstadt for so long, while he stays at Cologne, goes to Paris and later travels about with Herzbruder. The death of his wife is recorded without comment, except that he rejoices a little later in the thought of his freedom, and on the decease of his second wife, he " well-nigh laughed himself into a sickness," though in the second case, there was certainly good cause for relief. Towards the end, after he leaves Paris and falls in with Oliver, he begins to feel remorse at needless killing, though as the huntsman of Soest he had appeared as a sufficiently bloodthirsty person ; even then, however, he has let the impostor huntsman of Wesel off very lightly. The eventual resolve to quit the world, insufficiently motivated as it is, yet provides a satisfactory conclusion to a life of action such as that of Simplicius, and there can therefore be no hesitation in regarding *Simplicissimus* as a novel of development. It is just this element which is missing in the picaresque novels, where the reader is interested in the external incident, but is unable to perceive any psychological development in the character of the hero. Grimmelshausen is indebted to the picaresque novel for the use of the " I " form, which he employs in all the *Simplician Writings*, and also for the general biographical framework, beginning with a description of the parental house and the circumstances which force the hero out into the world at a tender age. Otherwise he owes nothing essential to literary sources, though an example of his wide reading is seen in the episode of Simplicius and the love-sick ladies of high degree in Paris, which is borrowed, though probably not directly, from Bandello.

The universal belief in witchcraft and magic is seen in the frequency with which Simplicius is taken for a magician. The Witches' Sabbath is described as though it were an actual occurrence, witnessed by the hero himself, and the reputation for being " frozen," *i.e.* invulnerable, was possessed by numerous individuals at the time of the Thirty Years' War. Oliver and the Provost-Marshal could not be killed by bullets, and Simplicius, as the huntsman of Soest, was believed by his enemies to be similarly protected. Great play is made with the prophecies of the elder Herzbruder and the conjuring tricks of the Provost, and there are frequent allusions to the prevalent superstitions. When the huntsman of Wesel goes sheep-stealing, his servant tells him that he must first of all see " if Bläsy is at home or not," that is to say, St. Blasius, the patron-saint of domestic animals. It was only necessary for a man to be a prominent scholar, to have performed some conspicuous and difficult feat, or even merely to be cleverer or more cunning than his fellows, in order to arouse the suspicion that he was in possession of supernatural powers, purchased from the devil at the price of his soul.

None of the great historical figures of the Thirty Years' War appears in *Simplicissimus*, for by the time the hero leaves the forest for Hanau, Gustavus Adolphus has already been killed at the battle of Lützen and Wallenstein murdered at Eger. Prince Bernhard of Weimar and Johann von Werth are barely mentioned. James Ramsay, the Scotch colonel in the Swedish army, commandant of Hanau, who is supposed to be the brother of Simplicius' mother, is well known for his defence of that town, but his connection with the hero of Grimmelshausen is, of course, fictitious, and the name Melchior Sternfels von Fugshaim, as it is sometimes spelt, is an anagram of " Christoffel von Grimmelshausen." If the course of Simplicius' career is compared with the actual dates of the various incidents of the War mentioned by the author, we discover some curious discrepancies. Simplicius was born just after the battle of Höchst, which took place on June 10th, 1622, when his father and mother were separated, so that the former resolved to become a hermit. He was ten years old when he came to the hermit, with whom he stayed for two years, and after the battle of

Appendix

Nördlingen, September 6th, 1634, he left the forest, his first real step out into the world, and arrived in Hanau, where he spent the winter of 1634–35, which was noted for being extraordinarily cold. In the early part of 1635, he was captured by Croats. During the siege of Magdeburg in 1636, he became acquainted with Herzbruder and Oliver. He took part in the battle of Wittstock, September 24th, 1636, and during the summer of 1637 he was active as the huntsman of Soest. Then came his capture and internment at Lippstadt, during the winter of 1637–38. He was invited to dinner by the commandant on Twelfth Night, 1638, and soon after that married and set out on his journey to Cologne. Then came the trip to Paris and the return to Germany, when he was compelled to serve as a musketeer in Philippsburg. On July 30th, of the same year, there took place the battle of Wittenweier, during August he was with the hangers-on of the army as a " Merode brother," and in December he was acting as a highwayman in company with Oliver. The meeting with Herzbruder, the pilgrimage to Switzerland and the journey to Vienna took place in the following spring. In March, 1645, both Herzbruder and Simplicius took part in the battle of Jankau, and this is the last exact chronological reference we find.

It thus appears that the huntsman of Soest was only fifteen years of age, and that he married before he was sixteen, at which tender age he experienced his amorous adventure with the Parisian ladies. It may be, of course, that the author intended to emphasise the youth of his hero, since he expressly refers (Bk. III, Ch. xi) to the fact that during his activities at Soest, he was unpopular with women, since he was like " a wooden statue, without strength or sap," but it would be better to take it as a poetic licence, since it is only apparent after careful correlation of Simplicius' adventures with the fixed historical references.

The so-called sixth book introduces Simplicissimus to us once more, leaving his hermit's retreat and setting off again on his travels. He wanders as far as Loretto, Rome, and Alexandria, is captured by robbers in Egypt, and is eventually shipwrecked on an island, which he resolves never to leave.

The first Continuation describes how Simplicissimus after his return to Europe acted as a writer of newspapers and almanacs, the second Contiuation tells how he left his island, and the third relates some anecdotes of the period after his return.

The story of *The Adventuress Courage* introduces the lady with whom Simplicissimus had a *liaison* at the Spa in the Black Forest. She declares that the child she had left at his door was not his at all, and that she had pretended that Simplicissimus was the father in order to spite him, hence the title, *Trutz-Simplex.* She unfolds a terrible tale, beginning with her service, disguised in boys' clothes, as page to a young captain, whose mistress she becomes when it is no longer possible to conceal her sex. She marries him on his death-bed, but becomes subsequently the mistress first of a count, and then of an ambassador. She marries a captain of dragoons, and takes part in various battles until her husband is killed, when she accepts the wooing of a lieutenant, who first tries to whip her into obedience and then deserts her, after which she continues to take part in battles and succeeds on one occasion in capturing a major. She abandons the army and returns to her former nurse, learns that she is of noble birth, marries another captain and goes to the Danish War, where she loses her husband, after having by her courage captured three of the enemy. Unfortunately, she is recognised by the major whom she had captured some time previously, and he takes his revenge by treating her in an unspeakably vile manner, until she is rescued by a Danish captain, who takes her to his castle in Denmark, where she is treated like a countess, but through the treachery of her host's relations soon finds herself back in Germany in misery. Another love-affair comes to an unhappy ending, for her lover is executed for killing his corporal, who had cast eyes on Courage. She makes the acquaintance of a musketeer, whom she calls Jump-in-the-Field, and goes with his regiment to Italy, where she finds occupation as a vivandière. Eventually, the army returns to Germany, where Courage leaves her companion and marries yet another captain, who is also soon killed, and it is while on a recuperative visit to the Spa that she meets Simplicissimus, with the result already related in the earlier book. Her last husband is a gipsy chief, and she ends her days as queen of the troop.

The Rare Jump-in-the-Field relates the life-story of the friend of Simplicissimus, who has already appeared as the

Appendix

latter's comrade during the adventures at Soest, and as the companion of Courage. The narrator of the story is a young unemployed secretary, who meets both Simplicissimus and Jump-in-the-Field, the latter now an old wooden-legged fiddler, in the guest-room of an inn. He describes a former meeting with Courage and the gipsies, and his adventures with them, and then Jump-in-the-Field tells his own story, which the secretary writes down. The last chapters relate the discovery of a magic bird's-nest, which has the power of making it's owner invisible, and this leads to the third sequel, *The Magic Bird's Nest*, which is in two parts. This unique object enables its possessor to pry into the intimacies of family life, as does Le Sage's *Diable Boiteux*. The most amusing incident is when one of the owners of the nest becomes enamoured of the daughter of a Portuguese Jew, whose acquaintance he has sought for the purpose of robbing him. He persuades her parents that the prophet Elias is present but invisible, and will with the young Jewess beget the Messiah, for whom the Jews are waiting. He plays himself the part of the prophet, and thus attains his object, but unfortunately the child turns out to be a girl. The nest is eventually thrown into the Rhine, and the owner turns his thoughts to repentance.

The Everlasting Almanac has only a nominal connection with Simplicissimus. It is a conglomeration of recipes, weather prophecies, lists of historical events, dialogues on astronomy and astrology, and a series of anecdotes having little or no real connection with Simplicissimus, but whose object seems to be to render him more adaptable to the popular taste. Much of the material is borrowed from other almanacs.

In *Courage* and *Jump-in-the-Field*, Grimmelshausen enlarged his picture of the Thirty Years' War by presenting two counterparts to Simplicissimus, and in *The Magic Bird's Nest*, he rounded off the picture by depicting social life after the declaration of peace. The *Simplician Writings* present therefore an incomparable picture of a period of which Grimmelshausen was the only German writer of the century to appreciate the literary value.

WILLIAM ROSE.

May, 1924.